We hope you enjoy this book. Please return or renew it by the due date.

You can renew it at www.norfolk.gov.uk/libraries or by using our free library app.

Otherwise you can phone 0344 800 8020 - please have your library card and PIN ready.

You can sign up for email reminders too.

Also by Natasha Lester

A Kiss From Mr Fitzgerald

The Paris Seamstress

The French Photographer

Her MOTHER'S SECRET

NATASHA LESTER

sphere

SPHERE

First published in Australia in 2017 by Hachette Australia
First published in Great Britain in 2018 as an ebook by Sphere
This edition published in 2020 by Sphere

1 3 5 7 9 10 8 6 4 2

A CIP catalogue record for this book is available from the British Library.

ISBN 978-0-7515-7310-7

Printed and bound in Great Britain by Clays Ltd, Elcograf S.p.A.

Papers used by Sphere are from well-managed forests
and other responsible sources.

Sphere
An imprint of
Little, Brown Book Group
Carmelite House
50 Victoria Embankment
London EC4Y 0DZ

An Hachette UK Company
www.hachette.co.uk

www.littlebrown.co.uk

What wouldn't you give to go back to the beginning, to be those people again, the future so fresh and promising that it seems impossible not to get it right?

Therese Anne Fowler

PART
One

Chapter One

The jar in Leonora's hand contained a substance as black as the sky on a new moon night. She unscrewed the lid, her friend Joan watching eagerly over her shoulder.

'It worked,' Leonora said.

'Try it on!' Joan said.

Leonora dampened her finger and rubbed it over the mascara she'd made the day before, creating a film of black liquid. She applied it to the curve of her lashes, cautiously at first, before dipping her finger back into the jar and adding some more. 'How does it look?'

'Wait.' Joan picked up a hand mirror and the copy of *Pictures and the Picturegoer* magazine that was lying open on the workbench in front of them. She held the mirror in front of Leo and the magazine, opened to a photograph of Theda Bara as Cleopatra, beside Leo's face.

Leo smiled at her reflection, green eyes made larger and brighter by the mascara. 'It's better than I hoped it would be. Here.'

3

She passed the jar to Joan, who coloured her lashes as Leo had done.

'I think next time I'll add some oil to make it shinier,' Leo said as she studied her face. 'Cleopatra's lashes definitely have more gloss.'

'Given it's the only mascara available for hundreds of miles around, I think it's a very good first effort.'

'Would you believe it's just soap flakes and lampblack? I tried Vaseline and lampblack, but it was too gooey. This is easier to put on, but I think I can make it even better.' Leo sighed, looking around the mess of the stillroom, workbench cluttered with salves and ointments and her cosmetic experiments. 'That's if I can find the time in between making medications for venereal disease.'

'I can understand why the boys do it though,' Joan said sadly. 'The ones I've nursed told me they were prepared to do anything to feel a bit of love in the midst of what they've had to face.'

Leo shivered, imagining Joan in the hospital of the army camp situated about a mile out of Sutton Veny, listening to such admissions while she bandaged wounded men. 'Are we awful, do you think? To stand here talking about the movies and mascara while . . .'

'Of course not!' Joan was emphatic, her Australian accent always more pronounced in moments of fervour. 'I spend twelve hours a day trying to keep men from dying and you spend just as long making medicines for the same purpose. Not to mention keeping up their morale; making the run to the chemist to collect supplies is the most popular job at camp.'

Leo blushed. 'Are we going to the cinema or not?' she asked.

'I just need some lipstick to go with my lashes.'

Leo passed Joan a jar filled with a glossy red cream.

'You're a treasure. I'm sure you keep the nurses here better supplied than the ladies of London are.' Joan dabbed some colour onto her lips, smoothed her hands over her brown hair, put a navy cloche hat on her head and nodded with satisfaction.

'What if Mrs Hodgkins sees us?'

Joan shrugged. 'What if she does? It's not illegal to wear mascara.'

'Not yet. But probably only because nobody understands quite how much we all want to.' Leo pointed at the magazine. 'Do you think "Theda Bara made me do it" is a reasonable excuse?'

Joan laughed. 'Let's go. Then I can tell you my news.'

'I'll check on Daddy first.' Leo flipped the closed sign on the door labelled *Harold East, Dispensing Chemist and Apothecary* and ran up the stairs to the flat where she and her father lived.

Harold East was sitting at the table, supposedly reading the newspaper, but he had taken off his glasses and his eyes were closed. He looked thin and even paler than usual and Leo wished for the thousandth time that she could get him the food he needed; rationing was fine for someone young like her, but not for her father, whose health had floundered from the effects of grief since his wife had died in childbirth, the strain and deprivation of war making him age all the quicker.

'Daddy,' she whispered, putting a hand on his arm.

He jumped, eyes flying open. 'What's happened?' he said, searching for his glasses.

Leonora found them beneath the newspaper and passed them to him, but he only held them in his hand and looked at her through eyes she knew were too foggy to see her properly. 'I'm sorry I scared you,' she said softly. 'Nothing's happened. I came up to say goodbye. I'm going to see a film with Joan, remember?'

'Of course you are.' Her father beamed and held out his arms.

Leo kissed the top of his head. 'You had some bread?'

'I even licked the plate clean of crumbs,' he said. 'You go off and have a good time. You spend too much of your life here with me.'

'How did things go in the shop this morning?'

'Fine. Some soldiers came in and were most disappointed to hear you were out tending to a luckier bunch of soldiers at Sutton Veny House. And you'll have to make another batch of Leo's Cold Cream. We've sold out again. Mrs Kidd told me it was even better than Pond's.'

'I knew they'd love it. Maybe now you'll let me sell lip colour too.'

Her father shook his head, but he was still smiling. 'Imagine what Mrs Hodgkins would say about that!'

Leo knew all too well what Mrs Hodgkins, who'd appointed herself responsible for Leo's moral upbringing, would say. She thanked God that her father hadn't put his glasses on and couldn't see her lashes. 'I don't need mothering from anyone except you,' she said.

Her father's eyes filled with tears, and Leonora knew he was thinking of her mother, who'd never even had the chance to hold her daughter. 'Well,' he said, voice quavering a little, 'it's your shop really. I'm hardly in it any more. You should do what you like in there. I might head off to bed, my love. I'm tuckered out.'

Leo watched him shuffle away, touching the wall once or twice for balance. Then she hurried downstairs to Joan. 'Sorry that took so long.'

'Is he all right?' Joan asked.

Leo shook her head. 'I don't know. It's like the war is draining the life out of him, making him frailer than ever.'

'Can I do anything?' Joan squeezed Leo's hand.

'No.' Leo dabbed at the dampness in the corner of her eye. 'Let's go.'

They set off along the high street, Leo waving to her neighbour, Mr Banks, who did a slight double-take when he saw them, though he waved back nonetheless. Leo felt her shoulders relax. It was nice to go out for the night and forget, for a short time, what the world had become. It was nice to add a little colour to her face to compensate for the fact that her dress was four years old, faded to a dirty grey, and had been mended so many times it felt almost as if it was made from thread rather than fabric. It was nice to laugh with Joan, rather than being always on edge, waiting to hear who was the latest of the boys from the village to die.

As they walked, their feet crunched through the elm leaves on the road, leaves that appeared in autumn as quickly as the new gravestones in the cemetery. Leo opened her mouth to ask Joan for her news when a group of soldiers from the army camp came streaming towards them. The presence of soldiers, Australian nurses like Joan, and an army camp was so familiar to Leo now that she could hardly remember what the village had looked like before the neat rows of identical huts, and the hospital where Joan worked had been erected. In the distance, she could see the butts on the shooting range, rectangles of white, like hankies set out to dry. A biplane flew overhead, preparing to land in the grass near the camp but Leo still ducked, still unwilling to trust anything that fell from the sky.

All of a sudden, Joan grabbed Leo's hand. 'Quick,' she hissed. 'Mrs Hodgkins is over there and if we don't move, she'll see you.'

The crowd of soldiers, so many that the villagers going in the opposite direction had to stand aside to let them pass, provided Leo and Joan with a good place to hide.

'Leonora!'

At the sound of her name, Leo smiled up at the familiar face of the boy – well, he was a man now – in army uniform who she'd known all her life as Albert from Gray's Farm. He'd taken her for a walk the last time he was on leave, and also to a film. When he'd escorted her home, he'd kissed her hand and Leonora had closed her eyes and willed herself to feel it, the bolt of lightning that always struck lovers in books when they touched. But all she'd felt was a wish to be elsewhere – back in London, perhaps, where she had spent three years at school before the war had started and she'd returned home, bringing with her a yearning for more than was hardly satisfied by running a black market in lipstick between the chemist shop and the nurses at the hospital.

Albert didn't reach for her hand this time. 'What have you done to yourself?' he asked, eyes wide with bafflement at the sight of her darkened lashes.

Leo felt the joy she'd painted on her face fade away.

What *had* she done? Making mascara while men were fighting to save her country. She stared down at the pavement, shame at her own frivolity flooding through her.

'You look like a . . .' He stopped himself just in time. 'You'll make yourself a laughing-stock, Leonora. What will your father think?'

What will your father think? Of all the things Albert could have said, that was the worst. Her own shame she could bear, but not her father's.

'Excuse us,' Joan said crisply. Taking Leo's arm, she led her into the Palace Cinema, where she chose seats right up the front, a safe distance from the soldiers who tended to occupy the back rows.

As Leo sat down, her spirit reasserted itself. 'Honestly, why is there such a fuss made about a little bit of make-up?' she said, vexed that she'd been so affected by Albert's judgement. 'It's all right for a man to contract VD from a French prostitute – who's probably wearing lipstick, I might add – but a woman isn't allowed to do something as innocuous as make her lashes darker?'

'Don't pay any attention to him.' Joan lit a cigarette and offered one to Leo, who shook her head. 'You look beautiful and he's scared of that.'

'Do you think, one day, everyone will stop being scared?' Leo asked. 'That Mrs Hodgkins will ever stop bleating about the horror of so many ankles on display beneath the nurses' uniforms, that Mr Ellis won't ask me to *turn off that rubbish!* when he comes into the shop and hears Marion Harris playing on the Victrola instead of "Oh! It's a Lovely War!"?'

'Probably not any time soon,' Joan admitted.

The newsreel flickered onto the screen and the lights dimmed. Leo had just settled back in her seat when she had a sudden thought. 'Why is Albert back?' she whispered. 'And so many other soldiers?'

'They shipped an entire regiment back this morning,' Joan said, ignoring the reproving stares of their neighbours. 'That's what I wanted to tell you. Pete wrote that he'd be here in a few days.'

'Really?' Leo asked.

She was reprimanded with a loud 'Shhhh!'

'Maybe the war is nearly over,' she whispered.

'Maybe.'

Leo grinned. 'If that was true, I'd cartwheel around the theatre.'

'Pete asked me to move to New York with him when he's discharged. That made me feel like cartwheeling to the moon.'

'New York! But what about Sydney?'

'Shhhhhh!' Even more people scolded them now.

'I'll tell you after the show's over,' Joan said.

They turned their attention to the screen, but Leo couldn't concentrate. She could see New York in her mind, the legendary city, a place filled with love and hope and skyscrapers-in-the-air; buildings that reached into the solid foundation of the ground so that the dreams they flung into the air must surely become real, as they had both bedrock and backbone to support them. If the war was nearly over, then the future might come after all; life would begin again, rather than being stalled as it had been for so long. Then what might she do?

Her smile remained on her face throughout the shorts, the feature and back out onto the street, where a soldier whistled. Even then, Leo couldn't stop smiling. Who cared if it looked like she was flirting? Wasn't it wonderful that she was here and that the soldier was still alive and that they *could* do something as simple as flirting?

'Did you say yes?' Leo asked, threading her arm through Joan's as they stepped onto the pavement, walking fast to escape the November wind biting viciously through their cloaks and mittens. 'To New York?'

'I did and you should come with me.'

'I can't,' Leo said. 'Daddy wouldn't survive a journey to New York and he certainly wouldn't survive if I upped and left him.'

'Joan!' A shout from behind made Joan and Leo whirl around, straight into the wind that had swept up like a cavalry charge, pounding their cheeks.

'You have to come back,' a nurse panted as she caught up to them.

'What is it?' Joan asked.

'Spanish flu,' the nurse said sombrely.

With those dreadful words sounding like a requiem in the night, Joan was off into the darkness and the wind, leaving Leo shivering.

Influenza. Not again. Not now, not when the boys were coming home, when the war was so close to ending. They'd been through it once already, back in the spring, and Leo and Joan had both been laid low for a fortnight with it. But she'd heard whispers from the towns and villages it had already struck that this one was worse.

She hurried the rest of the way home, unable to shake off the worry that fluttered relentlessly in her stomach. The first thing she did when she arrived, even before she took off her cloak, hat and gloves, was to creep along the hall to her father's room. She opened the door a crack and could see his huddled shape in the bed, could hear him snoring loudly, lost in a deep and lovely sleep. She smiled, throwing off her cloak and her fears.

The next morning, Leo woke early and went downstairs to the stillroom at the back of the shop. If influenza had come to the army camp, she'd be in for a busy day. She made certain she had enough liniments for chests and tinctures for coughs before she took advantage of the quiet dawn hour to pull out the stepladder and reach up to the highest shelf, which held her father's books. Chemistry books, science books – books filled with long and seemingly obscure words, but Leo had found that, if you spent time getting to know those words, they were among the most enchanting in the English language. Petrolatum was both an unctuous and hydrophobic mixture of hydrocarbons, but add some lampblack and you had mascara. She ran her hand along the spines and stopped when she reached her treasures: an enamelled Fabergé powder compact in which was nestled a swansdown puff, and a Coty perfume bottle, made by Lalique in the shape of a dragonfly. They were the most precious things Leo owned, both because they had belonged to her mother, and because Leo wished her cosmetics could be placed inside something just as lovely, lined up in rows on the shelves of a shop. She climbed down the ladder decisively. Provided this influenza wasn't too bad – and in the pale gold light of an autumn morning it didn't seem possible that it would be – she really would put some lip colour in the shop rather than just joking with her father about it, and who cared what Mrs Hodgkins had to say about that!

She took out a saucepan and wooden spoon – her crude version of a mixing kettle – and heated and stirred beeswax, carmine, almond oil, blood beet and oil of roses until it was the perfect shade of red. She poured the mixture into several small jars to set – soupçons of beauty in the midst of the horror in which they lived.

Then she went back upstairs. 'Daddy?' she called.

'I've slept in a bit today, love.' Her father's voice came from his room. 'Be there in a minute.'

Leo boiled two eggs, put out a slice of bread for each of them, then made the tea, with just half a scoop of leaves rather than the three her father liked; tea had become as rare as good news these last few years.

When her father appeared, he sat down heavily in his chair, body shaking.

'You're cold!' Leo cried. 'Let me get you a blanket for your lap.'

'Don't fuss. I'll be fine after my tea.'

Leo passed him his cup. 'Drink up then,' she said mock sternly. 'And I'll make you another.'

'You're a good girl, Leo. How was your night?'

'I saw Albert. His regiment's been shipped back.'

'I'll wager he was glad to see you,' her father said in a tone Leo couldn't quite decipher.

'I don't know. I was wearing mascara. He was a little shocked.'

'Pffft!' her father scoffed. 'He's been in a trench at war but he gets shocked by black stuff on your lashes? He's not the man for you. None of them are.'

'You're just being a protective father,' she teased.

'I'm not,' he said decidedly. 'He'll ask you to marry him, mark my words. And you're to say no. Don't let yourself get stuck here. As soon as the war is over, I'll find a way to get you back to London, you see if I don't.'

'I won't leave you, no matter what you say.'

The sound of church bells sang through the window, interrupting them. 'It's not Sunday,' Leo said.

She ran to the window and threw it open, heedless of the cold air that streamed in.

The bells rang on and on, and people thronged the street. The sound they were making was unfamiliar to Leo's ears at first. Then she realised – they were laughing.

'What is it?' she called down to Mr Banks, who was standing outside his solicitor's office next door, beaming.

'The war is over!' he shouted back.

Leo flew to her father and squeezed him so tightly he began to cough. 'It's over!' she cried.

He clapped his hands and laughed. 'Well, don't stand around here,' he said. 'Off you go!'

Leo pulled out her handkerchief and wiped the tears of relief off her father's face. 'I love you,' she said.

Then she tore down the stairs and outside, hoping to find Joan and dance with her in the streets. But it was almost impossible to move, as with every step she met a soldier who wanted to take her hands to twirl her around or lift her high in the air. One even tried to kiss her and she let him because it was a day when proprieties had ceased to matter.

'Thanks,' he shouted, grinning at her before running off.

The town went mad that morning: shops were left unmanned, cows unmilked, breakfasts uneaten. The church was full of people giving thanks, the Woolpack Hotel proprietor passed mugs of frothing beer out to anyone who waltzed by, the policemen ignored such flagrant violations of the rules and even the trees seemed to join in the celebrations, dropping leaves like blessings onto Leo's red-gold hair and the heads of all the villagers gathered together in an impromptu celebration on the high street.

Leo was sipping a beer and joining in an improvised circle dance when someone tapped her shoulder. 'Miss, my mum needs something for her cough.'

The words were like a slap on the cheek and Leo realised that she hadn't seen Joan, that very few nurses were out enjoying the revelry. But look how many soldiers had come into town. The influenza couldn't be too serious. Still, unease made her sober. 'I'm coming,' she said to the lad in front of her.

As she turned towards the shop, it began to rain. Her skirt was quickly muddied, the hem weighed down with clay and water. Back at the shop, she gave the boy some medicine for his mother, asking him about symptoms, frowning as he described fevers and coughs and headaches. After he left, she ran upstairs to see her father, who was still sitting at the table where she'd left him.

'The influenza's come,' she said without preamble. 'You're to stay up here. I couldn't bear it if you caught it.'

'Don't be a goose,' her father said fondly. 'I'll be right as rain. But I might lie down for a bit till that cup of tea oils my joints.'

Her father safely in his room, Leo returned to the shop. The flow of customers that afternoon was steady, but not overwhelming. A few coughs and fevers, but it *was* autumn. She closed the shop at six, made her father eggs and toast again for supper and went to bed, only to be awoken at five by a loud knocking on the shop door. Dread made her dress hurriedly, knowing that only those caring for the very ill would seek help so early.

'What is it?' her father called from his room.

'Just a customer whose clock mustn't be working.' She made her voice sound light, as if it was a minor inconvenience having to get up at dawn, nothing more.

But there wasn't just one customer; there were many. Their faces were dazed with the bewilderment that they'd beaten one merciless opponent – the war – only to have another that might be just as brutal land on their doorstep. They all wanted something Leo didn't have: a cure. A miracle. A way out of the hell this world had become.

In the space between yesterday and today, influenza had reached out its hand and gripped as many as it could by the throat, and it wasn't letting go.

Leo did her best all that long, long day, frantically making up more liniments to ease coughs. She gave away all the muslin masks she had left, not charging a penny for anything. She'd thought the worst moment was when the baker's wife ran in, eyes wild, shouting that her husband had turned purple. Leo knew it meant the end was nigh; the cyanosis that was such a distinctive feature of this flu had set in. There was nothing Leo could do.

'Be with him,' Leo whispered, hugging her.

But then the news came in that Albert – Albert, who'd never done anything wrong – had succumbed too.

After that, Leo turned off her thoughts. She concentrated on helping those she could, advising everyone to keep their hands washed, to thoroughly clean all bedding and handkerchieves, to stay off the streets. By mid-afternoon, there was nowhere to go anyway. Most shops had closed. The church was closed. The Palace Cinema. The Woolpack Hotel. There would be no more celebrations of the armistice. Instead, their village of five hundred people, already decimated by war, would start to bury more dead, until the dead almost outnumbered the living.

When night fell, she hurried upstairs to her father. She expected to find him at the table with a pot of tea for a companion but the flat was in darkness. Surely he wasn't in bed already?

Then a sound reached her ears. A wet, hacking cough. Dear God. Leo threw open the door to his room. 'Are you all right? I thought I heard . . .' She couldn't bring herself to say it.

'I have a fever,' her father rasped.

Black fear clogged Leonora's heart. 'You'll be fine,' she said, aiming for cheeriness but falling a million miles short. 'I'll make you some broth.'

'No. I'll sleep it off.' His eyes closed, but rather than finding peace in sleep, his lungs rattled with every hard breath in and out.

Leo fetched a cloth and basin then sat down beside his bed. She laid the damp cloth on his forehead. She rubbed his back when he coughed so hard he seemed almost to lift off the bed, holding a basin to catch the sputum, washing it out and returning just in time for the next spasm. She changed his sheets when they became soaked through with sweat. Occasionally he quietened and she perched on the edge of her chair, fingers worrying a hole the size of a handkerchief into her skirt. Then another violent paroxysm of coughing racked him, not stopping for what felt like hours. For its long duration, Leo's father clung to her, as if he was her child, and she held his hand and tried to sing him into sleep, just as a mother would.

It was dawn when she realised the only sounds she could hear were roosters and the delivery boys' carts. The relief that her father's coughing had settled made her woozy; the room tipped a little at the edges and she breathed in deeply and slowly to set it to rights. Through the first sliver of morning light creeping under the curtains, she could just make out his shape, curled on his side, resting peacefully.

She tiptoed from the room. She'd make him some porridge while he slept; it would warm him, give him strength. She even tipped in a little precious sugar. When it was steaming hot, she carried it down the hall, sure he would have smelled it cooking, that he'd be waiting with a hungry stomach for this unexpected feast.

But he hadn't moved.

'Daddy? I have some porridge for you.'

No response.

'Daddy!' The word cracked in two.

She knew she could move to the bed, touch his shoulder, watch him jump awake and flounder for his glasses. Or she could remain where she was, in a space that existed out of time.

She could stop the future from coming, if only she waited there long enough. A tear fell into her father's porridge. Then another.

She shook her head. It was her silly imagination, an imagination that Mrs Hodgkins had often said should be kept in check. Well, check it she would. She marched down the stairs, out the front door and knocked at Mr Banks's house.

But when Mr Banks answered, she found that the bravado she'd mustered had deserted her. She stood mute, eyes damp, hands clenched into fists.

'What is it?' Mr Banks asked.

'Father,' she said. 'Influenza.'

'Oh, Leo.' Mr Banks embraced her and she stood stiffly in his arms, wanting nothing more than to break down. But that would only make it true.

'I'll go and see,' Mr Banks said.

Leo nodded. She followed him into the flat and waited in the kitchen while he went to her father's room. She'd left the cooker on, she realised, and the kettle was still whistling. But her father hadn't come out to turn it off. The minutes scraped past.

Then Mr Banks appeared. He shook his head.

It felt like a knife had been plunged into her very core, shearing off everything that had ever made her Leonora East.

She hurried into the bedroom, pulling back the sheet that Mr Banks had drawn up over her father's face. That precious face, a face that was more familiar to her than her own, had vanished in the night, leaving behind something cold and livid. And his mouth — it was stretched open as if he'd been calling for her when he'd passed. But she hadn't heard him, would never know what he had wanted to say.

She sat by her father's side all day, wordless, tearless, holding his cold, cold hand. From all over the village, she thought she could hear coughing, people choking on the crimson fluid that filled their lungs, fluid that had suffocated her father. She pushed away the Bible someone tried to put in her hands. Who wanted God? Instead she raged at God, that He would do this to her, to Daddy, to everyone. She called God every bad name she could think of, including words she'd never said before.

Then they came to take her father's body away. 'No!' she hissed, jumping up from the chair. 'You can't have him.'

'Hush,' Mr Banks soothed her, holding her tightly in his arms so she couldn't stop the people lifting her father out of bed. 'You have to let him go.'

'How?' Leo whispered. 'How can I ever do that?'

Only when her father had gone did the tears start to fall, hard and fast, like iron bullets shooting into her father's now, and forever, empty bed.

Chapter Two

*D*eath and silence. Later, that was all Leo would remember of the next three months. Dead leaves unswept from the streets and left to rot. Silent customers with wooden stares, too exhausted for small talk. The brown slush of winter taking all colour from the world. And through it all, one song, the only sound Leo heard:

> I had a little bird
> Its name was Enza
> I opened the window
> And in-flu-enza.

The children's chanted words echoed as they skipped rope in the streets. And Leo found she couldn't shake the tune from her head. She hadn't been able to stop and grieve; people needed a chemist. So from November to January, she passed out masks and liniment and let her neighbours weep on her shoulder as everyone around them succumbed to that awful violet death. Meanwhile, her grief waited patiently in the pit of her stomach.

Until the influenza finally relented. Until the flow of customers to the shop slowed and she had long, ghastly moments of idleness in which she would see around her more signs of despair: the thick dust on the wooden shelves her father had built himself and that he used to dust every day. *There was no need for Boots' style tea rooms and libraries if you had clean shelves.* Leo could hear his voice as clearly as if he'd been standing right before her and she looked around for him, but then remembered he was gone, and that time stretched out relentlessly before her, empty of her father.

One day in February, Mr Banks and Joan, who came most days to check on her, found her sitting on the floor, weeping. She'd knocked into a stack of boxes, sending glass jars shattering to the floor where they spilled their contents, red like fresh blood.

'Are you hurt?' Joan exclaimed, seeing the pool of red around her.

'It's just lip colour,' Leo said.

'Thank God,' Mr Banks said, reaching out a hand to help her up.

'I made it that morning in November,' Leo explained haltingly. 'When I thought the influenza wouldn't be very bad. I was going to put it in the shop window. To try and sell it. I can't believe I was thinking that when I should have been . . .'

Joan hugged her. 'You weren't to know,' she said fiercely. 'You're not to blame.'

'But I feel guilty for even being alive when so many others aren't. Don't you?'

'Your father would be very glad that you're alive, Leo,' Mr Banks said. 'Otherwise, what was his life for?'

'I don't know,' Leo whispered, looking around at the mess she'd made of everything: the dust, the boxes, the unrolled bandages, the dirty stove, the unstoppered bottles. It was not how it used to be. Nothing was. 'I need to clean up,' she said suddenly. 'I need dusting cloths, and a broom, a mop, buckets.'

'Now?' Mr Banks asked doubtfully.

'We'll help,' said Joan.

Within fifteen minutes they were hard at work, Leo wiping the shelves and unpacking boxes, Joan scrubbing the stove and Mr Banks lining up products in orderly rows. The last job was the floor, which Mr Banks swept and Leo and Joan scoured with brushes, then mopped.

As Leo was wiping away the last of the red lip colour, she said, 'Imagine what Mrs Hodgkins would say if she knew we were so fast that even our floors were adorned with lipstick.'

Joan looked over at her and grinned, which made Leo smile. Then she began to laugh helplessly, bent over, holding her sides, almost unable to breathe. Joan joined in, both girls overcome with hilarity. Mr Banks put his head into the back room and said, 'I missed the joke,' which only made Leo laugh harder.

Eventually she wiped her eyes and sat down on the now clean floor. 'I needed that,' she said.

'You did,' Mr Banks replied. 'I'll get some tea.'

Five minutes later he returned bearing a tray of tea things and some bread and jam. He eased himself down beside Leo and passed cups and saucers around.

Leo sipped her tea, closing her eyes briefly as the warmth hit her. 'That tastes good,' she said.

'I made it exactly the way your father liked it,' Mr Banks said. 'Extra strong. Now, have some bread. You're too thin.'

Leo took some. 'Do you know, you're the only people who ever speak to me about him?' she said. 'Everyone else clucks around me like broody hens, or else they avoid talking about him, which is worse, because how can they pretend he never existed?' She tilted her head back and looked up at the orderly shelves, everything just the way her father would have liked it. And that knowledge made her only a little sad; the relief of talking about him, of remembering him, of letting him be more than a ghost smoothed a line or two from her forehead, lightened the weight inside her.

She kept going, words spilling out now. 'The villagers all seem to think that I'll become Miss Leonora East, eccentric spinster chemist. They pat my hand when they come in and say, *such a shame*, as if my life had ended too.'

'Your father wouldn't want that; he made his wishes very clear,' Mr Banks reminded her.

Mr Banks, as her father's solicitor, had presented Leo with a letter from her father at the reading of the will. It exhorted her to: *Sell everything. Take the money and do something, just like I've always wanted you to do, just like you've always wanted to do. Don't give your life to Sutton Veny. You're meant for something more.*

'I'm leaving in May,' Joan said. 'Pete's going earlier but I said I'd stay here until the camp's demobilised. You *should* come to New York with me. It's the perfect place for both of us, full of laughter and good times. There's work to be had. And I bet the people over there are more broad-minded than the ones here.'

'It's so far away,' Leo said sadly. Then she stopped. 'It's so far away,' she repeated slowly. 'It might be nice to go far away.'

'It might be,' Mr Banks agreed.

New York. Could she really do it? There was nothing holding her to Sutton Veny, or even to England. 'I promise to think about it,' she said.

Joan squeezed one of her hands. Mr Banks squeezed the other. And, sitting with them on the floor of her father's shop, Leo felt like a child taking its first step, away from the past, away from mourning. A step into the future. She shivered with a mixture of fear and excitement at the thought of striding out into the unknown.

Two weeks later, Leo arranged a pyramid of small pots in the window of the shop. In front of them, she propped up a sign which read: *Lip colour and mascara for beautiful women.* She smiled. Making up these pots of colour had been so much more gratifying than mixing infant teething powders. This was what she wanted for her future. Only one question remained: *where* would she do it?

Her cosmetics were met with a deathly silence. Few people crossed the threshold of the shop over the next three days, and they did so only when it was absolutely necessary. The pots remained untouched, except by the few remaining nurses at the army camp. Villagers darted sideways glances at the display, but then they'd hurry on, whispering to the person beside them, shaking their heads at Leo. Even though it was what she'd expected, it still hurt more than she cared to admit. All the work and all the love that she'd put into each jar, all the beauty that lay within, shunned. Worse than shunned: disdained.

'If your father could see what you're doing.' Mrs Hodgkins' disapproving presence filled the doorway, her eyes sweeping over both the window display and Leonora with contempt.

Leo looked at the sour expression of one of Sutton Veny's hide-bound and Victorian matrons and knew she never wanted to become the same. Never wanted to live a future prescribed by the rules of the past.

'You should come to mass tomorrow,' Mrs Hodgkins said. 'Speak to Father Lawrence.'

Leo smiled. Not out of gratitude, but because Mrs Hodgkins had given her the gift of a decision. 'No thank you. I think my father would be proud of me.' She ushered Mrs Hodgkins out, locked the shop and walked away with her back straight, her confidence growing so much that, after a few steps, she broke into a run. She ran all the way through the village, then past the flimsy huts, like creations from children's brick sets, to the end of Hospital Lane.

'I'm coming!' she cried the instant she saw Joan. 'I'm coming with you to New York.'

'Oh, Leo.' Joan put her elbows on the desk at the nurse's station, propped her chin on her hands and shook her head. 'Pete's a cheat. He's taking some other girl to New York with him. Not me. I'll probably just go home to Sydney when I finish here.'

Leo hugged her friend. 'Oh no! Are you all right?'

Joan nodded wearily. 'I'm fine. I think I'm more disappointed about not going to New York than I am about Pete,' she admitted. 'Especially now that you're going. Are you really?'

Leo faltered. Could she go without Joan? 'I want to.'

The gloom of dusk threatened to dull the edges of Leo's enthusiasm as she walked home. It would be much nicer to have Joan with her in New York, but she supposed she *could* still do it on her own. She definitely couldn't stay in the village and let the world shrink, become so small-minded that anything new posed a threat. Because then she might as well have died like so many others.

Her pace was slow as her thoughts churned. When she reached the high street, she went straight to Mr Banks's door. He might be able to help.

The words came out in a rush when he opened the door. 'Joan isn't going to New York after all. Just when I'd decided that's where I'd go. I want to make cosmetics. I could start a shop. But I need to work out how to get there.'

'That's a marvellous idea,' Mr Banks said. 'Come in. I may have a solution.'

In the kitchen, he didn't even wait for the kettle to boil before he began to speak. 'Do you remember my niece Mattie?'

Leo cast her mind back. Lady Mattie, she remembered. Mr Banks had an aristocratic niece. When Leo was about five or six, Mattie had come to visit her uncle and Leo had shown her how to find just the right spot to slide in the mud from the top of the hill behind Mr Banks's house all the way to the bottom without stopping. Mattie hadn't been impressed by these antics because they dirtied her dresses and mussed up her ringleted hair.

'Well,' Mr Banks said, 'Mattie and her parents are going to New York soon. They have some money troubles and they've heard that impoverished English gentry are treated more like royalty over there than they are here. I'll write to my sister and ask if you can accompany them. I'm sure you'd be the perfect travelling companion for Mattie.'

'That would be wonderful,' Leo said. 'But will they have me? Mattie is a lady and I'm just a country girl.'

'My dear, you've never been a country girl. I'll write to them this evening.'

'I'm going to New York!' Leo said, exhilaration causing her to crash her teacup into her saucer.

'To you, Leo.' Mr Banks raised his own cup. 'I wish you much adventure.'

Adventure. Leo grinned. How things could change in the space of a few months. Instead of worrying about war and death, now she was looking forward to a brand-new life in a brand-new place. A place where she could have her own shop. A place where it might be easier to show people that it wasn't a sin or a crime or the sign of a harlot for a woman to want to wear a little make-up. Because if enough women could buy it, could try it, then tradition and convention would have to give way. New York was a place where she could find out who Leo East really was. And who Leo East could really be.

Chapter Three

On an afternoon in late May that was unseasonably cold and dark, with storm clouds racing furiously across the sky, Leo took her first step towards New York, via Southampton. Two months had passed since the conversation with Mr Banks, during which time Mr Banks had finally found a buyer for the shop and the flat; few people wanted a chemist shop in the middle of a depleted country village. It gave Leo a little money, though rather less than Mr Banks had hoped for her.

The train rattled *away-away, away-away* beneath Leo as the Wylye Valley slipped past: first Warminster, then Heytesbury, Codford, Wylye. She spent the night in Salisbury, where the rain vented its fury on the roof of the inn and wind lashed the windows. The following day had barely taken hold when the sun was shut out by the darkest of clouds. Back on the train, Leo soon drifted into the sleep she'd been unable to find the previous night, but was woken by the sensation of falling, falling from her seat and onto the floor as the train braked suddenly.

The conductor arrived with news. 'Storm's brought down half the trees in Hampshire. The tracks are blocked and won't be fixed until tomorrow afternoon at the earliest. We're to walk on to Dunbridge for lodgings. Leave your luggage here.'

Reluctantly, Leo stepped outside, tying to quash her impatience at the delay. Within seconds she was drenched with rain, one of a straggling line of passengers trudging through water that reached her ankles and seeped into her boots, huge forks of lightning flashing around them. It took nearly two hours to walk to Dunbridge, where there was just one inn to house all of the passengers.

A mass of people pressed into the tiny reception room. Leo was at the back, barely inside, and she couldn't hear the landlady. She saw a dark-haired man walk up to the entrance, courteously tip a river off his hat and onto the lawn instead of bringing the water inside with him, although the rest of him was so wet it hardly seemed to matter. 'Damn weather,' he said as he reached the steps.

'I agree,' Leo said feelingly. 'I'd much rather be on a ship to New York than stuck here.'

The stranger smiled. 'Although this weather would be enough to make anyone seasick.'

'You're probably right.' Leo smiled back.

The reception room was quiet now; most people had moved off to their rooms. A few stragglers took to the stairs and then it was just Leo and the man still to be housed.

'Dearie me, why didn't you speak up when I asked for the women?' the landlady demanded when she saw Leo.

'I didn't hear you,' Leo said.

'I've no more rooms,' the landlady told her crossly, as if it was somehow Leo's fault. 'And it's not as if I can ask you to share because you're the only woman travelling. I suppose I'll have to go upstairs and ask a few of the men to shift, although

I've already got so many in each room I don't know what I'll do with them.'

'I'll wait in the parlour,' Leo said. 'I'm sure we won't be here for long.'

'That's very optimistic,' the man said, glancing out the window at the curtain of water drawn over the land.

The landlady sighed. 'Well, there's a good fire in the parlour to dry you, and a sofa you can use, Miss. But you –' she turned to the man, eyeing his coat which looked as if it had been made of the softest cashmere and noting his obvious wealth, 'I'm sure somebody'll give up their place for you.'

'No need,' he replied. 'I can wait in the parlour too.'

'I don't know if that would be right,' the landlady said doubtfully.

'It's a public parlour,' Leo said. 'It'll be fine.'

'I suppose it'll have to be,' the landlady said at last, unmistakably eager to have the problem solved, leading Leo away to find her a dry gown.

When they returned to the parlour, the man was waiting in the doorway, neck tie loose, shirtsleeves rolled up.

'Everett Forsyth,' the man said, holding out his hand to Leo.

The landlady gasped. 'Of Forsyths of London?'

'That's right.'

Leo vaguely remembered a fancy London department store called Forsyths, though she'd never had the money to shop there. 'Leonora East.'

'Pleasure,' he said.

The landlady left after admonishing them to keep the door open.

'What does she honestly think two wet and weary travellers are going to do in a public room at an inn?' Leo said, more to herself than her companion.

Everett Forsyth smiled. 'She clearly has a better imagination than we do.' Then he added hastily, 'I didn't mean . . .'

Leo laughed. 'I know what you meant.' She moved over to the fire.

Mr Forsyth remained by the door, unspeaking. The silence stretched into awkwardness, then he moved across to the sideboard and picked up a pack of playing cards. 'Do you play bridge?' he asked. 'Although we need more than two people.'

'We can play double-dummy,' she said. 'My . . . my father taught me.' The sting of those words, reminding her that she would never again play bridge with her father. She sank into a chair.

'We needn't play,' Mr Forsyth said. 'I thought it might pass the time, since we seem to have plenty of it.'

'Yes. Let's play,' Leo said abruptly. 'I'll show you.'

She put out her hand for the cards and, once she had explained the two-player variations, they played a round in silence. Through the steady rhythm of the cards falling from her hand to the table, punctuated only by their bidding and a short congratulations from him to her at the end, Leo studied Mr Forsyth; he was tall – taller than her, which not many men could claim to be – with dark hair and blue eyes that were like a sun-shot sky. How Leo envied him, that his eyes did not tell a story of death.

She brushed the thought aside. 'You play well, Mr Forsyth,' she said as he beat her in the second round.

'Call me Everett. Nobody but the maid calls me Mr Forsyth.'

'I wouldn't know,' she replied, unable to resist poking fun at him. 'I've never had a maid.'

He didn't laugh at her jest, just watched her for a moment. She concentrated on dealing the cards, his steady gaze making her self-conscious.

'Why do you look so sad?' he asked.

Her breath caught on his question because he'd said it with such gentleness, as if it mattered. So she told him what had happened, her voice wavering on the words, willing herself to remain composed.

When she finished speaking, Everett took her hand, a spontaneous gesture of compassion. 'I'm sorry,' he said.

Leo jumped. Because there it was. The lightning she'd once looked for in Albert's touch passed suddenly and shockingly through her.

~

The rain pounded on through the night, as did the thunder. One moment Leo was sitting in her chair, listening to Everett Forsyth explaining why he was travelling, and the next moment she found herself waking on the sofa, covered in a blanket, head resting on a pillow. She propped her head up on her hand and saw a man sitting in a chair by the fire.

'What happened?' she mumbled.

'You fell asleep. While I was talking, which must mean I was being a terrible bore. I thought you'd be more comfortable on the sofa. The landlady, Mrs Chesterton, supplied a blanket and pillow.'

Leo blushed. 'You weren't a bore. I was tired. I haven't slept much since . . .'

'Since Armistice Day.'

'Yes.'

'I brought you some tea and toast from the dining room.' Everett indicated a tray on the table.

'Thank you.' Leo stood up and stretched. As she did, she caught sight of herself in the mirror over the fireplace, hair a fiery tangle down her back, face still white from the shock of everything – and Everett's face, reflected in the mirror, watching her.

The room was suddenly too warm. 'I need some air,' she said. 'I'll go for a walk.'

'The puddles will reach up to your knees.'

Leo looked out the window. The storm had not abated.

'We're not leaving until tomorrow at the earliest, apparently,' Everett continued. 'My car is still stuck and your train is still stranded. You might as well eat.'

'You've been very kind. Bringing me breakfast. Carrying me to sofas when I fall asleep.'

'I wanted you to know that I don't rely on maids for everything, which is how I must have sounded last night.'

Leo remembered her jibe. 'Truce,' she said, holding up her hands and laughing. 'I won't fall asleep while you're talking or tease you about having a maid and you won't remind me I did any of those things.'

He laughed too. 'It's a deal.'

Leo sat, sipped her tea and couldn't help asking, 'Did you fight in the war, or . . . ?'

'Or was I sitting with my feet up in a cosy office in Whitehall?' he asked, eyebrows raised.

'I thought we'd called a truce!' Leo said.

He smiled and she knew that this time he was teasing her.

'It's just . . . It's your eyes.' With her words, Leo felt the mood in the room become as sombre as the day outside. 'You still look happy, as if you hadn't seen anything that had hurt you.' As soon as she finished, she knew how silly she sounded. 'I'm sorry,' she added hastily, 'I don't know what I'm saying, I think I will go for that walk.'

She went to stand up again but Everett touched her hand.

'Please stay, Leonora,' he said.

Leo's breath caught and she wished she could remain in that moment forever, Everett's hand brushing her skin, a part of her that she hadn't known existed unfurling. 'Nobody calls me Leonora,' she said, subsiding back into her seat. 'I'm really Leo.'

'It suits you,' Everett said softly. He cleared his throat. 'But to answer your question, yes – I did fight. I was an officer in France. I fought at the Somme. And Ypres.'

'Were you ever injured?'

'Shot through the shoulder. I have a scar the size of a silver crown on my chest and on my back.' His voice was matter-of-fact but Leo knew a gunshot wound was no small thing.

'You're awake now, are you?' Mrs Chesterton appeared in the doorway with a tray and two steaming mugs. 'More tea for you both to keep you warm. Drink up, young lady, your bones are showing through your skin.'

Leo's hand moved to her chest at the landlady's words, up to the sharp points of her collarbones. Everett's eyes followed her hand.

'Now that we know you're all staying on tonight, I'm doing what I can to get you a room, Miss,' Mrs Chesterton said. 'It's only proper.' She looked at Everett, who fixed his eyes on his mug.

Proper. Leo shook her head. Who cared about things like that any more?

'Mrs Chesteron's right.' Everett spoke sharply and Leo realised how over-agitated her mind was. Imagining shared glances where none existed. Everett Forsyth was a rich man; he probably had ladies falling at his feet. What was Leo East to him?

'I'll be back when I've arranged things.' Mrs Chesterton left and Leo absent-mindedly picked up the deck of cards and began to shuffle.

'Would you like to play again?' Everett asked. 'Or I can leave you in peace if you'd prefer,' he added formally.

'No, let's play,' Leo said dealing out the cards. When she'd finished, she asked, 'How did you manage Forsyths during the war?'

'I didn't really,' Everett said. 'I was lucky to have a good manager. Whenever I had leave, I'd spend the entire furlough in the office. And at the front, while everyone was writing letters to their sweethearts, I was writing to the manager.'

Leo smiled. Unconsciously she put down her cards. 'So you must be glad to be back, managing things in person.'

Everett leaned back in his chair. 'Actually, I've left things in the hands of the manager. I know I have a man I can trust, which allows me to . . . chase after some dreams I conjured up while listening to shells whistle through the air.'

'How do you dream when you're in a situation like that?'

'It's the only thing that keeps you alive.'

Perhaps he was right. Her New York dream was the thing that had enlivened her. 'What dreams did you have?'

'To open a Forsyths in New York. New York is where the world's eyes will turn over the next decade, I'm sure of it. There's no rationing, and unlike ours their economy isn't struggling to recover from a war. I'm moving there in a couple of months; I've bought up a bankrupt store that I'll transform into a Xanadu. A place where people will go just for the spectacle – a place where women, who won't want to give up the jobs and the money they earned during the war, can buy fashions from Paris, silk stockings, perhaps even cosmetics.'

'I used to spend my nights working in my father's chemist shop, making up cosmetics for the nurses at the army camp.'

'Who'd have thought that beneath your demure exterior lay a woman who's been supplying the ladies of England with such scandalous items?' he teased.

Leo laughed. 'One day I heard the nurses complaining that they couldn't get any cosmetics and I realised I was probably the only person in the village who had all the necessary ingredients. So in between making liniments and burn salves, I made lipstick and rouge. Cold cream. And scent. I managed to make one that smells quite nice.'

'It does,' Everett said quietly.

Leo shifted in her seat and talked on, talked over the sense that a peculiarly charged feeling between them was heating up the air, a fire leaping out well beyond the grate. Because he'd given her an idea, a way to solve the problem of not really having enough money to set up her own shop. 'I'm on my way to New York now,' she said. 'Perhaps I could sell my cosmetics to the department stores there?'

'That's an excellent idea.'

'I think it is,' she said, smiling widely. She continued talking excitedly. 'When you do open your store, don't have a Toilet Goods department. Call it the Beauty Department. That would be a place I'd like to shop in.'

'I'll do that, Leo. And I want you to know I'd be very happy to help you.'

At Everett's tone, Leo ran out of words, lost in the gleam of blue from his eyes, which no longer looked like a summer sky, but darker, as if he was trying to disguise a hunger that she glimpsed nonetheless. Her gaze dropped to his mouth, and she understood now that what she'd wished for from Albert was out of mere curiosity, whereas what she wished for from Everett was driven of wanting.

'Right.' Mrs Chesterton's voice made them both jump. 'The weather's settled enough for me to move a few men out to stay overnight with the villagers, which gives me a room for each of you. They've started work on the road and the track and they say the train will be leaving at seven tomorrow. I've organised one of the local men to drive you out to your automobile at the same time, Mr Forsyth. And Miss East, if you come with me, I'll show you to your room.'

Leo stood. 'Thank you for keeping me company, Everett,' she said, trying out the sound of his name on her tongue.

'Goodbye, Leo.'

That was that. In the morning, he'd leave in his car, and she on the train. And she'd probably never see him again.

One thing Leo was grateful for that evening was the bath. She filled it to the brim and sank into it, letting the warm water wash off the mud and dirt and more of the sadness. She unpinned her hair and, as it swirled around in the water, she felt more eager than ever to begin her adventure. Especially now that Everett had given her such a wonderful idea. Everett . . . She liked the sound of his name in her head. Groaning at herself, she sank under the water to shut out the image of his face when he'd looked at her across the table, before Mrs Chesterton had interrupted them.

Finally the water grew cold and Leo stepped out. She went to stand by the fire to help dry her hair but it had burned down to embers and the woodbox was empty. She stood for a moment, unsure what to do, and then remembered the warmth of the parlour fire. It might still be lit. Everett would be in his room by now and Mrs Chesterton had warned her not to go near the dining room as the men had commandeered it for a poker game. The parlour should be empty.

She quickly dressed then went downstairs. The parlour fire was well stoked so she chose a book from the shelf, sat on the floor and turned her damp hair towards the flames. She started as the door opened.

'Leo!' Everett said. He sounded both surprised and pleased to see her. 'Would you like a drink?' He held up the glass in his hand. 'The cook has a much better liquor store back there than I would ever have thought.'

'I would,' she said.

Everett disappeared, returning a few minutes later with two glasses. He passed one to her and she took a sip.

'What is it?' she asked. She swirled the delicious liquor around in her mouth; its edge had been taken off with a dash of something both sweet and spicy.

'It's called an old-fashioned. Do you like it? Sorry, I should have asked what you wanted. I'll get you something else.'

Leo smiled. 'This is perfect. I wouldn't have had a clue what to ask for. My father's tastes were limited to whisky.'

'Well, there's a good shot of whisky in that. Which probably just reminds you of your father. I will get you something else.'

'No,' Leo said. 'It's a nice memory. So thank you.'

Everett sat in a chair beside the fire and Leo remained where she was, no more than two feet away, sitting on the floor. 'When I rudely fell asleep last night, you were about to tell me where you'd been going before the storm,' she said.

'To Southampton, like you. I have some business to do with family,' he said grimly. 'That's always the hardest.' He rubbed his face with his hand. 'After fighting in the trenches, family difficulties seem almost unreal. It should probably be the other way around.'

'I know exactly what you mean.' And she did. That death was so much a part of the every day, whereas commonplace family problems, or even just sitting in an inn before a fire having a conversation, felt make-believe. She didn't move her eyes away from his face as she spoke, even though the effort of holding his gaze felt as intimate as stretching out her finger to

touch the fine blue veins she saw on his wrist. 'I'm sure you'll
sort it out. You seem a decent man.'

'A decent man? Really?' Everett swallowed his drink. 'I'm
sitting alone in a room with you when I should be far, far away,
because you're the most beautiful woman I've ever met and . . .'
His voice trailed off.

All Leo could do was study the floor, unable to believe
what he'd just said. The fire crackled like her skin and her face
flushed with an emotion she'd never felt before but she knew
must be desire. And God it was strong – strong enough to make
her want to walk over to Everett, to have him kiss her, to feel
his hands on her body. She hugged her knees to her chest and
forced herself to stay where she was. 'I don't see how that can
possibly be true,' she said.

'It is.' Everett's voice was as soft and heady as a hand stroked
over a cheek.

Leo found herself standing and speaking. 'Since everything
that's happened – the war, the influenza, my father . . . It's true
that I could die tomorrow. All I can think is that the only way
to live now is headlong, to rush at everything before it's taken
away, to grab hold of the simple pleasures when they're offered
because otherwise . . .' The look on his face made her stop.
A man had never looked at her in such a way before.

'We're on dangerous ground here, Leo,' he whispered.

She stepped in so close that her knees grazed his. 'Do you
want to kiss me?'

'Very much.'

Leo held out her hand. Everett took it and stood up.

As he did so, the length of their bodies touched ever so
lightly, but it felt like a match had been struck on her skin. Her
lips flew up to meet his.

That first kiss was beyond all her expectations. It was scorching, a kiss that swept right through her, her tongue seeking his, needing to feel him, to know him, to be a part of him. She was dimly aware that her leg was curving around his, that his hands were sliding down her neck to her back so he could pull her more closely against him and she gasped at the sensation of her body held tight against his. 'Come upstairs,' she whispered. 'Come to my room.'

He leaned his forehead against hers, breathing deeply. 'Are you sure?'

'Yes. Come in a minute.'

She turned and ran up the stairs to her room, heart hammering. There she took off her dress; she didn't want it on, holding her in like the prison of war and death and illness that had bound her these last few months. As it dropped to the floor, there was a knock at the door and Leo opened it, wearing only her chemise and corset. She could hear Everett's breath catch as he looked at her. 'You're so beautiful,' he said.

The clouds had been swept away by the wind roiling outside and the brightest of moons shone through the window; Leo could see herself in the dressing table mirror and, in that moment, she almost believed him. He closed the door and stood behind her, waiting for one long and intoxicating moment before kissing her neck. Then his hands moved to her corset. In the mirror, her red-gold hair was a ring of fire, the spill of her cleavage flushed with pink, and she watched herself tilt her head back against him and raise her hand to touch his face. Green eyes met blue in the mirror and her breath came faster.

Slowly, agonisingly slowly and sweetly, he undid each hook on her corset. Then he spun her around to face him. The strap of her chemise had slipped down and his finger traced the line of her naked collarbone and rested at the top of the fabric, which she knew was so translucent that he would be able to see all of her if he moved his eyes away from her face.

His voice was low when he said, 'Are you absolutely sure about this, Leo?'

'More sure than I've ever been about anything.'

He groaned and drew her into his arms, and she kissed him again, deeply, so deeply it left her desperate almost, but for what she wasn't sure. He slipped off her chemise and his hand found her breast, cupping it, fingers teasing her nipple, and she thought perhaps this was it, the thing she craved, because it felt glorious. She wanted to feel the bare skin of his chest against hers so she undid the buttons of his shirt and pushed it away, exhaling as her flesh met his.

Then he let his mouth drift along the collarbone his fingers had traced earlier, to her breasts, and he caressed each nipple, gently at first, and then he took the whole of each nipple inside his mouth. A sigh escaped her lips. His mouth shifted lower, to her belly button and then lower still and Leo found herself doing something she could never have imagined, tilting her pelvis towards him, and she cried out when his mouth reached the juncture of her thighs and his tongue began to circle around. Her hips moved too, so his mouth could press harder and faster, and a sensation that was so delicious it was almost unbearable began to build from the place where his tongue was, through her stomach and all over her body, making her cry out, louder this time, heedless of the guests who might hear, unable to stop herself, unaware of anything except the exquisite sensation, this man, his tongue, her body.

'Leo.' He whispered her name and looked up at her. He said her name again, then lifted her against him, wrapping her legs around his waist, and carried her over to the bed where he finally sank inside her, hands in her hair, mouth pressed against hers to stop himself from crying out too.

Oh, the things they did that night! It was a grand night of exploration, of discovering one another's bodies, of indulging in everything that was sensual and erotic, leaving nothing undiscovered. Occasionally they rested, content for a time to lie together, Leo's head resting on Everett's chest, but then she would look at him and he would smile and pull her closer and they would begin anew.

Too soon the dawn light was threatening through the curtains. 'I could stay here with you forever,' Everett whispered. He kissed her gently, with something more than desire or passion, with something deep and honest.

'I could too,' Leo said.

'Thank God for the storm,' he said. 'But for that, we might never have met.'

Leo's eyes filled with tears at his words. She knew that what she felt for him had taken her over. It was as like love as she could imagine love to be. But how could they fit this night into the lives they were supposed to resume now that morning had come? 'When I asked you to kiss me I didn't know I would feel like this,' she said.

'I didn't either,' he said.

'But you have things you need to take care of.' Leo curled her back into his chest. 'You won't be in New York for a while.'

Everett wrapped his arms around her and he kissed her shoulder. 'I have to sort out this business. I'll come to New York as soon as I can. When I do, then . . .'

We can be together. The words danced in the air.

Leo closed her eyes, wanting to imprint in her mind how sublime this moment felt, lying in bed, the back of her body held against the front of Everett's, his fingers lightly stroking the skin of her arm. 'So what should we do?' she said.

'There's a cafe in Greenwich Village called Romany Marie's. It's full of poets and artists and creative people – inspiring people, fun people. We'll meet there for dinner on the second Saturday in July. Romany Marie's a gypsy fortune teller. She'll tell us our fortune – although I don't need anyone to tell me how I feel about you.' Everett kissed her neck and moved his hand up to stroke her breasts.

Leo rolled over to sit astride his naked body one last time. 'Nor do I,' she murmured. 'Nor do I.'

Chapter Four

*L*eo stopped outside the Dolphin Hotel in Southampton, studying the two big bow windows that curved far out over the street like misplaced turrets. It was a much fancier place than she would ever have chosen for herself and she instinctively straightened her dress, tucked a loose strand of hair behind her ear and touched her face. Her lips felt red and swollen from Everett's kisses and her cheeks were grazed from the stubble on Everett's chin and she hoped nobody would notice.

'In you go,' she told herself, and she hid her awe behind a straight back and a face more composed than her emotions.

Inside, the parlour was crowded with cushiony sofas, and tables full of china, and people, so many people. She wondered how on earth she'd locate Mattie, whom she'd last seen when she was six.

Leo moved deeper into the throng, misjudging the movements of a man in front of her who stepped back, causing her to crash into a table laid for afternoon tea. 'Sorry!' she gasped as scones wobbled and teacups sloshed into saucers.

'You should be more careful,' a woman scolded.

'I'm sorry,' Leo said again, wanting to slink away.

'No harm done,' another woman said with a gentle smile.

Then a young lady glided into the room, tugging her elegant silk cuffs, gloves impossibly white. Leo hid her own hands behind her back; her gloves, which had been white four years ago, were anything but now. The woman gave a compressed smile to one of the women Leo had offended and a memory stirred. Leo had remembered Mattie's hair as being blonde and this woman's hair was a deeper shade of light brown, but that smile was the same as the one on the little doll-girl she'd once met.

'Mattie?' Leo said uncertainly.

'I'm Lady Mattie,' the woman said crisply. 'You must be the girl my uncle has sent me.'

There was a lot to hear in that one sentence and none of it was welcoming. Leo's stomach tightened with the awareness that Mattie didn't want her. She forced herself to smile. 'I'm Leo,' she said.

As Mattie's gaze travelled from her head to her feet, Leo was suddenly conscious that her dress was muddy from the march through the storm two nights ago. She also realised she was half a foot taller than Mattie and that, next to her, she looked like the unsophisticated girl she was. But she kept her smile on her face.

'Thank you for letting me travel with you,' Leo said.

'I wouldn't turn away someone in need.' Raucous laughter erupted from a nearby table, interrupting Mattie. 'I can't believe this hellhole,' she sighed.

'It's not exactly a hellhole,' Leo said, watching liveried staff slip past, carrying trays of champagne. Above them soared vaulted ceilings and beneath their feet were sumptuous rugs so thick they almost swallowed Leo's feet.

'I'm glad you think so because the first sailing of the ship is full and we have to wait a fortnight until it returns. There aren't enough ships released from war duties; all that's available is a ridiculous austerity service on the *Aquitania*.'

'Austerity service?'

'It means there is only *one class*. All in together, if you can believe it.'

Leo's spirits sagged. 'I don't think I can afford to stay here for a fortnight,' she admitted. 'I'll need to find another hotel.'

And, as they stood there, Leo suddenly saw the situation from Mattie's perspective. Being sent someone like Leo, whom she couldn't very well refuse because of what Leo had been through, and having Leo turn up, dirty and ill-equipped for long stays in luxurious hotels. No wonder Mattie looked strained.

'There's an inn next door. Why don't you have something to eat with us and then we can make some enquiries,' Mattie said, more kindly than before.

'Thank you.' Leo smiled, and Mattie's smile finally broke its banks too.

'Let me introduce you to my mother and father, Lord and Lady Monckton.'

Leo squirmed with embarrassment when she realised that Mattie's mother was one of the women whose tea she'd upset. 'How do you do, Lady Monckton?' Leo said. 'I really am sorry about your tea.'

'It doesn't matter,' Mattie's mother replied airily. 'I've sent the waiter to fetch some more.'

Mattie's father nodded and their companion – the woman who'd told Leo there was no harm done over the tea – gave her the friendliest smile she'd had since arriving in Southampton. Leo smiled back and sat down.

Mattie piled a plate with scones and began to chatter. 'I'm so bored. We've already been here for two days. I miss all the people in London. The parties. I hope they'll organise some dances to pass the time. There's someone in particular I'm very keen to dance with.' The waiter poured their tea. 'What about you? Have you left someone special behind?'

Leo was so relieved to be sharing a cordial moment that the words bubbled out. 'Well, I met someone on the way here actually.'

'Do tell. What's he like?'

Leo searched for the right words to describe her encounter with Everett. He was the first man who'd kissed her with passion, open-mouthed; the first man who'd brought her body fully to life. The first man who'd made her understand what love was. But she couldn't say that. 'I saw the ocean for the first time on the way here,' she said, remembering the furiousness and beauty of the waves, that she'd felt both terrified and breathtaken by the water. 'Meeting this man was like being swept out to sea and never wanting to return.'

Mattie waved a hand. 'Being swept out to sea is all very romantic, but what does he do for a living? I'm as good as engaged, you know, and luckily Rett is very wealthy; if there's one thing the war taught me, it's that you should be very sure of a man's pocket before you concern yourself with his heart.' Mattie stared accusingly at her father.

'Rett?' Leo said, a shiver of fear prickling her skin.

'Yes, my fiancé — well, almost my fiancé. And here he is at last, come to accompany us to New York. I thought you must have got lost,' Mattie called, as she waved to a man walking towards them.

And Leo realised that the man Mattie had called her almost-fiancé was none other than Everett Forsyth.

Thank God she was sitting down. Otherwise her legs would have given way from the shock. She clutched her bag so tightly the clasp bit into her skin and she stilled every muscle in her face so that nothing exposed the awful truth: that she'd been lying naked in his arms just a few hours earlier.

Everett's eyes met Leo's and he stumbled back, away from Mattie, who was advancing on him. He began to say Leo's name but he quickly transformed his words into a fit of coughing, which caused him to hold out an arm to Mattie, to ward her away. He turned his back in order to recover from his cough and when he faced them again, he shook his head when he saw that Leo was still sitting there.

'You look as if you've seen a ghost,' Mattie said. 'And that cough had better not be influenza. I don't want to catch it.'

Leo gasped at Mattie's flippant tone, as if influenza was an illness to be scoffed at, a trivial nuisance. She saw the shock on Everett's face shift to concern and she knew he understood that Mattie's words had stung her. But why would that bother him if he was planning to marry Mattie?

Mattie offered her cheek up to Everett, who gave it a perfunctory kiss. Both Mattie and Lady Monckton frowned.

Leo felt a hand on her arm.

'Are you all right, my dear?' The woman who'd given her a friendly smile touched Leo's arm with concern. 'We haven't been properly introduced. I'm Abigail Forsyth. Mother of that handsome young man.'

'Sorry, I don't feel well,' was all Leo could manage. 'Please excuse me.'

She stood up and hurried away. She didn't have time to look for another hotel right now, not when she needed to find a quiet place away from these people, so she paid for a room for one night and went upstairs. Then she lay on the bed and stared at the ceiling.

I don't need anyone to tell me how I feel about you.

At the memory of Everett's words, Leo rolled onto her side. She curled her knees into her chest and wrapped her arms around them, holding herself together. Because she had nobody else. She was utterly alone. She'd been a notch on a bedpost. A port in a storm. And far from being a decent man, Everett was a liar.

The sobs started then, deep gulping sobs that reached right down into her stomach, bringing up all the anguish and loss and heartbreak of the past six months. It hurt – it hurt so much that it left her gasping, unable to move, unable to do anything more than lie awake on the bed in an unfamiliar room, eyes occasionally closing. Then the memory of Everett's lips meeting hers would jolt her brutally awake and she'd remember him walking into the room downstairs and Mattie's words: *Rett. My fiancé.*

Leo woke early the next day, determined to find somewhere else to stay. She was so relieved to find that the inn next door was vastly cheaper and had a small room available that she almost cried while talking to the manager. She collected her things and was crossing the foyer of the Dolphin Hotel when she heard someone call her name.

'Where are you off to, my dear?' Mrs Forsyth asked, hurrying over. 'I thought Mattie was escorting you to New York.'

'I'm going to stay next door – I can't afford this place,' Leo admitted, shame colouring her cheeks.

'Don't be embarrassed,' Mrs Forsyth said, placing a gentle hand on Leo's arm. 'I'm glad I caught you before you left. I'm hosting a dinner tonight and I'd like it very much if you would come along.'

'Oh n-no,' Leo said. 'I couldn't possibly.'

'It would make me very happy if you did. Please?' Mrs Forsyth studied Leo's face with blue eyes so like her son's that Leo felt the tears prick her eyes once more.

'Of course,' Leo said, just to get away.

It was with grave misgivings that Leo read the note Mrs Forsyth sent to her with details of the dinner. She'd finished by saying: *I understand your father died recently and I know you might feel like staying in your room, but I really would love you to come.*

Leo crumpled the paper in her hand. She knew she was going to have to spend time with Mattie and her family on the ship. She had to get used to seeing them. And refusing to go to the dinner would seem so rude. She'd go, she decided. But she'd leave early and, for the rest of the time in Southampton, she'd claim tiredness and grief as an excuse to be by herself as much as she could. Then she sat down and wrote a letter to Joan, pouring out her heart. At seven o'clock, she dressed in the nicest thing she had, a cream-coloured lawn afternoon dress at least three seasons out of date and slightly yellowed, and walked back to the Dolphin Hotel and up to Mrs Forsyth's suite. She knocked at the door.

Of all people, Everett answered the door. 'Thank God, Leo, I was hoping it'd be you.'

'I don't think I can speak to you,' she said stiffly, trying to push past him.

'Please read this,' he begged, slipping her a folded sheet of paper.

'Rett! I need another drink,' Mattie called from within.

'Excuse me,' Leo whispered, hiding the note in her purse and stepping into the room.

She was appalled to find that she was seated beside Mrs Forsyth at dinner. Everett was seated beside Mattie's father, in a bizarre affront to the custom of alternating males and females. Mattie was seated beside her mother and a young man Leo didn't know.

The first course was oysters, which Leo had never eaten, and she looked around the table surreptitiously to see what she should do with the gelatinous-looking objects in front of her.

'Just slide it straight in,' Mrs Forsyth advised quietly. 'Tell me what you think.'

Mortified to have been discovered, Leo did as was suggested and tipped the first shell to her mouth. Expecting to be repulsed, she was pleasantly surprised by the strong and salty taste. 'It's better than I expected,' she admitted.

'A woman after my own heart. They're an aphrodisiac, you know.'

'I didn't,' Leo said, cursing her fair skin, which had the propensity to show every blush. 'Are you going to New York?' she asked, to change the subject.

'I think I am.' Mrs Forsyth sighed as if she wasn't looking forward to it. 'Lady Monckton is a very old and dear friend of mine and she's been having some difficulties of late. She's asked me to go with her to help her settle in. I expect I'll only stay for a month or two, although my son might just persuade me to stay longer.' She smiled over at Everett, whose eyes moved from his mother to Leo.

'But Everett's not going to New York right now is he?' Leo squeaked.

By unhappy coincidence, the other guests had fallen quiet, meaning Leo's words were heard by all.

Mattie frowned. 'He is. He's coming with me. I've convinced him not to wait.' Mattie fluttered her lashes at Everett in a gesture straight out of a movie and Everett shifted uncomfortably in his seat. Mrs Forsyth shook her head almost imperceptibly at Mattie and Leo wished she could hide under the tablecloth. Fortunately, conversation around the table resumed.

'He's being very generous,' Mrs Forsyth said. 'Lord Monckton needs some . . . assistance, and Everett has agreed to help him.'

'And he'll want to be with Mattie,' Leo said morosely.

'Why don't we have a break between courses?' Mrs Forsyth suggested to the table. 'Leo, I'll show you now.'

Leo stood up, bewildered. Show her what? She had no idea what Mrs Forsyth was talking about. She followed the older woman into another room and Mrs Forsyth closed the door.

'I hear you have a fondness for Lalique perfume bottles and I thought you'd like to see this one.' Mrs Forsyth took out a bottle whose stopper was delicately crafted into a crown of briar roses.

'It's lovely,' Leo breathed before registering Mrs Forsyth's words and realising that Everett must have spoken to his mother about her.

'I've always been close to Pamela – Lady Monckton,' Mrs Forsyth said casually, as if she was picking up a conversation they'd started at the dinner table, 'and because our children were born so close together and because one was a boy and one was a girl, we had an understanding that they'd marry when they were old enough. We spent such a lot of time together when the children were young and they did enjoy one another's company, as children do – always eager to be with anyone who prefers playing hide-and-go-seek to sitting quietly in a room with adults.'

This was so much worse than Leo had anticipated. Mattie and Everett had been promised to each other from birth and had a long-standing friendship.

'Everett is paying for their passage to America,' Mrs Forsyth continued. 'For their hotel rooms. He's even found them a house to rent in Manhattan. Lord Monckton has spent all his money, you see. Everett hadn't planned to accompany the Moncktons but now . . .'

'I understand,' Leo said haltingly, only to be interrupted by a loud crash of china from the next room.

'Excuse me a minute,' Mrs Forsyth said.

Before following her out, Leo took Everett's letter from her purse and threw it onto the fire. She didn't want to know any more about how deeply he was tied to Mattie, didn't want to read excuses for his behaviour; his mother had made everything crystal clear.

She stepped into the dining room in time to hear Mattie's father shout, 'Stop badgering me!' at his daughter. He banged a hand on the table and scowled at Mattie. 'If I feel like a walk, I'll go for a walk.'

Gracefully, Mattie's mother removed herself from the room, leaving her daughter and husband to it. Lord Monckton stood up, blundering a little, clearly having had more than enough wine.

'Stay away from the Red Lion Inn,' Mattie hissed. 'And the sailors. You're to come back with as much money in your pocket as when you left.'

'Can't a man even go out and buy himself a drink?' Lord Monckton snapped, and Leo flinched. That a man could speak to his own daughter that way. No wonder Mattie looked strained.

Mattie watched her father leave, lips pursed. Then she gave herself a visible shake and stuck a small smile on her face.

Impulsively, Leo reached for Mattie's hand. 'Are you all right?'

Mattie's laugh was brittle. '*I'm* perfectly fine. But you should buck up. You'll be miserable company otherwise.' She withdrew her hand and strolled over to Everett. 'You can see why we need your help,' Mattie said, eyes filling with tears. 'I can't follow him to whatever inn he ends up in and drag him out when the gambling starts.'

'I'm truly sorry, Mattie,' Everett said.

Leo had to leave. To witness their intimacy was more than she could bear. She strode towards the door.

Sleep was absent again that night. Leo kept her fingertips pressed to her eyes to stop any more tears from falling. She had to stay away from Everett. It shouldn't be too difficult. They weren't staying in the same hotel. The ship would be large. She'd make sure she only went to dinners with Mattie's family that were held in public places. There would be no occasion for her to speak to Everett ever again. If only she could excise him from her mind as surely, could stop seeing, behind her closed lids, Everett's eyes, Everett's hands, Everett's mouth.

After the longest fortnight Leo had ever known, finally it was time to board the ship. Leo followed the Moncktons to the gangplank, trying desperately to keep her eyes off Everett's back. He'd returned to London the day after the disastrous dinner – tying up business matters, according to Mattie – and he'd only arrived back in Southampton that morning. Which meant Leo had never been so glad in all her life to hear a familiar voice shouting her name. She spun around and saw Joan flying along the pier, clutching her hat to her head, bag thumping against her legs.

'Joan!' Leo cried, waving madly. 'What are you doing here?'

'I realised I don't need Pete as my excuse to go to New York. And I couldn't let you have all the fun,' Joan said as she flung her arms around Leo. 'Besides,' she whispered, 'your letter made it sound as if you needed a friend.'

'You're coming with me?'

"Course I am.'

Leo kissed Joan's cheek. 'Thank you. I feel better already.'

And she did. She stepped onto the gangplank, arm in arm with Joan, laughing at the people around them, many of whom – the well-dressed and obviously wealthy – were complaining about the proximity of those who would normally be out of sight in steerage. One woman who was nothing less than beautiful, her rich blonde hair threaded with strands of auburn and cut short in a blunt line that swung along her jaw as precisely as the foot of a marching soldier, was saying to a man in a loud and jocular voice, 'Hand me a gasper. The scent of the unwashed is killing me.' Her accent was unmistakably American.

'Faye!' Mattie called and the short-haired woman turned around.

'You're stuck on this puritanical tin can too, are you?' Faye grinned, stopping in the middle of the gangplank without a thought for the queue of people behind, waiting for Mattie to catch up and kiss her on the cheek. 'Well, at least that means we'll have some fun.'

'You remember Everett,' Mattie said, taking Everett's hand and forcing him to stop walking.

'I sure do,' Faye purred so flirtatiously that Leo's mouth fell open. 'How nice that you're stuck here with us.' Faye held out her hand to be kissed.

Everett simply shook it. 'I think we're in the way,' he said, moving past both women.

'No flirting with him,' Mattie said to Faye, giggling. 'He's mine, remember?'

Chapter Five

The next morning, wearing a striking silk dress as green as the phosphorescence trapped in the waves, Faye approached Leo. She almost jumped out of her deckchair, nervy anyway, having been up all night holding a basin for poor Joan, whose stomach and the ocean were bitter foes. When at last Joan had fallen asleep, Leo had taken the chance to get some fresh air, away from the odour of disinfectant. She'd patted powder onto her face, rubbed rouge onto her cheeks and coloured her lips in an effort to appear as if nothing at all was the matter. But now here was this woman, a friend of Mattie's, standing before her looking like she had something she wanted to say.

'Yes?' said Leo.

'Scram!' The woman's voice was so imperious that the person in the deckchair beside Leo stood up and scurried away obediently. 'I'm Faye Richier,' she said. Around her neck was a strand of oddly shaped pearls – misshapen moons – that gave off a silvery glow in the sunlight.

Leo shook the proffered hand reluctantly.

'I've been rubbernecking at your lips all morning wondering where you got that colour,' Faye said bluntly. 'It's the exact shade of red I've been wanting since I was old enough to wear it. But everything I've ever found washes away with one sip of champagne and is so insipid that I look like I still want to be twelve years old. Yours is the berries.'

Leo laughed despite herself. 'I made it myself,' she replied.

'You didn't tell me your name.'

'Leonora East.'

'Well, Leonora East, with that lipstick you're far and away the most interesting thing about this ship, although that's selling you a little short.' Faye paused long enough for Leo to blush at being the subject of such scrutiny, and then she waved to the man Leo had seen her with on the gangplank.

'Benj!' Faye called. 'Come and meet Miss Leonora East. This is my brother, Benjamin Richier.'

'Leo is fine,' Leo said, standing and shaking hands.

'Leo's joining us for dinner tonight,' Faye said.

'Oh no, I couldn't,' protested Leo.

'You have other plans, stuck on this crate of sardines?' asked Faye, her eyebrows raised. 'I can't let you out of my sight until we reach dry ground and I can get you to make me some of that.' She pointed at Leo's lips.

'Please ignore my sister,' Benjamin said. 'She's very used to getting her own way and, as we've discovered, her directness isn't what most Londoners are accustomed to.'

'Well, I'm not a Londoner, so she can be as direct as she likes,' said Leo, smiling at Faye who was impossible not to like.

Faye laughed and clapped her hands. 'See? Leo'll be much more fun than those dreary dowagers we sat with last night who talked of nothing but dead people. I'm tired of the war. It's time we forgot the whole thing.'

'Faye!' Benjamin spoke sharply to his sister.

But Leo interrupted. 'I'm tired of the war too. I'd love to join you for dinner.'

It was all very well when one was on deck on a sunny day, mesmerised by a woman in a bright green dress, but another thing entirely when Leo returned to the cabin. 'I think I just made a huge mistake,' she said to Joan.

'You and me both,' Joan groaned, looking anything but the sunny girl from Sydney Leo was used to. Even Pete's cheating hadn't been able to fell Joan as effectively as the sea had. Joan's light brown hair was almost black with sweat, her skin even paler than two years in England had brought about, her many freckles standing out distressingly dark on her face. 'Why did I think this voyage would be any different to the one from Australia?'

'At least this one's shorter,' Leo said, smiling.

'That,' said Joan, trying to sit up, 'is a blessing. But what's your mistake?'

'I just agreed to have dinner with Faye, Mattie's friend. Why did I say yes?'

'This might make you feel better.' Joan held out a note, addressed to Leo.

Leo saw that it was signed with an E, meaning it could be from only one person. 'That doesn't make me feel better,' she said. 'I'm not going to read it.'

'I dragged myself out of bed to take it from his mother, who's in the room next door, so you're bloody well going to read it,' Joan said firmly. 'Besides, if I'd spent a night with a man who looked like that, I'd be doing my damnedest to find out what was going on.' She opened the letter and read it aloud. '*Leo, please let me talk to you. It's not what you think; nothing is. I thought that by the time I returned from London, you'd have replied to my note but now*

I wonder if you even read it. I'll be down on what used to be the third-class deck at ten tonight. Please come. E.'

Leo held out her hand for the note.

'Right,' said Joan. 'You're going to dinner and then you're meeting Everett at ten. No arguments.'

'Do you think he means it?' Leo said slowly. 'That it's not what it seems?'

'Only one way to find out.'

There was a knock on the door and Leo found a steward there, holding out a dress the same colour blue as Everett Forsyth's eyes. 'Yes?' she said.

'I was asked to bring you this.'

'Are you sure it's for me?' Leo said doubtfully.

'Are you Miss East?'

'I am.'

'It's for Miss East.'

'Oh.' Leo took the dress. 'Thank you.'

Joan let out a squeal loud enough to deafen the fish. 'What is that gorgeous thing? And where did it come from?'

Leo unfolded the note attached to the dress.

Dear Miss East,

My sister Faye has decided to turn the upper deck of the ship into a nightclub for tonight's dinner. She has more dresses than she could ever possibly wear and I hoped you'd be happy to wear this, since we've been so rude as to turn a dinner into a party on such short notice.

Benjamin Richier

'My God,' was all Leo could say.

'Who,' Joan demanded, 'is Benjamin Richier? And why is he sending you beautiful dresses?'

'I don't really know who he is, besides being Faye's brother. I met him on deck this morning.'

'Well, you must have made quite an impression on him.'

'I can't wear it.' Leo dropped it onto the bed. 'What will he think if I do?'

'Put that thing on,' Joan said. 'You're going to a party.'

~

Leo did as she was told. Besides, she desperately wanted to wear the lovely dress, which reminded her of an oriental kimono, with batwing sleeves and a wide silk sash that tied around the waist. She shrugged off her browns and slid into the blue. She redid her hair, plaiting and coiling it into her own take on the traditional pompadour, which she knew might look maidenly next to Faye, but it was all she could do. She touched her lips with the colour Faye had admired and rubbed some onto her cheeks, blackened her lashes and sprayed herself with scent.

'You look beautiful,' Joan said approvingly. 'You should make the most of it. The Richiers are obviously wealthy, and friendly. Some friends like that could do you and your cosmetics idea a world of good.'

'Maybe,' Leo said. 'I wish you could come.'

'There's no way I could eat anything. You have fun.'

Leo kissed Joan's cheek and said goodbye before she could change her mind, then walked to the upper dining room, which was full to bursting with people. Leo could see the grandeur the room had once possessed, visible in the columns at the entrance that stood antique and white like bones stripped of their skin. The room looked tired, yet another thing diminished by war. But the deck, when she stepped onto it, was another thing altogether.

'Get a wiggle on,' Faye called. 'The party's started without you.'

At a table set up by the rail of the ship were seated Benjamin Richier, Mattie and her parents, Mrs Forsyth and Everett. Leo kept smiling and made sure she didn't flinch, thanking God and the Richiers for the dress.

'I believe you know everyone here,' Faye said. 'Mattie and I met in London a couple of years back and we've been friends ever since, and when I invited her to come to my little party, she asked if she could bring her poor, orphaned friend Leonora and I said, "Whaddya know? Leo and I are already acquainted."'

Mattie stiffened. So did Leo.

'Faye!' Benjamin said sharply.

'Everything looks beautiful,' Leo said, wanting to move the conversation away from herself – though everything Faye had said was true.

The deck had been transformed from the crowded space of the afternoon, where people had jostled for a position in the sun or on a deckchair, and into a floating paradise. Tables had been set out and covered in white cloths, with hurricane lamps glowing gently on top. The guests on the deck were dressed up and there was even a gramophone playing a song Leo wasn't familiar with. She thought she could make out the words 'I wish I could shimmy like my sister Kate'.

As Leo took in the re-styling of the deck, her eyes met Everett's. Tonight he looked more handsome than Leo had thought it was possible for a man to be, in a tuxedo, dark hair combed back neatly.

She snapped her attention back to Faye. 'How did you make this happen?' she asked, gesturing to the deck adorned with beautiful people, starlight and unsentimental music.

'I had a little chat to the captain.' Faye grinned. 'I told him I could provide the gramophone if he let me have a soiree that re-established life on a ship the way it should be.'

'You brought your own gramophone onto the ship?' Leo asked.

'I wasn't going to leave it to die a terrible death in England, killed by one too many renditions of "Oh! It's a Lovely War".' Faye sang a line from the song in a ridiculously overblown English accent and everyone began to laugh. 'Besides,' Faye continued, 'you never know when you might need a gramophone, as tonight shows. Take a seat.' The rest of the table began to talk among themselves and Leo was glad to sit near Faye, in the furthest possible seat from Everett.

Faye poured champagne into glasses. 'So, are you going to tell me why you're on a ship to New York?'

'Where did you get champagne from?' Benjamin interrupted.

'I'm not meant for austerity, Benj. Posterity, maybe.' Faye laughed. 'The captain was more than willing to supply it when I explained my inability to swallow food without the help of a glass of champagne.'

'I won't ask what you did in order to get it,' Benjamin said.

'Tsk-tsk,' Faye reprimanded. 'Leo will think I'm badly behaved.'

'Well then Leo would be right.' Benjamin leaned over and offered Leo a cigarette. She took one, grateful to have something to do with her hands.

'And I noticed how smoothly you drew the conversation away from the question I was asking Leo,' Faye said to her brother. 'Leo won't mind telling us why she's leaving that godforsaken island behind.'

Did she dare? Leo drew on the cigarette, and took a sip of champagne for courage. And then, spurred on by she didn't know what — the champagne; the unfamiliar gramophone music dancing away into the wide open dark; the need to ignore Everett, only a few feet away; or the feeling of being nowhere, in the middle of the sea, landless, homeless — she told them. 'I'm going to make cosmetics,' she said. 'Lipstick. Lash darkener. Rouge. I'm going to make people see that make-up isn't something that should only be ordered covertly by mail order. If most women are anything like me, they're tired of being told that red lipstick makes them fast; I want them to be able to buy it if they choose to. And I think they will.' She waited for the hysteria that would likely follow such a proclamation, but there was only silence, which was almost worse.

'Well, I'll be damned,' Faye said finally. Then she flung her arms wide and knocked all three glasses onto the deck, where they shattered. 'Atta girl! Then I'll be able to get my hands on that red. Best idea I've heard in ages. Don't you think?' She nudged her brother.

Leo became suddenly and uncomfortably aware that Benjamin's eyes were fixed on her. She tapped her cigarette on an ashtray.

'Cosmetics,' he said slowly. 'That *is* an excellent idea.' He smiled at her, leaning in closer.

Faye swivelled her head between Leo and Benjamin, raising an eyebrow at their nearness. She blew a long stream of cigarette smoke out into the night air and fingered her pearls. 'Cosmetics isn't really my brother's area of interest.' Her tone was chilly, exuberance gone. 'He's a boring industrialist who'd rather he didn't have to rescue his sister from England, where she's been stuck for the last four years.'

'How did you get stuck in England?' Leo asked, uncertain whether Faye's frostiness was directed at her or Benjamin, hoping to restore the camaraderie.

'I ran away to England for a man I suspected was a rake and he didn't disappoint me,' Faye said. 'Then the war started, leaving me stranded there.'

The conversation was interrupted by the arrival of dinner, over which Faye seemed to relax, and Leo found out that the Richiers lived in a house with a ballroom and that Benjamin ran a large manufacturing business in New York.

'You don't look old enough,' Leo couldn't help saying once Faye had finished.

Benjamin smiled. 'I'll take that as a compliment. Our father died eight years ago. I was seventeen and Faye just thirteen. I took on his business and I made some lucky decisions. Of course, the war helped.'

'Benj is being characteristically modest,' Faye said. 'He took on a business laden with debt and with only a few worthwhile assets and he's now one of the most successful men in Manhattan. Which comes with a price. Don't look now, but Dorothea Winterbourne is approaching. Dorothea –' Faye said in a voice that was obviously designed to carry – 'knew us and spurned us when our father was in debt but seems to find us more interesting now that we're loaded.'

'Faye.' Dorothea's voice was cool, like her blue-black hair and pale grey eyes. 'I was coming to see your brother.'

'I know you were.'

'But I'd just asked Miss East to dance.' Benjamin held out his hand to Leo.

All heads turned to Leo, including Everett's. Faye and Dorothea were both wearing frowns that gave the icebergs stiff competition for frostiness and Leo couldn't read Everett's expression.

She stood, reminding herself that once, long ago, she had learned at school in London both how to be a lady and how to dance. Now she was about to find out if she remembered any of it.

She stepped away from the table, then heard Faye say to Mattie, 'Looks like your charge is planning to hook herself a big fish.'

Leo winced, hoping to God that nobody, especially Benjamin, had heard.

But he only said, 'Thank you for saving me from Miss Winterbourne,' as they took their places on the dance floor.

'She doesn't look pleased.' Leo risked a glance in Dorothea and Faye's direction and couldn't help shivering when she met Faye's watchful eyes.

'She never is.'

Leo smiled, not expecting someone like Benjamin would dismiss a woman as pretty and clearly wealthy as Dorothea. 'You're very different from your sister.'

'I have to be. Imagine if there were two of us like Faye. Nobody would speak to us. And we'd be broke.' Benjamin smiled.

'But you love her just the way she is.'

Benjamin studied Leo's face. Their eyes were almost level; he was only an inch taller than she was. He was handsome, she decided, in an American kind of way. Blond hair, good looks that were almost too perfect. Preppy, she thought they called it over there.

'I do,' Benjamin said. 'Faye's been my responsibility for so long. And while I'd prefer not to have had to come to England to rescue her, I always will.'

'How nice that she has you.' Leo was aware that her voice wasn't quite steady as she spoke. She saw Benjamin notice, saw the question on his face and was glad that he didn't ask.

Instead he said, 'You look like a mythic siren with the moonlight behind you.'

Leo realised that her hair had blown loose, that the wind had picked up, and strands were streaming behind her as she danced. She was quiet, unable to think what to say in reply.

'In *Antony and Cleopatra*, Cleopatra had the sails of her barge drenched in perfume so that not only Mark Antony but even the winds were lovesick with the scent,' Benjamin continued.

Leo nodded, unsure where this turn in conversation was going. 'Yes. She cast a spell with rose oil and neroli and Mark Antony couldn't help but fall in love with her.'

'Which means perfume and cosmetics can be very influential.' It was too dark for Leo to read his expression so she didn't know if he was talking in generalities or if he was talking about the scent she was wearing. 'Let's talk more about your cosmetics idea in the morning.'

Leo was too stunned to say anything more. What did he mean? But he didn't elaborate and they finished their dance in companionable silence, witnessing the manoeuvrings at their table every three beats as they turned around: Mattie whispering hotly to her father. Her father shaking her off and moving over to join a group of men playing cards with piles of money on the table before them. Mattie looking beseechingly at Everett. Everett standing up to join Lord Monckton, hovering over the older man as if he was Lord Monckton's warder. Three beats later Everett had disappeared.

The dance finished and Benjamin led her back to their table. 'Excuse me,' Leo said, when she caught sight of the time. It was a quarter past ten and she realised that she was late for her meeting with Everett.

~

'I was worried you weren't coming,' Everett said, emerging from the shadows at the far end of the deck where he'd been smoking a cigarette, and he looked so happy to see her that she had to hold her hands rigidly at her side to stop herself reaching out to him.

'So the business you were to attend to in Southampton was an engagement,' she said shortly.

'No,' he said, shaking his head. 'It was the exact opposite.'

'Yet you're on a ship to New York with Lady Mattie, who calls you her almost-fiancé, but you told me you weren't sailing for a while.'

'I'm so sorry I hurt you.' His voice sounded gentle and genuine and Leo was glad of the darkness; he couldn't see that he'd caused tears to fill her eyes. 'Please let me explain.'

'You have five minutes,' she said.

And he began to tell her the story of an agreement between Mrs Forsyth and Lady Monckton, of a childhood friendship.

'Your mother has already filled me in,' Leo said.

'My mother,' Everett said wryly. 'She told me she'd tried to help but that she'd just made things worse.'

'She was certainly eager to explain your connection to Mattie.'

'But that's just it,' Everett cried. 'The connection isn't what you think and that's what my mother, in her lovely, bumbling way, was trying to say. Once I went away to school, I hardly saw Mattie at all. I'd forgotten about the agreement until the day after I came back to London from the war. Lady Monckton came to see me, to remind me of what she called my responsibility.'

'It seems a little unfeeling to call on you so very soon,' Leo said, wondering what kind of woman would press her daughter's claim on a man who'd been home only a day from a long and bloody war.

'In her mind, it was a matter of urgency. They were out of money. And I felt sorry for her, to be begging, almost, for a way to save her daughter. So I promised to take Mattie out, and to help Lord Monckton . . .' Everett sighed. 'Who just gambles everything away.'

Leo waited, beginning to feel the small scraps of faith she'd had in Everett, a faith she hadn't quite been able to let go of, stitch back together.

'It took only a few dates before I knew Mattie and I weren't suited. I told my mother and she understood. I told Mattie, and I thought she did too. But then some mutual acquaintances told me they'd heard her say I was joining her in New York. That there would be a wedding. I went to Southampton to ask Mattie to stop saying those things. Mattie had invited my mother there, thinking she'd help her cause. And now I've ended up on the ship babysitting Lord Monckton, trying to get him to New York without losing any more money. I've told the Moncktons I'd help set them up in Manhattan, but I won't be marrying Mattie.'

I won't be marrying Mattie. The relief of those words made Leo grip the rail. 'Thank God,' she said. 'I thought . . . I thought . . .'

'I know what you thought.' Everett stepped closer to her, his voice husky. 'I would never have done what we did if I was engaged to another woman. You're the only woman I want.'

Leo wiped her eyes and smiled at him, at Everett, the man who wanted her.

'You look beautiful tonight,' he murmured. 'And I wish I could hold you . . .'

'But you can't,' Leo finished for him. 'Not until everything is sorted out.'

Everett sighed. 'Out of respect for my mother's friendship with them, I probably shouldn't see you until I get the Moncktons established. But I feel like I can survive the crossing now, can survive until . . .'

'The second Saturday in July at Romany Marie's.'

'You remembered.'

'Of course I did.'

The next moment was wordless, but like the waves beating against the ship's prow, Leo heard the sound of Everett's ragged breath, the thud of her heart.

'I need to go back to steering Lord Monckton away from card games,' Everett said reluctantly.

'Goodbye,' Leo said softly.

As Everett passed, he stretched out a finger towards her. She let her hand trail across his. His eyes met hers and the desire that flared in her was the most overpowering thing she'd ever felt. It was like being back at the inn and standing before the mirror while he took off her corset and she felt powerful and beautiful and wanted. It took all her willpower to tear herself away.

Chapter Six

*L*eo awoke much later with a jolt; the noise of running feet and raised voices had trampled through her dreams. And the ship was no longer moving. She scrambled up, rubbing her eyes and hurrying out of her cabin along with other guests, a stampede of silk pyjamas and smoking jackets drawn to the commotion, all thinking of icebergs and sinkings.

Instinct made her run for the upper deck, where the party had been held. She reached the dining room and saw Everett standing in the archway leading onto the deck, his face blanched of colour. Mattie was sobbing loudly on his shoulder. Faye was rubbing Mattie's back. They were all still dressed in their party clothes: Faye in red, Mattie in lilac, Everett in his tuxedo. Beyond them, the hurricane lamps had been blown out, a tablecloth was tossed by the wind into the sky, like a ghost departing, and the stench of alcohol and something else, something ominous, fouled the air.

'There's no sign of him, sir,' the ship's steward reported to Everett with an anxious face.

'It's been four hours since he was last sighted.' It was the captain now, speaking to Everett in a low tone, but Leo was right at the front of the crowd of people and could hear every word. 'I think we have to assume . . .'

Mattie sobbed loudly and put a hand on her stomach. 'I'm going to faint. I need to lie down. Otherwise the baby . . .'

The word *baby* jerked Leo awake with even more force than the commotion that had brought her upstairs and an instant silence descended on the passengers.

Then Mattie's legs gave way and Everett caught her, picked her up, and carried her away from the crowd. Three people followed. Faye. Everett's mother. And Mattie's mother.

A hubbub began. *What had happened? Who hadn't been sighted for four hours? And had Lady Mattie really all but said she was pregnant?* The crowd didn't know which question was the most toothsome: a possible tragedy or the scandal of Mattie's condition. Leo pushed her way out of the throng, nausea rolling through her.

When she reached her room, Joan wasn't there. An hour ticked by and Leo sat on her bed, staring at the door, hearing people pass up and down the hall. Finally Joan appeared.

'Where have you been?' Leo asked. 'You look terrible.'

Joan's face was white. She ran to the washbasin and threw up.

Leo held her hair out of the way and tucked her into bed when she was done.

'It's Mattie's father,' Joan said once she was lying down. 'He's vanished.'

'What?'

'They think he fell overboard and they needed a doctor in case they found a body in the water. But the doctor was so drunk they couldn't wake him and they asked me to help instead. I was told that Lord Monckton played cards for hours, giving out IOUs because he was being thoroughly beaten. Apparently Everett tried to stop him but Lord Monckton punched him.'

'What!' Leo said again.

'Then Lord Monckton vanished. Everyone thought he'd gone to bed. But they've been searching since midnight and there's no sign of him.'

'Did he fall?' Leo asked. Then a terrible thought struck her. 'Or did he . . . ?'

'I don't know,' Joan whispered.

'Poor Mattie. How is she?'

'Sleeping now. I gave her what I could from the doctor's bag, but with her being . . .' Joan stopped.

Leo made herself say it. 'With child?'

'That's what she said.'

There was a knock at the door. Leo opened it to find a steward there.

'We need the nurse again,' he said.

'I don't think she's well enough,' Leo replied, casting a worried look at Joan.

But Joan stood up. 'I'll come,' she said, following the steward out.

Leo began to pace. Mattie's father had disappeared. And Mattie was pregnant. To whom?

Then she heard a door close and Mrs Forsyth's voice say, 'I need a drink.'

'So do I.' Everett's voice, in reply, sounded grim.

Leo realised the adjoining door between the rooms had been left ajar, probably by a steward, meaning she could hear every word passing between mother and son in Mrs Forsyth's cabin next door.

Ice tinkled in glasses.

Mrs Forsyth spoke again. 'Even without tonight's gambling debts, Pamela just told me that the only house they have left is so heavily mortgaged to the bank that Mattie could work for a lifetime and never be able to pay back the money owed. And

Mattie has no skills that anyone would employ her for. They're worse than penniless; they're indentured for life to debt.'

'Damn it!' Everett swore. 'What about the father of the baby? Surely he'd want to help the mother of his child.'

The most awful fear in Leo's heart vanished. She'd been unable to believe he was the father, but nor had she known what else to think.

'Mattie says she doesn't know who the father is,' Mrs Forsyth said.

'How is that possible?'

Mrs Forsyth sighed. 'I gather she was rather sociable in London, and very careless.'

'What the hell am I supposed to do?'

A long silence followed Everett's question.

'The gossip is already spreading around the ship,' Mrs Forsyth said haltingly. 'People assume you're the father of Mattie's child. You were standing beside her when she said she was pregnant and she'd told people that you were going to New York to be with her.'

'Which Mattie could easily refute.' Everett's voice rasped with barely contained anger.

'I've asked her to. But she won't.'

Another silence. Leo sank noiselessly to the bed, pressing her lips together to stop herself from crying.

Everett's next words were said so low that Leo almost couldn't hear them. 'Do you think she did it deliberately? Or was she just so upset that it happened to come out in front of everyone?' A glass slammed onto a table. 'I can't believe I'm even asking that.'

'I honestly don't know, my love.'

The endearment made Leo's throat tighten. Mrs Forsyth was clearly heartbroken for her son and the conversation was going in only one possible direction.

Everett's next words confirmed it. 'So I can be the man who abandoned the grieving, pauperised and pregnant woman everyone thinks I'm promised to, right after her father possibly killed himself. Or I can marry Mattie.'

'I don't want to influence your decision. But if you do the former, nobody will ever speak to you again. Or do business with you. Your dream of a shop in New York wouldn't get off the ground. The gossip would destroy you.'

'Perhaps I don't care.'

'Perhaps Leo is worth that,' his mother said gently.

'Leo is worth anything.' Everett's voice broke on the words. 'But then there's the right thing to do.'

'Yes.'

'I can't do it,' Everett whispered.

But Leo knew Everett was too fine a man to abandon Mattie now.

⁓

Leo walked out onto the deck, placed her hands on the rail of the ship and felt the cold air stream against her face. She leaned out as far as she could, taking the full force of the wind on her cheeks. Then she opened her mouth and screamed until she had no breath left to scream any more. She turned her back to the sea and leaned against the rails until her breath levelled out. Now, perhaps, she could do it.

She stopped first at the bar. 'Two old-fashioneds, please.'

'Coming right up.'

'I didn't know anybody else in the world drank those things.'

Leo froze. It was Mattie's voice. 'An American soldier gave me a taste for them,' she lied, wincing as the barman passed her two drinks.

'You must have quite a taste for them if you're planning to drink two.' Mattie stared at the drinks through eyes that were not quite as red as Leo had thought they would be, and she'd also found time, amid the grief and chaos, to dress immaculately and have her hair done.

'I'm sorry about your father,' Leo said. 'I know it doesn't feel quite real to begin with.'

Mattie gave a short, high-pitched laugh. 'Oh, it's real enough.'

'I was angry when my father died. Angry at him for leaving me alone.'

That barking laugh again. 'I don't expect Mother and I will ever stop being furious with my father. But at least now he can't keep gambling everything away. That's something to be grateful for.'

How awful for Mattie, to have a father who'd made her so resentful that his death would seem a blessing. Leo felt her own eyes fill with the tears Mattie wouldn't let herself shed.

'Have you seen Everett?' Mattie asked.

Leo shook her head and Mattie swept out of the room.

Leo picked up the two drinks. Should she still look for him now that she knew Mattie was looking too? But it had to be done and she'd make it quick; to drag it out would be more than either of them could bear.

She found him, as she knew she would, on the lower deck, staring out to sea as if he'd just seen all his men mown down in the no-man's-land that lay before him. She was unable to stop the tremor in her hands, a tremor that rattled the ice cubes and made him turn around. The instant he saw her, his mouth curved into the beginnings of a smile and his eyes lightened a little.

'Leo,' he said. 'You have no idea how good it is to see you right now.'

Thank God for the drinks. If she hadn't been carrying those, against all sense and reason, she would have flung herself into his arms. 'You too,' she said softly. 'I thought you could use one of these.' As she passed him the drink, their fingers touched and, instead of taking the drink from her, he kept his hand on the glass, letting that one small moment of contact linger.

But even that slight touch began to build into something beautiful and dangerous. He took the drink from her and had a long swallow.

'I needed that.' He put down the glass. 'Leo.' He said her name again, wretchedness scraping against her ears.

Of all the griefs she'd gone through, this one was almost too much. But she stared hard at the water, stretching far, far away from this place of sorrow, and she made certain her voice was level. 'Don't say anything,' she said. 'You have to marry Mattie. I understand why. It wouldn't ever feel right if we were to be together after this. I don't want to ruin our one perfect night because you feel obliged to me.'

'Obliged doesn't describe at all how I feel about you.' His eyes glittered.

'You can't say things like that. It only makes it harder.' Her voice wobbled despite her best efforts and she knew that if she let even one tear fall, he would hold her to try to take the pain away. But she could never, ever touch him again.

'Never in my life have I been less willing to do something that is supposedly the right thing,' he said.

'But you will do it because you're an honourable man. It's one of the many reasons why I . . .' *Why I love you*, Leo didn't say.

'Leo.'

This time, she let herself go. Let herself cling to him as he clung to her, deep in his arms, head tucked against his neck until she could resist it no longer and she raised her chin and kissed his lips as hard as she could, needing him to know exactly how she felt in spite of everything. And he responded the same way, gathering her as close against him as he could, imprinting himself on her so that she knew, no matter how far their lives strayed from one another, she would never forget this moment, never forget him.

She pulled back before her body completely overwhelmed her. 'I hope you can be happy,' she said, turning away in time to see Mattie walk onto the deck.

'There you are,' she said impatiently to Everett. Then she saw Leonora.

Mattie's eyes moved between Everett and Leo, taking in the two glasses, the wild look on Everett's face, the tears that had finally begun to stream down Leo's cheeks.

'What's going on?' Mattie said sharply.

Leo didn't answer. She couldn't. She kept walking resolutely on, past Mattie, who repeated more loudly, 'What's going on?'

What's going on? Leo repeated to herself as she escaped the deck and went to her room. How could anyone ever explain what had gone on between Leo and Everett? There weren't enough words, not the right words, in any language, to describe it.

Chapter Seven

*L*eo stayed in her cabin with Joan for the next two days. But the cabin soon became claustrophobic and she ventured out, found a deckchair, nibbled a croissant and watched a woman take a powder compact out of her purse and pat her nose. Leo knew she was staring but she couldn't help it; she'd never seen anyone do that in a public place. Indeed the few passengers on deck so early all reacted; an older couple exchanged horrified gasps and turned away, and a younger man almost lost his eyeballs over the side of the boat. But Leo was also fascinated by the compact; it was so big and unwieldy, as were most compacts. How she would love to make something more elegant, portable and unobtrusive.

'I know it seems out of place amid all the tragedy to say something like this, but Faye tells me nobody has a lipstick like yours.' Benjamin had appeared in the deckchair beside hers and was following her gaze.

'Imagine being able to make a compact that would fit in the palm of a hand,' Leo said, indicating the other woman.

'Imagine if you had the money to do that.'

'That would take a miracle,' Leo replied drily.

'Perhaps you're looking at your miracle.'

'What do you mean?'

Benjamin relaxed back in his seat, crossed his ankles and lit a cigarette. 'I mean that if Faye wants your lipstick, so will every other woman in Manhattan. I want to invest in you.'

'To do what?'

'To make cosmetics.'

Leo's brain was incapable of forming a rational thought or sentence.

'Of course, it's not as simple as that,' Benjamin went on. 'Just a couple of years back, a sales clerk at Macy's was fired for wearing rouge to work. It was all over the papers.'

Leo stood up. 'I need to walk. This isn't a sitting-still conversation. Because that's what makes me mad. That people can lie and cheat and . . .' She stopped, the direction her words were taking intensifying the ache in her chest. 'People do far worse things than colour their cheeks,' she said at last. 'At least rouge never hurt anyone. Why shouldn't a sales clerk wear it to work if she wants to? What right does anyone have to say that she shouldn't?'

'So you need to change the world?'

Leo sighed. 'Where would I even begin?'

'My factories can stop making bullets now that the war is over. I have spare capacity. I've been looking for something to fill it.'

'You made bullets for the war?' Leo interrupted. 'Bullets are so much more wholesome than rouge,' she couldn't help adding sarcastically.

'But rouge would hardly stop a trench full of Germans,' he joked.

Leo didn't laugh.

Benjamin sighed. 'Passion and business don't mix, Leo. Which is something you'll need to learn.'

'But . . .'

'I want to expand my interests,' Benjamin went on, not giving her a chance to protest. 'And I want Faye to stop running off after unsuitable men. She'd have to work with you. She needs something to do.'

'So, Leo makes the cosmetics. Benjamin gives Leo the money. And I show my very rich friends how fabulous the cosmetics are and they all buy them. Everyone's happy. Is that right?' Faye's mocking voice, coming from right behind them, punctured the conversation.

'Cosmetics makes good business sense,' Benjamin said to his sister. 'The end of the war is going to propel Americans into years of forgetting, of spending, of indulging themselves. Which makes cosmetics a product women will want more of. I know nothing about cosmetics, but I know you do, Faye. And Leonora wears her lip colour with elegance, and I know that she looks very beautiful.'

Leo had no need for rouge after that. Her eyes fled from Benjamin's face and landed on the water. 'It seems a large risk for a prudent businessman,' she said.

'You don't become filthy rich by playing small and safe,' Faye said, enunciating the words *filthy rich* as if she was testing Leo.

Benjamin winced. 'I'm sure I could have said that more tactfully. But Faye's right – it's the chancy opportunities I'm most interested in.'

I'm a chemist's daughter from a village in England who knows nothing about New York and whose only experience of cosmetics is making lip colours and mascara for the nurses at the local army camp. It's not a very solid foundation on which to build a business, Leo wanted to say. But why should she dismiss herself like that? She'd told Everett that she'd started to believe in herself. Shouldn't she behave as if that was true?

'We won't lose,' said Benjamin. 'Richier Cosmetics.' He moved his arm in an arc, as if he was writing the words in gold letters across the sky.

'Richier Cosmetics,' Leo repeated, entranced. 'I like the sound of that.'

'I bet you do,' Faye drawled. 'Interesting, isn't it?' She unfolded a newspaper and pointed to a picture of Benjamin's serious face. 'Here's an article that says the only thing Benjamin needs to be truly successful is the perfect wife. Now that Everett and Mattie are engaged, you aren't strolling the deck with them. Instead you're up here with my brother.'

Leo felt suddenly hot, as if the sun was burning her cheeks. So Everett *had* proposed to Mattie. But had Mattie told Faye what she'd seen: two drinks and two people crying on the deck of a ship?

'I heard there was a gold-digger with auburn hair aboard and I wanted to make sure it wasn't you,' Faye continued.

'You're being unbelievably rude, Faye,' Benjamin said sharply.

'I should go. I'll think about your offer, I promise,' Leo said to Benjamin before she hurried away.

Leo peeped into the room, in case Joan was still sleeping off the seasickness. 'You're awake!' she said, relieved to find her friend on her feet.

'I usually start recovering in time to disembark,' Joan said wryly.

'You won't believe it, but Benjamin Richier said he'd help me start a cosmetics business.' Leo dropped onto Joan's bed.

'And what does Faye think about that?' Joan asked shrewdly.

'I think she just wanted some lipstick that nobody else had and now she's worried I'm going to spend all their money.'

'I don't think that's the only reason she's unhappy.'

'I think Mattie might have told her she saw me talking to Everett.'

'So what?' Joan shrugged. 'You did the right thing. You left him to marry Mattie. Besides, that's not what's got her so riled up. She's jealous.'

'Jealous?' Leo just about fell over laughing. 'Why?'

'Because you've caught her brother's eye and she doesn't like it.'

There it was, the thing Leo feared, said aloud. 'Do you think he's only offering to help me because he expects something in return?' Leo fretted at a loose thread on the blanket. 'He's handsome and seems nice but I can't quite work out why he's so interested in me.'

'Well, let's see. Perhaps he's interested in you because you're beautiful. And you're completely different to Faye and to that Dorothea Winterbourne you told me about. Which is probably why Faye thought she was safe introducing him to you. What are you going to do?'

What was she going to do? It was a question Leo turned over in her head all night. She'd lost Everett, of that she was certain. But before she'd ever known Everett, she'd had a dream. He'd helped her shape it a little, and her conversation with Benjamin had helped her to see just how much she wanted to do it. Men could kill one another at war, could gamble away their family's entire fortune, could drink so much that they couldn't perform their medical duties on a ship and it would be seen as valiant, or it would be hushed up, or it would be ignored, but a woman might wear a little rouge to work and it was a national disgrace. Leo was in the mood for a fight. And she had nothing to lose.

The next day, Leo sent a note to Benjamin asking him to meet her on deck. She made her face up carefully for the meeting, armour on, becoming a different Leo East to the one who existed six months ago, one who was prepared to withstand anything in order to do what she wanted. One who was braver and stronger than she'd ever been.

At the appointed time, Benjamin approached with a smile. 'I looked for you at dinner last night. I hope Faye and I didn't frighten you away.'

'I skipped dinner. I've been doing a lot of thinking.'

'Oh?' His tone was light but there was a question in his eyes – and something else, an emotion Leo wished she didn't recognise: hunger.

'Thank you for offering to invest in me. But as much as I want to say yes to you, I can't. I want to try to do it by myself. To know that I *can* do something extraordinary.' She let the words take off like the bewitching notes of tiny songbirds across the Atlantic Ocean. 'I'm going to find a job in a department store. And I'm going to look for a workroom where I can experiment with formulas. When my cosmetics are the best I can possibly make them, I'll take them to the finest store. And I hope they'll agree to stock them.'

'You're a very determined woman. I know better than most that determined people can make it in Manhattan.'

'Like you did.'

'Yes.'

Leo exhaled a long breath and smiled. 'Thank you for understanding. I thought you'd laugh at me.'

'On the contrary,' he said, brushing a curl behind her ear. 'I admire you.'

Leo stepped backwards. But she was immediately annoyed at herself for behaving like the weaker one.

'Where will you go when you reach New York?' he asked. 'I hope you'll let me know where you end up. I'd like to see you again. And the offer of help will always be there when — or I should say if — things don't work out.'

Oh, it could so easily have been a slip of the tongue. *When* things don't work out. But Benjamin was a shrewd businessman. Not the sort to make slips of the tongue. 'Thank you,' Leo said, smile pasted on. 'That's very generous.'

'I'm glad you think so. I'll see you at dinner?'

'Yes, you will.' Leo kept smiling until he'd gone. Then she turned around and faced the sea and this time, instead of screaming, she said, 'Daddy, this might not have been what you had in mind, but it's what I want to do. If you're out there anywhere, I hope you'll give me your blessing. Because I don't want to fail.'

At last the day came when the ship was due to arrive in New York. It seemed to move faster, pushed onwards by the visible excitement of the passengers, some of whom, like Faye, had been stranded in England for years. Leo's excitement grew to such a state that she found herself not thinking of Everett for long stretches of time. She stood on the deck, watching eagerly for a sight of the vast country that would be her new home. Even Joan managed to struggle up onto the deck to join her.

'Land!' There was a cry from the prow of the ship and several hands pointed across the water to the looming shape of a city.

Leo could see silver towers reaching up into the sky like the wings of strange and unusual birds. She rushed forward, watching intently as Manhattan began to take shape. The harbour was alive with traffic: ferry boats, canal boats, fire boats, tugboats, picnic barges, yachts and giant floating platforms for loading grain. A gunshot made Leo jump, but another passenger said it was the sunset gun from Governors Island and, as if on cue, the Statue of Liberty's torch was lit, flaming like Leo's hopes across the New York City skyline.

Benjamin appeared at her side. 'Look!' Leo cried, pointing to the statue that Benjamin must have seen a thousand times before.

But he followed her gaze and his face lit up too; he was clearly happy to be almost home.

'It's magnificent,' Leo breathed.

Benjamin took her hand in his, raised it to his lips and kissed it. 'As are you.'

She laughed, too caught up in the excitement of their arrival to mind. 'I'm definitely not ready to be compared to the Statue of Liberty. But thank you.' They were both quiet a moment, Leo wonderstruck at the sight of evening falling over Manhattan, which was like lying back and staring at the night sky, witnessing each star of light begin to shine from the buildings near the harbour. The things she could do in this city, she thought. The things she *would* do.

Then she noticed Mattie and Everett standing a few feet away. Mattie wasn't wearing mourning, but if a face could wear mourning, then Everett's was.

Faye stepped up beside her brother, and Joan took her place beside Leo. Leo realised that Benjamin was still holding her hand, and that Mattie had slipped her hand into Everett's. Six people facing the city, sailing towards the future, lives now hopelessly entwined. And the baby riding with them, Mattie's baby, the baby who'd gained a father while taking from Leo the love of her life.

PART

Two

PART

TWO

Chapter Eight

JUNE 1919

*L*eo knew that nothing would ever compare to the feeling of standing on the edge of New York City for the very first time. Possibility carolled from every clock tower, soared from the skyscraper spires reaching for greatness, glowed from each window of light that banished night-time from the city.

'Look!' Leo called to Joan as automobile after automobile raced by: omnibuses and taxis and private cars, all going somewhere, filled with sparkling people. And, 'Look!' Joan cried in return when a thunderous noise erupted overhead, causing Leo to cower, thinking it must surely be a cannon firing, only to discover it was a steam train, a colossal and filthy steam train on a steel lacework of tracks, sending down clouds of black snow. But nobody, besides her and Joan, seemed to think it anything out of the ordinary.

'We can drive you somewhere,' Benjamin offered.

Leo shook her head and took Joan's hand, eyes shining, feet hankering to move through the city that would now be her home.

'It's an adventure!' Leo said to a more pragmatic Joan, who looked to be on the verge of accepting Benjamin's offer. 'We can't go in a car. We'll collect our luggage later.'

Joan relented and Benjamin shook his head, clearly at a loss to understand why Leo preferred to walk on into nowhere, when his jaw-dropping Rolls-Royce with driver was waiting like a carriage in a fairytale to sweep them away.

'I'll let you know where we end up,' Leo called over her shoulder, grinning.

She promptly bought the *Ask Mr Foster* map of New York City from a street vendor, then she and Joan stepped boldly into the seething, thriving hullabaloo of Manhattan, heading for Chinatown, because an American friend of Joan's from the hospital had said that was the place to find cheap rooms. It took them more than an hour to walk there because they had to stop so often to take in the sights: Buddhist temples, a Chinese theatre, half-plucked chickens hanging by their feet in neat rows in a shop window, and the constant rattle of the El train overhead, up and down the Bowery. Above it all, a host of sheets and clothes wafted like angels caught on the washing lines strung between buildings.

They found a room for eight dollars a week in a gimcrack building on Hester Street, right on the edge of Chinatown, in an area where many of the buildings were tenements, four windows across and four windows high. The strangeness of Chinatown suited Leo from the first because it was so unlike Sutton Veny and could not possibly remind her of her childhood home. Sutton Veny smelled of lavender and earth and fresh bread from the bakery whereas Hester Street smelled of fish shops, incense from the joss houses, bitter melon and mustard greens in the produce stalls, chop suey restaurants and hand laundries.

The next day, Joan and Leo began to look for work. After a week of scouring the newspapers, of walking the streets and looking for signs, Leo at last found an advertisement for a job in a department store: *Window dressing assistant wanted*. She didn't know what window dressing was, but if it brought her close to a high-end department store then it was perfect.

She walked up to midtown and rapped on the door of a tiny office, home to the Fortunate Display Company. She had an interview with a woman called Fortune and, because most other women wanted to work in the typing pools of the big companies, not work nights in an obscure job that required skills such as sewing, cleaning and errand-running, was told to report for a trial at Lord & Taylor at half past five the following Monday afternoon.

Lord & Taylor on Fifth Avenue turned out to be a kingdom of mahogany sales counters and sparkling chandeliers, of marble staircases and gloved elevator attendants, of luxuries chosen to make women swoon.

The floorwalker approached, his expression making it clear that Leo was out of place among the crowds of shoppers, arms adorned with shopping bags, shoulders draped in mink. 'May I help you?'

'I'm here to meet Fortune. I'm looking for the goods entrance.'

The floorwalker sniffed. 'Please leave by the main doors. You need the Thirty-Ninth Street entrance.'

Leo did as she was told, dreaming of the day when she'd enter a store like this and see her lipsticks displayed. When she wouldn't have to take the goods entrance.

'So you turned up,' Fortune drawled as Leo appeared. 'Last girl decided five minutes into the job that she'd prefer life in an office, clacking away on a typewriter. Let's see how long you last.'

'Well, I can't type, so that shouldn't be a problem,' Leo joked, but Fortune just drew on her cigarette and motioned for Leo to follow her down into the bowels of the building.

As they walked, Leo observed her new boss. Fortune looked to be in her thirties, and she didn't wear a wedding ring – or a corset, judging by the way everything jiggled about. Her hair was a shade of blonde that couldn't possibly be natural.

'How much d'you know about windows?' Fortune asked as they marched on.

'Nothing,' Leo admitted.

Fortune sighed dramatically, as if there was no helping Leo, but she deigned to explain. 'Fifth Avenue windows are a prime piece of real estate and their fitting out requires as much con-sid-er-ation as a bride's choice of a fancy frock.'

'Do we work here at the store, or at your office?' Leo asked.

'We work here – but we aren't *really* here.' Fortune smirked.

'But we *are* here,' Leo pointed out unnecessarily.

'This one's got a lot to learn,' Fortune said as she turned into a room.

The first thing Leo realised was that there was another person present to whom Fortune was talking. The second thing she realised was that she must have taken a wrong turn and walked into a room in the sky where rainbows were made. Rolls of vividly coloured silks and organzas lined one wall. Stacked against another wall were hundreds of boxes containing dyed ostrich feathers, seashells, bright tissue and crepe papers, paint pots, electric bulbs in every hue, clay, cardboard, wire, paper and glue.

'Lottie,' Fortune said, 'meet our newest recruit.'

Lottie glanced up at Leo with dark brown eyes made large and striking by her haircut, which was as short as a boy's. She stood up, and Leo saw that what she'd thought was a skirt was actually a pair of trousers, made with pleated legs that folded together to resemble a dress. Culotte skirts, Leo had heard they were called, worn by women who rode bicycles around the city. Lottie's face was arresting but dispassionate, as if she was reserving judgement. She was a far cry from Joan who, the first time she'd met Leo, had gossiped non-stop about the soldiers' shenanigans.

'According to Messrs Lord & Taylor, and the owners of every other department store in America, the display men make the windows.' Fortune lingered over *display men* as if they were dirty words. 'Women can't be display *men*, so women can't trim windows. Got it so far?'

Leo nodded.

'But seeing as how men know just how to ruin a group of mannequins dressed for evening by putting hats on them made for daytime, the men need a little help. Unofficially, of course, because the secret society – the International Display Men of America – won't let us work here any other way: women are too precious to work nights and lift heavy things and hammer a nail into a wall, aren't we, Lottie?'

'Yes, I might hurt my finger and then I'd cry and cry,' Lottie said sarcastically.

'So you and Lottie don't work for Lord & Taylor,' Fortune continued. 'You work for me: the undisputed and unacknowledged Queen of the Windows.'

'Where are the display men?' Leo asked, unable to imagine a man amid all the colour and splendour of the room they were in.

Fortune snorted. 'They're in the carpentry room with their tools. And we're here designing the windows, adding the style and casting a spell to make it all look as pretty as the proverbial picture.' Fortune waggled her fingers at Leo like a witch.

Leo smiled. 'So what's the first spell we need to cast?' she asked, unable to resist reaching out to run her fingers through a tray of shining glass beads that tinkled like a song made for dancing.

'There'll be a Victory Parade in September,' Fortune said, cigarette hanging from her mouth as she spoke. 'Twenty-five thousand soldiers marching down Fifth Avenue past our windows, plus one hundred thousand or more cheering them on. We gotta provide a bit of colour to liven up all the khaki.'

Lottie pulled out some sketches that were unlike anything Leo had ever seen. Four women were arranged on a carpet of burnt orange and copper autumn leaves. Their dresses were a striking contrast of emerald, sapphire and violet set against the russet tones of fall. Butterflies, wings coloured to harmonise with the gowns, fluttered gaily out of reach. In the background, most eye-catching of all, was a cream car, the kind you might see pulling up outside a stately home in the country. Leaning against it was a man, laconically smoking a cigarette, pretending to be oblivious to the admiring gazes the women were sending his way. The illustrations weren't flat, lifeless things; they were a living story taking place before Leo's eyes, a story she would have been happy to step into, which was obviously the point.

This was selling, Leo suddenly understood, something she knew nothing about. But she'd need to if she was going to have any chance of convincing a store like this to sell her cosmetics. She really had come to the perfect place to learn what she needed to know.

'It's beautiful,' Leo said. 'I feel like one perfect leaf is about to fall from the tree and maybe he'll pick it up and pass it to one of the women and she'll know he prefers her. Then maybe they'll go for a drive and . . .' She stopped, blushing. She'd let her mind and her mouth run away with her and now Fortune and Lottie were staring.

'So we've got a romantic on staff. That'll make a change,' Fortune said, stubbing out her cigarette and promptly lighting another.

Lottie eyed Leo appraisingly, waiting for her to say more.

'I just think,' Leo said, studying the illustrations, 'that I wouldn't be able to help but look at a window like that.' She leafed through the drawings and saw that each window of the six that ran along Fifth Avenue unfolded in much the way Leo had imagined. There was the man passing the woman a star-shaped leaf. There they were walking hand in hand. There they were driving away, the woman's goldenrod scarf streaming behind her.

'For that, you can help me work out a way to make autumn leaves from silk,' Lottie said, walking over to a work table and beckoning for Leo to follow. 'The last girl couldn't see a story in a book of fairytales.'

'I'll see what I can do about the car!' Fortune called after them.

'Will you really put a car in the window?' Leo asked Lottie. 'How?'

'Fortune can sweet talk her way into borrowing anything,' Lottie said. 'Then we drive it into the basement and it goes up on the hydraulic lifts and into the window one night. In the morning, there it is, and everyone thinks it's magic.'

'It sounds like magic.'

'That's retailing for you. But it's really rabbits in false-bottomed hats. Autumn leaves made from silk. A tiny red light in the tip of a cigarette so it seems as if this fella's smoking. Berry juice rubbed on the mannequin's cheeks to make you think she's blushing. That's why we work nights. Nobody's meant to know about the Lord & Taylor windows until the grand unveiling.'

Leo grinned. Beauty and invention, masquerades and enchantment. 'I think I'm going to like this.'

'No,' Lottie said, her grin matching Leo's, 'I think you're going to love it.'

~

It was hard to tell who was more excited that night in the tiny room on Hester Street. Joan had arrived home first, with a bottle of gin, in a flagrant but well-received violation of the wartime restrictions that were in place until the Eighteenth Amendment took effect. She had two glasses waiting when Leo came through the door.

'I have a job!' Joan said triumphantly.

'And I survived the first day at mine,' Leo said with a laugh as they sat on the bed with their legs tucked beneath them and clinked glasses. 'Tell me about yours.'

Joan sobered a little. 'It turns out I'm not the only one who fell for a man who talked marriage but just meant sex, which means a lot of unmarried girls are now stuck with babies they can't keep. I'm just lucky I made Pete wear a rubber.'

Leo put her glass down on the floor, euphoria gone. A voice she'd heard whispering in her ear over the past week, a voice that had been easy to ignore beneath the cacophony of Manhattan, grew suddenly louder.

Joan chattered on. 'Annabel – she's the one who suggested we look in Chinatown for a room – told me about a place over in Hell's Kitchen where they take in pregnant girls, let them stay for a couple of months until they have the baby, and then adopt the babies out to rich families who can't have their own. Problem solved. It pays me more money than a hospital job would and I feel as if I'm helping people who really need it.'

'My monthlies are late,' Leo said slowly, as she finally let herself hear that appalling, insistent voice.

'How late?' Leo heard shock in Joan's tone.

'At least two weeks. Do you think it's just stress or grief?'

'Have you ever been late before?'

'Never.' And that one word made real the truth of Leo's situation.

'Oh, Leo.' Joan was by her side in an instant, wrapping an arm around her shoulders.

'I should tell Everett.'

Joan reached across to the dressing table, to the pile of newspapers they'd accumulated in their search for jobs. She pulled one out, opened it and passed it to Leo. 'Mattie and Everett were married on the weekend.'

Leo's eyes ran over the words. One hundred guests. Formal reception at the St Regis Hotel. Bride looked delighted. No honeymoon. Groom busy with business interests.

So it was done. Even though she'd expected it, the news hit Leo so hard she felt like doubling over, and it answered her question. It was too late to tell him. The image of Everett's desperately sad face on the ship was all Leo could see before her. That and a baby with his blue eyes. 'What should I do?'

Joan hesitated. 'You could always . . .'

'I won't abort it.' Leo was adamant.

'If we took the baby to the lying-in home I'm working at, nobody need ever know,' Joan said matter-of-factly, presenting the only other possible solution for an unmarried woman with child.

'I will know.' Leo's voice cracked. 'I'll know that somewhere in Manhattan there's a child of mine, a child of Everett's.' Oh God! As she said the words – a child – she felt the most over-whelming rush of love. In their one night of enchantment, she and Everett had conceived a child. 'How can I give it away?'

Her last sentence was a wail, a lament for a baby she suddenly realised she desperately wanted.

'You have to,' Joan whispered, sitting down and rocking Leo back and forth. 'There's no other way.' Neither spoke for a minute then Joan went on. 'You wouldn't be giving up the baby,' she said emphatically. 'You'd be making sure it survived. If you kept it, you'd be an unmarried woman with an illegitimate child and nobody would give you a job or rent you a room. Most girls who keep their babies end up working as whores because that's the only job they can get, and the ones too stubborn to do that end up on the streets with a child in the middle of winter, hungry, sick and very soon dead.' Joan tightened her embrace. 'Giving the child away is an act of love. I promise.'

An act of love that felt anything but. Leo's throat constricted with sadness and shame – shame that she would even consider relinquishing her own precious child, and sadness that, if she did, she would never have a chance to know it; it would call somebody else Mother. She traced a finger over her stomach, offering the baby the only caress she could.

'The birthing home is expensive. Rich mothers only want the babies of well-off sinners, not poor ones.' Joan's tone was brisk and efficient, a nurse addressing a medical issue. 'So you can't go there to have the child. But I've birthed babies before. I know what to do. You can have it here. I'll tell the lady who runs the home about you, assure her that you're not a germ-infested pauper. I'm sure she'll take the baby.'

Leo knew she should just agree. What other choice did she have? She'd already vowed not to abort the child. And Joan was right; if she kept it, both she and the baby would be on the streets, and how could a child survive that? Above all, Leo wanted her child to thrive.

As if she'd read Leo's mind, Joan said, 'It's the only way to keep it safe.'

'Then I'll do it,' Leo said sadly. 'I'll hate it. But I'll do it.'

On the weekend, Leo walked out of the boarding house, determined. The baby was probably due in about seven months. She'd most likely have to go into hiding in four or five months. So that was all the time she had to get some samples made up and get them into a department store.

She walked up the Bowery and across to Fifth Avenue. Then she methodically worked her way through every street in midtown, searching for pharmacies, asking if she could pay for the privilege of using the backroom on a weekend. From what she'd seen so far of New York, anything could be bought. Dim sum cooks rented corners of tea houses, apple carts jostled for space on sidewalks, cigarette and soda stands protruded from tailors' stores and she'd even seen a barber and a dentist cohabiting, as if trimming hair and taking out teeth went together like Fifth Avenue and crowds.

But everyone shook their heads at her. Those less polite laughed. 'Not to a woman,' they said, eyeing her as if she was proposing something criminal.

Dejected, she walked back to Chinatown at dusk; she'd have to try another part of the city tomorrow. She was so lost in thought that she walked too far, reaching a street called Pell, which she thought was a couple of blocks past the boarding house. 'Damn,' she muttered. As if her feet weren't already tired enough. Then a sign caught her eye: *Chinese Medicine*. That had to be something like a pharmacy, surely? She pushed open the door.

Once inside, she stared about in wonder. Behind the counter was a wall of wooden drawers, each about the size of a shoebox. Sets of brass scales hung from some of the handles. Above the drawers, up high, touching the ceiling, were jars filled with herbs, labelled in the beautiful and delicate script that Leo had seen everywhere on the streets around the boarding house. She recognised some things: chrysanthemum flowers and honeysuckle, a type of mushroom she couldn't identify, apricot kernels, berries. But there were so many others she was unfamiliar with and she studied them eagerly, wishing she could open all the drawers and the jars. Strange and exotic scents filled the air with a wild and heady perfume that was equal parts floral, spice and danger.

'Can I help you?' The Chinese woman behind the counter, who looked only a little older than Leo, spoke perfect English, with the accent of a native New Yorker.

Leo couldn't keep the surprise from showing on her face.

'Relieved I speak English?' the woman asked testily.

Leo nodded, abashed. 'I'm from a village in the middle of England,' she said apologetically. 'You're the first Chinese person I've ever spoken to in my life.' Her voice trailed away. She wasn't off to a good start.

'Mama!' A small boy ran into the shop through a curtained door.

The woman hushed him. 'I have a customer,' she said, then added something in Chinese that sounded like a term of endearment. The boy smiled at his mother and the action pricked Leo's heart.

'What a lovely child,' Leo said, eyes fixed on the gentle waft of curtain through which he'd disappeared. 'What's his name?'

The woman's eyes lit up. 'Jimmy. He's four. What do you need?'

'You have so many things,' Leo said, stepping forward. 'It's wonderful. Like a treasure cave.'

'Some you'd know. Camellia.' The woman opened a drawer as she spoke, then another. 'Aster.'

'And you use all these for medicine?'

The woman laughed. 'It's not quite that simple. I'm Jia, by the way.'

'And I'm Leo.' Leo hesitated, then plunged in. 'I need to find a workroom to use on weekends to make up some cosmetics. Like this lip colour.' She took what she had left of her supplies from Sutton Veny out of her purse. 'I'm happy to pay rent, and I'd be sure to clean up after myself. The only thing I might need help with is ordering in what I need. I don't yet know where to find supplies in New York.'

Jia studied Leo. 'You've tried everywhere else and they've said no?'

'Yes,' Leo admitted. 'But if I'd known about this place, I'd have come here first. It smells exactly the way I'd like my lip colour to smell when you open the lid. Inviting – no.' Leo shook her head. 'More than that. Exhilarating.'

'Well, you sure know how to get someone on your side. Why not? I could use the money. There's something I'd like in return though.'

'What?'

'That.' Jia pointed at the lip colour.

'It's yours.'

Jia opened the lid and dabbed some onto her lips with her finger.

Leo frowned. 'That looks terrible,' she blurted.

Jia searched for a mirror to see her face.

'I didn't mean it like that,' Leo added hastily. 'Just that it washes you out.'

Jia passed the pot back to Leo. 'I thought it was too good to be true.'

'Wait!' Leo cried. 'Don't give up on me yet. I have fair hair and pale skin, so the colour suits me. But you're completely different.'

'Thanks for pointing out the obvious.'

'No, no. You've given me an idea.' Leo looked at the vast array of ingredients around her, the variety of herbs and flowers and leaves, things she could try, could play with, have fun with. 'I thought that all I needed was the perfect red. But maybe I need lots of perfect reds. Different shades, so women can find the right one depending on how light or dark their skin is or the colour of their hair. Do you see?' Leo could feel her whole face bright with elation and she hoped Jia could sense it too. 'I'll make you a lipstick so stunning that, next to you, Manhattan will look like an old maid.'

'Then we have a deal.' Jia extended her hand. 'Four dollars a week rent and I'll even show you what's in the drawers. There are things you could use that you probably don't even know about.'

Four dollars! Leo flinched. That was what she paid for her half of the room at the boarding house. Her job with Fortune only paid eighteen dollars a week. She'd have very little left to buy supplies.

'If you're not interested . . .' Jia shrugged.

'I am,' Leo said, thinking quickly. She was at Lord & Taylor from half past five to half past eleven every night. She'd get a daytime job too. She might have to forgo sleep but maybe that was just as well. Then she wouldn't be able to dream of Everett.

'Done,' Leo said, shooting out her hand. 'Can I start today?' She opened her purse and took out four dollars before she could change her mind.

Leo spent the next two weeks looking for another department store job, but she had no luck. She was running out of money, unwilling to dip into her savings, eating the bare minimum she needed, feeling a little sorry for herself.

Which was why, on the second Saturday in July, she decided to go to Romany Marie's. She knew Everett wouldn't be there; he was a married man now. Joan was working late and Leo was alone so she set off along the Bowery.

The Bowery at night was not a place for the faint-hearted. On no other street in Manhattan were the wartime alcohol restrictions, still in force, flouted so openly. Liquor was cheap on the Bowery, and it was strong, and the saloons were packed tighter with men than any church on Sunday.

Those men who were still able to walk when they left the saloons staggered to the flophouses with fancy names, like the Savoy, which were nothing more than a place to pass out with a roof over one's head. Above it all hovered the El, a roof that blocked out the stars and the moon, enclosing them all in a kind of hell lit by conflagrations of light from the theatres, the restaurants and the drinking establishments. It was a place apart, a subterranean New York, which made Leo feel as if the real New York was happening elsewhere. Like the St Regis, where Everett had married Mattie in what was sure to have been a grand party, or at Romany Marie's, which Leo found at the top of a cramped staircase in Greenwich Village.

A log fire burned in the first of two rooms, even though it was July, chasing away the shadows of the world Leo had come from. A singer crooned in a language Leo didn't understand, but she recognised absolutely the meaning: it was a song about what it meant to be heartsick and Leo slipped into a chair, both entranced and disbelieving that a stranger could have understood her so well. Then someone else took the stage and played a rowdy folk song, the room threw off its melancholy and everyone danced, even those who, before, had been aware of nothing other than the chessboards on the tables in front of them.

'You're Leo.'

'Yes,' Leo said, startled, looking up into the face of a black-haired, olive-skinned woman, dressed in crimson, an exact replica of a romantic gypsy figure, cigarette poised between her fingers. 'You're Romany Marie.'

'I am.' Marie blew out a stream of smoke that hovered blue-grey in the air. 'I have something for you.' She held out an envelope addressed in the most precious handwriting to Leo East.

Leo took the letter and placed it on the table. But Marie didn't leave her alone to luxuriate in Everett's words.

'You should open it,' Marie said, stubbing her cigarette out on Leo's table.

She so desperately wanted to. What did it matter if Marie was there to witness? Leo slipped her finger under the seal and took out a single sheet of card. *I love you. E.*

Leo drew in a sharp breath.

'He wasn't sure you'd come; I told him you would,' Marie said.

'How did you know?'

'I see the future. Your baby will thrive. The other will suffer.'

With that, Romany Marie melted away to another table to impart her eerie clairvoyance and Leo fled down the stairs and back out onto Christopher Street feeling nauseous, her skin clammy. She loosened the top button on her shirtwaister but the night was too still and the fire had overheated her skin. She dropped onto a nearby bench.

Slowly, the nausea subsided. Her skin cooled. But she couldn't shake Marie's voice from her head: *Your baby will thrive. The other will suffer.*

Which other baby? The only one Leo knew of was Mattie's, the child that would become Everett's in a few months' time. But how would Marie know about that? Leo rested her hands on her belly, feeling nothing out of the ordinary, but knowing that something remarkable lay beneath her skin. *You will thrive,* Leo whispered, as if her child could hear her. Thank God for that. It was ridiculous to believe the words of a gypsy woman who probably wanted nothing more than an easy dollar, but Leo tucked those words into her chest, let them beat in her blood and down to her baby so it would know, no matter what Leo had to do, that she loved it with all her heart.

Chapter Nine

The next day, Leo awoke feeling revived and full of ideas. She'd been too blinkered; there were other places to work besides department stores. Like a salon. She'd heard the stories: Elizabeth Arden had started as a cashier for a rival beautician. Then she'd taken a jar of cream and turned it into a business. Now she ran the Red Door Salon. Her products were sold in some department stores too. It would be perfect – if only Leo could bluff her way into a job.

She tucked some feigned confidence into her purse along with her handkerchief and set off for the gleaming red door on Fifth Avenue. It opened a little abruptly and Leo jumped back as a young woman dressed in a white uniform and nurse's shoes and with a pink ribbon in her hair hurried out, crying. Puzzled, Leo watched the girl go, wondering why someone would leave a place of such glamour with tears on her cheeks.

Then she stepped into the famous Oval Room, which was ostentatiously decorated in white and gold. It was like being trapped inside the egg of an exotic bird. Chaise longues were set along the walls, a place of repose for the wealthy customers, tired out by the walk from their car to the salon. Mirrors made the room look palatial and the gold silk of the drapes was so glorious that Leo wanted nothing more than to snip it down and fashion a dress from it. The room spoke of luxury, privilege and discretion.

Leo approached the cashier and turned on the cultured voice she'd learned so many years earlier when she was at school in London learning how to be more than a simple village girl. 'I've recently arrived from England, where I worked at a salon,' she lied outrageously. 'I thought you might be interested in someone with my expertise.'

The cashier looked at Leo exultantly. 'Oh yes! The girl who left just now was overly sensitive to Miss Arden's tongue and I have a list of clients I was going to have to cancel, but if you could start today then you'd save my skin. Otherwise I'll be the one on the wrong side of Miss Arden's tongue. I'll make sure someone else does the consultations so you'll just be in the treatment rooms and I can get one of the other girls to take ten minutes to show you what to do. And,' she lowered her voice, 'some of the girls earn forty dollars a week here, what with all the tips.'

Forty dollars a week! Leo almost had to hold on to the counter top to steady herself. 'I can start right now,' she said eagerly, knowing she'd have to wing it; she couldn't let this chance pass her by. She'd made creams, she'd sold creams, she'd used creams. Hopefully that would help. Or else she'd also become familiar with Miss Arden's tongue.

'Let's get you a uniform and you'll be all set.'

Soon she was wearing a spare white uniform and a pair of soft-soled shoes that were a little too small, she'd dressed her hair with the pink ribbon as requested and the hush and calm of the salon, where you could have heard a fly sneeze, relaxed her a little. Her palms were sweaty when she received her first client behind the white voile curtain, but all she had to do was smooth a Youth Mask onto the face of a woman who had nothing of youth about her, and who would hand over two hundred dollars for a course of treatments that probably wouldn't alter her a jot. Leo was incredulous. So much money! She surreptitiously sniffed the cream and thought it was probably nothing more than beeswax and lanolin, along with something sharper – pine bark, perhaps.

Leo finished the treatment and ushered the lady back to the Oval Room, where she promptly fell upon another woman of a similar age and they began to compare jowls. 'It's making such a difference, don't you think?' Leo's client said.

Leo bit her tongue to stop herself saying, *Wax and lanolin can't work miracles!*

But the other lady nodded enthusiastically. 'You look ten years younger.'

'As do you,' her friend replied, and they both sipped their cups of tea.

As Leo walked back to the treatment room, she began to understand something, an idea she'd glimpsed while working on window displays with Lottie. Those women believed the cream she'd put on their faces had transformed them. It didn't matter that it probably hadn't done a thing. Leo needed to remember she wasn't just creating a lipstick; she also had to create a promise. A promise any woman would pay to have kept.

⁓

Now that she and Joan were settled into their new lives, Leo sent Benjamin a note with her address, knowing it was a connection she couldn't afford to lose. The very next day, a reply came, with an invitation from Benjamin to take them both out. 'Am I the chaperone?' Joan grinned, before Leo threw a pillow at her. But she'd replied in the affirmative, fixing on a Saturday night in August.

Then she and Joan stayed in most weekend nights making themselves something to wear – if there was one thing the war had been good for, it was improving their sewing skills. Leo had regularly turned old dresses into something new with the addition of a ribbon or lace taken from a dress that could no longer be mended. But this time she dipped into her tiny stash of money to buy some cherry red jersey fabric and a pattern for a dress that had a draped cowl neckline, a dropped waist emphasised by a belt with a rhinestone-studded buckle, and a skirt that sat an inch above her ankle. On the shoulder, she pinned a piece of delightful frippery: a little burst of red and black feathers. She used a leftover piece of red jersey to re-trim her hat and, that night, when she ran the hand mirror down her body, seeing herself in pieces, she hoped she was dressed up enough. It was still early enough in her pregnancy that the baby didn't show, which she knew should be a blessing – but she wanted, foolishly, to see her stomach round, to know that the baby was growing, to feel it move.

She sighed and put the mirror down, turning her attention to her lips. She made them redder than she ever had before, applying layer after layer until the colour matched her dress. A flick of black on her lashes and she was ready.

'Perfect!' Joan said when Leo did a final twirl.

'You too,' Leo said, smiling at her friend, who'd chosen a bright colour too – violet – and whose crepe-de-Chine dress had lovely, floaty chiffon sleeves.

The sound of a car tooting from the street below carried through Leo's open window, as did Faye's voice: 'Ready or not, here we are!'

'I was wondering whether she'd let her brother out on his own with you.' Joan raised an eyebrow at Leo.

Leo didn't reply, just made for the stairs, trying not to worry about whether they'd find nice Faye or frosty Faye in the car.

'Ladies.' Benjamin had stepped out of the Rolls and opened the door for them, waving the chauffeur back into the car. He kissed both their cheeks, but it was only to Leonora that he said, 'You look beautiful.'

'Why have you set yourselves up here?' Faye asked, coming straight to the point, as was her way. She wrinkled her nose as a waft of Chinatown's peculiar odour of anise and menace drifted through the open door. 'The Roller doesn't like filth and murder. Nor do I.'

Leo laughed as if Faye had made a joke, although the hard glitter in Faye's eyes belied the possibility. 'We've survived for over a month without being murdered. Besides, you didn't need to collect us. We could have caught the subway.'

Benjamin took Leonora's hand in his and gave it a squeeze. 'As usual, ignore my sister.'

But Faye was on a roll. 'The subway! No other woman in Manhattan would refuse a ride with Benj. We've got ourselves a rare one here.'

Benjamin didn't let go of Leo's hand and she wished for a moment she could feel the urgent need that swept over her whenever she'd touched Everett, but all she felt was gratitude for his attempt to protect her from his sister. 'Where are we going?' she asked.

'Tex's place,' Faye said, as if that was explanation enough.

Leo tried to catch Joan's eye, to see if she'd understood, but Joan was staring at Leo's hand in Benjamin's and grinning. Faye also glanced at their joined hands, but she didn't smile.

Leo retreated to the safety of the window, watching the parade of buildings fly past. The flower stands and confectionery counters of midtown were deserted now; the men who bought the flowers for their best girls had left work, as had the stenographers who lined up in pretty rows at lunchtime for a fix of candy. The four-dial tower clock of the Metropolitan Tower rang out the notes of Handel's Cambridge Chimes and two flashes of red sliced through the night sky, declaring that it was half past the hour.

'I have two jobs,' she said, wanting to share her news. 'One at Lord & Taylor. I'm just an assistant window dresser for now. But it's giving me ideas about things I didn't even know I needed to understand – about selling, and having a story.'

'Jesus!' Faye looked aghast. 'You'll be the only shopgirl at the party tonight.'

Luckily, they'd arrived at a tiny speakeasy on West Fifty-Fourth Street and there was no time for Leo to reveal to Faye that she was also a salon girl.

'Tex!' Faye shouted. 'This is Texas Guinan,' she explained to Leo and Joan. 'She used to be a movie star.'

An immense tigress of a woman greeted Faye with a continental double kiss and the words, 'Hello, suckers!'

Faye relished in explaining to Leo, as if she was a gauche girl from the country – which Leo knew she was – that 'suckers' was a term of endearment reserved for those Texas deemed suitable to belong to the esteemed 300 Club – a membership as fluid as the Hudson. Her man dealt with those who weren't.

Inside the club, Leo could see actresses Pola Negri and Gloria Swanson sitting at a table, and businessmen Reggie Vanderbilt and Walter Chrysler, whose faces were familiar from the newspaper, standing by the bar. A jazz band played in the corner and the air was fogged with cigarette smoke. Tables were pushed right up against cloth-covered walls shimmering with a luxurious blend of sage, gold and pale rose. Illuminated pictures of parrots decorated the walls, burnishing the marcelled heads of the beautiful people gathered beneath. It was a wild jumble of styles, put together with such virtuosity that it somehow worked.

Leo could see that hers was the least like an evening dress, besides Joan's, but it was still red and bold and it made her feel good. If she smiled and pretended she didn't care, then perhaps no one would notice it was really a day dress staying up late.

Tex led them to a table near the front. 'Ginger ale?' she asked with a grin and produced a bottle of champagne.

Faye took the proffered bottle and downed its contents in several swallows. 'That soldier's dead,' she declared, pushing the near-empty bottle away.

'What soldier?' Joan said.

Faye laughed as if Joan had said something hilarious. She pointed to the champagne bottle. 'Dead: finished, run out, drained. As in, I need another.'

'Faye,' Benjamin began.

'Don't be a fire extinguisher, Benj,' Faye said. 'Loosen up. It's a party. I'll behave tomorrow.' She stood up and walked away.

'You can see why I think she needs something to keep her busy,' Benjamin said. 'Now, why don't I introduce you around?' He beckoned to Joan and led her away, leaving Leo sitting alone, not sure if she was supposed to wait for him or find something else to do.

But he was soon back, having left Joan chatting to a group of men. 'Now I have you all to myself,' he said, smiling.

Before she could reply, a man sat down beside her and slapped Benjamin on the back. 'Rich. Good to see you. But who's this?'

'I'm . . .' Leo started, but Benjamin interrupted.

'This is Leonora East.' Benjamin slid his chair closer to hers. 'She's the woman who's going to start a cosmetics business for Richier Industries, if I have anything to do with it.'

'But I'm not . . .' she began.

'Looks like she might be making something else for you,' the man cut in, leering.

Benjamin laughed.

'I bet you'd like a dance,' the man said, holding his hand out to Leonora.

'Pity I'd just asked her,' Benjamin shot back, standing and pulling Leo up with him. His arm snaked around her waist as he led her over to the dance floor.

Leo's smile had long since faded. Here she'd been thinking a night out would be fun. But so far Faye had abused her and Benjamin was acting like he owned her.

Then she was on the dance floor and she found the fun. There, everyone was laughing and talking and smoking and drinking. Young women like herself danced in dresses of the sort that hung in the Lord & Taylor windows, dresses that were definitely not homemade. They moved from one man to another at the change of every song, not like Benjamin and Leo, who were clasped somewhat uncomfortably together. Or so Leo thought, but Benjamin didn't seem to mind. Other women watched the movement from the sidelines, needing either a whiskey shot of confidence to join in or, Leo thought, just the right lipstick.

She saw a few women whose cheeks had spiders crawling down them but it was just that their mascara didn't have the right ingredients to allow it to cling to their lashes in the heat and the sweat. She saw women who'd tried to wear lipstick but either the dyes used were far too pale to begin with or they had no longevity, so they wiped off with the first sip of champagne. She remembered those details, stored them away, knowing those were the kinds of problems she needed to solve so that cosmetics might, one day, become indispensable.

The music slowed. Benjamin's hands slid down to the top of Leo's hips and drew her firmly towards him.

'I need the bathroom,' Leo said. 'Please excuse me.' She hurried away before he could offer to escort her.

She threaded through the groups of people in the room and came upon Faye, her arm linked through a man's. Leo couldn't see his face because Faye's body was blocking her view. She was whispering into his ear and giggling. Then the man said, 'Please don't,' and Leo saw him step back, away from Faye. As he did so, Leo's heart crashed through the floor.

'Leo!' Everett saw Leo a split second after she'd recognised him.

'I think you mean the wants-to-be-Mrs Richier.' Faye patted Everett's arm playfully.

'What?' Everett's face was white and Leo felt a tear leak into the corner of each eye. She saw Faye smirk at both Leo's eyes and Everett's face, which were more than enough to suggest that things between Leo and Everett weren't quite what they should be.

'Where's Mattie?' Faye went on gaily. 'At home is she? Of course, she's indisposed.'

'I'm not that indisposed.' A smooth English voice carried into the conversation and Mattie — now Mrs Everett Forsyth — appeared, sliding her arm through her husband's. 'Leonora,' she said. 'You look very . . . red.'

And Leo knew that her cheeks must match her dress and her lipstick. Mattie, on the other hand, was tranquil in ivory, which did nothing for her very pale skin. The dress looked as if it had been painted on, her body now so full-figured with child that she seemed to take up all the space in the suddenly shrinking room.

Then Benjamin stepped up behind Leonora and ran a finger down the bare skin of her neck. He smiled and said, 'Weren't we dancing?'

Leo nodded, not trusting her voice to come out steadily. She danced with Benjamin, watching Mattie withdraw her arm from Everett's and walk away without so much as a backward glance at her husband. Faye cosied into Everett's side again but Everett gave Faye a look so cold that even Faye stepped back, stung more than Leo thought she'd be, hand gripping the pearls she always wore. Then Everett strode off. Faye's eyes were on him the whole time.

By midnight, Leo was a little drunk. She'd excused herself after her dance with Benjamin and found Joan, who was gazing up at the man beside her. He hadn't noticed, being more interested in whiskey and cigars and the tasteless jokes he was telling his friends. She tried to catch Joan's eye, but Joan clearly didn't want it caught.

Then Benjamin tapped Joan's back urgently; Faye had been taken ill and he hoped Joan might be able to help her. Neither Leo nor Joan stated the obvious: that Faye had most likely had too much to drink. Instead Joan went with him and Leo wandered off to find the bathroom. She'd just stepped into the corridor at the back of the club when she felt a hand on her arm.

'Come with me,' whispered a voice Leo would know anywhere, and her whole face broke into a smile. Everett led her down the corridor and then out a back exit into a laneway that smelled of whiskey and woodsmoke, just as the inn at Dunbridge had smelled the first night they'd kissed.

'I think everyone's having too much fun in there to notice us out here,' Everett said.

'I think you're right,' she said lightly.

'It's good to see you.'

'You too.'

Silence was dangerous; it made the attraction between them louder, more difficult to ignore.

'How did you get mixed up with the Richiers?' Everett asked, taking them onto safe ground. 'Mattie met Faye in London but she doesn't seem like the sort of person you'd be friends with.'

'Faye liked my lipstick. And she seems fond of you,' Leo said.

Everett rubbed a hand across his jaw and sighed. 'She's persistent. The first night I ever took Mattie out in London, Faye waited until Mattie had gone to the bathroom and then she leaned across the table and took off my cufflinks, telling me she'd happily help me remove a few more items. She did it in front of a group of people, so I couldn't say what I really wanted to without embarrassing her. I was trying to save her dignity, which was pointless,' he said ruefully. 'I never did get those cufflinks back.'

'That sounds like Faye.'

'And Ben?'

'And Benjamin . . .' She stopped.

'. . . is obviously smitten with you,' Everett said.

Leo blushed. 'I don't think so,' she said. 'He wanted me to start a cosmetics business for him.'

'What did you say?' Leo heard apprehension in his voice.

'I said no.'

'He's a man most women would want to marry.'

'This one doesn't.'

'Don't ignore someone like Benjamin Richier because of me. You deserve to marry. To fall in love.'

'I don't feel anything for him beyond friendship. And that's not your fault. It's just the way it is.' Leo hesitated. 'Do you know him well?'

'Not really. I've met him at a couple of dinners. I've heard he's a man who goes after what he wants until he gets it. You have a good business idea. You're also beautiful.' Everett's smile was both tender and sad.

Leo longed to blurt out, *We have a baby*, to share the wonderful yet devastating news. But Everett had been strong enough to do the honourable thing. She should be too. 'Are you happy sometimes?' she asked.

'When I'm at work, yes.' His eyes lit up for a moment, a gentle blue. 'You should see how the store's coming along.' Then the storm rolled over his face. 'But life with Mattie . . . it has its ups and downs.' He paused. 'Did you get my note – from Romany Marie?'

'I did.'

They'd run out of words and now, without the shield of conversation to protect them, in the silence of eye meeting eye, of seeing his gaze drop to her mouth, her stomach clenched and a dangerous warmth flooded her body. 'I should go,' she said.

Everett turned away, but not before she saw that his face was a mirror of her own longing. 'Take care, Leo.'

'You too,' she whispered, before slipping back into the club and then out the front door and onto the sidewalk, where she breathed in huge gulps of hot summer air, scalding her lungs, trying to forget the ache in her chest where her heart pounded for no one other than Everett Forsyth – and their child.

Chapter Ten

*L*eo's life was soon divided into three parts: days at the Red Door Salon pampering ladies who had little to do and too much money to do it with; nights at Lord & Taylor; and weekends at Jia's store, which were her favourite times, especially as Jia became more and more interested in what Leo was doing. In fact, Jia's growing friendliness had given Leo the courage to ask for a remedy for nausea, which bothered Leo for the first couple of hours each day. Jia had produced a tea, thankfully without comment, which had made it easier for Leo to work through the pungent smells of the salon.

'What are you making today?' Jia asked, leaning against a bench near Leo one Saturday in late August, having left Jimmy, her son, napping upstairs.

'Lipstick. It's basically just wax, oil and colour. I used to use beeswax and almond oil because that's what we had at the chemist. But now I want to see which is really the best wax and oil. Then I can experiment with colour and scent.'

'Why would it make a difference?' Jia asked as Leo stirred hot wax on the stove.

'Try some of those over there and tell me what you think. They're not mine,' Leo added hastily as Jia opened the first compact and wrinkled her nose. 'I bought them to see what else was available. Which isn't much, as I suspected.'

Jia put down the compact. 'I'm glad you didn't make that. It stinks.'

Leo laughed. 'That's one of the problems. The ingredients used to make lipstick don't smell at all like something you'd want to put on your lips – which is why I need scent. Try the next one.'

Jia reached out dubiously and took up a lipstick tube. She pushed up the levers on the side and tried to apply it. But it was too soft and it squashed back into the tube without leaving any trace of colour on her lips. 'Well that's useless,' she said.

'Exactly,' said Leo. 'It's hot in here, right?'

Jia nodded.

'So I have to find a combination of wax and oil with a high enough melting point that it won't collapse in a puddle at the first sign of summer. If I was making lipstick in tubes, which I can't afford to do' – here Leo sighed, because she desperately wanted to make a lipstick rather than a compact, but the cost of materials and the problems of manufacture were far too great to surmount – 'then it needs to be strong; you don't want the lipstick to break when you apply it. But mine will be in compacts; they need to be soft enough to apply with a brush, but not so soft that the ingredients liquefy when it's hot.'

'And have you figured it out?'

'I think so,' Leo said as she began to pour her concoction into glass pots. 'But I also have to make sure that it tastes nice and that the colour doesn't come off the instant you have one sip of a drink. Or a kiss.' Leo looked up at Jia, who laughed.

'Look at you! You're the happiest I've seen you since I met you. You enjoy this, don't you?'

'I do. When I'm in here, mixing and making up samples, I feel like I can actually do this. It's only when I step outside and into a place like the Red Door Salon that I realise how much money I really need to make it work. But,' she added resolutely, 'I can't let that stop me. I just need a set of perfect samples, then I can convince one of the department stores to buy from me, and I'll use that money to make more things.'

'Carnauba wax,' Jia said suddenly. 'When you make lipstick in tubes, use carnauba wax. It's from the leaves of a Brazilian palm tree. It's one of the hardest setting waxes, but it also has softening properties and doesn't cause rashes.'

'That sounds perfect!' Leo said, eyes shining. 'Can we order some in? I'd love to see how it reacts with the other ingredients.'

'I'll get some on Monday,' Jia said. 'And when you have your first orders, I know a couple of factories that might be able to help. They make skin whitening creams, white face powders and all the other junk Chinese girls buy to look more American. They should have the equipment you need. They're run by Chinese though.'

'That doesn't worry me,' said Leo. 'If they're willing to help then I love them already. But I have another favour to ask you. I don't want to use rose oil as the perfume. It's too old-fashioned. I want something like I smelled the day I walked into your shop. Something that makes you feel as if anything could happen.'

'I might have to charge you extra for that.'

'Oh,' Leo said, crestfallen.

Jia laughed. 'I'm joking! As much as I love my store, this is the best fun I've had in years. We'll try jasmine perhaps. That's what you smelled the first day you were here.'

Leo grinned at Jia through the steam of the cooling pots. With Jia's help, and her own hard work, she really thought she might see her products on the shelves of a store like Lord & Taylor very soon.

———

Leo quickly discovered that the Red Door Salon was a revolving door of staff who disliked Miss Arden's brand of pep talk, which was why Leo had been able to get a job so easily. But, despite her acid tongue, Leo admired Miss Arden, who stayed late every night cleaning the salon, who tied the pink ribbons on the boxes of cream herself, and who was ruthless in following her own personal regime of massage, exercise, wax baths, hair removal and even sending electrical currents into her skin.

To look like I did twenty years ago was the wish of every customer, but that was impossible. Instead, Leo led the ladies to the treatment room and promised that the Ardena patter would firm the lady's face and the Francis Jordan roller, which in Leo's opinion looked like an instrument of torture, would disperse the fatty tissues and unearth the slender woman who used to lurk beneath the now-pouchy flesh. She applied the chin straps and the forehead straps which were supposed to remove frown lines and double chins but which only made the clients resemble Egyptian mummies.

Leo understood Arden's shrewdness, but everything was so earnest and staid and so bloody white. It was like working in a hospital, with the silence, the uniforms, the ridiculous pseudo-scientific treatments that were nothing more than bandages wrapped over a face with a bit of oily cream underneath. Where was the joy? As Leo pressed the patter over the deep lines on the forehead of the woman on the table, she felt a ripple of elation run through her. Joy. *That* would be her promise. Not youth. Joy and excitement and daring. She would sell a party in a tube of lipstick.

That day, she got her first tongue lashing from Miss Arden. She was smiling too much and only stiff and serious faces were permitted. Leo bore the reprimand and reined herself in for the rest of the day, then skipped off to Lord & Taylor in high spirits. She rushed into the workroom promptly at half past five and stopped short. In the middle of the room was the car. 'Oh!' she said, reaching out to touch the lustrous cream paint on the bonnet.

'If a car could ever be considered beautiful, this one is,' said Lottie.

Leo walked around it, seeing the soft leather of the seats which gleamed subtly, like pearls. The roof was off and the door was open and it looked as if it was inviting her to step inside. 'Shall we?' she asked Lottie, eyes sparkling.

Lottie nodded and took the passenger seat. Leo slipped into the driver's side. She peeled off her gloves and placed her hands on the wheel – more leather – and felt the richness on her palms. She closed her eyes and leaned her head back. 'Where would you go in a car like this?' she asked.

Lottie didn't hesitate. 'It'd be night-time and I'd drive over the Brooklyn Bridge into the city, then across to a jazz club in Greenwich Village. I'd wear a silver dress and I'd drink gin until I saw a man I wanted to dance with. Then . . . well.' Lottie stopped and smiled.

Leo opened her eyes. 'What make-up would you wear?' she asked.

Lottie laughed. 'I love the way you just assume I'd be brave enough to wear it.'

'But you don't believe mascara is only for actresses and ladies of the night?'

'Of course not. And now I can ask you a question I've been wanting to ask for ages. *Where* did you get your lipstick? I thought it must be from Elizabeth Arden because you work there, but I went and all she has is a ton of lotion.'

It was Leo's turn to laugh. 'I keep thinking Fortune's going to ask me to take it off, but we're here at night with no one around so perhaps she doesn't care. I'm not allowed to wear it at the salon. Too *unnatural*. As if it was one of the seven deadly sins. Anyway, I made it. It's what I want to do: sell cosmetics to department stores. Because if I want it and you want it and other women want it, then why can't we find it anywhere?'

'You don't need to convince me. *I'd* buy it.'

Leo let go of the wheel with a loud exclamation. 'That's it!'

'What's it?'

'Today I realised that my promise to women is fun, good times, a moment to be enchanting. But my make-up is not for the women who go to the Red Door Salon — it's for their daughters. Arden's clients are the grande dames of the city, but their daughters are the ones who want to wear rouge and *shimmy like my sister Kate.*'

'Girls!' The thunder crack of Fortune's voice had Lottie and Leo out of the car quicker than Faye could down a glass of champagne and standing demurely at their work tables by the time Fortune's body caught up with her voice. Leo noticed Lottie hurriedly sweeping together some drawings and she had a brief and startling glimpse of couples dancing, a woman standing confidently by herself at a bar, surveying the room. The drawings were definitely not for the Lord & Taylor windows, but what *were* they for?

'Leo, go up to Ladies' Wear and bring back an armload of dresses for the mannequins,' Fortune said. 'You obviously don't have any money since you wear one of the same two dresses to work every day, but at least those dresses have some style.'

Leo took the elevator up to the shop floor and walked straight over to examine the cosmetics, instead of the dresses. The first compact she picked up depicted a lady sitting at her dressing table, served by her maid, and it looked so out of place with the time Leo now lived in, when women had jobs and lived in boarding houses and went out at night without chaperones.

Then she went to Ladies' Wear, where she took her time selecting dresses, gloves, hats and shoes, the images of the women in Lottie's window designs fixed in her mind, wanting to do justice to their carefree elegance, the way their clothes and their poise arrested the eye. She took everything down to the basement, dressed the mannequins and stood back, satisfied, when she was done.

'Well, well, well,' Fortune drawled when she saw them. 'I think they look just about perfect.'

Lottie looked up from her work table. 'They do,' she said, smiling at Leo. 'Exactly how I imagined them.'

Leo beamed, delighted.

Later, after Fortune had left for the night and Lottie was packing up her things, Leo found the courage to ask, 'The drawings you hid earlier – what are they for?'

'They were nothing,' Lottie said dismissively.

'They were something,' Leo insisted. 'Can I see them?'

Lottie paused, then opened her drawer and felt around in the back. 'Gin?'

'Why not?' Leo fetched two glasses and, when she returned, Lottie had spread the pictures out on the floor. Leo sat down, back against the wall beside Lottie, and studied the women; they looked stylish and just a little arch, as if either fun or trouble could be around the corner in equal measures. 'They're beautiful.'

'Thanks,' Lottie said quietly.

Leo glimpsed an expression on Lottie's face that she'd seen in her own mirror: relief edged with doubt. Relief that something you loved had met with another person's approval, and doubt about whether it meant anything, whether it made any difference at all to the fact that they were sitting on the floor in the basement of a department store near midnight.

'What are we doing here?' Leo said with a sigh. 'You're much too talented to be hiding away in a basement, designing display windows. You should be . . . I don't know. Making your own lovely things.'

'That'd be nice,' Lottie said. 'Sometimes I think I'm going to be buried down here, alongside Fortune, and in a hundred years' time someone'll find our skeletons, but they'll just bury them beneath the foundations of another building because the skeleton of Lottie McLean won't be anything worth preserving.'

'One day, when I have more money and can pay you what you deserve, will you draw pictures to be printed on my compacts? Pictures exactly like the ones you've drawn here.'

'Not like this you mean?' Lottie stood up, opened her purse and pulled out a compact with the words *Stein's Face Powder* printed on it in ugly red lettering, the only concession to beauty being a few old-fashioned roses decorating the edge.

'No.' Leo laughed. 'Definitely not like that.'

'Tell you what,' Lottie said. 'I'll draw something up for you anyway. You don't have to pay me for it. It'll just be a rough. But you can take it in to show the department stores what you're aiming for.'

'Would you really? I will pay you one day, I promise.' Leo sipped her drink and then said wistfully, 'I like working with

Fortune but I don't want to do this forever. Do you think we will get out of here? Some days I think I will and other days . . .' Her voice trailed away.

Lottie reached over and clinked her glass against Leo's. 'After talking to you tonight, for the first time in my life, I think we just might.'

Leo had seen Faye and Benjamin only twice since the night at Texas's club. On one of those occasions, she and Joan had gone to the Richiers' for a party and discovered that their home was indeed a mansion, enthroned on Fifth Avenue and overlooking Central Park, like a king surveying the peasantry.

'Benjamin bought it for me,' Faye had said when they arrived. 'When the Dickinsons finally died, I told him I wanted it for my birthday. And he gave it to me with the front door wrapped in a red bow.'

'That's very generous,' Leo replied, which, as far as understatement went, was like calling Faye a firecracker.

Benjamin was so busy with his guests that night that he only kissed Leo's cheek and danced with her a couple of times. There'd been another night at the 300 Club, but Faye had again taken ill early on and Benjamin had had to take her home. Leo watched Joan's concerned eyes following Faye and Benjamin out of the club and into a cab and had squeezed her friend's hand. 'I'm sure she'll be fine, Nurse Joan,' she said teasingly. 'Probably too much to drink, like last time.'

'Yes, just like last time,' Joan responded drily.

Then Benjamin had gone to Washington for business for a month and Leo hadn't seen him since. But one Saturday in late September, when summer was still clinging to the city, unwilling to make way for fall, and the air was so thick with humidity that it seemed to settle like a cloak on everyone's skins, Benjamin arrived unexpectedly at Jia's store and Leo cursed her stupidity for giving him the address. Her hands were black, her forehead was sweating, and every time she wiped the sweat away, the black on her hands transferred to her face. She'd been trying to finesse her mascara formulation, but instead she'd made black mud.

'What *is* that?' he asked, pointing to the gloopy mess in front of her.

'You don't think it looks like anything a lady would want to apply to her face?' she quipped.

Benjamin didn't reply. He simply stood there, calm, neat and assured in the midst of one of her most colossal failures. Leo drew in a breath to stop herself from leaping into the chasm of silence before them and babbling. She shrugged ruefully. 'It's supposed to be mascara. I want it to be less dry than the Maybelline but now I've gone too far the other way.'

Benjamin walked around the room silently, picking things up and putting them down. He passed no comment, which made Leo angrier and angrier. How could anyone look at the six lovely pots of lip colour, each a glorious variant on red and designed to suit different skin tones and hair colours, and not say anything?

Leo picked up a mascara cake, not her own, and made sure to keep her voice level. 'You can make mascara in two ways,' she said. 'You can use oil, lampblack and a stearate to aid emulsification, so that when a woman dips a wet brush into the cake, the mascara forms a paste and adheres to the brush and then her lashes. Or, you can add water to the formula, which gives you a product that is even better at mixing to a liquid, and easier to apply to the lashes.'

She knew her hands were waving around as she spoke but she couldn't help it. 'Women are scared of mascara. It either runs down their faces at the slightest hint of rain or it clumps on their lashes so they look like chimney brushes, or it's just too damn difficult to transfer from the cake to the brush to the lashes. I have to solve all of those problems, because I know that if what I produce is anything less than perfect, it'll just make women more fearful of wearing it. I have one chance to convince them. So I have to experiment. And fail from time to time.'

As Leo spoke, she felt more confident. She *knew* what she was doing. She'd studied every book on cosmetic chemistry that she could find at the New York Public Library, she'd delved deep into her father's books and reread them all over again, and she'd been out to see Mr Chim, an acquaintance of Jia's, at his factory in upstate New York and had learned all about the different stearates she could try that were kinder to the eyes than the widely used sodium stearate.

Benjamin appeared to be listening, so Leo kept talking. 'I need to use a wax that makes the mascara stick to the lashes and look lovely and glossy, but not so much wax that it won't emulsify. Enough water so it does emulsify properly, but not so much that the cake dries out, shrinks and flakes. And the perfect amount of a stearate that won't sting the eyes, that creates a paste when water is applied, but that won't just slide off the lashes in a shower of rain – or sweat,' she finished, wiping her brow again.

'Damn,' she said as she realised she'd probably added yet another black mark to her face. Then she began to laugh. What must she look like? A face covered in lampblack, ranting at Benjamin about waxes and emulsifiers and things he'd have no idea about. But she felt good for having said what she wanted to, for not letting his silence and self-possession get the better of her.

'If your face wasn't so black, I could kiss you right now,' he said.

Leo stopped laughing abruptly. All she could think was: if Everett Forsyth was standing here, he wouldn't care if she was covered in lampblack from head to toe. *He* would still kiss her.

'You weren't expecting me to say that?' Benjamin asked, smiling at last.

'I wasn't.'

'Which is just one of the many reasons why I like you,' he said. 'Every other woman in Manhattan would be kissing *me*, in the hope it might lead to marriage. And my money. Let me take you out. Just the two of us.'

Leo put the mascara cakes down on the workbench. She needed more time. She needed to get to know Benjamin better; at the moment she felt as if she was grasping at his shadow, trying to discover the person to whom it belonged. 'I'd love to,' she said. 'But not for another month or so. I have to spend all of my spare time on this mess and transform it into something worthy of being called cosmetics. Once I've taken it to the department stores, then we can go out. And celebrate my success,' she added determinedly, hoping a wish spoken aloud was one that would come true.

Benjamin sighed. 'All right. Then I'll take you to the Empire Room at the Waldorf Astoria for dinner. And we *will* have that kiss.'

With that, Benjamin rolled the mascara sludge back and forth in the tin, sniffed it, and set it down. Then he left.

Leo's bravado vanished with him, as quickly as the crabs escaping their buckets and scuttling along the streets of Chinatown. She walked over and picked up the tin Benjamin had inspected, seeing what he'd seen. The only blessing was that he hadn't voiced his disappointment aloud, but it lingered in the room, coating everything as darkly as the lampblack on Leo's skin.

~

Eventually fall swept into Manhattan, the Lord & Taylor windows began to attract the admiring glances of all the young women across the city, the Victory Parade marched down Fifth Avenue with hundreds of men in full combat gear, and all the girls in the Red Door Salon had rushed outside to watch. The humidity had blown clean out of the city and Leo needed a coat to go outside and wore thicker dresses, which was just as well; they hid her growing stomach, the baby Joan told her not to think about. The baby Leo stroked every night in bed.

Then, by late November, everything was ready. Leo had an appointment to take her samples to Lord & Taylor.

Jia and Joan, who'd met through Leo many times and were by now good friends, had decided that, in honour of such a momentous occasion, they should blow some of their cash and go to the Oriental Restaurant on Pell Street. They met in the huge dining room that spread over two floors.

'We'd like a booth, please,' Jia said to the waitress and they were ushered past wooden tables decorated with lustrous mother-of-pearl inlays to a booth fashioned from red lacquer and silk-embroidered panels. Above their heads hung lights from which dripped brightly coloured silk tassels and cloisonné dragons that pranced and fought across the pendants.

'It's amazing,' said Leo, looking around in wonder.

'The real Chinese eat at Hang Far Loo down the street, but I figured you'd find this more impressive,' said Jia as they sat down and an orchestra on a small stage began to play.

The waitress poured some tea, which smelled delightfully pungent. Leo sipped hers with satisfaction. 'Will you order for us?' she asked Jia. 'Besides the noodles your mother makes for me, I have no idea about the food.'

'We'll have chow mein – that's the fried noodles my mother makes for you – and moo char siu, which is roast pork and mushrooms, rice, and maybe some chop suey as well, with baby plums and carrots,' Jia said. 'How does that sound?'

Leo and Joan both agreed it sounded delicious, and it was. Leo ate with relish, pregnancy having given her an increased appetite. And how good it felt to be sending these delicious vegetables and soft pieces of pork down to her baby for nourishment.

Midway through the meal, Joan lifted her teacup. 'Here's to you, Leo. Good luck tomorrow.'

'I think I'll need it,' Leo said.

'They'll love everything,' Joan said.

Jia remained silent.

'You heard what Benjamin said that day when he came in, didn't you?' Leo said suddenly to Jia. 'Or what he didn't say.'

'I saw him walk in smiling and walk out frowning,' Jia said. 'That's all.'

'It was the worst day for him to visit,' Leo sighed.

'Who cares what he thinks?' Joan retorted. 'He's not the person at Lord & Taylor you need to impress.'

'He made me see my cosmetics as a stranger might,' Leo admitted. 'And now I have a terrible feeling that I've taken so much time perfecting the formulas that I haven't paid enough attention to the packaging. That they look like a pathetic excuse, rather than something that might attract notice in a department store. But I don't have the money for anything else. I keep thinking that if women just try the products, it won't matter about the packaging. But I think in my heart it *does*.'

'Despite all that, he still wanted to kiss you,' Jia said.

This caused Joan to explode. 'What? You never said anything about a kiss!'

'Calm down,' Leo said, laughing, 'or you'll end up on the ceiling with the dragons. There was no kiss. Have we finished? I need to go for a walk after all that food.'

The baby had an uncomfortable foot wedged in her ribs. She slid awkwardly out of the booth, trying her hardest not to hold her stomach, knowing suddenly that she was nearing the end of the time when she could get away with it. Joan tried to shield her discreetly and help her up, but Leo felt Jia's eyes on her.

They walked further along Pell Street, past the shops filled with back scratchers, jade ornaments and colourful cheongsams. On Mott Street, the sickening smell of opium drifted out of a den, and at Soy Kee's they feasted their eyes on dragon drums, embroidered slippers that Joan declared too pretty to only wear inside, straw baskets and lacquer boxes. A group of children with shiny black hair played in the street, singing nursery rhymes in English. Leo stopped to watch them play. And then she felt it: the baby's first kick. 'Oh,' she gasped, unable to stop the impulsive leap of her hand to her belly.

'I have some herbal medicines that are good to use during labour,' Jia said conversationally.

Leo and Joan stared at her.

Jia nodded at Leo's stomach. 'You're having a baby. Joan might like some help when it's ready to come.'

Leo reached out a hand to Jia, blinking hard. 'Thank you. I just felt it move. Here.'

They stood there for a moment, Joan's and Jia's hands resting on Leo's stomach, feeling the baby rippling below the surface, all with teary smiles on their faces. But Leo also knew that, if Jia had noticed, then soon others would too. Everything had to go smoothly tomorrow, because it wasn't long before she'd have to shut herself away from the world.

Chapter Eleven

Leo had made herself a new dress for her meeting at Lord & Taylor. Sky-blue charmeuse fell in a fitted skirt to mid-calf and was overlaid with a shorter, fuller skirt which disguised her pregnancy. The sleeves were blue chiffon and a red sash around the waist gave it a touch of fun. She lined the brim of her hat in a matching red so that, beneath the royal blue, a touch of colour peeked out. And, of course, her lip colour matched the red of her sash and her hat exactly.

Once she was ready, she put on her cloak and felt a huge thrill of excitement. This was it. Soon she'd have her very first order to fill and her cosmetics would be in the hands of the young women of Manhattan. She tucked her samples into her bag carefully, each one representing hundreds of hours of work.

When she arrived at Lord & Taylor, she was shown to the office of the buyer, who gave her an appreciative look. 'Please take a seat. What can I do for you?' A thin, mustachioed man, he spoke with just a little too much insinuation in his tone, as if hinting there was something Leo would be very welcome to do to him.

Leo pretended not to notice, just opened her bag and plunged in. 'I have some cosmetic samples to show you.' She pulled out the jar of lipstick – her star product – and opened the lid to show him the colour. 'I have six different shades of red,' she explained, 'so women can more easily find one that suits them.' She was about to take out the mascara cakes when the buyer held up his hand.

'I've seen enough. It's not what we want at Lord & Taylor,' he said.

Leo could feel her daring melt away like one of her failed mascara attempts. But she forced herself to speak. 'I know they don't look like much on the outside,' she said, 'but the products inside are better than the ones you currently sell.'

'Really?' he said, feigning surprise. 'The beautifully boxed powder compacts we sell aren't as good as yours?'

Blood rushed to Leo's cheeks, making her humiliation all too apparent, but she kept going, pulling Lottie's illustrations out of her bag, skin cooling slightly at the sight of the gorgeous designs. 'I just need an order and then I'll have the funds to make the packaging as lovely as the products. See?' She pointed to a colourful image of a woman dancing with a man, bold red lips curved in a smile. 'These drawings will be on the compacts themselves. They're sophisticated and stylish and they show women doing the things they want to be doing. I know it might be hard to imagine now, but I promise they'll be irresistible.'

'We have enough cosmetics. Thank you.'

His voice was as disdainful as Benjamin's silent disapproval had been. Leo fumbled with her bag and the pages of illustrations, dropping a pot of lip colour on the floor. But she stayed where she was, knowing how it would look if she scrambled around for it. 'You don't have enough cosmetics,' she said firmly. 'Not for the market I intend to reach. You might have Elizabeth

Arden, but that's for wealthy older ladies. It's not fun.' Leo's words buoyed her spirits. She knew she was right. She might lack cash, but she'd spent more hours with cosmetics over the last few months than this man would ever spend in his lifetime. 'Young working women like me wouldn't buy the cosmetics you stock if you paid them,' she finished.

The ensuing silence felt like a great canyon whose rim Leo was teetering on, ready to fall ingloriously and finally away from her fantasy of doing something extraordinary. The buyer moved to the door. 'Why would I take a chance on something that hasn't yet been manufactured to any scale? It would be a poor business decision, which you'd understand if you knew anything about business. Good day.'

And Leo heard the truth in his words. What a fool she was, walking in here with her pathetic little pots, hoping someone would understand what it was she could see when she closed her eyes and held a jar of her lip colour in hand. 'Thank you for your time,' she said. Her voice sounded only a little strained and she was glad about that, she didn't want the buyer to see that she was cut through the bone and into her very heart, because that was what she'd put into these samples.

Once outside, she didn't know what to do. She'd blown everything. She couldn't just move on to another store. Nobody would take a chance on her amateurish samples no matter how good the product inside might be. They wanted to see the whole story as a solid and substantial thing, not a vision in her head. But for that she needed cash, and lots of it. Not a window dresser's wage, or that of a salon girl, but piles of money. Her head dropped and her shoulders sagged with the absolute impossibility of it all.

She wandered southwards for a time and then, when she'd nearly stepped onto the street in front of a car, she decided to take a cab for her own safety. 'Uptown,' she said to the driver, not wanting to go downtown, where she would have to tell Joan and Jia the whole sorry tale. 'Just take Fifth Avenue uptown.'

The taxi drove past the Flatiron Building, the Waldorf Astoria, on the corner of Thirty-Third, and then hit the chaos of New York's busiest street corners at Fifth and Forty-Second, where they slowed to a crawl. It took fifteen minutes and a symphony of horn-blowing to negotiate the swarm of pedestrians and the battalion of cars, but Leo didn't care. She had a whole day to fill somehow. An unsolvable problem to confront. A dream burned out before it had even begun.

Soon, the Gothic spires of St Patrick's Cathedral loomed over her and Leo saw a sign that made her shout, 'Pull over here.'

The taxi screeched to the kerb and she stepped out in front of Forsyths department store, which had opened three weeks earlier with windows designed to make passers-by stop and stare. And stare they did, gathering on the pavement to gape, to peer through a peephole into a private party. Mannequins were arranged in groups, adorned in evening gowns, champagne glasses in hand. A gramophone played in one corner, the music passing into the feet of the spectators so that everyone's shoes began to tap a little. A chandelier sparkled above, and a mannequin couple sat close, thighs touching, leaning towards one another as if on the verge of a kiss.

In the next window, a real live human couple were dancing in a way Leo had never before seen and she was captivated. Arms and legs gracefully akimbo, fast and loose, joyous. Leo wanted to step into the window and join them, to be swept away to this untroubled world.

The sound of more music drew her into the store. She made sure her cloak draped completely over her stomach to conceal it, just in case, and stood watching the jazz band playing on the shop floor. The female shop assistants were dressed in emerald green, the men in pinstripe suits and boaters. There were no patronising floorwalkers in black frock coats with pink carnations in their buttonholes, no guttersnipes advertising what goods could be bought within the store, no pullers-in — the young men often stationed outside department stores shouting out prices and hustling in customers. Forsyths stood apart, elegantly modern, knowing it didn't need to hustle; the right people would come through the doors and then everyone else would follow.

A waterfall of cocktail glasses greeted her, thumbing their noses at the alcohol restrictions. Perfumes were dabbed on wrists, scarves were taken out from behind counters and wound around ladies' necks, everyone was beautiful and young and carefree. There was no mahogany or wood, no partitions or cabinetry to obscure the goods that were for sale, and no overstuffed shelves. The glass cases and counters and the abundance of space seemed to indicate that only the most fabulous merchandise had been selected as good enough for Forsyths customers.

This was what she'd wanted to make. This was what she'd failed to do. But Everett had done it and, despite her own catastrophe, she felt so proud.

Then Leo saw, like a punch in the stomach, a sign saying *Beauty Department.* Another punch came with the sound of a voice saying, 'Leo,' just behind her. She pasted a smile onto her face, buried the morning's shame, and spun around. 'It's magnificent, Everett,' she said feelingly.

'Do you really think so?' Everett asked, and she could see that he didn't quite believe it, hadn't quite grasped what he'd done, nor the way New Yorkers were responding to it.

'Of course I do. Everyone else thinks so too. Look!' She pointed to the crowds of people, arms hung with shopping bags, purses emptying of money. 'And you have a Beauty Department,' she couldn't help adding wistfully.

'Waiting for your cosmetics,' he said, studying her face, and she turned away, pretending to look at the store in case she wasn't hiding her disappointments as well as she'd hoped.

'That would be much too complicated,' she said. 'And would probably get us both into a lot of trouble.'

'A nice sort of trouble though.'

Leo risked a sideways glance and saw a wry smile on his face. 'But you're married,' she said. 'And this conversation is likely to lead us into the same sort of trouble. So I should go. But congratulations on what you've done. It really is spectacular.'

Everett touched her arm. 'Sometimes I remember that night and I think I shouldn't have done it because, in the end, all I did was hurt you. But I can't ever make myself wish that it never happened.'

This is what despair looks like, Leo thought: the smudge of grey beneath each of Everett's eyes which said that he didn't sleep as much as he ought. The line cut into his forehead, between his brows, which said that he frowned more than he smiled. The penumbra of grief colouring his eyes blue-grey, rather than the brilliant blue that had first turned her way at the inn in Dunbridge. But Everett was soon to become a father. He needed to smile, needed to show the child eyes tinted with nothing but joy. She felt again the absolute conviction that she could never tell him about their baby because the shadows would only become blacker, the eyes gunmetal, the lines omnipresent. She could never tell him about this morning's failure, because then he would want to help her. To tell him any of it was selfishness; Everett had his own family to help, his own business to run.

'I've never once wanted to undo that night either.' Leo smiled as she said the words, then slipped out of the store. She walked all the long, long way from Forsyths on Fifth Avenue to the boarding house on Hester Street. And as she walked, the reality of her situation beat against her ears more loudly than all of the cars and carts and buses and trains thundering around the city of Manhattan.

In just under three months she would be having a baby. It was no longer something she could hide.

It was time to lay low. It was time to forget about making cosmetics. One woman alone in a Chinese medicine store could not possibly make a lipstick that a store like Forsyths would want to sell. She caught sight of a white ball of moon, hanging in a daytime sky, up near the sun and the light, and all of her hopes seemed just like that moon; always there but almost impossible to see in the clear light of day, meant only for nights, the time of dreaming, to be all but forgotten in the morning.

She walked on, hand resting on her belly, the energy of faith and belief drained out of her. The only thing left was a determination to get through the next three months for the sake of the baby. Against all reason, she wanted it, the last reminder of her night of passion – and of something more: love – with Everett to survive. It deserved every chance Leo had blown.

Chapter Twelve

*L*eo was already curled up in bed when Joan arrived home that night. 'I've telephoned the salon,' she said. 'And Fortune. I've quit my jobs. I won't go anywhere now. And I need your help, if you're still willing.'

Joan crossed the room in a second. 'Of course I'm still willing, you goose! In fact, Mrs Parker, who runs the home, asked me about you today. She wanted to know whether you were still planning to go through with it. Shall I say yes?'

Leo nodded.

Joan looked around the room, eyes stopping on Leo's bag, still full of the samples that Lord & Taylor were supposed to have taken. 'Do you want to talk about your meeting?' she asked.

'Not yet.' Leo rolled onto her back so she could see Joan a little better. 'I've decided —' she paused, struggling to say the words '— I've decided I'll use the money from my father to pay the rent for the next couple of months while I don't have a job. I'm just glad I can't see his face now,' she whispered. 'Can't see how disappointed he would be if he knew how I was spending his money.'

Leo clambered out of bed and walked over to the one tiny window high above the street. Beneath her, she could see the fur shops, the snuff shop, the start of the chicken market at Hester Street and the steeple of St Mark's church in the distance. How was it that, just last year, on any given Sunday she'd have been walking to church with her father. Now God wouldn't let her in the door. 'This is so far from the life I thought I'd have,' Leo said.

'You can start again. In a couple of months, this will all be over.'

'Will it ever be over? Will I ever stop thinking about it?'

'How about I go down to the newsstand? We can read magazines and not think about the whole damn mess for a couple of hours.' Joan picked up her purse.

Leo nodded, swiping at tears. 'Thank you.'

'You don't need to thank me.' Joan squeezed Leo's hand before she left.

A week later, realisation dropped like a stone in Leo's stomach when a letter arrived from Benjamin. She'd said he could take her out. But there was no way she could see him, not now. When Joan arrived home, Leo showed her the letter.

Dear Leonora,

I take it your cosmetics weren't the hit you wanted them to be with the department stores otherwise I'd have heard from you. But a date is a date. Remember, I said I'd be here when things didn't work out and I meant it.

We'll still go to the Waldorf Astoria. Maybe we'll be able to celebrate you taking my offer seriously at last. And you promised me a kiss.

Benjamin

'I don't know what to say. I can't see him. Perhaps after . . .' *After the baby's born.* She swallowed those words. 'But how do I explain disappearing for weeks?'

'Mumps!' said Joan triumphantly.

'Mumps?'

'Mumps are highly contagious. You need to stay away from people for at least two to three weeks. And it leaves you weak for a good while after that. A man like Benjamin definitely won't want to catch mumps.'

'What if he's already had mumps? Then he wouldn't care less.'

Joan frowned. 'But you'd still be too ill to go out with him. And our landlady would never allow a man in the boarding house, so he can't visit you. It'll work.'

'Almost three months of mumps?'

'Well, it's nearly Christmas. So perhaps say that it's unlikely you'll be well enough until after New Year. Then it's only a few more weeks until February.'

'But what about everything he's said?' Leo pointed to the letter.

'Yes, how awful that he wants to take you out for a lovely dinner and help you,' Joan said sarcastically. 'I don't see the problem. You never know when you might need a man like Benjamin Richier. Maybe you need to forget about Everett and think about what you do have – the handsome and wealthy Benjamin Richier inviting you to dinner – rather than what you don't have. What you might never have.' Joan said this last as matter-of-factly as always, as if they were discussing what to have for dinner instead of the devastation of love.

Leo didn't reply. *Might never have. Might never have.* Words she tried not to think, not ever. Words that sounded so bleakly and utterly final. But the fact that she was sitting in a boarding house soon to have the baby of a man who knew nothing about it gave an unwelcome ring of truth to Joan's words.

So Leo wrote Benjamin a letter in which she told him a story about mumps. Then, about a week after she'd sent it, she was looking longingly out the window at the life that continued to go on, imagining the smell of cinnamon and duck blood that would be swirling in the December wind, when she heard the door open. 'You're home early,' she started to say, thinking it was Joan. She was struck dumb when she saw that it was Faye Richier.

'Surprised to see me?' Faye drawled.

Oh God! Leo looked around desperately for a coat, for something more concealing than the old suit she was wearing that stretched awfully over her stomach and which she'd decided to wear for as long as she could and then throw away when she eventually split the seams.

'That doesn't look like a mump,' Faye said nodding at Leo's stomach.

'Why are you here?' Leo asked tiredly, noting that Faye's wild nights seemed to be catching up with her. She looked pale and, beneath a heavy cloak, she was carrying the weight of the dozens of glasses of champagne she quaffed every night.

'I found these on my brother's desk.' Faye held out two pieces of paper. 'A note from you to Benjamin, and one from him to you.'

'You read the letter I sent to Benjamin?' Leo said, trying to match Faye's sallies; the only alternative was to quaver beneath Faye's accusatory tone and Leo was damned if she was going to show Faye anything of how wretched she really felt.

'Of course I did.' Faye didn't even sound ashamed. 'And I asked myself: what's the real reason a woman would need to hide herself away for a few weeks, making special mention of the fact that Benjamin wasn't to visit? Mumps seemed a little too trifling for such a big fuss. And now I know.'

'How did you even get up here?' Leo asked.

'Your landlady is very amenable to bribes. I expect she'll be wearing a new dress tomorrow.' Faye blew smoke at Leo.

'And I suppose you're going to tell Benjamin – to protect him from my shameful immorality,' Leo bit back.

'I sure am.' Faye grinned. 'It turns out you were a much easier problem to get rid of than I'd thought. Have a nice life, Leo.' With that Faye walked out.

Leo's hands trembled. Faye hadn't asked who the father was. Which could mean only one of two things: either Faye had no natural curiosity, or she thought she already knew.

⁓

When Joan arrived home that night, her face was as long as Leo's.

'What's wrong?' Leo asked, almost glad to forget about her own problems.

Joan shook her head. 'Nothing really. A woman turned up just before I was due to leave, a patient. We knew she was coming in but she's just . . . difficult. I was glad to come home. After yours is born, I think I'll go back to hospital work.'

'You should leave now. Don't stay there just for me,' Leo cried.

'It's only a few more weeks. It'll be fine. And I'm sure half the reason she was so trying today was because she was as sozzled as a snake when she came in. Mrs Parker doesn't allow any alcohol though, so now she's checked in, that won't be a problem. Enough about me.' Joan pulled off her gloves. 'How was your day?'

'My day?' Leo forced a smile. 'The same as always. Nothing to report.' Joan had enough on her mind. She didn't need any more of Leo's problems to deal with.

On February the thirteenth, Leo woke not long after she'd gone to bed with a pain low down in her belly. 'Joan?' she whispered.

'I'm here.' Joan was out of bed in an instant, turning on the light, using her stethoscope to check on the baby. 'I'll go get Jia. We'll be back soon.'

She hurried off and, not long after, Joan and Jia arrived back and the secret birth began. Silence was imperative; nobody in the building should find out what they were up to. So Leo sweated through each pain, then as they came on stronger and faster and lasted beyond the point at which she thought she could endure it, she held a pillow over her own face and sobbed into it, unable to be absolutely quiet, unable to stop one or two small moans escaping. Then one escaped that was loud – so loud that Jia and Joan exchanged worried looks.

Jia gave her a few more drops of arnica but it didn't seem to help; or perhaps it did – perhaps it would be even worse without Jia's concoction. But if that was the case then Leo didn't know how anybody would ever go through labour more than once.

'I really can't do it,' she cried. 'I just can't.'

'You have to,' Joan said grimly. 'Besides, it's nearly done.'

Which was a lie. Midnight passed. Valentine's Day 1920 began with no arrows from Cupid, just one engulfing shaft of pain rolling from Leo's chest and into her stomach, through her lower back and even down into her thighs. The early morning hours felt like days and at least a dozen more groans broke free, so that the landlady knocked on the door to see what was the matter and Joan called out something about food poisoning.

Finally, at dawn, Joan said, 'It's time.'

'Let me hold the baby after it's born,' Leo said, taking the pillow away from her mouth, pushing her sweaty, sticky hair off her face and looking pleadingly at Joan.

Joan shook her head. 'If you hold her, it'll break your heart.'

It's already broken, Leo tried to say, but Joan doused her with ether.

Then Leo began to dream, an unintelligible stream of jumbled memories – the child Leo running along the road to the camp hospital; Everett's face when he'd said goodbye to her that morning at the inn; the sound of her father's deathly cough hacking through the long night of rain; Mattie saying she was pregnant; dancing with Benjamin on a boat wearing another woman's dress; Faye smirking; a red lipstick that had started it all and that she'd had to forget because of this, her unforeseen but nonetheless adored child.

When she woke she was still alive. Her stomach was smaller. She was bleeding, but not too much. Joan was gone. So was the baby.

'Where . . .' Leo's voice broke on the question.

Jia smiled. 'You had a girl. And she's beautiful.'

Beautiful. She'd had a beautiful baby girl. The bittersweet relief of those words. 'Thank God.' Then Leo's mouth screwed up and the sobs came, so loudly that Jia had to pull Leo's head into her shoulder to muffle the sound.

'She's gone,' Leo wept, and Jia nodded.

Gone, gone, gone. The words pounded agonisingly with every beat of Leo's heart. Her child was gone. She hadn't held her. Hadn't seen her. Hadn't smiled at her and told her how she was loved. Hadn't had a chance to say that giving her up didn't mean she was unwanted. It meant just the opposite. That she was the most beloved, most precious thing ever to grace this world.

Jia stayed with her that day and then, when Leo began watching the door intently, waiting to pounce on Joan to ask about the child, Jia said, 'I'm supposed to give you this if she's not home by evening.'

Leo stretched out her hand. Letters always held bad news and this one felt drenched in it, a cloying, suffocating waft of the untenable rising from the paper.

Dear Leo,

Please don't hate me. I couldn't bear it if you did. Something's happened and I can't stay with you any more. The baby is beautiful. You'd be so proud of her. Mrs Parker will send her to a wonderful home. She'll be loved, I promise.

Please take care of yourself, and forgive me if you can.

Love,

Joan

Speechless, Leo passed the note to Jia.

'That would explain why none of her things are here,' Jia said.

Leo looked around. Jia was right. There was no trace of Joan in the room. 'Where did she go? And why would she go now?' Leo felt her throat tighten and tears threaten once more. 'I need her.'

Jia took Leo's hand. She opened her mouth to speak, then closed it again.

'What?' Leo asked.

'I want to tell you something but I don't know if now is the best time.'

'You're not leaving too, are you?' Leo asked, horrified, her stomach tight with dread.

'No, that's not it,' Jia said. 'I'm sticking around. It's something about Jimmy.'

'Jimmy? Please tell me.'

'Okay, I will. But stop me if you decide you don't want to hear it.'

Leo nodded.

'Jimmy's father . . . forced himself on me. He was a son-of-a-bitch who used to extort money out of every store on the block so he could sleep the day away in an opium den. Jimmy wasn't conceived out of anything that could be called love. Jimmy was not my plan. But I love him more than I ever thought I could love another human being.'

Leo took some time to reply, struggling to make sense of what Jia had said. That someone could have done that to her. That she'd survived a fate that was considered worse than death. 'How?' she asked stupidly.

'How have I kept Jimmy?' Jia snorted. 'My mother married me off to a distant cousin in China. He's slow, so no one will marry him. And I'm damaged goods, so no one will marry me. It's a match made in heaven. It was all done in an exchange of papers. I've never even met him, although my mother insists to everyone that we had a lovely honeymoon in China and that he has to stay back there for his work. Every day my mother prays for my rotten soul. Every day I go to work in the shop and pray that the customers, who don't quite believe the story, will come back.'

'That's why you needed my money,' Leo said.

Jia shrugged. 'I did.'

'I'm glad I gave it to you. I would have given you more, if I'd known.'

'That's the trouble with you, Leo,' Jia said. 'You're too damn nice. You'd never have asked for rent from a girl who came into your store wanting to use the stillroom. But I knew I had to. You *can* do everything you want. You just have to be prepared to do it a different way. To be a little tougher.'

'What happened to Jimmy's father?' Leo asked. 'Did he go to jail?'

'Jail!' Jia said incredulously. 'Why would he go to jail? I've never told anyone because nobody would care. Since the Chinese Exclusion Act, I'm not even allowed to be a citizen in the country where I was born, so why would anyone raise a sweat about a dirty Chinese slut with a baby? No, he didn't go to jail. Someone shot him. He died alone in a filthy laneway. So there is some justice in the world.'

Dear God. So much death and loss and pain and prejudice. 'I'm so sorry,' Leo whispered, knowing her sorrow didn't help Jia at all. No – Jia had helped herself.

Later, after Jia had left, Leo reached out her hand to the bedside table and picked up a jar of lip colour that she hadn't touched since her disastrous meeting at Lord & Taylor. She opened the lid and inhaled the glorious waft of jasmine and peony. She dipped her finger into velvet, soft and smooth, a shade of cerise that wouldn't look out of place in Saks and Company silks. So yes, there was also beauty and joy and even a touch of the divine still left in the world. Like her baby.

She passed a long, long night of searching deep into her soul and finding things she was proud of, and things that she wasn't. Why had she brought a baby into the world if she herself was too scared to do what she'd vowed on the boat: to be braver and bolder and smarter than she'd ever been. There were things she could do that would truly take courage. Things she would ordinarily flinch from. But not any more.

Chapter Thirteen

APRIL 1920

'Ben, it's lovely to see you again.' Leo smiled.

'Leonora! You look . . .' Benjamin stopped, searching for a word that hovered just beyond his grasp, his eyes raking over Leo's body, taking in her rather fabulous slim black skirt and the black jacket with the V-neck and glamorous wide collar. It was cinched in tightly at the waist and fell, handkerchief-style, to sit only a few inches above the hem of her skirt. Her shoes twinkled with a star of rhinestones just above the heel, and her hair blazed, flame-coloured, when she removed her hat. She waited for Benjamin to finish, as if she didn't understand at all that her appearance was causing him to stutter.

'Indescribably good,' he finished, leaning in to kiss her cheek.

Leo held out her hand. 'As this is a business meeting,' she said, 'I'd prefer we shook hands. Let's save the kissing until we know where we stand.'

Benjamin gave a startled laugh. 'Just so long as kissing is still on the table.'

Leo kept the smile on her face, hiding all traces of confusion. Hadn't Faye told him about Leo's pregnancy? Surely he wouldn't flirt with her like this if he knew that she'd given birth barely two months ago? 'Perhaps we should also save the flirting for later,' she said lightly, sitting down in a chair and taking a cigarette from her purse.

Benjamin was immediately by her side with a lighter. 'Allow me.'

'Thank you,' she said. Perhaps this wouldn't be as hard as she'd thought. The same instant, the door to Benjamin's office opened and in walked Faye. Leo almost dropped her cigarette but the self-command she'd donned that morning along with her new outfit held firm, and she relaxed into a chair as if there wasn't anything in the world she'd like more than to have Faye at this meeting too.

'So you did show up,' Faye said, helping herself to one of Benjamin's cigarettes. 'You're braver than I thought.'

'And you look so much better than the last time I saw you,' Leo said coolly, reminding herself that she'd come here to play all her cards and folding wasn't an option. Besides, Faye did look much improved, appearing slimmer and fresher than when she'd visited Leo before Christmas.

'I invited Faye,' said Benjamin. 'You know I've always wanted her to be part of any cosmetics business I decide to set up, so she should be here for this meeting.'

'Of course,' Leo said. 'Shall we begin?'

'You have the floor,' Benjamin said, sitting down and gazing at Leo with bemusement, clearly unable to reconcile the elegant and purposeful creature before him with the woman he'd last seen amid a blackened mess of mascara in Jia's store in Chinatown.

'Thank you.' Leo stood and placed three jars of product and three beautiful colour illustrations on the desk in front of Benjamin and Faye. One picture showed a lipstick in an elegant silver levered canister, with the word *Richier* engraved in a flourish along the side, and a rhinestone sparkling at the top. The next showed a petite powder compact, its lid adorned with an utterly modern illustration of a couple dancing; it was an image that wouldn't have looked out of place in a fashion magazine. And the last one showed a mascara cake, also gingered up with a striking picture, the word *Richier*, and the signature rhinestone.

'I went to Lord & Taylor a few months ago with flawless products in terrible packaging,' she said. 'I told a story about cosmetics that promised fun, excitement and daring to young women. But they wanted evidence. I can't afford to make evidence. What I can bring you are my impeccable products, and all of my ideas about how to sell them and who to sell them to. What I need are the resources to make the products look beautiful, and to advertise those products in a way that will make women want them as much as they all want to read *This Side of Paradise*. In that book, Fitzgerald describes the air as *thick and exotic with intrigue and moonlight and adventure*: so are Richier Cosmetics. And the woman who wears them.'

Leo could see that Faye was quite literally sitting on her hands to stop herself from reaching out to try one of the products. Leo picked up the mascara. 'You should make sure that it really is as good as I say it is.'

She passed it to Faye, who left the room with it, uncharacteristically short of a wisecrack. Leo didn't speak to Benjamin while they waited for Faye to return. Once upon a time she'd have prattled on unnecessarily, nervously; this time she'd smoke. She took out another cigarette and Benjamin again leaned across to light it.

She inhaled a long, long breath.

'It's damn good.' Faye stood in the doorway, one hand on the doorframe, one hand on her hip, looking for all the world like the most perfect model with her short hair and thick, glossy black lashes.

Leo met Faye's eye. 'Thank you,' she said. 'But before I say too much more, there's something you need to know.' She turned to Benjamin. 'I had a baby in February. Not mumps. I thought you'd want to know that before you made any decisions about whether or not we could work together.'

It was Benjamin's turn to reach for a cigarette. 'Where's the baby now?' he asked slowly.

'I don't know.' Leo studied her hands. 'I couldn't keep it.'

A leaden silence took up all the space in the room. Leo could almost hear thoughts humming in the stillness. Faye wondering how to get rid of her again. Benjamin wondering God only knew what.

'Shall I tell you more about Richier Cosmetics?' Leo asked, looking up. 'Or not?'

Benjamin nodded. 'Tell me more. For now.'

So Leo did. She told him what products she thought they should manufacture. She told him about the factory she'd need. She told him that she wanted, more than anything, to see her products in the hands of women and that, given the money she was asking him to invest, the Richier name should be on the cosmetics. Of everything, that part hurt the most. But Leo knew she'd suffered hurts before and, here she was, still standing. It was a small price to pay: another piece of her heart in exchange for her cosmetics carrying somebody else's name.

'I'd like to be responsible for the day-to-day running of the business,' she concluded in a quiet but determined voice. 'And I'd like to employ two people: Lottie McLean, who'd be responsible for designing the packaging, the compacts and overseeing the advertising, and Jia Liang, who'd help with the manufacture and formulations.'

'A Chinawoman,' Faye said disdainfully. 'I couldn't work with an Oriental.'

'You know all about carnauba wax, do you?' asked Leo. 'And bromo-acid dyes?' She kept her eyes on Faye as she spoke.

'I think we can safely say Faye doesn't know anything about them,' Benjamin said at last. 'Perhaps we do need staff. On a trial basis though. I want to see what they've done at the end of a month and then I'll decide if they stay.'

'Oh, you'll want them to stay,' Leo said. 'But does that mean you're . . .' For the first time, her nerves got the better of her and she couldn't finish the sentence.

'Interested?' Benjamin said. 'Yes.'

Leo's dignified facade collapsed. 'Really?' she exclaimed.

'Really,' Benjamin said.

'Thank you!' Leo jumped up and kissed his cheek.

'Thank *you*,' he said, smiling.

'I'd like to know the details.' Faye broke through the moment like a hail storm in summer. 'Before *we* decide.' She moved to sit on her brother's desk, one hand reaching up to finger her pearls, though Leo noticed she wasn't wearing them for once. 'After all, it would be a change of direction for Richier Industries. I might not work day to day in the business but I know enough to know that we've always been more about industrial goods, not consumer goods.'

'Of course,' Leo said, slipping back into her suit of sang-froid. 'I don't believe the department stores will take a chance on us until we've proven we can manufacture to scale, so we should start our own salon. A cosmetics salon. A place where women can come to try the products, where we show them how to use everything, where we can overcome their fears about mascara and rouge. Faye is the perfect person for a salon: she'll greet the customers and make them feel as if they're having a good time. And the products are so heavenly, nobody will be able to resist once they've tried them. Smell that.' Leo opened the powder compact and held it out for both Benjamin and Faye to sniff.

'It smells like a beautiful woman,' Benjamin said, eyeing Leo.

Despite her best intentions, Leo felt her cheeks flush. She pushed on, wanting to leave with all the details finalised so that nothing could be changed if Faye worked on Benjamin later. 'In return for my expertise and formulations, I should own ten percent of Richier Cosmetics. You and Faye can split the rest as you wish.'

'Ten percent!' Faye said incredulously. 'For a bit of colour in a pot?'

'You've found a red like this somewhere else have you?' Leo asked.

'Have you?' Benjamin asked his sister.

'No.'

'So Leo does have something of value.'

'Besides a propensity to sleep with men she shouldn't,' Faye bit back.

Leo's intake of breath echoed through the room.

'That was beneath you, Faye,' Benjamin said sharply.

'Didn't you once say you'd followed a rake to England? I assume you didn't just hold his hand,' Leo said.

If the silence in the room had been dense before, now it was absolutely impenetrable. Leo exhaled. 'I'm sorry,' she said. 'That was beneath *me*. I want this to work and that means we have to figure out a way to get along.'

'A bottle of champagne with breakfast wouldn't tranquillise me enough for that to happen,' Faye said.

'Then perhaps you'd better have two,' Leo said.

Benjamin laughed. 'I don't mind a bit of competitive spirit; it'll keep you both on your toes. But ten percent is too much, Leo. You can have five.'

Damn. If only they'd had this conversation at the start of the meeting, before she'd let Faye agitate her. 'Five percent?' Leo repeated.

'I'm putting down real money. You're not.' Benjamin's voice was firm.

But I'm putting in my heart. Leo held back the words, which would make her the most vulnerable person in the room.

'I don't want to be a shopgirl,' Faye said adamantly. 'No salon. We'll take the products to Forsyths. Mattie's a good friend of mine; so's Everett. I'm sure he'd take them if I asked him.'

'The stores won't take a risk on us until we've proven ourselves,' Leo reminded her. 'We'd be wasting time if we approached them again.'

'You were a nobody who went to one store with a bunch of amateurish products. I'm a Richier, and you'll make the products look like that –' Faye pointed at the illustrations '– before I take them in. They won't say no to me.'

'You have the casting vote,' Leo said, turning to Benjamin, wondering if this was what it was going to be like: Faye and Leo agreeing on nothing and Benjamin coming in to referee every decision.

'Let me think about it,' Benjamin said. 'Come back tomorrow, Leo. I'll have the paperwork drawn up for you to sign, giving you five percent of Richier Cosmetics. Faye will have thirty. And I'll have sixty-five.'

Meaning Benjamin would be the one deciding everything. But Leo knew it was the best she could do for now and she was lucky he was even speaking to her. It was a start. A place from which her cosmetics dream could finally grow.

'He said yes!' Leo rushed into the apartment above Jia's store, where she now lived with Jia, Jimmy and Jia's mother.

'Hurray!' shouted both Lottie and Jia, who'd been waiting at the kitchen table, consuming copious amounts of tea and cigarettes to quell their nerves. Jimmy clapped his little hands.

'You're both on trial for a month though,' Leo said, 'so you have to decide if it's worth it. I'll do everything I can to make sure you stay on. Besides, once Benjamin sees what you can do, he won't want you to go anywhere.'

'Of course it'll be worth it,' Lottie scoffed. 'I'm not staying in the belly of Lord & Taylor for the rest of my life.'

'Let's go out,' Jia said. 'We have to celebrate. What about the Oriental?'

'The last time we went there, it was with Joan,' Leo said, her elation dimming. Every day she wondered where Joan had gone and why; that her disappearance might only be temporary had become harder to believe as more time passed.

'We'll go somewhere else,' Jia said quickly. 'What about that place in the Village you told me about, the one with the fortune-telling gypsy?'

'A fortune-telling gypsy?' Lottie grinned. 'Oh, we have to go there.'

'Romany Marie's it is,' Leo said. 'I hope she's serving whiskey with her coffee. I could use a drink.'

'Was it that bad?' Lottie asked sympathetically.

'Selling my soul, you mean?' Leo smiled. 'No. I'll tell you about it at Marie's.'

The three quickly changed, made up their faces and, leaving Jimmy with Jia's mother, piled into a cab.

The salon at Romany Marie's was lively with people, and the foot-tapping folk music Leo remembered from last time played loud and fast. They squeezed around the last free table and her friends listened as Leo recounted her meeting. Both Jia and Lottie groaned when they heard that Faye had been there.

'I haven't met her, but I don't think I want to,' said Lottie.

'You'll have to if we're all going to work together,' Leo said. 'But don't judge her on what I've said. She can be fun. You might like her.'

'Like corpse lilies,' said Jia drily. 'Best admired from a distance.'

'Stop!' Leo laughed, then nudged Lottie. 'There's a man over there with his eye on you. By the time I get back from the bathroom, I expect to find you dancing with him.'

Leo crossed the room, catching Marie's eye and giving her a small wave, not really expecting Marie would remember her. She returned to the table to find Lottie dancing with the man and looking quite pleased with herself.

'Now we need to find someone for you to dance with,' Leo said to Jia.

'And you,' Jia said.

'I don't dance.'

'You should.'

'Look what happened the last time I met a man.' It was the first time Leo had referred to the baby since the night of the birth and she'd meant to sound comic, but the words came with the added complication of a tear in each eye.

'I know you know that dancing doesn't lead to babies.'

'You're right.' Leo blinked. 'Who do you suggest I dance with then?' She cast her eyes around the room, thinking for a moment that maybe she should just throw caution to the wind and dance with a man, when she realised that Everett Forsyth was standing just a few feet away.

He came over to the table. 'Well that makes sense,' he said.

'What does?' Leo asked, unable to believe that of all the nights she chose to come to Romany Marie's, so did he.

'Marie telephoned me. She told me I was needed here.'

'She saw me earlier.'

'And obviously decided to look up my number for some very unsubtle meddling.' Everett smiled at Leo. 'I'll leave you to it.'

'Oh no,' Jia interrupted. 'You should stay. Besides,' Jia went on, avoiding Leo's glare, 'Leo was just saying she wanted some whiskey and you look like the type to have a flask on you.' Jia pulled a spare chair over from the next table.

Everett hesitated and looked at Leo.

'You might as well stay for a drink,' she said. 'Otherwise you've wasted an evening.'

'I haven't at all,' he said as he sat down, his eyes fixed on Leo, who was trying her hardest not to meet his gaze but failing miserably. 'I'm Everett, by the way,' he said, holding out a hand to Jia.

'Jia Liang,' she said. 'I don't remember Leo ever mentioning a friend called Everett.'

Leo didn't elaborate.

Everett broke the silence, saying, 'I do have whiskey. I'll go see if Marie can help me out with some other ingredients.'

'Better make it four,' Jia said. 'Lottie's coming to see what's going on.'

'Of course she is,' Leo said, half laughing now and shaking her head.

On his way to find Marie, Leo saw Everett smile at Lottie and say hello, which made Lottie stop dead and swivel her head to follow him with her eyes across the room. Then she raced over to the table. 'The most air-tight man just smiled at me.'

'He's a friend of Leo's,' Jia said. 'He's getting us all a drink.'

'Why have I never met this gorgeous friend of yours?' Lottie spluttered.

'He's married,' Leo said simply.

'Oh,' Jia said. 'That explains an awful lot.'

'Where's that drink?' Leo said desperately.

'Right here.' Everett returned and slid a glass across to her. 'I take it your tastes haven't changed?'

'Not a bit,' Leo said, unable to repress the ridiculous smile that she always seemed to wear when Everett was around. She sipped her old-fashioned. 'That tastes good.'

'It does,' said Jia. 'A man of good looks and good taste. You're a rare one.'

'Jia!' Leo said.

But Everett laughed, along with Lottie and Jia. 'Thank you,' he said. 'So why are you all here tonight?'

'We're celebrating,' Lottie said. 'I'm no longer a window dresser. I'm a . . . what am I, exactly?' she asked Leo.

'You can be the Manager in Charge of Making Things Beautiful,' Leo said.

'I like the sound of that,' said Lottie, grinning.

Everett looked at Leo with a question in his eyes.

'I can't do it on my own; I need money,' Leo said. 'So I went to Benjamin Richier with a proposal. Jia and Lottie are part of the package. Meet the team behind Richier Cosmetics!' Leo raised her glass.

'Congratulations,' Everett said warmly.

'I negotiated a share of the business too,' Leo said. 'Five percent.'

'Benjamin got a bargain.'

'When I walked into his office, I had nothing. I left with more than that.'

'Where's Joan? Did you manage to find a role for a nurse at Richier Cosmetics too?' Everett asked teasingly.

The man Lottie had danced with came back to try again, saving Leo from having to explain Joan's absence, as did Jia, who said mock pitifully, 'If only someone would invite me to dance.'

Everett stood up. 'Shall we?'

'I thought you'd never ask,' said Jia.

Leo groaned. 'The cocktail seems to have gone to your head,' she said to Jia.

Everett smiled at Leo. 'Old-fashioneds have a habit of doing that,' he replied as he ushered Jia out to the dance floor.

Leo's stomach clenched. Yes, old-fashioneds did. Especially in the rain before a fire with Everett Forsyth. She watched him dance with Jia, watched Jia flirt outrageously, and smiled as Everett took it all in his stride.

Then the music changed and another man tapped Jia on the shoulder and she moved on, leaving Everett free. He returned to the table and held out his hand. 'One dance before I go?'

Leo stood up. 'One dance.'

She took his hand, feeling the shock of skin meeting skin, and she heard him catch his breath. They danced at a respectful distance from one another, but still one of her hands was on his back, just as his was on hers.

'Faye might come to see you,' she said to block out the sensation of nearness. 'I want to start a salon. She doesn't. She wants to try department stores. I think we need to prove ourselves first.'

'You know I'll take on Richier Cosmetics, no matter what.'

'You wouldn't normally be involved in a decision like that, would you?'

'Not usually, no.'

'Then don't do it for me. Let your department manager decide as he ordinarily would. I don't want to rely on favours.'

'Are you sure?'

'I am.'

Slowly, their bodies moved closer. A few inches still separated them, but their proximity made her cheeks burn, and the pulse in Everett's throat beat visibly.

'Mattie had the baby?' Leo asked, hoping that would dull the heat.

'She did. Alice. She's beautiful.'

Leo watched his face as he spoke. It was transformed. The strain was lifted; his eyes were clearer and he looked every bit as joyful as Leo had hoped he'd be. 'You're in love.'

'I am. She's the most precious thing. I wish you could meet her.' Everett smiled and it was too much. They were too near.

They both stepped back at the same time.

Which was lucky, because Faye and Benjamin Richier and a crowd of soused and rowdy people chose that moment to enter Romany Marie's. As Leo and Everett had been dancing right near the doorway, there was no way they could avoid notice.

'Forsyth!' Benjamin said when he saw Everett. Then, 'Leonora? What are you doing here?'

'I'm with Lottie and Jia. I told you about them today.' Leo indicated the table where Jia and Lottie now sat, watching the scene unfold.

'Yet you're on a dance floor with Everett. Where's Mattie?' Faye drawled, making a big show of looking around the small room.

'At home,' Everett said. 'Which is where I'm headed. Say goodbye to Lottie and Jia for me,' he said to Leo before taking his hat from the hook. 'Goodnight.'

'Goodnight,' she said, trying not to watch him walk down the stairs, on his way back to his wife and daughter.

'That was peculiar,' Faye said. 'A bit like this place. It could do with some jazzing up.'

'I'm sure if you find a bottle of champagne and a space on the dance floor, you'll have it jazzed up in no time,' Leo said drily.

'It's not worth the bother. Being artsy and bohemian isn't a patch on being rich. C'mon, Ben, let's scram. And you lot!' Faye commanded her friends. 'We're going back to Tex's.'

'Have fun,' Leo said.

'Why don't you come with us?' Benjamin suggested. 'I don't want you to have to resort to dancing with married men.'

'I don't want to leave Jia and Lottie,' she said. 'But I'll see you tomorrow?'

He studied her, ignoring Faye who was hollering at him to get a wiggle on. 'Come at nine.'

'I'm looking forward to it,' she said, and she meant it. Because in signing the papers tomorrow, her cosmetics business would be born.

∼

Leo arrived at Benjamin's office on Wall Street at nine sharp, with a dull headache and a throat raspy from too many cigarettes.

'Lucky Strike?' he offered, opening a gold cigarette case.

'I think I had too many of those last night,' Leo said.

Benjamin leaned back in his chair, lit a cigarette and gestured to a set of papers sitting on the desk between them.

Leo picked them up and turned to the last page, where she found her name.

She signed with a flourish.

'It's really happening,' she said, looking up at Benjamin with an uncontainable smile on her face.

'I have champagne,' he said, indicating a bottle resting in an ice bucket on a sideboard. But he didn't move to pour it into glasses. Instead he asked, 'Are you going to tell me more about the baby?'

'I might have a cigarette after all.' Leo picked up Benjamin's cigarette case with a hand that was noticeably unsteady. But then she couldn't get the flint on the lighter to catch. After watching her fumble a couple of times, Benjamin got up and walked around the desk to sit beside her, took the lighter and made it strike perfectly the first time.

Leo drew on her cigarette. 'I'm not going to tell you any more about the baby,' she said flatly.

'I can make it a condition of working with me,' he said. 'That you tell me.'

This was where she would ordinarily fold, give way, but she thought of what Jia had told her the morning the baby was born. It was all very well to swan into a meeting with a new dress and a show of attitude and give a nice speech, but what toughness really came down to was the ability to deal with the unexpected. She put her cigarette in the ashtray and looked Benjamin directly in the eye. 'You could,' she said levelly. Then she waited.

Benjamin waited too. When it was perfectly clear that she didn't intend to say anything else, he took up her cigarette and inhaled. 'I won't though. Besides, I prefer a woman with experience.'

Then he left her to chew on that while he opened the champagne bottle at last, pouring two glasses full of golden bubbles. He handed one to her. 'To Richier Cosmetics.'

'I will definitely drink to that,' said Leo. 'And thank you.' But all she could think was: what the hell have I just signed over to Benjamin Richier?

Chapter Fourteen

The next day, Benjamin picked up Leo, Lottie and Jia in the Rolls-Royce and had the chauffeur drive them upstate to where he had a factory waiting idle for Leo's cosmetics. He manoeuvred Jia into the front beside the driver and Lottie near one of the doors. Leo sat in the middle with Benjamin by her side. He slipped an arm around her shoulders and Jia, watching, raised an eyebrow at Leo.

'You'll all have offices at Richier Industries in the city,' Benjamin said as they drove. 'Just let my secretary know when you're going out to the factory and she'll organise a driver.'

'An office! And a driver!' Lottie was almost bouncing up and down in her seat. 'You know you're our favourite man in the whole world right now, don't you? Have I said thank you enough times?'

Benjamin laughed. 'You've all said thank you more times than you need to.'

Leo smiled. Benjamin could be so nice when he chose to be. Like right now, delighting her friends.

'I like seeing you happy,' he said into her ear.

170

'I think you'll only be seeing happy Leo from now on,' she joked. 'I can't wait to get my hands on that factory.'

'Every other woman in the world would be wanting to get her hands on mink coats and jewellery,' Benjamin said.

'We wouldn't say no to those either,' Jia quipped, and everyone laughed.

They arrived at the factory in a state of high spirits and good humour which only increased when they saw the vast space awaiting them.

'This is all ours?' breathed Lottie.

'Sure is,' said Benjamin. 'I need the factory to do something, otherwise it just weighs down my bottom line.'

'Then we'd better get started!' said Leo. 'We'll need a colour grinder, a mixing kettle and a moulder – and that's just for the lipstick.'

'Talk to Reg,' Benjamin said. 'He's the foreman. He'll get in the equipment you need, set it up, hire the staff for you. But you need to decide when you're going to start manufacturing, I don't want a whole lot of staff sitting here idle.'

'I want samples, like the ones you showed us, ready by the end of the month.' Faye's voice bullied its way into the conversation.

'Faye,' Leo said. 'Glad you could join us. But what exactly do you think we can make those samples on when we don't yet have any equipment?'

'I don't care.' Faye didn't even bother to acknowledge Jia and Lottie. 'That's your problem. I want to deliver Forsyths a sockdallager right between the eyeballs before their Beauty Department gets overfull.'

'I need to do more work on the lipstick formulation,' Leo said. 'The colour doesn't last long enough. I don't want to rush in with imperfect products.'

'End of the month.' Faye turned to her brother. 'Let's blow this joint. Ride with me back to the city.'

'Now you have your deadline,' Benjamin said to Leo. 'Reg'll be here soon. You can fill him in on everything you need.'

With that the Richiers breezed out of the factory, clothes perfectly pressed, hair impeccably groomed, demeanour absolutely untroubled. Faye especially left behind a distinct waft of stand-offishness.

'I take it that was Faye,' Jia said.

'It was,' Leo said with a sigh. 'Don't worry about Faye. That's my job. What we need to do is to make the impossible happen. Are you ready for the first of many, many challenges, or do you want to leave right now?'

Lottie snorted. 'Are you kidding?'

'I'm not leaving.' Jia crossed her arms. 'But you need to tell us what's going on with Ben.'

'I don't know,' Leo said honestly.

'If things fall apart with him, where does that leave us?' Jia asked.

'There's nothing between us, so nothing will fall apart,' Leo said, uncertain whether that was the truth or not. She opened her arms to the room in front of them. 'Look what we do have! An entire factory. Maybe in a couple of weeks, we might actually be making products. Then selling products. Imagine walking into a ladies' room and seeing a woman applying a Richier lipstick. How will that feel?' A smile was back on her face, and Lottie's. Only Jia's was less than radiant.

'I want that too,' Jia said. 'But not just for the duration of an affair between you and Ben. Faye looks as if she'd be happy to blow us all off like coal dust at the first sign of trouble.'

'I know what you're saying,' Leo said, pressing Jia's hand.

'But please don't worry. I'll do whatever I have to do to make sure this works.'

~

'Eosins!' Leo cried about a week later as she raced into the factory where she, Lottie and Jia spent most of their time, eschewing the offices on Wall Street.

'Well that sounds like either a profanity or a disease I don't want to catch,' Jia said. 'Which is it?'

'Neither.' Leo led Jia over to the workbench where they conducted small-batch experiments before running everything through the factory lines. 'I think I've solved our lipstick problem. The pigments we've been using don't last. But eosins make an indelible stain on the lips so the colour stays on no matter what you do. I've been reading about it here.' Leo pointed to the pages of a chemistry journal and continued. 'And apparently good old castor oil is the perfect solvent for the eosins because it's so viscous. So that's what we'll use. Of course it smells terrible, which is where you come in.'

'We'll need a stronger scent,' Jia said.

'I think so.'

A sudden squeal made them both turn around. Lottie ran over to them, waving something in her hand. 'It's the first compact,' she shouted. 'Look!'

Lottie passed Leo a stunning silver powder compact, the lid of which had been decorated with one of Lottie's illustrations.

'It's beautiful,' Leo breathed, and it was. Lottie's drawing of a woman boldly surveying a room, her lips red, cheeks rouged, lashes darkened, dress elegant, cigarette in hand, had been perfectly transferred onto the metal case. It was already an object of desire, even without opening the lid.

'It's enough to make anyone want to go out dancing and not come home until three in the morning,' Lottie said jubilantly.

'It really is.' Leo took Jia's and Lottie's hands in hers. 'Can you feel it? It's really happening. We have the compacts. I think we've solved the only problem we had with the lipstick. And look at that stack of mascara cakes over there. It's not a dream any more; it's real.'

'It sure is,' said Lottie.

'It sure is,' echoed Jia, surveying the room like Leo was doing, taking in the kettles mixing, the moulds being poured, and the samples set out for testing of perfume stability, breaking point and ageing. 'But did you read in the newspaper that they've proposed a law in Utah to fine or imprison any woman who wears a skirt higher than three inches above her ankle? What if that makes women even more scared of something like mascara?'

'What if it makes them want it more?' Leo responded wickedly.

Jia laughed. 'You have an answer for everything.'

'That's my job. Speaking of which, we have to get to our meeting, Lottie.'

'We're going to an advertising agency,' Lottie told Jia. 'Imagine having advertisements too!'

'Benjamin's giving you a lot of money,' Jia said to Leo.

'I have a budget, which I'm sticking to. That's all.'

Benjamin's driver took them back to the city to the offices of J. Walter Thompson. Leo and Lottie used the drive to pore over magazines, finding only advertisements which did the opposite of what they thought was right for a Richier customer.

'Look at this one,' Leo said, pointing to a picture of Odorono deodorant and the advertising copy that insisted the product would protect ladies from losing all of their friends and suffering social disgrace. 'We don't want to shame women into buying lipstick; we want them to feel wonderful about it. Emboldened.'

'How about this?' Lottie said, reading aloud, '*If you are twenty — and your skin is dull and lifeless and the outline of your face is drooping — you are old.*'

Leo frowned. 'Surely we can do better.'

But as they sat in the green carpeted boardroom of J. Walter Thompson, at a heavy and traditional mahogany table, Leo wondered if she was wrong. The first thing the agency had shown her to prove their expertise in the fledgling beauty industry was the very Odorono advertisement that Leo had rebelled against. The man presenting it was very formal and polite, but there was an undertone of condescension that irritated Leo, as if he knew better than she how to encourage women to buy lipstick.

'Do any women work here?' she interrupted.

Mr Goodwin paused mid-flow. 'Ah, yes. We have some women working here.' He looked across at Mr Buchman, who Leo assumed was his boss, for approval to deviate from the script he'd prepared.

'Could you bring one of them in, please? Someone young,' Leo said. 'If you don't mind.'

Mr Buchman tilted his head slightly at Mr Goodwin. 'Bring in Miss Delancey.'

Mr Goodwin disappeared, returning with a woman who looked as if she'd have been right at home on the dance floor of the 300 Club.

'Miss Delancey?' Leo asked. 'Would you mind telling me, as a young woman at whom these advertisements are presumably directed, what you think? Do they make you feel uplifted? As if you can't wait to rush out and buy this product?'

Miss Delancey looked first at Mr Buchman, then at Mr Goodwin, then at Leo. Leo could tell that she had something to say, but wasn't sure it was worth the risk.

'Gentlemen,' Leo said in her sweetest voice, but with steel in her eyes, 'Could you leave us for a moment?'

Mr Buchman began to bluster but Leo stopped him. 'It would please me greatly if you did.'

He gave way reluctantly. As soon as he'd gone, Leo turned to Miss Delancey. 'I'm Leo. I hope you don't mind us calling you in.'

'I'm Lil. And no, I don't mind. Are you sure you want to hear what I think?'

'Very much.'

'Well, playing on female insecurity might be profitable but it's not what I'd do. I read your letter when it came in. You want fun and good times. You know that Mrs J. Pierpont Morgan and Mrs James Roosevelt have banded together with a group of other biddies to rally against dresses with an excess of nudity and improper ways of dancing?'

'I had heard,' Leo said. 'But how does that help us?'

Lil's eyes sparkled. 'We use it to make lipstick even more coveted.' She scribbled some words on a piece of paper and showed it to Leo: *The low-cut gowns, the rolled hose and short skirts are born of the devil and his angels and are carrying the present and future generations to chaos and destruction.* 'Those are the words of President Murphy of the University of Florida. We print that next to a picture of a beautiful woman with rolled hose and a short skirt and a low-cut gown and a face made dazzling with make-up and we see just how many women might prefer to be on the side of the devil.'

'Do we dare?' asked Lottie, looking at Leo.

Leo grinned. 'Oh, yes. Yes we do.'

Everything was ready to go two weeks later than the deadline Faye had set, which Leo still thought was a miracle. On the morning of the meeting at Forsyths, Leo put on the chic black suit she'd worn the day she presented Faye and Benjamin with her plan and she waited in her office for Faye. The meeting at Forsyths was at eleven and, at a quarter to, she began to pace.

At ten minutes to eleven, she hurried into Benjamin's office, ignoring the secretary who wanted to announce her. Benjamin was in a heated discussion on the telephone.

Leo shifted impatiently while she waited for him to finish. After another minute, he replaced the receiver with a crash. 'What's wrong?' she asked.

'Damn workers at the steel factory are striking again. They've only been back at work a week and now they want more. Everyone wants more, Leonora. You get used to it eventually but this is costing me money.' Benjamin's brow was etched with frown lines.

'So why are you here?' she asked.

'What do you mean?'

'Why aren't you down there talking to the men?'

'My lawyer is there.'

'Benjamin, you can be very charming and persuasive when you want to be. Believe me,' she said with a smile, 'I've felt the full force of the Richier charm once or twice. Like on the boat when you first said the words *Richier Cosmetics*, as if it might one day be something real.'

'And now it is,' he said, smiling back.

'Which is why you should go down there. Make them feel what I felt that day.'

He studied her face for a moment and she felt herself softening a little towards him, despite the fact that he'd sided with Faye about the department stores. He looked like she felt half the time: worried, uncertain, tense, never knowing exactly what to do but having to make a decision and do something anyway, always hoping it would turn out to be the right thing.

'Maybe I will go down there,' he said. 'Thanks for the advice.'

'You're welcome.'

'Now what did you want to see me about?'

'I'm looking for Faye.'

'She's gone out to lunch with Mattie Forsyth.'

'Oh,' Leo said, sinking into the nearest chair without waiting to be asked.

'How well do you know Mattie?' Benjamin asked, a question that seemed too forced to be real, a question that brought back to Leo's mind the memory of dancing with Everett at Romany Marie's and Benjamin seeing them together, a question that bruised the momentary softness she had just felt for Benjamin.

'Mattie's family accompanied me to New York. You must remember that.'

'You obviously know her husband too.'

'Yes, I know Everett,' Leo said.

Benjamin lit a cigarette. 'Do you know him well?'

Better than anyone on this earth, besides myself, Leo thought. 'I saw Everett occasionally on the ship.' It wasn't a lie, but the truth was too precious a thing to place in Benjamin's hands. 'If Faye's at lunch, what happened to the meeting at Forsyths?' she asked, changing the subject.

'She had it at nine this morning.'

'Nine? She told me it was eleven.'

'She had to reschedule. Besides, you didn't want to approach department stores. She didn't want your doubts to become apparent in the meeting.'

It took all of Leo's strength not to explode. 'Richier Cosmetics is like a piece of me. I'd manage to curb my doubts in any meeting because I want it to do well. I can't believe she didn't tell me, and that you didn't either!'

Leo realised that she was standing. And shouting at the man who was her boss, who could shut down the whole operation with one click of his fingers. 'I'm sorry,' she said, resuming her seat. 'I just . . .' Her voice trailed off. *I just wanted to make sure Faye said the right thing.* Because Faye didn't know how the products were made, or the details of the advertising campaign; Faye didn't have the blood of Richier Cosmetics flowing through her.

'You look very beautiful when you're passionate,' Benjamin said. 'Let's go for a drive.'

'A drive? Now? But how did Faye go at Forsyths?'

'I'll tell you. If you come for a drive.' Benjamin held out his arm.

Leo stifled a groan of frustration. 'Fine,' she said, slipping her arm through his, knowing she needed to calm down before she put Benjamin out of humour with her.

They didn't speak as the driver took them to the Tenderloin district in midtown, where they stopped and Benjamin got out of the car.

'Why are we here?' she asked. The sidewalks around them were quiet at this time of day; the ladies of the night who plied their trade in the streets were still sleeping off the night before and the men who bought their services were earning their daily bread. There was nothing lovely about any of it, no hint of what lay several blocks beyond: the promenade along Fifth Avenue to wealth and glory. Here, way off Broadway and far from the ritzy

Upper East Side, the bright lights had ceased to shine and the pawn shops and junk shops beckoned those in need of dollar bills to trade in their furs for cash.

The Sixth Avenue El rattled overhead, sprinkling their heads with soot. Benjamin waited until it had passed before he spoke. 'Forsyths said no.'

Even though she hadn't wanted to approach Forsyths in the first place, Leo's stomach still lurched at what seemed like yet another failure. 'Why?'

'For exactly the reasons you said. We haven't manufactured to scale. They don't want to take so large a risk when they've just opened the store.'

Leo put her hand on a chair that sat abandoned outside a bar with boarded-up windows. No one else was around; it was just Benjamin and Leo, squaring off outside a rundown saloon.

'You know, Leo, you could have very easily found a way to sleep with me on the boat or soon after you arrived in New York. Then you could have blamed the baby on me, forced me to marry you, made me do the right thing.'

Leo couldn't help laughing. 'Benjamin, the idea of someone like you marrying someone like me is ridiculous. You belong with a Fifth Avenue socialite – someone like Dorothea Winterbourne. And Faye would cast a kitten at the thought.'

'Don't worry about Faye,' Benjamin said dismissively. 'My point is, here you are worrying about the future of Richier Cosmetics just because one meeting with a department store didn't go to plan. You should be jumping up and down for joy because now we have no choice but to open a salon.'

'Really?'

Benjamin pointed to the saloon behind Leo. 'That was the first business my father bought. We made our money out of liquor, before he moved into manufacturing. I sold off all the saloons when I took over the business because the city had moved north, away from the areas he'd bought into. And now look at the place. Would you ever have thought that everything I have could be traced back to this?'

Leo stared at Benjamin in astonishment. 'I had no idea.'

'It's not something I advertise. But I come here every now and again when things are tough.' Benjamin took out two cigarettes, lit them and handed one to Leo.

She moved over to stand beside him and they both smoked in silence for a moment, backs against the rickety wall, Leo enjoying the moment of camaraderie, of honesty, of seeing the heart beneath the suit of the businessman. 'You know, I really do like you when you talk like this,' she said.

'If I'd known that bringing you to the Tenderloin would make you like me more, I'd have done it a lot earlier,' he said, smiling. 'The Tenderloin is the way to a good many things about a woman, but who knew it could also be a way to her heart?'

Leo laughed. 'Now you're flirting,' she said, not really minding for once, touched by this new image of Ben as a man who'd fought his way out of a saloon business and into one of the largest industrial conglomerates in America. The man, she reminded herself, who'd been fatherless for years, who'd all but raised Faye. A man who might tend towards ruthlessness in business, but why shouldn't he? Perhaps that was how he'd been able to survive.

'Faye isn't going to like the idea of starting a salon,' Leo said. 'But I'll talk to her. You don't need to do it for me. I want her there; she knows the right people. She'll be good at it, despite what she says about "shopgirls".'

'Well then, let's get back to the office. I'm sure you're itching to start planning your salon.' Benjamin held out his hand to lead her back to the car and Leo took it with a smile.

'First, I need to find the premises. Imagine seeing the words *Richier Cosmetics* emblazoned on an awning on Fifth Avenue.' Leo tightened her grip on Benjamin's hand in her excitement.

'I know just the place.' Benjamin leaned forward to speak to the driver. 'We'll take a look now.'

Fifth Avenue, with all of its traffic and shopping and people, was a welcome reprieve from the Tenderloin and soon the car stopped outside a building that Leo knew instantly was perfect. It was a couple of blocks from Forsyths and far enough uptown that the women Leo wished to lure would be happy to shop there.

'When can we look inside?' Leo said, leaning so far out the window that a gust of wind almost blew her hat onto the sidewalk. 'I want it to look like the annexe to a nightclub. An intimate space where a woman might make herself beautiful before stepping out into a real speakeasy.'

Benjamin laughed. 'I'll have my secretary call the agent and see if we can take a look this afternoon.'

'This afternoon!' Leo said, pulling her head back into the car. 'I'm not going to be able to think of anything else all day. But won't it be horribly expensive?'

'You'll just have to make sure the business starts earning some money.'

'It'll be my motivation – knowing I need to pay the rent. Thank you. I thought this day started out terribly and now I don't want it to end.'

'If you wait long enough, you always get what you want,' Benjamin said, studying her face. 'I didn't think for a minute that Faye would succeed at Forsyths. So now she doesn't have a choice about the salon. You win bigger when you let the other person make the mistakes.'

Leo felt her hand, which had been squeezing his with all the joy of the morning, go limp. 'Is that what you did?' she whispered. 'With me?'

Benjamin shrugged. 'I knew you wouldn't be able to do what you wanted without money. That if I waited . . .'

'I'd come begging,' Leo said. 'So everything you said on the boat about determined people and admiring my decision was a lie?'

'On the contrary. I knew if you were determined enough, you'd eventually see past your scruples and take me up on my offer.'

There was that streak of ruthlessness again, always pushing Leo back five steps just as she'd taken a large stride towards him. 'What is your offer dependent on though?'

'I don't think I've made any secret of the fact that I want you.' Benjamin kept his eyes fixed on her face, and this time he didn't even try to hide his desire.

'Then I need to tell you something,' Leo said. 'It's my turn for honesty.'

'Let me make it easy for you,' he said. 'You're not in love with me. Someone broke your heart. I'm not after love. Because maybe you're not the only one with a broken heart.'

Leo saw something flicker in his eyes behind the desire. It was a deep hurt that she knew all too well because it lingered at the back of her eyes too.

'We'd make quite a match,' he said. 'You have a head for business.'

He hadn't answered her question. So she asked again. 'But how much of the business is dependent on a match? Would you still do this, even if there was no chance . . . ?'

'Is there no chance?'

'I don't know.'

Benjamin shrugged. 'Well, at least that's not a no. Besides, business is business. I want to make money, will always want to make money, no matter what happens.'

She chose to believe him, happy to drop the subject entirely. She'd asked, he'd given an assurance. She'd be able to tell Jia that everything would be okay.

The car pulled up at the Richier Industries offices and Leo opened her door.

Benjamin's hand stopped her. 'You're not waiting for Everett Forsyth are you?'

Leo's whole body froze, except her breath, which came too fast for speech.

'I don't think Mattie Forsyth is the kind of woman to let her husband go,' he said. 'Especially now he has a very successful business. Money. And a child. I should have said that only some things will come to you if you wait long enough. Not everything.'

Leo forced herself to speak calmly. 'I need to do some work,' she said, stepping away. 'After all, I have money to make for you, don't I?'

Chapter Fifteen

The salon opened its doors in September 1920. On that day, Leo stood in the main room with Jia and Lottie, surveying what they'd done, feeling so proud. The gramophone played Al Jolson's 'Avalon', she'd had the walls decorated with prints of the images that adorned the lids of the Richier compacts and she'd placed the cosmetics in stations around the front room, compacts open and ready to have fingers dipped into them, begging to be tried on. The only sadness was that Joan wasn't there too; how thrilled she would have been to see how far Leo had come since that first pot of black mascara they'd tried on in the chemist shop. Leo pushed the thought away. Joan wasn't coming back; she knew that now. In asking Joan to help her with the baby, she'd demanded too much, and had lost her good friend forever.

Wrenching her thoughts away from the past, Leo poured out three glasses of champagne and passed them around. 'Here's to Richier's Salon becoming one of the most visited places on the Upper East Side.'

'Hear, hear,' Lottie and Jia chimed in.

Leo put down her glass and smiled ruefully. 'It has to; I'm just about broke.'

'Aren't you drawing a wage?' Lottie asked, horrified.

'Twenty dollars a week. Benjamin keeps saying I should take more, so it's not his fault,' Leo reassured her. 'But I don't want to, not until the salon is making money.' Leo sat in the nearest chair. 'Every night I go to bed terrified that I'm spending Benjamin's money and nothing will come of it. That nobody will like the products. That there isn't a space in the market because Elizabeth Arden already has it covered.' She shook her head. 'Is that the worst pep talk I could give on opening day?'

'We just need to get people in the doors,' Lottie said confidently. 'And with our advertisements, that's bound to happen.'

'And don't forget we have Faye to rely on too,' Jia said drily. 'Do you think she'll turn up for opening day?'

'She wouldn't miss it,' Leo said. 'Either to rub our noses in the fact that nobody comes or to take all the glory when they do.'

They all laughed. Then a woman hurried up to the door, knocked, and Leo let in Lil Delancey, the woman who'd helped create their infamous advertising campaign. 'I came to get some mascara,' she said with a grin.

'Of course,' Leo said, grinning back. She pulled out mascara, rouge, lipstick and powder from the display cases, put it all in a bag and handed it to Lil. 'Take this.'

Lil opened her purse but Leo shook her head. 'It's a gift,' she said. 'To say thank you.'

Lil's smile widened. 'Thank *you*,' she said. 'Thank you for making mascara something that I don't have to buy in secret by mail order, as if it's right down there with opium and moonshine. I think your salon will make a big difference, Leo.'

Leo beamed. This was what she'd wanted: to give women choice and opportunity. To make them feel happy rather than wicked, sinful and ashamed when they wore cosmetics.

She watched Lil skip out, delighted, and saw a car pull up and a man step out carrying an enormous bouquet of deep red roses. He waved to Leo. She opened the door again, this time to let in Everett Forsyth.

'Congratulations,' he said, giving her the roses and a chaste kiss on the cheek.

'Thank you.' Leo knew her joy at Everett's gesture was written all over her face but she didn't care. 'They're my favourites.'

'I remember you once told me that.'

'Let me take those out the back and put them in some water,' Lottie said.

'I can do it,' Leo said.

'No, you stay here. I have to go and do some work anyway.'

'And I need to go to the factory. Bye, Everett.' Jia waved and left the salon.

Leo laughed. 'Was that their not-so-subtle way of leaving us alone?'

Everett laughed too. 'I think so.' He paused. 'Do they know?'

'I haven't told them. But I think they've guessed.'

Everett shifted towards the door. 'I wanted you to know I was thinking about you today. I won't stay. I was worried Ben might be here.'

'I have a funny feeling he's waiting to see whether or not it's a success before he comes in. I suppose I understand. Nobody wants to be associated with a failure.'

'It won't be a failure, Leo,' Everett said gently.

Leo dared to look at him properly and regretted it immediately. It was too much, seeing the lips she'd once kissed with abandon, the body she'd once held beside hers, the man she still wanted to spend the rest of her life with. 'Thank you for believing in me,' she said.

'I still think you should ask for more of the company,' he said. 'Now, before it really takes off. You deserve it. What's Faye really done? And Ben?'

'Well, there's the small matter of all the money he's put in,' Leo said.

'And the not so small matter of all the hours and expertise I bet you've put in. Don't sell yourself short.'

Leo sighed. 'It's complicated, asking for things from Benjamin.'

'Because he wants something in return?'

'Maybe. And something he said makes me think he always knew he'd get me cheaply when I was desperate enough. He might not be prepared to pay more for something he already has.'

'Do you mean that you and he . . . ?'

'Oh no!' Leo was quick to say. 'We're not lovers. I was talking about our business relationship. Which is just as tricky.'

'I asked Mattie for a divorce.'

'Really?' Leo whispered, hating herself for the flicker of hope she felt at his words; divorce was a painful thing, she knew, not something to wish for.

'I've given Mattie everything she needed.' He rubbed his face tiredly. 'But we just don't get along. I've done what I said I'd do for her. Now it's time for me to go after what I need. That's if you're still . . .'

'Of course I am.' She smiled at him and saw on his face a matching joy. 'But what did Mattie say?'

'She refused to discuss it. But I expected that, the first time I raised it. I'm sure I can talk her round. I'll pay her anything she wants; I don't care how much it costs. All I want is Alice.'

'How is Alice?'

'Beautiful,' he said with a smile. 'She's in the car. The chauffeur's with her. Do you want to see her?' He held up his hand. 'Of course you don't want to.'

'I do,' said Leo.

Everett led the way out to his car, which had one door open for air and a chauffeur standing guard. On the back seat, asleep in a basket, was a little baby girl. A perfect baby girl. Leo felt her heart quite literally squeeze, her blood stop pumping. She clutched Everett's arm to steady herself. 'How old is she?' she whispered.

'I'm sorry.' Everett shook his head. 'I didn't mean to hurt you.'

'You haven't.' Leo tried to smile. 'It's just so many feelings all at once.'

'She's seven months old,' Everett said proudly.

Seven months. Around the same age as Leo's baby would be, wherever she was. Leo was glad of Everett's arm holding her up. Because in this child, she'd seen a ghost. A ghost of the baby she'd given away. A ghost of the little girl Leo looked for every time she saw a baby, never seeing one that she recognised definitely as her own. She knew she probably never would. 'Why isn't she at home with Mattie?'

'The nurse is sick. And Mattie finds looking after Alice by herself . . . difficult.'

Leo winced at the thought that Mattie could disregard a child she'd been lucky enough to keep, whereas Leo thought about her child almost every minute of every day: she'd be checking cosmetic samples and there, floating on the edge of her vision, would be a baby sleeping. Or smiling. Sometimes, although only rarely because it was so very painful, Leo would see herself holding a baby.

'I often take Alice to work with me,' Everett continued. 'She sleeps in my office. Forsyths has lots of female employees so she gets cooed over all day.'

The baby wriggled, stretched and opened her eyes. She blinked a few times, then saw her father and the most natural, unrestrained smile spread over her face. She kicked at her blanket, giggled and reached out a hand to Everett.

'Look!' Leo said, entranced.

Everett leaned into the car to pick up his daughter. She snuggled into him as if his shoulder was the most comfortable, safest and loveliest place in the world.

Leo stroked Alice's cheek. 'She's beautiful. You've done so very well.'

'Leo.' Everett looked at her over his daughter's head.

And it hurt so much to see him like that, a man she was in love with, now a father in love with his child, but married to another woman.

A car swept past, jolting Leo out of her thoughts. She shouldn't be standing on Fifth Avenue with Everett, stroking his daughter's cheek. 'I should go back inside,' she said. 'Thank you for the flowers. And for coming.'

'I wouldn't have missed your opening day for anything. And I'm going to keep talking to Mattie about a divorce. I promise.'

'I want to wish you good luck but that seems like an awful thing to say.'

'It's not as if there was ever any love between Mattie and me.'

As Leo watched the gentle way Everett bent over to tuck his daughter back into her basket and the smile Alice gave him, she saw a perfect moment of shared love, confirmed by Everett's next words. 'Despite everything, I'm so glad I have Alice,' he said.

'I'm boiled as an owl and hitting on all sixes!' The door whooshed open at two minutes to nine and in danced Faye, dress sporting a rip, make-up an utter mess, and reeking of liquor.

Leo stared. How could Faye turn up on opening day looking like that? 'You need to go home. I can manage without you for the morning.'

'I'm not going to miss this for all the world,' Faye declared. 'I just need a new frock, a new face and a glass of champagne.'

'I think you've had enough of those already,' Leo said, taking Faye's arm and leading her out the back to the offices, away from the doors where customers might enter in just a few minutes. 'I have a dress you can borrow.'

Leo took a coat hanger off the back of her door. She kept a spare dress at work because she often worked so late into the night that it was easier to stay rather than go home. The dress was an exact replica of the one she was wearing; she'd copied a Worth design, a column of silk with a skirt of tiered panels that fell like a waterfall to just below mid-calf. She'd made one in rose pink and one in blue and she passed the blue one to Faye.

'We'll look like a set of twins,' Faye said, laughing. 'People might think we're related.' She waggled a finger at Leo. 'Which is what you want.'

'Faye, you need to fix your face,' Leo said, ignoring her. 'Are you sure you shouldn't just go home?'

'Oh no. I want to be here to see what happens.'

Leo hurried out, feeling the composure that she'd worked so hard to maintain begin to crack. *It'll be all right*, she told herself. Faye wouldn't deliberately sabotage the opening, because then she'd have Benjamin to answer to.

She waited in the salon, fidgeting with pots that didn't need to be straightened, tidying brushes that were already in order. All was quiet out the back — too quiet, given Faye's state, so

Leo went to see what she was up to. And what she found was Faye, bent over Leo's desk, one finger pressed against a nostril while she sniffed up a quantity of a white powder that certainly wasn't make-up. Leo knew what it was; one didn't have to live in Chinatown long before being given an unwelcome introduction to cocaine.

Leo closed her eyes. This couldn't be happening. Of all the contingencies she'd planned for, Faye loaded to the muzzle with more than just champagne on opening day was not one of them. Then a bell tingled – a customer, presumably. Perhaps Faye would fall asleep and leave Leo to it. She fervently hoped so.

She stepped into the salon with a smile on her face and held out her hand to two young women. 'I'm Leo East. Welcome to Richier's Salon.'

'So this is the place where the morals of an entire generation are likely to be ruined,' one of them said.

Leo laughed. 'You've seen the press?'

'We have.'

The advertisements that Lil Delancey had created for them had been running in *Vogue* for the past fortnight. The newspapers had picked up on them instantly, coupling Richier Cosmetics with F. Scott Fitzgerald and flappers, unscrupulous people mired in all kinds of sin, which Leo thought was the kind of publicity she could only have dreamed of.

'I'm Gloria Morgan,' the woman said. 'This is my sister Thelma.'

'Please have a seat,' Leo said, trying to quell her excitement. The Morgan sisters were money with a capital M. They ran New York Society, even though they were still in their teens. It was well known that Reggie Vanderbilt was wooing Gloria and it was rumoured that a prince had his eye on Thelma.

'We're about to turn sixteen,' Thelma said. 'We're having a party and we want to give something beautiful and unique to the guests as a party favour.'

'I see you've met the Morgans.'

Leo's stomach contracted. It was Faye's voice.

'Faye. Nice to see you.' Gloria smiled at Faye, a smile that was not quite real, and Leo sensed there was no love lost between Faye and the Morgan sisters.

'I'll get champagne,' Faye said. 'Then I can show you around my salon.'

Her salon. The words stung Leo. But of course they were true. It wasn't Leo's name on the door.

'Leo's looking after us very well,' Gloria said.

The salon bell tinkled again and Leo's stomach did more than contract – it just about turned inside out when she saw Mattie Forsyth sail through the door.

'It looks like Leo has another customer to help,' Faye smirked. 'Mattie will want your expertise. You make the stuff. You'll know what would best keep the eyes of the hotsy-totsy Everett Forsyth fixed on a woman.' With that, Faye ushered the Morgans into chairs on the other side of the room, popped the cork from a champagne bottle, turned up the gramophone and began to sweep piles of make-up onto the table in front of her.

Leo thought she might be sick and wondered how it was that Faye didn't feel the same given all the drugs and champagne. 'Mattie,' she said. 'How can I help?'

'I'd like more colour,' Mattie said imperiously. 'Childbirth leaves one rather washed out.'

Leo picked up some rouge. 'Perhaps if we start with highlighting your cheeks? Your skin is lovely and would suit a peachy colour.'

'I thought rouge was for harlots,' Mattie replied, staring at Leo's rouged cheeks, which Leo knew were rosier than they should be.

'Oh no,' Leo continued, hoping her voice wouldn't fail. 'Many young women are starting to wear rouge to highlight their natural beauty.' She sounded wooden, like she was reciting a pre-prepared spiel. She tried again. 'Shall we just put some on, then you can see what you think?'

Mattie nodded and Leo began to powder Mattie's face. The powder was soft and luscious, and smelled like an exotic garden.

'What is that delightful smell?' Gloria Morgan asked, walking over to Leo. She picked up the silver powder compact from the table. 'Look at this, Thelma! It's good enough to eat. And it smells like it's just wafted in from the Orient.'

'I find it pungent,' Mattie said.

Faye sat and drank her champagne, watching the fun unfold.

'I bet if I wore this to the 300 Club I'd have men trailing after me like I was the Pied Piper,' Gloria continued.

'If that's what you like,' Mattie sniffed.

'Wouldn't you?' Gloria said. 'What woman doesn't want a secret charm to make men fall at her feet?'

'I thought that was called money,' Faye snorted.

Leo didn't know whether to laugh or cry, but the Morgan sisters laughed and Leo wondered how she could inconspicuously remove the bottle of champagne from Faye. But the Morgans were drinking it too, even though it was only half past nine, and so it'd have to stay.

'Here's the rouge I'd suggest,' Leo said, holding out a compact to Mattie, who feigned shock.

'That's much too bold,' Mattie said.

'But if you just dab the smallest amount here' – Leo touched it to the apples of Mattie's cheeks '– then it will look like you're glowing, nothing more.' Leo held out a mirror to Mattie.

Thelma clapped. 'Oh, that's fabulous! You're transformed!'

Mattie stared at herself critically. 'It's not for me,' she snapped. Leo prayed that the Morgans would see Mattie for what she was, a woman with a chip on her shoulder, and that they wouldn't be put off their quest to find a party favour.

'More champagne!' was Faye's way of breaking the silence, ever the lalapazaza – the life of the party – and for once Leo didn't care. She only wished Mattie would take a sip herself and loosen up. She desperately wanted to know what Faye was showing the Morgans. Why did she have the powder puffs out, for instance, when they were clearly not the right thing?

Gloria moved back over to Faye and Leo heard her say, 'We wanted something more special. Something nobody else has.'

'You know as well as I do that among the Upper East Side set, there's no such thing. We all have everything,' Faye said.

Leo stood up, even though she knew she was supposed to be serving Mattie. She took a rouge compact from her pocket and held it out, showing the Morgans the picture of the couple dancing, the woman's head tucked into the man's shoulder as if she'd found a place she never wanted to leave.

'We could make these for you,' Leo said. 'With a bespoke image of both of you, dancing, as if you were at the 300 Club with a line of men trailing behind.'

'That would be the cat's meow,' Thelma said breathily. She kissed Leo's cheeks but Leo didn't have time to smile because Mattie was saying, 'I thought you were helping me.'

'Of course I am,' Leo said soothingly. 'Let's start again.'

'If only that was possible,' Faye said, sniggering.

'Faye, perhaps you could write down how many we should make and when the party is?' Leo said coolly.

'Exactly what I was about to do,' Faye slurred.

Leo saw the Morgans look at one another and she knew that if it wasn't for the beauty of the compacts, they would probably walk right out.

Leo removed the make-up she'd applied to Mattie's face and began again. A few minutes later, the Morgans stood up, without thanking Faye, but they both stopped at Leo's side. 'It was lovely to meet you,' Thelma said.

Then both sisters swept out of the salon, two young women with more self-possession in their little fingers than Leo thought she'd ever have.

'Perhaps Faye can help me now,' Mattie snapped.

'If that's what you'd prefer,' Leo said politely.

'Let's go to town,' Faye hiccoughed, plonking herself down opposite Mattie. 'Get me some mascara will you?' Faye said to Leo.

'I don't think Mattie will want mascara,' Leo said.

''Course she does,' Faye said. 'It'll be fun,' she cajoled Mattie, who nodded.

Leo fetched a mascara cake from the other side of the room. Both Faye and Mattie lowered their voices but Leo was still sure she heard the word 'Everett'. She returned to the table, mascara cake in hand. 'Here you are.'

'We don't need it any more,' Faye said. 'Mattie's upset and it'll only run all over her face if she starts blubbing.'

Mattie didn't look at all upset. She was as tranquil as an Upper East Side drawing room and equally overdressed. 'Is something the matter?' Leo asked.

'Not any more,' said Mattie. 'Faye just reminded me of something: that children should stay with their mothers. And that if a man loves those children, then he'll stay too.'

Mattie's words dripped with more subtext than a piece of high literature. And Leo knew she should just go away and smoke a cigarette. But the last thread of her patience finally snapped. 'I'm not sure that Richier Cosmetics makes the kind of products that suit you, Lady Mattie.'

Mattie and Leo exchanged a stare which Leo held and Mattie couldn't. Mattie covered it by saying, 'Rouge is definitely for harlots,' before she strode out.

'Well, I'm off to have coffee.' Faye smiled broadly. 'A bit of a pick-me-up.'

The last thing you need is a pick-me-up, Leo shouted in her head as Faye skipped through the door. Then she picked up a glass and, heedless of the freshly painted walls, threw it. It crashed in a splinter of pieces, marking the wall with the dregs of champagne.

The sound caused Lottie to appear. 'What was that all about?'

Leo walked over to the table where Faye had sat, supposedly taking notes. She held up a piece of paper. 'This is meant to be a list of quantities and delivery dates for a large order of rouge compacts for the Morgan sisters to give to their party guests – the very people we want as our customers.'

'It's blank,' said Lottie.

'No telephone number, no delivery address, no order details, nothing.' Leo pointed to the table. 'Here's the rouge I created.' She pointed to the pictures on the wall. 'Those are the advertisements you worked on.' She picked up another compact. 'Here's the mascara cake Jia helped refine. Faye's contributions to the business are empty champagne bottles, lipstick-smudged glasses she never washes, and the unwritten order for our largest customer so far. With only Faye to rely on, Richier's could go out of business within a month.'

'Can't you get rid of her?' Lottie asked bluntly.

Leo shook her head. 'I'm her employee. *She* can get rid of *me*.'

'Talk to Ben then.'

'I don't want him to think I can't manage Faye.'

'Can you manage Faye?'

Damn, damn, damn, Leo thought. She didn't want Lottie to doubt her. Didn't want to cringe every time Faye walked into the salon. Didn't want to run to Benjamin every time things went wrong and ask him for help. And, most of all, she didn't want to think about what Mattie had said about children and their mothers, the way she'd doused that little flame of hope Leo had felt after her meeting with Everett.

*C*hapter *S*ixteen

*L*eo had Lottie draw up a compact design for the Morgan sisters. Then she took it to their home that afternoon, along with a gift box of products for each, and a bagful of apologies. Luckily, she managed to convince them that only Richier Cosmetics would do for their party favour, although they weren't all that hard to convince once they'd seen Lottie's design.

She left their home happy, with an order in hand, knowing it was a break she needed. They wouldn't be able to sell enough products from one salon to make much of a difference. But if they made such a name for themselves that women began to ask for Richier Cosmetics at department stores, then they'd be in business.

At the corner of Fifth and East Fifty-Ninth, the smell of hot buttered corn made her stomach growl. She'd just paid the corn man for one of his freshly roasted cobs when she heard someone call her name.

'I was just coming out of the Plaza,' Benjamin said, 'and I saw you. How's the first day been?'

'Great,' she said, holding some paper under the corn to catch the dripping butter. 'We're making party favours for the Morgan sisters.'

'Really?' Benjamin seemed surprised. 'That is something.'

'I know,' Leo said proudly.

'Sounds as if you should have been the one celebrating at the Plaza.'

'I'm happy with corn from the wagon. What were you celebrating?'

Benjamin took the corn from her hand and threw it in the nearest bin. 'You deserve oysters,' he said. 'I was celebrating the end of the strike. You were right; I went to the factory and talked to the men and now we've ironed out a new agreement with the union. So why don't we go out tonight? My car's here. Come back to my house. Borrow something of Faye's. We'll go to the Empire Room at last.'

Leo pushed away every misgiving. What if the doubts she had about Benjamin were simply because she didn't know him and was comparing him to Everett? She'd never given him a chance, whereas he'd given her part of a business. He'd trusted her. Shouldn't she pay him the courtesy of doing the same? Because, despite what Everett had said about a divorce, after Mattie's visit she was starting to wonder if being with him was more of a fantasy than ever.

Benjamin led Leo up the stairs to Faye's room. At the door, Leo paused. 'I don't think she's going to be pleased to see me. Or to lend me a dress.'

'She'll do what I ask her to,' Benjamin said.

As we all do, Leo thought, then shook her head. She was here to get to know Ben. To see what he was really like as a man. To see whether her heart could feel anything for somebody else.

Leo opened the door to find Faye pulling armfuls of dresses out of the wardrobe and flinging them onto the bed.

'Why are you here?' Faye asked mid-throw.

'I'm going out with Ben. He said I should borrow something of yours. We're going to the Empire Room.'

'Are you now?' Faye asked, eyebrow raised. She took a sip from the ever-present glass of champagne. 'Take whatever you want when I'm through.'

Faye rifled through the pile of silk, then twirled around with a gorgeous indigo frock, the colour of the Manhattan sky just before the sun disappears and the city lights began to shine. 'Wave my hair,' she snapped at the maid.

Then she began to wrap something around her breasts and Leo couldn't help asking, 'What *is* that?'

'Boyshform. You know. Breast flattener. Bubs are so Edwardian. You should try it. All the better to show off your lipstick.'

Leo shook her head and approached the bed, sorting carefully through the clothes. The maid left the room to fetch something that Faye had demanded and Leo looked up to see Faye watching her in the mirror, her expression unveiled, the toughness and hostility replaced momentarily by a kind of pain. Leo closed her eyes; she didn't want to see Faye laid vulnerable: the child of a saloon owner who'd died when she was a child herself, so desperate for love that she'd run away to England with a man whom she suspected was a rake, with a brother she adored but who was far more cavalier towards her than he ought to be. Perhaps the drink and drugs were a way to fill the empty space inside her.

'You never told Ben I was pregnant, did you?' Leo said.

'No.'

'Why not?'

Faye took a moment to answer. 'I thought the threat would be enough,' she said eventually. 'I didn't think you'd tell him.'

'I couldn't accept money to start a business without telling him.'

'Or you knew I would if you didn't, so you had to.'

A knock on the door broke the impasse. 'Are you ready?' Benjamin called.

'Almost,' Leo said, grabbing the nearest dress off the bed as Faye walked out. The dress slipped down over her body and she could feel the weight of the dollar bills it would have cost to buy such a thing. The label sewn into the back said Vionnet and a strap of black jet beads circled her neck, held up the tips of the bodice and continued on around to the back of the dress, the beads growing ever larger as they finished in the middle of her back beneath her shoulder blades. The waist was ruched with a sash that fell to one side and the skirt was made up of hundreds of tiny pleats that fell longer at the back and shorter, to mid-calf, at the front. The dress was black, and the neckline lower than any she'd ever worn.

She hurriedly made up her face and pulled her hair into a low, tight bun. She didn't look at herself in the mirror; she didn't want to lose her nerve.

Ben glanced up as she came down the stairs and took a step back in surprise. It took him a moment to speak. 'You look . . . I was going to say beautiful but that seems inadequate. Stunning.' He held out his arm. 'Shall we?'

'Yes,' Leo said, slipping her arm into his. 'We shall.'

The Empire Room was as imperious as its name suggested, and a dominion of the muted: muted conversations, pale-coloured silk dresses, conservative hair styles and definitely no rouge. Leo felt stares affix themselves to her as she entered the room and withdrew peremptorily when they saw Benjamin by her side, his presence obviously providing her ticket to entry.

They sat down. Benjamin ordered champagne, oysters and caviar. 'Here's to our long-anticipated date,' he said, raising his glass in a toast.

Leo clinked her glass against his and smiled. 'I need to tell you something that I probably should have said a while ago.'

'Okay, now I'm worried,' Benjamin said, putting down his glass.

Leo laughed. 'No, it's not like that. I wanted to say that you really are a remarkable man, taking a chance on me like this. I don't imagine many, or any, others would do the same. So thank you.'

Ben's face softened. 'And thank you,' he said. 'That's probably the nicest thing I've heard all day.'

Leo reached out and took his hand. He smiled at her and she smiled back, letting herself be charmed by this man who'd done so much for her. 'I suppose people don't often take the time to thank you when you own the company.'

'They don't. But I like it when they do.'

It was while they were regarding each other with something more like intimacy than they had ever shared before that a flashbulb blinded Leo.

'For the social pages,' a man said. 'Look out for it in the *Times*. A woman like you will definitely make it into the papers.' He gave Leo a cheeky grin.

The waiter appeared and set down their main courses with a flourish. When he moved away, Leo saw that at the next table a man was on bended knee, offering a blue Tiffany & Co. box to a woman who looked as delighted as if she'd fulfilled the dream of a lifetime.

'True love,' Ben said as he followed her eyes to the tableau. 'I wonder when they'll find out it's not as grand as everyone says it is.' He picked up his fork. 'You'll think I'm being cynical.'

'I think maybe true love is less grand than devastating.' Leo shook her head. 'I don't know why I said that. It's not really dinner conversation, is it?'

'But you're right.'

Leo saw on his face the same pain she'd glimpsed in the Tenderloin that day when he'd said she wasn't the only one with a broken heart. 'What happened to you?'

'Two years ago,' he said, 'I fell too hard and too fast in love. I thought she felt the same. But she was playing a game with two other men, taking as much cash as she could and enjoying the ride. She married the wealthiest of us and, after a while, she moved on to somebody else.'

There was just the faintest glimmer in Ben's eyes as he finished speaking, which he covered by removing his hand from Leo's and clicking his fingers for the waiter. 'We need more water,' he said, although they didn't.

'I wonder how many tycoons she's planning to make her way through before she stops,' Leo said lightly, sensing Ben wanted a change of mood.

He laughed, clearing the weight of heartbreak from the table. 'Luckily Manhattan has a plentiful supply. Now, what say we talk about something more prosaic. Like balance sheets.'

Leo laughed too. 'Let's.' And she began to talk to him about some of the expenses she was incurring that bothered her, especially some of the ingredient costs.

'Go out to tender again,' Ben said. 'Your order quantities have gone up so it's reasonable to expect a better deal.'

'I thought about that, but as we've only recently signed the order agreement, I thought I should stick to it for a time, out of good faith.'

'Not if it's costing you more than it should. You didn't agree to any set timeframe did you?'

'No.'

'Then stop being so accommodating. Go out to tender.'

'All right! I'll stop being nice.'

Ben smiled. 'Only in business, Leo. Not with me.'

It was the first time he'd called her anything besides Leonora. And it felt like a shift, as if whatever gap there'd been between them had now been fully bridged. Who else, besides Lottie and Jia, could she ever sit down with and talk about her business in such a way? The number of things that she and Ben had in common was growing each day. 'I think I can manage that,' she said warmly. Then she realised they were the only people left in the restaurant. 'That went fast.'

'You sound surprised.'

'I wasn't sure how it would go,' she said honestly. 'But I don't think it could have gone any better.'

'There's one thing I can think of that would make it better,' Ben said. He leaned over the table and kissed her gently on the lips.

It didn't last long, just a few seconds, and it was warm, pleasant even. 'That was nice,' she said.

'I'll settle for nice,' Ben said. 'But I'm definitely aiming higher. We might have to try again another night and see what happens.'

~

The picture was in the social pages, front and centre, Leonora and Benjamin staring at one another like lovebirds. A delivery to the salon of expensive hot-house orchids from Ben followed, along with a magnum of French champagne which Faye promptly fell upon.

'That takes care of breakfast,' she said.

Leo picked up the flowers, which had come in their own porcelain vase. The delivery man had placed them beside Everett's roses of yesterday, which made the orchids look thin and insubstantial, whereas the roses looked as if they could bloom forever.

The salon was quiet that morning and Leo flicked through the pages of the *Atlantic Monthly* for something to do, stopping with an audible gasp at a page titled 'Polite Society', written by a Mr Grundy. The piece was apparently the first in a four-part series the journal intended to run about the younger generation, and Leo couldn't help reading aloud the first paragraph that struck her eye: '*If woman resorts to barbaric methods of conquering young men, old men must retaliate by adopting uncivilized warfare to subjugate woman. It is for us middle-aged fathers and uncles to do our share toward restoring social law and order — peaceably if we can, forcibly if we must.*'

'Uncivilised warfare and force,' Leo said with barely disguised contempt and to no one in particular. But her voice was loud enough to draw Lottie out of the office and Faye away from her champagne. 'To battle the *barbarism* of dancing, flirting and lipstick. I see men hit their wives or their children almost every day down by the tenements and nobody blinks an eye. But a woman dares to rouge her cheeks and they cry out for guns to defeat her.'

'Gimme a look at that,' Faye said. She scanned the page then snorted. 'Get a load of this.' She adopted a serious tone as she read, '*We must encourage mothers to tell their daughters truthfully and simply the effect of some phases of their social laxity on the men whose moral fibre they are weakening.*'

Lottie made a scornful noise. 'Of course we're weakening the moral fibre of men. Men would all be upstanding and virtuous if it wasn't for us barbaric women.'

'And our mascara,' Faye added.

'Can you believe it though?' Leo said. Then she shook her head. 'I don't know why I asked that. I can believe it all too well.'

'What about this bit,' Lottie said, leaning over Faye's shoulder and pointing.

Faye put her ridiculous voice back on and read, '*Let them dance and flirt and be frivolous and gay; only let them remember that the girls with whom men like to dance and whom they like to flatter are not necessarily the girls they will choose as friends, still less as wives. The popular adjective for the popular girl today is "jazzy," — the word carries its meaning in the sound — and the quality seems to have superseded the gift of charm which womankind used to desire as the indefinable social magnet.*'

'We have to use that,' Leo said. 'In the next advertisements: *The popular adjective for the popular girl today is "jazzy"*. Accompanied by a picture of a very jazzy girl dancing and laughing and perfectly lipsticked.'

'Let's do it,' said Lottie.

'Sooner the better.' Faye was in agreement for once, and they all smiled.

The first day the advertisements ran, Leo heard a commotion outside the doors. A well-dressed matron was handing out leaflets to any women approaching the salon.

'Who's that?' Leo asked Faye.

'Hell,' Faye swore. 'That's Mary Weston. Purveyor of chastity belts and Victorian morality.'

'Why is she outside our salon?' Leo asked.

'Dunno,' Faye said.

Leo stepped onto the sidewalk. 'Can I help you?' she asked.

Mrs Weston shuddered and turned her back on Leo.

'May I have one of those?' Leo asked, indicating the leaflet.

Mrs Weston continued to ignore her.

'Would you mind?' Leo asked a young woman who'd had one of the leaflets thrust upon her. The woman passed it to Leo, who read it, screwed it up in her fist and marched back inside.

'She's demanding that people boycott the salon!' Leo cried, waving the balled-up paper at Faye and Lottie. 'She says we sell products designed to lure women into wickedness, debauchery and licentiousness. That we're bootleggers, peddling devilry instead of alcohol.'

Faye laughed. 'That's a lot of power for one little lipstick.'

'It's not funny, Faye,' Leo said. 'If she stands out there, nobody will come in. She's not the kind of gauntlet anyone will want to run.'

'She'll be gone soon,' Faye said with a shrug. 'Ignore her.'

But she was still there two hours later and no customers had dared enter the salon. 'Right,' said Leo at last. 'If she can stand out on the sidewalk, then so can I. Lottie, if you wait halfway down the lane, I'll stand on the corner and direct customers down to you and you can take them in the back entrance. If Mrs Weston wants to call us bootleggers, then let's take our customers through the secret entrance and into the Richier den of iniquity.'

'You can't stand on a street corner,' Faye said, aghast.

'I can and I will,' Leo said. 'I'm not too proud to help our customers get past Mrs Weston.' With that she searched around until she found a piece of cardboard. 'Can you make this say "Richier's Salon this way" in a design nicer than my scribbled writing will look?' she asked Lottie.

'Sure.' Lottie set to work and within five minutes had made a cheeky sign showing the face of a girl giving a mischievous wink.

'Perfect!' Leo cried.

'You're going to stand out there holding a sign?' Faye said. 'What are we, a dime store?'

'No,' said Leo. 'We're women who'll show the Mrs Westons of the world that there are far worse things to worry about than a bit of mascara and rouge.' With that, Leo flounced out of the salon and positioned herself on the corner, ahead of Mrs Weston and her leaflets. Lottie waited halfway down the lane.

It wasn't long before a woman stopped to talk to Leo. 'I thought the salon was that way,' she said, pointing to the canopy.

'Today we're using the secret entrance.' Leo smiled. 'It seems we're a little too outrageous for some, but we won't let that stop us, will we?'

'Golly, no,' replied the woman.

'You just need the password,' Leo said. 'Today it's *iniquity*. If you give it to the lady down there –' she pointed to Lottie, who gave a wave '– she'll show you through.'

'Okay,' the woman replied with a grin. 'I should have brought the other girls along. This is almost as much fun as a night out.'

'It'll be even better in the salon. Quick,' Leo urged, 'Mrs Weston's looking!'

The woman scurried off down the lane laughing, and was ushered inside by Lottie. And so the day went on, Leo and her sign doing battle with Mrs Weston and her leaflets, the pile of which grew no smaller in the face of passwords and secret entrances and mascara made more covetable by being branded licentious.

'I hope you're prepared to pay the consequences with our Lord for what you're doing,' Mrs Weston huffed when it became all too apparent whose wares were the more popular.

'I'm more concerned about the men who think it's acceptable to use uncivilised warfare to subjugate women. Why should we be subjugated?'

'The Lord says we should,' Mrs Weston inisted.

'Well the Lord is wrong,' Leo said, turning her back on Mrs Weston's gasp and directing another young woman on to Lottie.

Soon after, Mrs Weston gave up, but not before a news-paperman had snapped a photograph of Leo and Mrs Weston standing side by side with their various inducements. 'I think you're just giving us more publicity, which is probably not what you want,' Leo said. With that, Mrs Weston took her leaflets and her judgements and left.

Leo went back into the salon with a sigh of relief. 'We can go back to business as usual,' she said.

'But I was enjoying my new role,' Lottie said.

'It was fun, wasn't it?' Leo said with a grin.

'Fun!' Faye exclaimed. 'Demeaning is the word I'd use.'

'Did we sell some products this morning?' Leo asked her.

Faye shrugged and Lottie chipped in, 'Did we ever! I think we need to make a new batch of rouge we sold so much of the stuff.'

'Well then,' said Leo, 'it wasn't all that demeaning, was it?'

'I'm going home,' Faye said, picking up her purse.

Leo began a quick stocktake and was almost finished when the telephone rang.

'What's going on?' Benjamin asked when she picked up the phone. 'I've had a reporter and Faye both tell me you spent the morning standing on a street corner brandishing a sign.'

'I wasn't brandishing anything,' Leo said indignantly. 'Why don't I tell you the real story.'

He listened in silence and said at the end, 'I agree with Faye. It was a cheap stunt.'

'What was I supposed to do? Let her stand there and drive away all of our customers? She was right in the doorway, blocking the entrance.'

'She'd have gone eventually,' Benjamin said.

'Or she'd have stayed there longer because her tactic was working!' Leo cried. 'We turned it into a game — a game the customers were more than willing to play. And we sold more this morning than we have on any other morning, so I can't see that anyone was offended overly much by my cheap stunt.'

Benjamin's silence made Leo hear how loud her voice had been. 'We had a problem,' she said, more quietly. 'We came up with a solution, which proved successful. Besides, do you think it's right to say that women should be subjugated by warfare just because we wear lipstick?'

'No. But next time, run it by me,' Benjamin said.

Leo slammed the phone down. So that was how it would be. Every man in the city would either condone or ignore Mr Grundy's views. And the women of Manhattan would all become just that little bit more scared of doing nothing more sinister than wearing mascara. The irritation stayed with her all afternoon and into the early evening, when Jia appeared at the salon.

Leo smiled. 'I'm not done here yet. You should go on home without me.'

'There's something I need to tell you.' Jia's voice was bleak.

'What's wrong?'

'I can't make the rouge for the Morgans. We're out of money.'

'I checked the account last week. We have enough.'

'It's gone.'

'Gone?'

'Gone.'

'Where?' Leo asked, trying to keep her voice from sounding desperate, panicky. 'Tell me.'

'I don't know. I'll go back to the factory and see what I can do. But unless we find a pile of money sitting on the doorstep . . .' Jia stopped at the sight of Leo's face.

She knew she was as white as the walls. 'We have to make those compacts.'

'I know,' Jia said.

Leo stood up. 'There's been a mistake, that's all. I'll sort it out and we'll be ordering the materials we need by tomorrow morning at the latest. And thank you; I know you could have just telephoned. You didn't have to come in here to tell me.' She hugged her friend, willing a confidence she didn't feel to pass from her arms and into Jia.

Once Jia had left, Leo called the bank. Surely it was a monstrous error.

Her banker was blunt. 'There is no money in the account, Miss East.'

'But where did it go? It was there two days ago. I know we have spent some since then, but only a very little of the total amount.'

'You have spent it all.'

'I have not.'

'You have not but the other signatory to the account, Miss Richier, has. She has charged some money to Bergdorf Goodman, some to Saks & Company, some to various restaurants and has taken the rest as cash. She has, in fact, overdrawn the account and you now owe us almost nine hundred dollars.'

'Nine hundred dollars!' Leo couldn't stop the exclamation. Then she gritted her teeth. 'Thank you for explaining. You'll have your money returned to you shortly.'

Leo hung up the phone and walked back into the salon – *her* salon, not Faye's: the salon she was about to lose if she didn't find a way to both repay the debt and buy the materials she needed to fulfil the Morgans' order. 'Damn, damn, damn,' she swore. So Richier Cosmetics was Faye's money pit, a way to finance her dinners and her dresses and her drinks and her drugs without Benjamin knowing what she was up to. And Leo was so damn stupid for not having realised it sooner.

She sat down, rested her elbows on a table and dropped her face into her hands. Why had she ever thought that going into business with Faye was a smart thing to do? Faye could be brilliant, when she wanted to be. Now Faye was a demon, the flaming millstone around Leo's neck. What Leo needed was money – money of her own. But where the hell was she going to get that? She opened one of Faye's champagne bottles and didn't bother with a glass. She just lifted it to her lips and drank it down as if it was water. Her head spun and her throat burned.

Her eyes settled on an article in the social pages of the newspaper, spread out on the table before her, about the Morgans' forthcoming birthday party. It listed the guests: Mary Pickford, Pola Negri, Zelda Fitzgerald. All of whom would have Richier Cosmetics placed in their hands at the end of the party if only Leo could afford to make the party favours.

Leo turned over each page of the newspaper. She'd been looking every day but hadn't yet seen an article about the Forsyths' impending divorce. Did that mean it wasn't going to happen? Why was it all going so wrong?

But then Leo heard Everett's words, spoken the day they opened the salon, echo around the room: *Don't sell yourself short.* Was it possible that he was right, that she was worth more than five percent? Perhaps it was finally time to fight for what she deserved.

Chapter Seventeen

E arly the next morning, Leo went to the Richier Industries offices on Wall Street.

Benjamin's secretary hadn't arrived by then, and nor had Benjamin, so she let herself in, sat down in a chair and waited. At eight o'clock, the door opened to reveal Benjamin, who smiled when he saw her.

'This is a nice surprise.' He kissed her cheek. 'I'll get Anna to make coffee.' He ordered the coffee, then sat beside Leo. 'You look like a woman who needs to get something off her chest.'

'I do.' She hesitated. 'Let's wait for the coffee though.' It took forever for Anna to come back with a coffee pot and two cups, to pour the coffee, to add milk and sugar, to check if they needed anything else and then, finally, to leave.

Leo plunged in before her confidence vanished. 'I've told you how important the Morgans' order is for the business?'

Benjamin nodded.

'I need to place an order for materials this morning but we have no money. Faye . . .' Leo had tried all night to think of a way to say this that didn't sound accusatory, but she hadn't come up with anything. 'Faye has made some purchases that have used all our cash. I need . . .' Leo's voice trailed off. *I need money.* She sounded so weak, so pathetic. *I need, I need*; it was all she ever thought, all she ever felt, this constant need for something more, something she was as yet unable to provide for herself.

'Faye came to see me last night,' Benjamin said.

'Oh?' Leo's stomach fell through her silk stockings and into her shoes.

'She said you were broke. She had a list of purchases that had been made with company money: dresses, shoes, restaurant bills.'

Damn you, Faye, Leo thought. Damn you to hell and to everywhere bleak and black and without champagne. How dare she blame her frivolous spending on Leo?

'Which is why, every time I see you, you're wearing one of the same three dresses,' Benjamin went on. 'And the same pair of shoes.' He smiled. 'A woman who'd spent two hundred dollars at Bergdorfs would probably want to wear her new dresses.'

Leo could have cried with relief. He knew it was Faye. He was on her side. Perhaps she could say it then. 'Because Faye owns so much of the company, she can spend what she likes. There's nothing I can do to stop her.' She paused. Benjamin loved Faye; if she said too much she could easily anger him.

'Faye also told me you'd probably ask for more of the company to be transferred to you.'

If there was a worse place than hell she could damn Faye to, she would. Leo's hand wanted desperately to pick at a loose thread of embroidery on her dress. But she reached for a cigarette instead. 'My choices are to keep running to you every time I need money, which is both demeaning and a waste of everyone's time. Or I take a larger share in the ownership of Richier Cosmetics, in exchange for my expertise and good management of the business. Then issues like this won't arise.'

'So what's your proposal?'

'That I own as much of the business as Faye.'

Leo waited for Benjamin's shocked gasp but either he was a good actor or he hadn't heard her properly. 'If you give me twenty-five percent of your share, then Faye and I have thirty percent each. You still have the most, at forty percent.' Still no reaction. 'I'll keep drawing the same wage I am now, which is lower than I could expect in the same position elsewhere. I'll do that for a year, in part payment for your shares. The rest of the payment is in the form of the cosmetic formulations I've created. It's a fair exchange. The shares are worth little at the moment.'

'But they'll be worth more in the future, I'd hope.' Benjamin exhaled smoke in a thin, deliberate stream.

'Of course.'

'More coffee?' Benjamin asked, deftly avoiding giving Leo an answer.

Leo shook her head.

Still, he rose, walked over to the door and called for more coffee. 'And biscuits,' he said to Anna. 'All this talking is making me hungry.'

There was another silent interval of waiting for the coffee jug and biscuits to be brought in. Finally it was all laid out in a way that would have put the Waldorf Astoria to shame.

'If I agree to what you're suggesting, then as the owner of a large share of the company you'll be a woman who needs to set an example,' Benjamin said. 'I've told you before that you're beautiful, but on the wage you're drawing, you can't afford to buy the clothes, shoes, jewellery and other adornments you need to look like the ideal Richier woman. Like Faye.'

'I don't think I look shabby,' Leo said defensively.

'No, but you could look more glamorous – like you did the other night.'

'When I was wearing Faye's Vionnet gown that probably cost a year's wages, you mean?' she said coolly.

'Yes.'

Leo hugged her coffee cup closer to her. There was no conceivable way that she could buy gowns like that, not even on an ordinary salary, much less on the pauper's salary she now drew. 'Does it really matter?' she asked.

'Of course it does,' said Benjamin. 'And you shouldn't be seen hustling for business on street corners.'

Leo's hands squeezed the china cup so hard that she wondered why it didn't crack. He was probably right though. She couldn't imagine the Vanderbilts or the Rockefellers or Henry Ford doing what she'd done. But it had worked. Wasn't that what mattered?

'Let me think about it,' Benjamin said. 'I'll let you know within a fortnight.'

'And the money I need right now for the Morgans?' Leo made herself ask.

'See Anna on the way out. She'll arrange to have it transferred.'

⁓

Leo had to wait until the salon was closed before she could speak to Faye, who had, Leo conceded, been only tipsy enough that day to ensure that all the customers had a good time and that no one left empty-handed.

'Thank you,' Leo said to her as she locked the door. 'You helped sell a lot of product today.'

'*I* know how to talk to the gals from the Upper East Side,' Faye said.

'You do,' Leo said, refusing to rise to the bait. 'And because of that, I'd like to make a deal with you.'

'You'd like to make a deal with *me*? Well, I can't wait to hear what it is.' Faye poured herself into a chair, lit a cigarette and waited expectantly.

'We had some trouble with money, which I think you know about.'

'Oops. Fur coats can be so expensive.'

'I'm sure they can be,' Leo said drily. 'So, the deal is this: you can keep spending some of the salon's money on your habits. Not as much as before, but some. All you have to do is confine most of your drinking and . . . other indulgences to the evening, outside of salon hours.'

'If I hadn't seen you and your little pot of red on the ship you wouldn't be here right now.'

'You're welcome to ask Benjamin for the money you need for your "fur coats".' Leo kept her voice level, doing her damnedest to keep her feelings of revulsion at having to fund Faye's habits a secret.

'Sure, I'll accept,' Faye said gaily. 'Anything to see that look on your face every time you check the transactions and find I've been doing a little spending.'

'What did I ever do to you?' Leo asked in frustration.

Faye cackled. 'Perhaps I just like a relationship with a bit of fire. Keeps things interesting.' She stood up. 'Ciao! I'll be in around noon tomorrow. Got some shopping to do in the morning.' She swept out of the salon.

~

Besides the altercation with Faye, the next two weeks were an ever-spinning roulette wheel where the ball kept landing on the right number. The Morgans had their party and business more than doubled in the following days. The Lord & Taylor buyer placed an order. Then the Saks & Company buyer did the same.

The actresses at the Morgans' party took the rouge back to California and two department stores on the west coast placed orders too. And the days ticked down towards the deadline that Benjamin had set for making a decision.

Leo called a meeting with Lottie, Jia and Faye to discuss how they were going to manage the orders. 'We need a sales team,' she said. 'And demonstrators for the department stores. We need to increase our advertising while things are going so well. What else?'

'We need another mixing kettle for the factory,' said Jia. 'The lipsticks are the product most in demand and to fill the orders we need more capacity.'

Faye decided to chime in. 'None of that sounds cheap.'

'No, but we aren't cheap, are we?' Leo said. 'And we weren't prepared for this quantity of orders so early on.'

'Whose fault is that?' Faye eyeballed Leo through a cloud of cigarette smoke.

'It's mine,' said Leo. 'But as I've never forecast sales for a business before, and I didn't want to overstate things, I underestimated demand. Benjamin's accountant halved the numbers I gave him. So now we're in a situation where we have a level of orders that wasn't expected until mid next year, but the orders are sitting on my desk right now.'

'So it's Benjamin's fault,' drawled Faye.

'It's no one's fault and we're wasting time. We obviously need your approval to increase our expenditure this month.'

'I don't see why we need a sales team. Or demonstrators.'

'Are you going to travel around the country demonstrating in stores?' Leo exploded. 'Elizabeth Arden has her own training facility, for God's sake. All I'm asking for is a few people, who I'll train in my own time to sell the products rather than leaving everything to sit on a shelf where it will be overlooked.'

'You're also asking for a new mixing kettle.'

'Do you want me to call these stores and say we can't fulfil their orders?'

Faye didn't reply.

'Then we need to do something. I'm already here from six in the morning till midnight. Lottie and Jia are putting in the same kind of hours. It's not as if Jia can leave the factory and turn demonstrator. And it's not as if Lottie can leave off managing all the advertising and design work and catch a train over to California. Perhaps I should go myself, but then who's going to do my work?' Leo realised she was leaning over the table, that her voice was raised, and that Lottie and Jia were watching in a kind of awed fascination. She sat down, folded her hands in her lap and shut the hell up.

Faye let the silence drag on and on. She stubbed out her cigarette. Lit another. Took a long, slow drag. 'It's not the kind of thing I can decide on the spur of the moment. Write me a report. Best do it by the end of the day. Then I'll have all the information I need to make a decision.' With that Faye stalked out, and Leo knew she was being punished for her outburst. And that she'd also unwittingly involved Lottie and Jia.

She let out a groan of frustration. 'Now we're going to have to sit in here all day writing a report to justify fulfilling existing orders! When's everything else supposed to get done?'

Faye's head reappeared. 'And I'm off to lunch so you'll need to be out in the salon, Leo. Bye!'

'Of course,' Leo muttered. 'Who doesn't go to lunch at ten in the morning?' She sighed. 'Okay, I need to be in the salon. Jia, can you telephone the factory and let them know you're working from here today? Then, if you break down the current lipstick orders and pending orders, showing how much we can make with the existing mixing kettles versus how much we need to make, that would be great. Lottie, I don't need much from you in the report, just an overview of the advertising we'll use on the west coast. I'll pull it all together tonight.'

'She's not going to make us do this every time we get a new order is she?' Jia asked in disbelief.

'Who knows?' Leo said.

'Do you think she'll even read it?' Lottie asked.

'I have no idea. But she might and we don't want to give her any excuse to say no. So we have to do it properly.'

'Can't you just ask . . .'

Leo cut Jia off. 'I'm not going to ask Benjamin. Let's play it her way, and perhaps we'll get what we want.'

But Leo knew the business couldn't run like this. If she owned thirty percent of Richier Cosmetics, then she'd be ordering mixing kettles and employing demonstrators, rather than prevaricating, writing reports, justifying the only sensible course of action.

Jia and Lottie stayed with her as she finished the report, clacking away on the typewriter as slowly as a child learning to put shapes into a sorter. But the report was something to be proud of. Jia's figures were an argument in and of themselves, Lottie's advertising breakdown was magnificent and Leo wove it all together with a story of what Richier Cosmetics could be with just a little more investment.

'It's excellent,' she said when she typed the last word and rolled the sheet of paper out of the typewriter.

'She can't say no to that,' Jia agreed.

'She'd better not,' Leo said grimly as she lay the report on Faye's desk, ready for whenever she decided to turn up in the morning.

Chapter Eighteen

*L*eo had hoped to arrive at the salon the next morning to find the report sitting on her desk stamped *Approved*. Instead, she was met by an article in the business pages of the *New York Times* all about Richier Cosmetics. The article praised the business acumen of Benjamin Richier, who had seen a space in the market and created another national enterprise to add to the Richier Industries portfolio. Faye's involvement was mentioned but not Leo's. It was as if Leo didn't exist. As if she and Richier Cosmetics were two separate entities that could operate without each other, which she knew wasn't the case. Because without Richier Cosmetics, what did she have?

She sat at her desk, pressing her fingers against her temples, the question – *What do I have?* – repeating over and over in her mind. She had Lottie and Jia: two friends she wouldn't trade for all the world, two people she knew she could rely on. But that was it. She had no family. She had lost Joan. She lived in a tiny bedroom in Jia's mother's flat. She had a job that paid her very little. Four homemade dresses, which Benjamin had all but labelled second-rate. And the tiniest star of hope, like a snowflake already melting, that Everett would divorce Mattie and they might somehow be together.

The telephone shrilled, making her jump. 'Did you see the *New York Times*?' Benjamin asked.

'I did,' Leo said. 'Congratulations.'

'That's the kind of press we need – not a piece in the *Sun and Herald* about a Fifth Avenue stoush between you and virtue.'

Yes, because our customers often read the business pages of the Times, Leo thought, but she didn't dare say it aloud. 'I think all publicity helps,' she said evenly.

'And now it's time,' Benjamin said.

'Time for what?'

'To have a proper launch. To show New York we're serious about cosmetics.'

'I think we're overdue for one,' Leo said wryly.

'I'll have Faye organise it.'

'I can do it.'

'You're busy enough,' Benjamin said. 'We'll have it on Friday night. Our special date.'

The date when he was supposed to give her an answer to her proposal about the business. 'But that's two days away,' she said. 'It's not enough time.'

'It's plenty of time,' Benjamin said.

At that moment, Mattie Forsyth breezed through the door, arm in arm with Faye.

'Mattie needs more powder,' Faye told Leo, who was hanging up the phone. 'Can you get it?'

'Of course,' Leo said, forcing a smile to her lips.

'I'm supposed to be going to a ridiculous charity event for some hospital or other for luncheon,' Mattie said to Faye. 'It's a children's hospital, so somebody had the bright idea that the luncheon should be for families. Husbands, wives and children!

Isn't that why we go to luncheon – to get away from the children? But Mrs Astor invited us so I have to attend.' Mattie laughed and so did Faye. Leo fetched a powder compact for Mattie.

Mattie opened the compact, dabbed powder onto her nose and cheeks and snapped it shut. 'Everett's walking down from the shop to meet me,' she said. 'I was going to collect him on the way but he was on the telephone and I couldn't wait for him.' Mattie smiled smugly at Leo and Leo knew she was about to have her nose rubbed in the fact of Mattie and Everett Forsyth.

'I might go out for a bit,' she said to Faye tiredly. Then she wouldn't have to watch Mattie and Everett together, wouldn't have to try to guess from the way they spoke if Everett was any closer to convincing Mattie about a divorce.

'You can't do that,' Faye said. 'You'll need to look after any other customers who come in. I'm busy with Mattie.' She took out some glasses and a bottle. 'Let's have champagne while we wait,' Faye said to Mattie.

'I don't think I'll survive the luncheon any other way,' Mattie said.

Leo left them to it and sat down at her desk on the other side of the salon. She was itching to ask Faye if she'd read the report, but she knew better than to bring it up now. She shuffled papers around on her desk for a time and looked up to see Everett coming down the sidewalk. He stopped when he got close to Mattie's car and turned his head as if he was listening to something. Then a look came over his face that Leo had only seen once before – on that grim night on the ship when he was livid at having to become engaged to Mattie. He flung the car door open, bent down and scooped out a baby. The baby was screaming, its face red and wrinkled with misery.

Everett cradled Alice, kissed her, then flung open the door of the salon. 'How long has she been in there while you've been drinking champagne?'

Leo didn't know how he managed it, but he kept his voice level. His rage showed only on his face.

Mattie looked up in surprise, the howling baby having done nothing to draw her attention, as if it was a sound she was used to blocking out. Leo thought it best to disappear into the office out the back, but she could still hear every word.

'Babies cry all the time,' Mattie said airily. 'There's nothing wrong with her.'

'You left her in the car by herself for God knows how long!'

'It's only been twenty minutes. Isn't the chauffeur there?'

'William is waiting at the salon door for you. Alice was by herself.'

'I couldn't bring her in here. Her basket catches on my gown.'

'You could take her out of the basket,' Everett said stonily. 'Pick her up. Show her some affection. You can't leave a child alone like that.'

'She'll never know.' Mattie sounded completely unconcerned. 'It's not as if she can talk or understand anything. What a lot of fuss about a little bit of crying!'

'It's time to go,' Everett said.

Mattie stood up. 'Faye, you'll have to excuse my husband for being so rude. Thank you for the powder.'

Leo heard the door open and close. When she was sure they were gone, she slipped back into the salon.

'What a charming family scene,' Faye said with a smirk.

'Have you read the report?' Leo asked, hoping her voice would come out smoothly.

'I haven't had time – you've seen me, busy with customers like you always want me to be.'

'Could you read it soon?' Leo asked, knowing how desperate she sounded. 'I need to let the California department stores know about demonstrators.'

'But I'm off to organise our launch venue. Which, you've got to admit, is the priority now that the launch is on Friday.'

With that, Faye waltzed out the door, leaving Leo trying to climb out from under the knowledge that had dropped on her like a stone: if what she'd just witnessed was the way of things, and it seemed irrefutably to be so, Everett would never abandon Alice to Mattie for the sake of his own happiness. And Leo would never want him to do that to a child. But it would also mean he was utterly lost to her, a thought too painful to allow into her head. She took advantage of the quiet afternoon to drink a Faye-sized quantity of champagne. But it didn't help.

Because Faye was in charge of the venue, the launch was held at the 300 Club. Because Leo had contrived it, each invitation was sent out with a tube of Richier's Reddest Red lipstick, which Leo hoped some of the guests might see their way to wearing on the night. And boy, did they ever.

In a banquette, spotlit by one of the Chinese lanterns hanging above, stood Pola Negri, letting fly with her movie-star smile, lips glossy with Leo's lipstick. Leo knew she couldn't have stage-managed it any better and, seeing that victory was a possibility, a smile lit up her own face, growing ever larger when she saw Zelda Fitzgerald point at Pola's lips with a covetous finger.

This is the moment, Leo thought as she grinned at Jia and Lottie, who were standing by the bar staring at all those red lips. *This is how it starts.* Because if women saw those they emulated and admired wearing cosmetics so freely, then they might try it too. An ordinary woman like Leo herself was, like Jia was, like Lottie was, like the women typing out letters in an office on Wall Street – all those ordinary women might see that they could, if they wanted to, wear mascara, feel beautiful and that it was up to them, not society, to decide that it was okay.

Leo said hello to Texas and kept moving through the long room of the club, which was tight with people, torn between wanting to join Lottie and Jia and wanting to rush over and kiss Pola on the cheek with her own set of Reddest Red lips. Tonight, for the first time, Leo was standing at the top of something as astonishing as Niagara Falls and it looked as if, far from falling, she might at last fly.

'Shall we dance?' Benjamin asked, appearing at her side.

'We should,' she said, smiling at him and squeezing his hand. 'Thank you again. For everything. I wouldn't be here tonight if it wasn't for you.'

'I think you might have had something to do with it too,' he said.

He drew her close to him on the dance floor and she let him, let herself dance with this handsome man who'd been the one to help make her dream come true. And the charm of the evening, the intoxication of knowing all those people were there to celebrate Richier Cosmetics, of seeing movie stars wearing a lipstick she'd created, one that had begun life in a chemist shop in Sutton Veny, made her rest her cheek against Ben's, made her hold him a little tighter. Made her try as hard as she could to let go of the other hand that still, ghost-like, held hers: Everett's hand.

Right at that moment, a cigarette girl in shimmering blue trousers knocked into her.

'You need to apologise,' Ben said sharply to the girl, whose composure fled as fast as the cigarettes falling from her tray and onto the ground.

'I'm fine,' said Leo, putting a placating hand on Ben's arm.

'Clean those up,' Texas barked, and the girl selling the elaborate dolls that New York men liked to buy in clubs for their grown-up dolls rushed over to help.

'Here come the real dancers,' Leo said. 'Let's sit for a bit.'

It was the safest thing to do when faced with a line of barely dressed girls carrying baskets of cherries and singing some kind of crazy homage to fruit. The chorus got the waiters and the the club patrons involved, crying out 'Cherries! Cherries!' and Leo had to bite her lip to stop from laughing aloud at the ridiculous sight of the rich and glamorous – and liquored-up – Manhattanites calling out like the Italian fruit sellers along Bleecker.

Then the girls began to wind through the room, popping cherries into the men's mouths, ruffling their hair and letting one or two kiss their fingers and Leo couldn't help rolling her eyes at the sight of grown men turned into panting schoolboys at the touch of a cherry on their lips. Ben was watching the girls and so, somewhat bored, she cast her gaze around the room and felt herself jump back in her seat when she saw a man at the bar whose blue eyes she'd once compared to a sun-shot sky.

Ben chose that exact moment to stand up, clanging two glasses together to demand silence. The girls stopped popping cherries, and the noise dimmed to a murmur.

'Thank you all for dragging yourselves down to Tex's tonight, although I know most of you just about live here,' Ben said.

There was a cheer of assent, and champagne made its way down most throats. Except one. Leo watched as Everett took a sip of a drink she knew was an old-fashioned.

'We're here to celebrate my new interest in cosmetics, which will take New York by hurricane if my sister Faye has anything to do with it.' A round of laughter followed. Ben continued with his speech — a speech Leo could see was perfectly tailored for this audience, because most people in the room were nodding as he spoke, laughing at the jokes sprinkled throughout, listening attentively. He really was a man to admire . . . but so was Everett. Leo pushed the thought away.

'I want to end by doing something I've been wanting to do ever since I first saw this woman on a moonlit night on a ship sailing across the Atlantic,' Ben said.

Leo smiled up at Ben and her feet danced under the table. He was going to acknowledge everything she'd done for Richier Cosmetics. To say that, while the line might carry his name and Faye's, it was Leo's in every other way. She prepared to stand up.

But Ben put his hand into his pocket and pulled out a small, square box on which the word *Cartier* was embossed.

Through a haze of dancing girls who hadn't waited for their cue and who were now distributing snowballs to the guests, Ben spoke again. But Leo couldn't hear him because everyone had started to fling the snowballs, as was the custom, at the man or woman they wished to, at the very least, neck with in the alleyway, but preferably have escort them home.

As the clamour died down, Leo heard Ben ask her to marry him.

He opened the Cartier box. Inside was the biggest diamond Leo had ever seen, although her experience could only be called limited. And there was more than one. The largest was at the centre of the ring and it alone dazzled the eyes. But the platinum band was set with six more square-cut diamonds on each side of the main jewel.

She lifted her eyes back to the bar. Everett Forsyth nodded at her – not a formal nod of leave-taking, but a nod that seemed to suggest he was giving her his blessing to go ahead and marry Benjamin. But his eyes told a different story; no longer a sun-shot sky, they were darker than a thunderstorm and damp too. Just like Leo's eyes. And she knew it was over. That the threats she'd suspected Mattie might make about Alice had come to pass.

Ben slipped the ring onto her finger and pointed to a scroll of paper in the ring box which proclaimed Leo the owner of thirty percent of Richier Cosmetics.

Leo saw Everett leave the club. Saw Faye snatch one of the dancers' pink ostrich feather fans, slide the straps of her dress down below her shoulders, and lead a line of dancers winding through the room, stopping every now and again to press her body against a man's or steal someone's glass of champagne. The men in the room descended upon Benjamin, thumping his back and congratulating him. Leo sat at the table with a ring on her finger and the most precious piece of paper in all the world in her hand, while the most precious person to her in all the world went home to his wife and child.

She stood and pushed through the crowd to the bar, where she took a seat and ordered an old-fashioned. She finished it in one swallow as Jia and Lottie appeared at her elbow.

'What might some women do for a ring like that?' Jia mused. 'Especially when it comes from a handsome fella we need on our side.' She eyeballed Leo.

Leo passed the scroll of paper to Jia.

'Thirty percent!' Jia exclaimed. 'No more reports for Faye.'

'Really?' Lottie leaned over to take a look, head bent beside Jia's, Leo's two friends and true business partners, women who deserved to see their hard work rewarded with certainty – the certainty that would come if Leo married Ben.

'That's right,' Leo said quietly. 'Thirty percent.'

'What about Everett?' Lottie asked, sitting beside Leo.

'Everett has to look after his daughter,' Leo said. 'He can't get divorced because he could never leave Alice to be raised by Mattie.'

'And Ben's quite a catch,' Jia said.

'But he's not Everett,' Lottie said, taking the words from Leo's mouth.

'He's not,' Leo said. 'But why should I punish him for that?'

She slipped off her seat and made her way back to Ben. She tapped him on the arm with the hand now adorned with his ring.

'Do you like it?' he asked.

'It's enormous.' She paused. 'Let's sit down. We need to talk.'

And so, beneath the noise of the club, as their guests celebrated around them, Leo said, 'I'm sure there's a woman out there who can give you a lot more than I can.'

'And fleece me in the process,' Ben said bitterly. 'Seeing the way you've lived over the last few months, I know you'd never burn through all my cash. I know my heart is safe in your hands.'

Which wasn't saying much.

'I don't intend to fall in love again, ever,' he said.

The wretchedness in that one word – *ever* – made Leo's heart weep for him. 'Ben, you can't say that.'

He held up his hand. 'I don't need pity. I thought you felt the same.'

'I never wanted to give up on love,' Leo whispered.

'But you have now.'

I haven't, she wanted to say. *I've given up on ever being with Everett. But not on loving him regardless.*

Ben studied her face and she wanted to close her eyes so he couldn't see what she was thinking. 'Love and marriage are incompatible,' he said. 'We get along well, Leo. You're beautiful, the embodiment of the kind of wife I need; a man in business is considered more trustworthy with a wife at his side and the press has been eager for me to find one for a while now. But, more than that, you're smart. Your advice about the strike was just what I needed. We'd have a lot to talk about, to help each other with, over the rest of our lives.'

'What about sex?' she blurted.

'I'd be very happy to have it.' He grinned. 'I think the existence of prostitutes is enough evidence to signify that one doesn't need love to enjoy sex.'

A yelp of incredulity escaped Leo. 'I need a cigarette.'

Ben lit one and passed it to her. 'Would marriage to me really be so bad?'

'Of course not!' Leo said, hearing the note of uncertainty in his voice, understanding suddenly how vulnerable he'd made himself – proposing to her in front of all these people. 'It wouldn't be bad at all. You're right, we *do* get along well. Most of the time,' she amended with a quick grin and he gave her a half-smile in return. 'And we do have a lot to talk about. Dinner the other night showed me that. I just wanted to be sure that you really wouldn't prefer to wait for someone who loves you with their whole heart.'

'I wouldn't. In every way, I think you're the perfect wife for me.'

And maybe Benjamin Richier was the perfect husband for her. Someone who wanted to take her on despite the fact that she could offer only an imperfect love. Someone who'd given her new life in the form of a business. 'Then my answer is yes,' she said.

There was silence after that, as if neither of them could quite believe it.

'Two weeks,' Benjamin said. 'We'll be married by the end of the month. Let's get it done.'

'Let's,' said Leo. And this time she leaned over and kissed him. Because if she was going to do this, then she'd damn well try to do it properly. To forget Everett now that he was bound to Mattie forever for the love of a child.

Ben kissed her back hungrily, pulling her up out of the chair, showing her that, while he might not love her, he wanted her very much.

Chapter Nineteen

Despite Lottie's and Jia's protestations, Leo asked to be left alone while she dressed at the Richier mansion for the wedding.

She slipped on her Worth wedding dress, a daringly strapless sheath of ivory silk, ruched over one hip and falling to just above her ankles in the front and spilling into a delicate train at the back. The pièce de résistance was a turquoise sash that wrapped around her head, with a row of crystals positioned at the centre of her forehead. Then the sash drifted down the back of her neck before falling over the front of one shoulder and behind the other, one side dropping to the floor, the other side wrapping back around the front, pinned with crystals at her hip. The contrast of the ivory silk and the turquoise was dramatic, and Leo had found ivory shoes trimmed with flirty turquoise bows to match.

She looked at herself in the mirror and felt like an imposter – a sophisticated and elegant facade painted on top of the girl who used to run through the autumn leaves with her hair streaming behind her.

Her one concession to being herself was the pot of eyeshadow she'd made up and that she knew would fly out the door when they began selling it the following week. Named 'Cat's Meow', it was the perfect shade of dark teal to make green eyes like Leo's look like the pathway to seduction.

Then the door opened unexpectedly to admit Faye, who was wearing a dress with the lowest back Leo had ever seen, and an astonishing fluted ruffle that curled from the back of the dress to the front, standing up like a fan on Faye's right hip. She made dynamite seem tame.

'So you got what you wanted,' Faye slurred, and Leo could see that she was drunk at the very least, and most likely something more.

Leo didn't reply.

Faye tapped a cigarette out of a gold case and lit it, blowing smoke at Leo. 'I invited Everett and Mattie to the wedding. They'll both be there to watch you become Benjamin's wife.'

Leo's shoulders sagged but she said, 'Faye, I have a wedding to get to. I don't have time for this.'

'Sure you do.' Faye smiled. 'You definitely have time for this.'

There was something in Faye's voice that made Leo sink into the armchair nearest the door with a feeling of dread. She tapped her foot impatiently, feigning calm, but the minute Faye began to speak, Leo's foot stilled.

'Guess who Mattie's baby really is,' Faye said.

'Everett already told me he's not the father.'

Faye's grin widened. "Course he did. And the only way he would have told you something like that is if you two were like this.' She crossed the index and middle finger of her right hand together. 'So you just proved what I've always suspected. But there's more to it than that.' She strolled over to the chiffonier and poured herself a whiskey. 'One for you?'

Leo shook her head, even though she felt like downing the bottle.

Faye held her glass up in the air as if to salute Leo. 'Mattie's baby is mine.'

The room was so quiet that Leo could hear the grandfather clock downstairs. It ticked and then chimed, telling her she was supposed to be at the church. She could hear a lonely bird calling for a mate; could hear her own heart pound the black blood of fear around her body.

'Cat got your tongue?' Faye sipped her whiskey. 'Too much to take in on a day that's meant to be joyful? I'll tell you the rest of the story tomorrow. Don't want you to be late for the wedding.' Faye moved over to the door.

Leo's hand shot out and held Faye's wrist. 'Tell me now.'

Faye tossed her cigarette onto the floor and ground the ash into the carpet with her shoe. 'I had something Mattie wanted. I gave it to her.'

'You were pregnant?'

'Same time as you were. We both had babies. But Mattie didn't.'

'What happened to Mattie's baby then? You're being ridiculous, Faye.' Leo stood up.

'Mattie was never pregnant.'

'What?' Leo's voice was so faint she couldn't be sure she'd even spoken. 'She said . . . on the ship . . . I don't understand.'

'Then let's sit down and I'll give it to you straight.' Faye stared at Leo, challenging her.

Leo dropped back into the armchair.

Faye took her time arranging herself and her dress and her ridiculously stiff ruffle into a chair. Then she lit another cigarette. Took another sip of whiskey. 'She said she was pregnant to make sure she got Everett. She needed his money to rescue her mother and the family name. And herself; Mattie's far from selfless,' Faye added with unnecessary sarcasm. 'Nobody else was going to take on a woman laden with debt like she was. And even if she did find another man, it would have taken months; she didn't have the money to survive for months in the circles she'd have to move in to lasso a fella with enough dough that he'd buy her the kind of frocks she was used to, let alone pay back the bank.' Faye laughed. 'She also thought that once she was engaged to Everett, she'd fall pregnant soon enough – she didn't realise he was immune to her charms and would never go to bed with her, no matter what she tried.'

Leo winced at the thought of Mattie trying to seduce Everett.

Faye noticed, grinned, and continued. 'She meant to have a fall after the wedding and pretend to lose it. But then I told her about my predicament. That's when she decided.'

'Decided what?'

'To take my baby as her own. It was perfect. She didn't have to fake a miscarriage; that would've just made Everett suspicious and he'd probably have divorced her. By that time, she knew Everett wasn't going to come near enough to her to find out she was carrying padding rather than a baby. And the timing was close enough. So she took my baby.'

How could this be? The plotting, the conniving, the deliberate effort to deceive Everett, to tie him to Mattie, to ruin his life was breathtaking. It had been bad enough when she'd thought Mattie had trapped Everett into marriage using a child that wasn't his, but to know that there'd never been a child, that Mattie had made the whole thing up, was wickedness beyond anything. Leo could feel her body doubling over, her breath coming in short gasps. This was so much worse than what Everett thought Mattie had done. Whereas before it seemed she'd been honest with him, at least – telling him of her dalliance – now it was clear she had lied and lied and lied again. And Faye had helped her.

Leo wanted to run to Everett and tell him everything, to slap Faye across the face, to scream like she had on the ship. Instead she stared at her hands, listening to the loud, loud sound of her breath.

'Why didn't you just . . .' Leo couldn't finish the sentence.

'Get rid of it?' Faye asked, one eyebrow raised. 'I did that once in London. Damn near killed me. I didn't want to put my life in danger again.'

'Who was the father?'

Faye shrugged.

And Leo believed that Faye might actually be the kind of woman who couldn't keep track of her lovers. 'Why are you telling me this now?' she asked tiredly.

'So you won't marry my brother.'

'You think I'll tell Everett?'

'Of course you will,' Faye said confidently. 'Why wouldn't you? Isn't it your chance to get him back? I still can't believe Mattie suggested I tell you, but Mattie's always been a slippery fish.'

'Mattie suggested you tell me?' Leo repeated. 'Why would Mattie do that?' And suddenly she understood. Telling Everett wouldn't change anything. He loved Alice. He thought of Alice as his. He'd never be able to get Faye to admit to what she'd done in a court of law. Mattie would lay claim to Alice if he divorced her because Mattie would say, as she had on the ship, that Alice was hers but not Everett's. And Mattie would tell Alice, the minute she was old enough to understand, that the man who loved her, the man Alice adored, wasn't her father. Everett already knew Mattie to be conniving, but if he knew just how wicked she was, he'd never, ever leave Alice to be raised by Mattie. And Mattie knew that. And she'd wanted Leo to know it too.

There was a knock at the door and before Leo could shout, 'Go away!' Faye had let the butler in.

'Madam,' he said to Leo. 'Your car has been waiting for half an hour.'

'I'm coming,' Leo said, standing up and forcing herself to breathe deeply so she wouldn't pass out.

'You can take me to the church too,' Faye said gaily. 'I can't wait to watch.'

'You can take another car,' Leo said.

'But Hampton won't let me do that.' Faye pouted at the butler.

'Hampton, as of today, I'm the mistress of the house,' Leo said, drawing herself up to the top of her not inconsiderable height.

She disappeared down the stairs and into the car before Faye had quite recovered.

It seemed only minutes later that the car stopped at the church. Leo knew Ben would be inside, wondering why she was so late. He'd be smiling at everyone, making them feel comfortable, easing their concern at her tardiness, but his jaw would be rigid with tension. And Mattie would be there, smiling, knowing there was nothing Leo could do.

So she'd step out of the car, put one foot in front of the other, make her mouth smile with gladness, not look at anybody in the pews, and focus only on Ben as she walked down the long, long aisle. Because Ben was steadfast. When they'd met on the ship, he'd promised her a cosmetics business. And he'd given her one, as well as his friendship. And he'd given her his name, despite all of her doubts. It was a lot for him to give and now she would give him the joy of this day. Their wedding day.

But as she approached the altar, she saw Mattie smiling at her, victorious. She'd won. She hadn't had to suffer the ignominy of a divorce. But, more than that, Mattie had made sure that Leo understood Mattie's lie on the boat more than a year ago had cost Leo the love of her life.

At the front of the church, with beads of colour from the stained-glass windows falling on her face and on Ben's, Leo took Ben's hand and whispered, 'I'm so sorry.'

His jaw relaxed. 'Are you all right?'

'Yes.' She made her smile wide. 'Let's get married.'

The wedding ceremony was something of a blur, a memory lost forever. Then there was the drive to the Waldorf Astoria, where the reception was to be held; it was only a short distance away and she barely had time to exchange a few words with Ben before they were stepping into the Grand Ballroom. Leo felt her head tip back so she could take in the elegance: the marble columns lining the room, the domed ceiling painted with murals of dance and music, the balconies full of beautifully scented flowers that Ben had had brought to New York especially for her.

Then someone summoned Ben to a telephone and he disappeared. When he returned, his face had changed.

His expression roused Leo from her stupor. 'What is it?' she asked.

'There's been a fire at one of my factories upstate. I have to go there. Hundreds of men are inside, possibly trapped, and it wouldn't look good for the man in charge to stand here drinking champagne when they might be dying. Do you understand?'

'Of course,' Leo said. 'I'll come with you. Perhaps I can help.'

'No. Stay and enjoy yourself. One of us should.'

Before she could demur, he hurried away, leaving her to be looked after by someone called Jeffrey who had been hastily recruited to ensure she had a good time. But she had no interest in the mousseline, the shrimps on lettuce, the foie gras or the turtle soup that Jeffrey kept saying she should try. The room was hot, unbearably so, and her cheeks were burning, her palms clammy, her dress now too tight.

'Excuse me,' she whispered and escaped the ballroom, searching for somewhere quieter.

She walked down a hallway and took a wrong turn into the Oak Room, the men's room, which was all leather and fireplaces and cigars. Leaning against the bar was Everett, and she saw his face in a way he hadn't meant her to, lacerated, pain etched into the new line on his forehead, the midnight in his eyes.

She almost cried out. But he looked up and saw her, and so she crossed the room to stand beside him, wanting to put her hand on his, to offer one small gesture of affection to soothe the ache in her heart and in his.

'Drink?' he asked.

'A large one,' she said.

'Leo!' It was Faye, of course. 'There you are. What are you doing tucked away in here when you should be out dancing? Rett, I command you to take me for a twirl and Leo, this is Mr Wright, who would love to dance.'

Mr Wright was sixtyish, fat and short, and he smelled as if he'd never heard of a bath. Her stomach turned.

She pushed her way past Faye. She didn't know where she was going but she soon found herself traversing the enormous lobby and passing through Peacock Alley, which joined the Waldorf and Astoria buildings. Then she was outside, on Fifth Avenue, staring at a near-empty street. She suddenly realised how cold it was, that she had no shawl, that she was alone on her wedding night chasing after something she'd told herself was in her past, and she sank down onto the step and leaned her head against a pillar. She heard nothing, no footsteps, just a voice saying, 'Leo?'

She looked up into the face of the man she loved. 'What am I doing?' she whispered.

'I don't know.' Everett sat down beside her.

'What a sight we must look. Sitting in the cold when we could be inside the city's grandest hotel. A woman in her wedding dress. And a man . . .' Leo stopped. How to finish that sentence?

She didn't mean to do it; her head took matters into its own hands, tucking itself against Everett's shoulder as if it had come home. And Everett picked up her hand and held it, wrapping his other arm around her, resting his head against hers. They sat like that, unmoving, because to move would mean stepping away from this perfect moment, a moment that could never happen again, a moment to be treasured and held on to for as long as they could make it last.

The soft touch of a salty tear landed in her hair.

'What have I done?' she whispered.

Everett squeezed her hand. 'You did what you had to do.'

'Like you did.' She wiped her eyes.

'Don't cry. I can't bear to see you cry.'

'Then you can't cry either.'

He held her to him more closely and Leo could hear him swallowing hard, reining in the sadness for her sake, just as she was choking back her sobs for his.

'Alice needs you,' she managed to say.

'I know,' he said simply. 'I'm sorry. I feel as if that's all I ever say to you. I should never have . . .'

'Yes, you should have,' Leo said. 'No matter how much this hurts, at least I've had the best kind of love.'

'You'll always have it. Even if I can't show it.'

She looked up at him again, knowing it would be the last time she'd ever see him like this, vulnerable, and so close to her that she could reach out and stroke his cheek. He smiled at her and for a moment he looked young, as if he really was only twenty-six and he didn't have a deceitful wife, and a child whom he loved, but who had been placed in his house as a yoke, shackling him to Mattie.

The hardest thing that Leo had ever done in her life was to stand up then, without kissing him, without allowing anything more to happen beyond an embrace and the exchange of a few words. But if he could be strong enough to endure life with Mattie for the sake of Alice, then she could be strong too. 'Is it possible,' she asked, once she was standing, 'to live in a loveless marriage?'

'With a child, yes,' he said.

With a child. A tear fell from one of Leo's eyes. A tear for their child, out there somewhere in the night, loved – please God, let her be loved – by another family. Leo's hand flew to her mouth and she turned away. 'Goodbye, Everett,' she said.

'I love you, Leo.' The words were a mere breath but Leo still caught them before they disappeared into the cold, hard October night.

Chapter Twenty

Time passed quickly. Richier Cosmetics opened salons in London and Paris, and by 1922 every department store in America sold the brand. Lottie had fallen in love and married but, against tradition, she had kept working and Leo had made her Richier Cosmetics' creative director. Jia and Jimmy had moved to a larger apartment, still in Chinatown and within walking distance of Jia's mother. Jia was now the operations manager at Richier Cosmetics. A company with three women in senior positions – it was unheard of. Even Elizabeth Arden still surrounded herself with men. And through it all there was the constant and arduous endeavour of avoiding Everett Forsyth, made all the more difficult because they moved in the same circles and were often at the same parties. Leo didn't know how he fared, but she knew that most nights she sank into bed with a headache from keeping her head studiously turned away from him, from the tension of her hand gripped tight to her glass.

Then, two years to the day since they were married, Leo woke to find Ben's arm curving around her shoulders, drawing her head onto his chest, lighting a cigarette for himself and one for her. 'It's your turn to go first today,' he said.

She took her cigarette from him, inhaled and breathed out, still warm and drowsy, cheek resting comfortably on his bare chest. It was her favourite time of day, the hour when dawn bruised the sky purple, when nobody and nothing was awake except them, when he was, for just a few moments, not her boss.

The dawn hour was a time apart from the world, a little space they'd cleaved off and held on to as their very own, a space where he became the man she could talk to, the man she understood and admired, the man who, briefly, understood her. And in that hour, everything about their relationship felt more intimate than the endless dinners and parties they went to each night, he the successful businessman and she his glamorous wife. It still irked her, even after two years and global success, that she was always referred to in the newspapers and in the article that ran in *Time* magazine, as Benjamin Richier's wife and hardly ever as the woman who ran Richier Cosmetics. But here, every morning in bed with Ben, that's who she was.

'I have nothing much to report, really,' she said. 'I was thinking about Australia though. Helena Rubinstein has salons there. Perhaps we should too.'

'Australia,' Ben said after a moment. 'Do they wear lipstick out there?'

Leo laughed. 'Well, if they don't, surely I can convince them.'

'You wouldn't have to go out there, would you?'

'Maybe for a bit. Why, would you miss the photos of Mr Benjamin Richier and His Wife in the *Times*?' she teased.

Ben was quiet for a moment before saying, 'Yes, that's what I'd miss.' He planted a kiss on her forehead and climbed out of bed. 'Don't forget we have dinner with the Schwabs tonight at Riverside. There are a couple of recalcitrant potential clients I hope you can impress for me. I'll order a dress from Saks for you.'

'I'm sure I have something in the wardrobe I can wear,' Leo called after him, but he was already in the bathroom and didn't hear.

⁓

That night there was indeed a lovely new Lanvin dress laid out on the bed for her. It was white, which terrified her; she'd probably drop her dinner on it and leave a dreadful stain. But it was also lovely – a long sheath of silk that fell to her ankles, decorated at the waist with a bunch of roses rolled from mauve silk, two lengths of which draped down to the floor. He'd even bought her – or his secretary had – a short mauve and silver embroidered cape to wear with it, made from a light tulle so delicate it felt as if she was wearing the gauzy webs of spiders.

He smiled when he saw her. 'You look beautiful,' he said and he kissed her gently, another of those tender moments Leo wished she could fall into but which were always snatched away so quickly she never quite dared. No sooner had she closed her eyes to the kiss than he'd drawn back and called to the butler to have the chauffeur bring the car around.

The party didn't pass in quite the way she'd expected. It was smaller, much smaller, than these gatherings ordinarily were; she felt Ben stiffen beside her as they walked in to find there were only four other couples present and that one of those couples was the Forsyths.

Leo tried her hardest to relax her arm, which was wound through Ben's, not to let her body tense even a little, not to let Ben know that the sight of Everett Forsyth still threw her entirely off balance. By some terrible twist of fate, Leo was seated opposite Everett, and after a couple of hours she felt an aching knot in her neck from the effort of keeping her gaze firmly fixed on the man beside her, the man Ben had asked her to charm. Usually when he asked her to do something like that, her spirit contracted a little more, but tonight she was glad he'd asked because it gave her a much-needed distraction.

Just as dessert was being served, and the gentleman beside her was occupied with directing the waiter's attention to the amount of cream on his plate, she moved her head back to centre. She lifted one hand unconsciously to rub the back of her neck and, as she did so, she caught Everett's eye. They both knew better than to hold any such glances and so it lasted only a second, but it was enough to know that he was as discomposed as she to be sitting an arm's length away, to know that if he stretched out his leg, it would find hers.

'Let's go,' Ben whispered to her not long after and she nodded, wanting nothing more than to escape.

He draped her cape around her shoulders, placing a hand proprietorially on the small of her back as he steered her through the goodbyes. He was quiet in the car on the way home and she sat close by his side, holding his hand, wondering if he would say anything about Everett, but thankfully he didn't.

Not until she had undressed and was sliding her nightgown over her head did he say anything.

'The way you still look at him . . .' Ben started to say, and then stopped.

Leo pulled her nightgown down, about to say something jocular – that he didn't really care about it because he'd never wanted her to love him anyway – when she saw, as she emerged from the satin and lace, his face. Oh God! She'd hurt him. She'd done what she never wanted to do, what she'd tried to make certain she'd never do by having him swear, on the night he proposed, that his feelings for her were no more than friendship. But the look on his face was that of a man cut to the quick by the woman he loved.

'Ben,' she said, coming around the bed to him, drawing him into her arms, holding him.

He let her for just a moment, then he pulled away. 'Don't pity me,' he said gruffly. He left the room and didn't come back for the rest of the night.

Leo lay in bed staring at the ceiling for the first hour, then she went to look for him. His study door was shut, but a strip of light showed beneath. She could hear the gramophone playing a symphony – not a rousing, triumphant piece, but one that was subdued and melancholy. She tapped on the door.

'I'm fine,' he called brusquely. 'You should go to bed.'

She knew better than to enter, not when he spoke like that, in the voice he used at work. He didn't want her to see him. He didn't want her to know how he felt.

Leo resolved to speak to Ben the following night. But he raced in the door at eight o'clock, shouting that he'd promised to pick Faye up at the Plaza – where she'd moved after Ben married Leo – at half past eight and that Leo needed to get ready.

So Leo did, reasoning that it might actually be easier to talk to him if they were both a little drunk; if his guard, and hers, were lowered.

In the car on the way to collect Faye he talked about work. When Faye climbed in, already many sheets to the wind, the conversation deteriorated to a ribald commentary from Faye about some acquaintances. They soon pulled up at the 300 Club and Faye was immediately the life of the party. The liquor flowed, the jazz played, people danced and Leo drank too much champagne. So did Ben; in fact, he was the one who kept refilling her glass, insisting she drink, until he was far tipsier than she'd ever seen him, drinking steadily and quickly, like a man who'd set himself a task.

Then George Gershwin started playing the piano and Rudolph Valentino was saying goodnight to Texas when the front doors opened and the cops came in.

'Hello, suckers,' Texas greeted them, in her usual way. 'What can I say? They brought the liquor with them. I'm just one woman; I can't strongarm every man who walks into the club with a bottle of whiskey under his arm.'

'Let's go,' Leo whispered to Ben.

Ben grabbed Faye's arm but she pouted at him. 'Why leave now?' she said. 'The fun's just starting!'

'We need to go,' Leo said; she wasn't too drunk to know that they didn't want to be caught in a raid. '*Now.*'

'You go. I'll find someone else to take me home.' Faye dazzled the man next to her with a smile.

'Leo, take the back exit,' Ben hissed. 'Catch a cab. I'll bring Faye in the car.' He stood up unsteadily.

'I'll wait for you,' Leo said.

He shook his head. 'I don't want you arrested. Go now, while you can. Let's not waste time arguing about it.'

He stared at her in a way so inscrutable she couldn't read at all what he was thinking. But he was right; she *was* wasting time. If she left now, then he could concentrate on getting Faye out.

'Be careful,' she said, leaning over to kiss him, but he turned his head at the last moment and the kiss landed on his cheek.

Then he moved off after Faye.

The police were rounding up the patrons at the front. Leo joined the people escaping out the back door and hurried off down West Fifty-Fourth towards Fifth Avenue, nausea rising in her stomach. Something had shifted with Ben and she knew she was the cause of it. Which meant that she could fix it.

She decided to walk home, to think. What if they took a holiday together? Left work behind, left everything behind. What if they were just Ben and Leo on a beach somewhere together for the first time ever? Maybe Ben would relax, would stop keeping her at a distance. Maybe she would do the same. What if he really was the man who appeared each morning at dawn, the man on whose bare chest she lay her head, the man who stroked her hair as they smoked their cigarettes, the man who was her husband. She felt something suddenly shift inside her too, the nausea gone, replaced by a different kind of ache. Loneliness. And something more. Yearning perhaps. Because the man who held her at daybreak was one she thought she could love. And after seeing his face last night, she was certain he felt the same. That he was only keeping her at arm's length because he thought she might break his heart.

She was roused from her thoughts by a sudden and terrifying screech, followed by a crash. It seemed to come from far behind her, metal smashing against metal with such violence that the sound had carried a long way. She shivered.

Not much further, she told herself; she was almost at the Richiers'. Once there, she would wait up for Ben, would propose a grand and glorious holiday, would convince him that they should just go, taking nothing with them but each other.

She passed the St Regis, the Cornell Club, the enormous Cornelius Vanderbilt House, the Hotel New Netherland and the Millionaires' Club, announcing the start of Millionaires' Row. Then the Astor house, the Whitneys', the Fricks', the Hebrew temple, the Clarks' – all the Manhattan moguls, mixed with a smattering of religion – and finally, on the opposite corner, she reached the Richier mansion. She raced up the front steps and let herself in, hurrying up the grand staircase and into her room.

She waited by the window, eyes on the street below, watching for Ben, but she was so tired that at last she sank onto the bed, still wearing her dress, and closed her eyes. She fell asleep, dreaming of a car falling from the top of a tall building. The car was on fire, burning like a demon, charred to ashes before it even reached the ground.

'Leo! Wake up!'

She was still dreaming. But the car had gone and Everett was talking to her.

'Leo!'

She could smell his cologne.

She opened her eyes and almost leaped off the bed. Everett was in her room, shaking her awake, and Ben must surely be about to walk in the door.

Leo scrambled up the bed, away from Everett. 'What are you doing here?'

Her eyes realised it was morning, that light was pushing in through the windows; she'd forgotten to draw the drapes. Where was Ben? What was Everett doing here? She remembered too much champagne. The raid. Ben sending her out of harm's way while he tried to persuade Faye to leave. She shook her head, trying to get her brain to make sense of the pieces of the night before.

Everett began to speak, then hesitated. Leo looked at him properly for the first time, daring to run her eyes over his face, and what she saw there made her skin prickle with fear. His eyes were bright with tears. 'Leo, if I could sit down on the bed beside you and hold you while I said this I would, but I know I can't do that. Ben was in a car accident last night.'

The violent screech and crash she'd heard. The plunging car burned to ashes before it fell to the street below. But that was a dream, a phantom collision her drunken mind had conjured into being. 'No,' Leo whispered. 'No.'

'Faye banged on our door last night, screaming,' Everett went on. 'She wanted to see Mattie but her eye was black and she had a cut on her head, blood everywhere. So much blood. She kept saying, *Where's Ben? He'll be all right*, over and over.'

Leo tried to follow his words. He'd said Ben was in an accident but he was talking about Faye. So, Faye had banged herself up, but she probably couldn't feel it given the amount of cocaine she'd sniffed.

'Faye told Mattie that . . . that Ben had been driving.' Everett's voice cracked. 'Along West Street, for some reason. He'd said he wanted to drive all night, into the wind. The roof was down. And Faye hadn't thought there'd be any cars on the road, because who would be driving along West Street at that time of night? So she grabbed the wheel; she wanted to weave from side to side, she said. She was bored with going straight. And she was lucky, in a way. There were no other cars. Just the end of West Street, which she didn't take into account, and they hit Battery Park going too fast. Ben was thrown out of the car.'

Not Ben. No. They were going on a holiday. They were just about to find out who Ben and Leo could really be. Weren't they?

~

He didn't look like Ben. His body was completely still, his mouth was open as though there was something important he wanted to say. His face was blue, the colour of rigor mortis, the sky at the demise of day.

She stood by his side, unwilling to touch him lest she inflict any more bruises on his beaten skin. All she could think was that when Everett had said the words – an accident – she'd never imagined this.

'Mrs Richier?' A doctor stood in the doorway.

Leo looked around the room, searching for the person who would respond to that name. But of course he was talking to her; she was Mrs Richier. She nodded.

'Perhaps you'd like to sit down,' the doctor said.

Leo shook her head.

'Mrs Richier, your husband has suffered an injury to his head, which has rendered him unconscious and caused a commotion of the brain. The brain is so shocked he is unable to wake up.'

'But he will.' Leo said this firmly, the way Faye would, the way that made people do her bidding.

'Technically, it's referred to as being in a state of coma. Depending on how severe the commotion is, he may not wake up.'

Leo turned away. She wouldn't listen to him. Ben was a Richier. Richiers were invincible. 'Of course he'll wake up,' she said.

'Is there someone you can telephone?' the doctor asked. 'Perhaps a lawyer or a friend . . .'

'We do not need a lawyer. What is being done for him?' Leo felt herself turning cold, her voice icing over, her heart slowing the flow of chilled blood through her body so that her extremities began to feel as numb as her senses. She would not allow the doctor to invent such stories about Ben. 'What are you doing for him?' she repeated, making herself hard like Faye, indestructible.

'You can see that we are using artificial respiration. Hopefully that will elevate his blood pressure. Atropine is also being used for the same effect. This morning we will try to relieve the pressure on his brain with trepanning.'

'Trepanning?'

'Are you sure there isn't someone who should be with you?' The doctor looked around desperately, as if hoping that somebody rational would appear from under the bed and shake his hand.

'What is trepanning?' she asked again.

'We make a small hole in the skull to relieve the pressure on the brain.'

With each word, Leo's chest tightened like a corset, squeezing the breath from her. She struggled for a long, long moment. But she knew she had to speak for Ben, who could not. She forced out the words. 'You will not do that to him.'

'If we don't, he will certainly die.' The doctor's response was curt.

'No. He will not.' The effort to speak cost her everything. All that was left before her eyes were tiny snowflakes of colour amid the darkness. 'Leave me for a moment, please,' she whispered, sinking into the chair beside her husband's bed.

The doctor's footsteps faded away. Leo groped for Ben's hand, a hand which had always been strong and elegant but which was now twisted and broken. She pressed it to her lips and, as she did, she caught the faintest scent of Ben, a scent which made consciousness flood over her, along with a strand of memories. Standing with Ben on the deck of a ship and watching as the Statue of Liberty flamed in the sky beyond. Ben's gift to Leo of Richier Cosmetics shares.

'It's my fault,' she whispered. He was drunk last night because he was hiding himself from her, desperate to conceal what he'd let slip the night before. How long had he felt like that? Why hadn't she forced the issue, gone into his study the previous evening and asked him about it?

Because she'd been afraid of what he would say and what she might say in return. Because they'd both been too damn scared of the colossal hurts that lurked in their pasts – and now he was hurt almost beyond repair. But she could have stopped this from happening. If she'd talked to him at the 300 Club, then they would both be on a ship to Paris now, not here in the hospital.

She held his hand against her lips, kissed it, then pressed it to her wet cheek. 'I forbid you to die,' she sobbed. 'You are my husband and I want you here.'

~

Leo was able to keep the news out of the papers for a few days. But then, there it was: RICHIER TYCOON DAMAGES BRAIN IN CAR CRASH. DOCTORS UNSURE IF HE WILL RECOVER.

It was served to her at breakfast, along with her eggs, by the butler.

'Take it away,' she said. 'And the eggs,' she added when the butler took only the newspaper. 'It's not true,' she said. 'Mr Richier will be sitting down to breakfast with us very soon.'

The butler nodded stiffly and withdrew.

Leo stood up and called for the chauffeur. She was too jumpy to drive herself. Today was the day. She'd been told she'd be allowed to see Faye at last. Finally, she could scream at her: *What the hell have you done to Ben? Why did you take the goddamn wheel from him?*

What would Faye say in return? *Whatever has been done to Ben, you've done it yourself, Leo.*

But no matter what Faye shouted at her, it couldn't be any worse than the things Leo had accused herself of over the last few days. Every day had been spent by Ben's bedside. Nothing had changed. She'd allowed the trepanning in the end. It hadn't helped. She should never have let them do it. What if it had made things worse?

Leo dressed for combat in a long flared coat of red kasha satin, trimmed with exaggerated cuffs of antelope and leopard skin. Then she stepped into the car and was driven to Bellevue Hospital, where both Faye and Ben lay.

The ward for the insane was too quiet. Leo's heels clicked loudly on the floor even though she tried to step lightly, to give Faye no warning of her approach. It was so typical of Faye, to pretend to be mad so she could escape the consequences of what she'd done.

A nurse showed Leo into Faye's room. The bed was empty. Where was Faye? And who was that person crouched in a chair, arms wrapped around her legs as if trying to shrink back inside herself?

'Let me know if you need anything, Ma'am,' the nurse said, leaving Leo alone in the room with the curled-up woman who had hair the same colour as Faye's, although it was greasy and lank and had not been marcelled into golden-red waves as Faye's should be.

'Faye?' Leo said, disbelieving. This person was not Faye; they'd shown her to the wrong room, surely.

The woman looked up and stared at Leo with eyes bright and eerie. 'Leo,' she whispered. 'Lovely Leo.'

'Faye?' Leo said again. For it was Faye – or what was left of Faye.

'Leo, Leo, lovely Leo. Leo, Leo, lucky Leo,' Faye repeated in a voice that made the words into a song, a childish nursery rhyme that one might sing over and over so that the words had no meaning, like the song Leo had heard in Sutton Veny: *open the door and in flew Enza.*

Where was the person she could shout at, scream at, the person she could blame for everything that had happened? Faye was not really here and that left Leo with only herself to hold to account.

'I shouldn't have come,' Leo whispered as she backed away, into the door and then out the door and down the corridor, Faye's song echoing in her ears: *Leo, Leo, lovely Leo. Leo, Leo, lucky Leo.*

This time last week Ben was still whole and Faye was just a woman with too much money and too many drugs, and Leo was a girl in love with a man she couldn't have, married to a man she could have, a man she should have been able to love, a man who'd given her more than a cosmetics shop; he'd given her the start of an empire.

What were they all now if they weren't those things any more? What was Faye, deranged by the knowledge that she'd destroyed her brother? What was Ben? Trapped somewhere nobody could reach him? What was Leo without either of them? She stopped outside the hospital and put one palm to the wall, one hand on her mouth to stop the useless sobs. Because she knew that, if she could, she might do what Faye had done and curl herself up so tight that she could no longer think: *Ben was drunk and wanting to drive all night because of you, Leo. Because he didn't want to go home and have you see in his face that he'd fallen in love with you.*

∽

Ben lived, if you could call it living, for two years after the accident. Two years of daily hospital visits, daily attempts to harangue the doctors into curing him, daily infection scares, and a daily trickle of tears that ran from Leo's eyes and into Ben's as she kissed his forehead.

But one day in late 1924, whatever part of his brain that had continued to function suddenly no longer did. He slipped quietly out of life, too quietly for such a man, and Leo walked out of the hospital with her fists clenched, the tears running unchecked down her cheeks. She strode down to the port, arms wrapped around herself, heart turned inside out, and she made a decision.

Everett came to Ben's funeral, as Leo suspected he would. She caught him as he came up the steps to the church and drew him aside. 'You have to leave,' she said. 'Whatever we had is over. Finished. Because it's hopeless. We're hurting people, killing people – and for what? For the sake of one night long ago.'

'That's not all it is, Leo. It's more than one night long ago,' he said quietly.

Leo drew in a sharp breath. 'But that's all it can be now. Ben saw me look at you at the dinner party at the Schwabs'. The next night, he got into a car with Faye and he died. I can't see you, be near you, or even think about you. Not ever again.'

She fled back into the church, hand clutching the pews, unable to see through the veil of tears. It was done.

PART
Four

Chapter Twenty-one

AUGUST 1939

'Leo Richier has singlehandedly transformed the cosmetics industry in America. It is largely due to her leadership and vision that it has grown from a forty-million-dollar industry to one worth over four hundred million dollars. Cosmetics have now become an indispensable part of daily life rather than a cheap adornment used only by women of questionable morality. Please welcome Leo Richier as our guest speaker today.'

The applause was subdued, which Leo expected; she was the first woman ever to address the Yale Club of New York City, and she knew most of the men in the room had come for the breakfast and not for her. After all, it was only a couple of years ago that *Fortune* deemed cosmetics and fashion to be non-vital industries, and declared that success in the sale of cosmetics meant nothing. 'Four hundred million dollars worth of nothing!' she'd exclaimed to Lottie when she'd slapped the magazine onto the desk.

So, today, she was determined to make the members of the Yale Club applaud with a great deal more enthusiasm by the end of her speech. Because, she reminded herself, the person they'd

just introduced was her. Leo Richier. Cosmetics visionary. Not
the widowed workaholic she saw in the mirror first thing in the
morning and last thing at night.

She'd spent extra time on her appearance that morning,
applying the shield of clothing, make-up and coiffure with even
more rigour than usual. Her lips were painted her favourite
red and her skin was flawless, helped a little by her latest face
powder. Her hair was impeccably styled, a touch shorter than
it had been when she was younger, and sat in big glossy curls
below her shoulders. She was sick of tea dresses and utilitarian
skirts and jackets, so she'd opted for a red peplum top that
flared out over her hips. It was cinched around her waist with a
matching belt and a daring triangle had been cut out from her
clavicle notch to finish at a point demurely above her breasts.
The narrow skirt fell to just below her knees.

She stepped onto the stage and waited. She didn't want to
ask for quiet. And she knew she'd chosen her outfit, her hair
and her make-up well because the silence was instantaneous.

'Imagine,' she said, holding up a lipstick. 'This small thing,
this trifle that your wives probably spend far too much money
on' – here there were chuckles of recognition from the men
'– imagine if this was to completely disappear.' Leo closed her
hand around the lipstick, hiding it from view. 'Imagine a four-
hundred-million-dollar hole in our economy. We all remember
the scrimping and saving of the Great War. The scrimping and
saving of the last decade of economic depression. The businesses
that collapsed because there just wasn't enough money to go
around. Well, next time your wife goes to the powder room
to touch up her lipstick, be very thankful that she is. Without
lipstick, many businesses in this room wouldn't exist. Who here
manufactures metal? Who owns a chain of department stores?
Who's involved in the petroleum business? You all need lipstick.'

Leo paused for a moment to watch the heads nodding in agreement. She held up a page from a magazine, a competitor's advertisement that she especially loathed. 'You're probably used to seeing things like this. Advertisements that tell your wife she should wear lipstick to look beautiful for her husband. But your wife knows better.' Leo paused again for the chuckle. 'She's wearing it for herself. Because she knows it makes her look good. And you should thank her. We don't want a four-hundred-million-dollar hole appearing in our economy now that we're on the brink of another war. So when your wife goes to the powder room to touch up her lipstick, don't sigh and complain about how long she takes in there. She's doing something far more important than colouring her lips; she's doing her patriotic duty for the whole of America!'

They were applauding now, clapping wildly. Leo smiled, even though she felt a mile away from happy: talking of another war when the last one felt as if it had happened only yesterday, making a speech about lipstick when, in a few months, men might be dying, knowing she had to talk about lipstick otherwise this roomful of men who made decisions about how the country ran wouldn't take her industry seriously, would take over her factories and ration her supplies and grind Richier Cosmetics into the dirt beneath their shoes.

She stayed for a while after her speech, spoke to the men she needed to speak to – the directors of International Paper, who might have to help her out with cardboard lipstick tubes if metal was rationed for the war; senators Wagner and Mead, who'd refused or been unable to promise anything to her over the telephone but who now seemed able to offer her the world. She gritted her teeth against one hand stroking her buttock, two different hands pressed into the small of her back trying to steer her around the room, and dozens of eyes talking to her breasts, as if that was the place from which they expected wisdom to flow.

She pretended to smile when one man said to her, 'We can't have a national shortage of glamour! That really would lower the morale of our men if they get called up to fight.' She refused several invitations to drinks, because the part of her that had once become entangled with men no longer existed, but when one was offered with the wink of an eye as if she needed prompting to understand he was really asking for sex, she couldn't help saying, 'Something a woman in business learns very quickly is that she's never thirsty.' She said it with a smile to soften the blow and hoped she was right, that he wouldn't understand, and he didn't because he grinned enthusiastically and said, 'Another time then!'

She left after that and drove back to the Richier mansion, which she still thought of by that name, checking the time, knowing the butler could let in the nurse, but Leo preferred to do it herself, to inform the nurse how Faye's night had been. The nurse stood on the doorstep, hand raised, ready to knock. But it wasn't the usual one. This nurse had light brown hair and looked awfully familiar, even though her face was more lined than the last time Leo had seen it.

'Joan?' she gasped.

'Leo!' Joan's hand flew to her heart.

Leo reached out to stop Joan tumbling down the steps and led her inside.

'Anne woke up with food poisoning, so they called me to fill in for a few days, but it was all such a rush that they didn't give me any names, just an address.' Joan's words streamed out.

Leo opened the drawing room door. 'I can't believe it's you.'

'And I can't believe it's you! You haven't changed a bit. You could still pass for twenty years old.'

Leo hugged her old friend. *You haven't changed a bit.* The facade was holding, it seemed, covering over everything inside her that had changed irrevocably. 'I don't think that's true, but thank you.'

In the drawing room, Joan tipped back her head to take in the ceiling, which was a magnificent trompe l'oeil of blue sky, adorned with puffs of white cloud. The two chandeliers hanging from the centre were Art Deco, without the traditional excess of crystal; instead, arches of glass with etched and scalloped edges curved upwards to a central spoke holding glass cups of light. Joan spun around and surveyed the honey wood on the walls, divided into geometric squares by silver trims, and hung with Man Ray's photographs of women with masks.

Joan whistled. 'This room looks better than the last time I saw it.'

'The party,' Leo remembered. 'That's right. I'd forgotten you've been here before . . .' Her voice trailed away. *Before I killed Benjamin. Before you disappeared.* 'Sit down. What about some coffee?'

'I'm supposed to be working for you, not chatting.' Joan hesitated. 'Who's the patient?'

'It's Faye.'

'I remember reading about the accident.'

Leo kept talking so she wouldn't have to discuss *the accident.* 'There's not a lot to do. Just make sure she washes, dresses, eats something. She won't leave her room. She'll just drink. I know I don't really need a nurse but I need someone to look after her when I'm at work, otherwise . . .' Another unfinished sentence. 'Well,' she said. 'A nurse seemed like the best solution. And it's really good to see you.' And it was. Leo almost wanted to reach out and squeeze her old friend's hand, just to be sure she was really there, but who knew how Joan felt, whether she still had any affection for Leo at all.

'I just do agency work now, filling in when people are sick. I have two children,' Joan said shyly, 'so I don't like to work nights at the hospitals.'

'Two children!' Leo exclaimed. 'That's wonderful. So wonderful.' Her smile belied the ache that Joan's news had caused, the awareness that she herself would never have children. That she'd given away the only child she would ever have. She stopped speaking, knowing her voice wouldn't be able to last like her smile.

A silence followed, laden with questions: *Where did you go twenty years ago? And why?*

'I have to tell you why I disappeared,' Joan blurted, as if she'd heard the unspoken questions. 'I don't want you to think I'm an awful person.'

'I don't think that.'

'But I want to tell you anyway.'

'I'll get coffee.' Leo went to the door and spoke to the housekeeper. Then she sat beside Joan on the sofa. 'What happened?' she asked gently, wanting to hear but also not wanting to — because what if she discovered that she'd unknowingly done some other awful thing that had caused Joan to leave her?

'It was because of Faye,' Joan said.

The hairs along the back of Leo's neck stood up.

'I wish I could tell you to run from her, run far away,' Joan said emphatically. 'But now she's sick and you're stuck with her. What exactly is the matter with her?'

Leo hesitated. 'I used to think Faye was stronger than anyone,' she said, remembering the woman who'd danced a conga line at the 300 Club, the woman who'd visited her in the boarding house in Chinatown and laughed mockingly at Leo's swollen belly. 'But it seems she's not. Nobody really knows what's wrong with her. Some doctors think she's mad, that I should send her to Rockland State Hospital, the asylum for the insane. But I went out there once to take a look. There were iron bars on the doors and windows and I could hear the screaming from outside. I couldn't send her there. I think that she simply doesn't know how to live in a world without her brother in it, or she feels so guilty that she can't face life any more.' Leo said all this as if she herself didn't feel exactly the same. Except Leo was technically living. She was running a business. She only curled herself up like Faye at night.

The housekeeper brought in the coffee. 'Thank you,' Leo said to her. 'I'll pour it.'

'I still can't believe you have someone to make your coffee,' Joan teased. 'After we started off in Manhattan living in a room smaller than your entry foyer.'

Leo smiled. 'It's almost unbelievable, isn't it? But I only have a butler and a housekeeper. I drive myself where I need to go. I'd move out of the house if I could, but I keep it for . . .'

'For Faye.'

'Yes. But half the time I don't think she even knows where she is.' Leo sipped her coffee.

Joan picked up her cup too and Leo could hear it rattling against the saucer. 'Back when I was at the birthing home,' Joan began, 'Faye was one of my patients. She was pregnant.'

Stop talking, Leo wanted to say. *I can't go back to that place where once upon a terrible time I could feel my child moving within me.* What she felt moving over her now were the footsteps of the past, creeping lightly along her spine, down her arms and legs. 'She told me she'd had a baby,' Leo said, eager to have this part of the story over. 'I know about it already. She couldn't wait to rub my nose in the fact that she'd given her baby to Mattie.'

Joan crashed her cup and saucer onto the table. 'What?' she whispered, staring at Leo as if either she or her words were some kind of phantasm.

'Faye had a blast filling me in on how she'd given her baby to Mattie to cover for Mattie's imaginary pregnancy.'

'No. That can't be right.' Joan shook her head, repeating the word: *No. No.*

'What is it?' Leo asked, taking Joan's hand in her own. 'You look . . .' She stopped. How to describe the way Joan looked. Buffeted, her sails turned inside out, stranded in a now windless lull.

Out it came, a torrent of heart-stopping words. 'Faye's baby was sickly,' Joan said. 'It wasn't breathing when it was born, didn't breathe for some time. I don't know for certain because I was looking after Faye, not the baby, but I thought it would have been damaged through lack of oxygen. Or else . . .'

Like time folding in on itself, Leo heard a voice murmur: *I see the future. Your baby will thrive. The other will suffer.* She stood up abruptly. 'Well, the baby must have been fine in the end. I've seen Mattie and Everett's daughter. She's very much alive and well. And none of it really matters anyway.'

'But it might,' Joan said slowly. 'Did you read the article in the *New York Times* yesterday? The one about Everett Forsyth?'

'I never read anything about Everett.'

'It was a long piece, not just about him and the Forsyths stores, but about his family.' Joan paused. 'It said that Alice Forsyth was born on Valentine's Day in 1920.'

Valentine's Day in 1920. Leo's mind repeated the words, recalled exactly what *she'd* been doing on Valentine's Day in 1920. 'That's when . . .' There was no possible way she could finish that sentence.

'When your baby was born.'

How uncanny, thought Leo. That the child Everett had raised had the same birthday as his real child. She shook her head. 'What does that have to do with why you left?'

'Nothing,' Joan said. 'It's just that I never knew Faye gave her baby to Mattie. Or that she told you she did. Faye's baby *was* also born on February fourteen and the newspaper says that Alice Forsyth's birthday was February fourteen. So Mattie must have taken home a child that day. Perhaps Faye told you the truth. But I can't quite believe that Faye's child was well enough to go anywhere the day it was born. Which would mean Mattie took home a different child.'

A different child. One that thrived.

Leo crossed to the mantelpiece and took a cigarette from a case. She managed to hold the lighter still enough for the flame to catch and inhaled deeply. The silence was shocking, excoriating; it left her feeling skinless. Even breathing hurt, but so did thinking. Denial was the only option. Because to move past denial meant asking a question that was at once so irresistible and so catastrophic that Leo couldn't begin to contemplate it. She stubbed out her just-lit cigarette in an ashtray.

But Joan asked the question. 'If Faye's baby was sick or impaired, could the birthing home have given your baby to Mattie?'

No. Leo's mind pushed back against Joan's words. Faye's baby might have recovered more quickly than Joan realised. It might not have suffered any ill effects from a lack of oxygen. Or else Mattie took home another woman's baby. Not Leo's. It was impossible.

'Joan . . .' Leo struggled to think of something to say that might bring this unendurable conversation to a close. 'How did Faye end up in the same birthing home where you worked?'

'I found out she was pregnant on that first night at the 300 Club. She was sick, remember?'

Leo nodded.

'She had a bad pregnancy. She was sick a lot. There was that other night at the Club too, when she had to leave. Well, the next day she came to the boarding house and asked for the address of the home where I worked. I think . . . I think she was scared. She'd had a botched abortion in England that nearly killed her and she seemed to want someone familiar around. When she came to the home, she wouldn't let any of the other nurses touch her. Just me.'

'And the day she went into labour?' Leo made herself ask. 'Were you there when someone adopted my baby? Or Faye's?'

'No. Mrs Parker, the lady who ran the home, organised the adoptions. She had the meetings in private. I gave your baby to her when I got to work in the morning. It was the last I saw of it because Faye was in labour and she haemorrhaged, which meant I never really saw what happened to her baby. I only know that it wasn't breathing. Sure, they might have got it breathing in the nursery. But would it be undamaged, or well enough to go home with a family the same day? I don't know.'

'But it might have been.'

Joan shrugged. 'Perhaps. But it also might not have been. Which means it's possible . . .'

Leo cut her off. 'Were any other babies born that day?'

'Not that I saw.'

So it *was* possible. It was possible that Mattie had taken Leo's baby, not Faye's. That Alice Forsyth was Leo and Everett's child. As soon as Leo had the thought, seductive and lovely, she pushed it away. Instead she said, 'But if you didn't know any of this, then why did you vanish?'

Joan sighed. 'Faye didn't want Benjamin to know she was pregnant. She trusted me enough to keep her secret up until the baby was born but, right after, she went a bit crazy. I think she was grieving, and getting mad at me made her feel better. She said that I had to stay away from you because it was the only way to be sure I didn't tell you. She thought if you knew about her baby, you'd run straight to Benjamin with the news. She also said that if I didn't stay away from you, she'd tell Benjamin that *you'd* had a baby. And I knew he'd offered you money, that he was interested in you. I didn't want to ruin everything for you – your chance with Benjamin, your dream of making cosmetics.'

Leo put her arm around her friend's shoulders. 'You should have told me. We could have worked out a way to deal with Faye. Besides, I told Ben about the baby anyway.'

Joan looked crestfallen. 'So it was all for nothing.'

Leo was quiet a moment. 'Do you think Faye knows any of this? Did she lie to me?'

'Why don't you ask her?' Joan said in her matter-of-fact way.

'Because . . .' Leo stood up. Because that would mean she was hoping for the slimmest of all chances to become a real and substantial thing. Which was sure to lead to the bitterest of all disappointments. 'I should take you up to see her.'

Leo led Joan up the stairs to Faye's room, opened the door and peered into the darkness, stomach turning at the smell. It was like the Lower East Side on a hot summer night: a swill of liquor and rot and everything unclean. 'I know I shouldn't let her drink but . . .'

Leo remembered all too well what had happened fifteen years earlier, before she'd hired a nurse to look after Faye, back when she'd refused to let Faye have anything to drink besides water and coffee. Faye had vanished for three days. Leo had called the police, called everyone she knew, gone to all of Faye's regular haunts searching for her until she finally received a call from a lock-up in Hell's Kitchen. What she'd found there was even less of Faye than had left the house; a barely conscious carapace of a woman intent on destroying herself with drink and drugs. So Leo had made a deal with her; she'd allow Faye a quantity of alcohol that would knock anyone else senseless, but that was all. It didn't matter how much Faye screamed and wailed through the night; nobody would bring her any more. And Leo didn't know what had happened to Faye while she was gone, but she never disappeared again.

Leo sighed, not wanting to burden Joan with the story. Joan's face remained impassive, as if she was used to such odours, as if she was used to seeing women who'd once been formidable and immaculate lying in a locked-up silence. Just like Benjamin when he lay dying, Leo always thought when she saw Faye. Once, in the early years, Leo had tried shouting, to see if Faye would jump or react, but she hadn't done anything and it was then that Leo had begun to believe Faye wasn't pretending, that everything that made her human had been eaten away by shame.

'I can't ask her about it,' Leo whispered, backing out of the room and retreating down the stairs. Grabbing her purse, she hurried outside, where she swallowed huge gulps of air, but it was thick with humidity and it didn't make her feel any better. She wanted to sit on the step, but if the neighbours saw her, they'd come out and fuss over their poor widowed neighbour, the woman who had all the money in the world, but no one to love. Leo knew what they said about her; she'd seen it in the papers and usually she shrugged her shoulders and turned back to her desk and dreamed up another product to add to the Richier Cosmetics' shelves.

Leo pressed her hand to her lips to stop a sob from escaping. What if Alice Forsyth was someone she was meant to love? She had to find out who Alice's mother was. And then she would have to decide whether or not she should tell Everett everything she'd learned.

Chapter Twenty-two

Alice Forsyth held her leg high, determined not to let it fall even half an inch. Every muscle was shaking from the strain and she thought she might be sick. One by one, almost as though it had been choreographed, each ballerina's leg dropped to the floor until it was just Irina and Alice still standing, legs held aloft. And Irina's leg didn't seem to be shaking at all.

Alice could feel sweat pouring down her back, dripping from her face onto the floor, but she held on, held on, held on, looking out beyond the room, beyond the mirror, beyond the sprung floors, the white walls, the barre and the ballerinas in damp leotards. She looked into nothing, a space beyond pain and muscle fatigue and impossible endurance.

She felt her leg slip a little and she struggled, if not to pull it back up, to maintain its position, but her will was not great enough and her leg collapsed, as did Irina's. But whose had fallen first? Alice wondered. She sighed and sank to the floor. Balanchine would let them know.

'Irina or Alice will be my *première danseuse*. You are excused,' Balanchine said.

Alice's smile was the opposite of nonchalant. She buried her face in her knees to hide it and would have executed a line of *grand jetés* across the floor if she didn't know better than to leave herself so exposed. She was about to stand up when she heard Balanchine's voice again. 'This is Jesse Valero. Our new *premier danseur* for the gala.' With that bombshell, Balanchine left the room.

A new *premier danseur*? Alice could hear the whispers of hatred run through the room. From Pierre especially. Now he had competition, just as Alice did. The new dancer didn't bow or acknowledge their shock. He just stood there, as if daring them to say something, to challenge his right to be swept into the School of American Ballet as *premier danseur* in the final month before the gala. But nobody did. In a ballet company, the fights were never held before an audience. They were hissed in undertones before the dressing room mirrors, so the victim could always see a reflection of what was going on, but never the real thing.

Jesse Valero was handsome, Alice thought as she studied him. None of that pale Russian skin and blonder than blond hair that so many of the male dancers had. Jesse's skin was tanned and she guessed that, with a name like Valero, he had Italy in his blood. His eyes were dark and his body was strong and lean and tall, taller than the other men in the room. His gaze drifted across to meet hers and she turned away, embarrassed to have been caught assessing him.

'I'll show you around.' Irina had moved quickly across to Jesse and bestowed on him a regal smile.

'Okay,' Jesse said, and Irina's smile turned to a smirk when she saw Alice watching.

Alice picked up her towel and wiped herself down, unable to avoid seeing herself in the mirrors all around – her face glowing like a Hallowe'en pumpkin from the strain of the rehearsal, her leotard decorated unbecomingly with the sweat of her hard work, her hair worming out of her bun and sticking out all over her head.

And she'd once believed ballet was glamorous! Now she knew that ballerinas worked almost as hard as the garbage collectors did to earn their keep. This last year, since the Metropolitan Opera had all but thrown out Balanchine and his dancers for being too experimental, her work had consisted mainly of the Broadway shows he'd choreographed. It wasn't the kind of work she wanted to do. The gala at the end of the month was the one thing keeping her going. Then she'd be done, her training completed, and she could pick and choose her ballet company and earn a real wage – but only if she was the one selected to be the *première danseuse*, the one in the spotlight, the one the recruiting ballet companies would notice. She stretched for a few minutes to cool down and then left the rehearsal room.

'Alice, this came for you.'

Natalia, Balanchine's assistant, held out an envelope. 'Take it before Balanchine thinks you're using his ballet company as your personal post office.'

'Thanks.' Alice smiled at her friend.

'It will be you,' Natalia said, pressing Alice's hand. '*Première danseuse*. Not Irina.'

'I really hope so.' Alice had given everything to ballet, her whole childhood; she was at ballet school against the wishes of her mother, who wanted her to marry Robbie Austin and have babies, and to treat ambition like a fresh snowfall – quick to melt away into nothing. She sighed and tore open the envelope.

Dear Miss Forsyth,

Richier Cosmetics would like to invite you to star in our next advertising campaign, to be the woman who represents our products to the world.

I've seen you dance many times and feel that your combination of beauty, grace and talent make you the perfect face of Richier Cosmetics. We would arrange to have photographs taken by Man Ray, which would then be used in magazine advertisements and on billboards.

If you could telephone me, I'd be very happy to answer your questions. I hope to hear from you soon.

Yours sincerely,
Leo Richier

This time, Alice did let her body dance out how she felt. She turned a perfect pirouette, ending in an arabesque which made her say, 'Oh no!' when she realised she'd kicked somebody with her outstretched foot, an obvious danger when pirouetting in the hall.

She twisted her head; she'd kicked Jesse Valero. 'Are you all right?'

'Your leg would need to be a lot stronger for it to have hurt,' he said.

'My legs are strong,' she snapped.

He smiled at her. 'I know that. You're a dancer. I just meant it didn't hurt.'

'Oh. Sorry. I'm just . . .' It burst out. 'I wanted to be the last one standing this morning. To be the best.'

'You nearly were.'

'Nearly isn't good enough.'

'I know.'

And she knew he understood that coming second was not an option for a dancer at their level. 'If Alicia Markova had been in my position, her leg wouldn't have dropped,' Alice said pensively.

'You don't know that,' he said, and his tone was suddenly gentle. 'She's brilliant now, but maybe when she was nineteen or twenty, she had an Irina to compete with too. Sometimes that makes you a better dancer.'

It was Alice's turn to smile at Jesse. 'You think Alicia Markova is brilliant? Everybody else here dismisses her because she's English. As if you can only truly be a prima ballerina if you're from Russia.'

'Well then we're in big trouble.'

Alice laughed. 'We are. Which company have you come from?' she asked.

'I've been dancing in Europe for six months. But there's a war coming. I had to leave while I could. My ballet master introduced me to Balanchine. He said he needed a dancer for his gala so here I am.'

'So simple,' she said, knowing he must be an excellent dancer to have had things happen so easily.

He reached out his hand then, and she thought perhaps he was going to brush away a strand of hair that had fallen across her brow, but at that moment Irina appeared. She'd changed out of her sweaty leotard, had made up her face and brushed out her shining white-blonde hair. She looked sleek and lovely in a way that Alice, who was tall and had wildly curling hair the colour of fire – yellow and gold and streaked with red – never would.

'Shall we go?' Irina asked Jesse.

Jesse nodded. 'We're going for a drink. Do you want to come?'

Irina's glare could have powered the whole of Manhattan. Alice knew better than to intrude. 'I won't. Thank you.'

'I'll see you tomorrow.' Jesse turned his attention to Irina, but Alice saw him glance back over his shoulder as he walked away. She held the letter from Leo Richier tightly to her chest. At least, she thought, I'm the one who might be starring in an advertising campaign. But her mood collapsed, like her leg had earlier, at the thought of telling her mother. Mattie would never let Alice do any such thing.

After a string of morning meetings, Leo arrived at her offices, which now filled the entire building above her original salon on Fifth Avenue. The salon still operated, but more for the sake of nostalgia than profit. Leo was now well and truly a manufacturer, not a retailer, making hundreds of products for thousands of stores across America, Australia and Europe.

She always entered her offices through the salon because the women loved to see her, to admire her lipstick, to shake her hand, to get Leo's own coveted advice on which shade would best show off the colour of their eyes. Today was no exception. But, soon enough, it was time to go up to the fourth floor, where she found Lottie, Richier Cosmetics' creative director, just back from a week in California, eager to see her.

'How did the speech go?' Lottie asked.

Leo beckoned her into her office. 'You'll cringe if I tell you what I said.'

Lottie shook her head emphatically. 'No I won't. Not if it means we never have to use these.' She held out some prototypes of the cardboard lipstick tubes Leo had asked her to work on. 'I like the undyed board best,' Lottie continued. 'We could make everything look very pared back so the lip colour is the hero of the product, not the packaging. But I'd rather stick to metal.'

'So would I,' Leo said. 'Hopefully it won't come to metal rations. But we need to be ready if it does. I'll take a look and let you know. And we should create a few shades of tan for ladies' legs, in case silk stockings are rationed too.'

'We really are preparing for war,' Lottie said soberly.

'I think we have to.' Leo sighed. 'I'll talk to Jia about the tanning cream. Maybe you could play around with packaging ideas. It'll keep us distracted.'

Lottie gave a small smile. 'I suppose you're right. Oh, and Jen's sick so I answered your phone while you were out. You had one strange message.'

Leo tried to look as if she had no idea what Lottie was talking about.

'It was from Alice Forsyth,' Lottie said. 'Isn't she Everett Forsyth's daughter? What's going on?'

'Nothing,' Leo lied.

'Everett Forsyth's daughter is calling you and nothing's going on?'

'Okay, something's going on, but I'm not sure what. Now, how's my gorgeous godchild?' Leo asked in an attempt to divert the conversation. Lottie had married years ago and had one lovely son. Jia had married too, so Leo's life was full of their children's christenings and birthdays, Thanksgiving dinners, school concerts and graduations.

'He's very proud since he discovered this morning that he's taller than me,' Lottie said. 'At fourteen!'

Leo laughed. 'Well, that is something to be proud of.'

Lottie waggled a finger at Leo. 'Don't laugh! He'll be taller than you before you know it. I'm going out to see Jia about these prototypes. Any messages for her?'

'No. Thanks.'

Lottie left the office with a wave and Leo sank into one of the two extremely comfortable wood and leather Weber airline chairs. Her office was an Art Deco showpiece of glossy chevron-patterned hardwood floors, an outlandish zebra print sofa, a chrome cocktail set and the walnut Marconiphone she had because sometimes music was the best way to get through the day. But she didn't look at any of it. Instead, she faced the window, which looked out onto the glorious bustle that was a Fifth Avenue afternoon, where life went on and on as if every day was the same and nothing would change. But something had changed.

For fifteen years, she'd remained true to her vow of not speaking to Everett. Her products had been sold in Forsyths for years but she'd never once spoken to him. Her sales manager did that for her. They were often invited to the same parties, some of which one or the other missed altogether or, if they were both present, Everett would stay near the bar with the men and Leo would talk to the women, which was actually the best research she could ever do for Richier Cosmetics. She'd heard more rumours about Mattie's liaisons and infidelities than she had fingers to count on; she'd heard nothing of the kind about Everett. Just that he remained married to Mattie.

But now Leo had sent a letter to Alice.

She picked up the telephone and called Jia. She talked about tanning creams and then asked, at the end of the conversation, in a truly awkward segue, 'Was my baby really perfect?'

Jia's reaction was too swift for untruth. 'Absolutely perfect. Why?'

'There was nothing at all wrong with her?'

'Leo, you're scaring me. But no. There was nothing wrong with her. Why?'

'Sorry.' Leo put on a smile, hoping it would sound in her voice, would reassure Jia and forestall any questions. 'I'm just being nostalgic.'

Jia's silence meant that she didn't believe Leo for one second, but she wouldn't pry. 'Come for dinner on the weekend,' Jia said. 'Jimmy's got some drawings he wants to show you.'

'I'm looking forward to it,' Leo said and she was. Jimmy's dream was to be the art director of an advertising agency, even though, for a Chinese man still subject to the Chinese Exclusion Act, that was just about impossible. For now, he'd refused all Leo's offers of employment, saying he wanted to start out on his own, and so he worked as a general dogsbody in the advertising department of the Bank of China, which he said was the world's most boring job but it allowed him to meet important people. He loved to show Leo his ideas for all kinds of products, from cars to cola. And she loved to see them.

As soon as she'd finished the call with Jia, she dialled the number Alice had left for her before she lost her nerve. It took some time for the receptionist at the School of American Ballet to track down Alice and, when she said hello she sounded breathless.

'Alice, this is Leo Richier. It sounds as though I've dragged you away from a passionate *pas de deux*.'

Alice's laugh was bold and genuine. 'No, just an incredibly difficult double *fouetté en tournant*, which is like standing one-legged on the edge of the Brooklyn Bridge, smiling as you look down at the rocks below.'

Leo laughed. 'Glad I'm not a dancer. Making lipsticks is decidedly less dangerous.'

'But very glamorous.'

'Sometimes.' Leo paused. 'Did you receive my letter?'

'I did. And I want to say yes. But my parents might not be so . . .' She hesitated.

'Enthusiastic,' Leo supplied.

Alice didn't speak for a moment, then blurted, 'My mother doesn't even want me doing ballet. Thank goodness my father won that fight. But I can't imagine what she'd say about advertisements. So I spoke to Robbie about it – we're dating and Mother wants me to marry him because his father owns Austin Ironworks, so he's wealthy – but he laughed and said I wasn't Claudette Colbert. I know that, but I can't be a dancer forever. I might have another seven years if I'm lucky and don't injure myself, so it'd be good to see what else I can do.' Alice paused, but before Leo could speak, she continued, 'And now I've chattered on like the silly nineteen-year-old girl I probably am and you won't want me to be in your advertisements any more.'

Leo kept her voice level, betraying nothing of how she really felt, which was as flustered as Alice sounded. 'Perhaps you just have a lot to say and no one to say it to. Why don't you come and meet me and we can talk about it? You can ask all your questions and then you can decide if it's what you really want to do.'

'I can come after rehearsals tonight,' Alice said eagerly. 'I can be there by five o'clock.'

'Do you know where the salon is?'

'Of course I do! Every girl in New York knows where Richier's Salon is.'

As Leo put down the phone, her heart was thumping like a jazz band at the Cotton Club. Because beneath every word that she'd said was, of course, the real reason she wanted to see Alice.

The salon door opened at exactly five o'clock. Leo drew in a breath when she found herself face to face with a stunning girl who was all the more remarkable because she was nineteen and still growing into herself and had yet to develop her confidence. Alice Forsyth seemed to hold the shadow of the woman she would become in the contours of her face and it was an impressive foretokening.

Leo had seen Alice dance several times; she'd been a patron of Balanchine's School of American Ballet since it began, before Alice was ever a part of it. One night, two years earlier, she'd seen a dancer *glissade* onto the stage with the *corps de ballet*, a dancer who attracted Leo's notice simply because she had presence, that elusive combination of charm and magnetism. Then she'd checked the program and been stunned when she'd read the dancer's name: *Alice Forsyth*. But Leo had never intended to approach her – until the conversation she had a week ago with Joan.

'Alice.' Leo extended her hand. 'Lovely to meet you. Have a seat. Would you like a drink? It must be time for champagne.'

'Thank you.' Alice sat on the sofa and stared at the walls of the salon, which were decorated with black-and-white photographs, all taken by Man Ray, and all of dancers, as was the Richier tradition – Ziegfeld Follies dancers, as well as Gilda Gray, Zelda Fitzgerald, Josephine Baker and Ginger Rogers. In the pictures, each woman looked to have been caught forever in the moment of her beauty.

'Those are the kind of photographs I'd like to have taken of you,' Leo said. 'Pirouetting or flying through the air, black-and-white and beautiful, so the focus is not on the individual lipstick that made your lips red or pink or peach, but on the fact that you're magnificent from head to toe. The photographs will be a work of art in themselves and the only words on them will be *Richier Cosmetics* placed discreetly in the corner. There'll be no products shown. Just you and the Richier name.'

'That's very daring,' Alice said, eyes shining with excitement.

'I think we're about to be entrenched in another war. Despite what everybody says, I can't help thinking it will be like the last one: long and deadly. It's not a time to be frivolous, but small moments of beauty are often welcome when all else is tragedy,' Leo said quietly.

'Robbie says any war will be over quickly and that nobody need lift more than a finger to defeat Hitler. But he has a habit of bombast.' Alice fiddled with the stem of her glass.

'You mentioned Robbie on the telephone.'

'My mother wants me to marry him.'

'What do you want?'

'You're the first person ever to ask me that.' Alice's voice was pensive. 'I want to be a ballerina. Balanchine is having a gala at the end of August and if I can be the *première danseuse*, I'm sure to be offered a position at a ballet company. I'd earn a wage. I could rent an apartment. Step out of what I know is the very sheltered life I lead in my parents' house on the Upper East Side. But if I marry Robbie, that's all I'll ever have.'

'I remember what it was like to want more. Once upon a time, I thought my whole life would play out in an English village, perhaps married to a farmer. But here I am.'

'Gosh, that's a wonderful story. And if you can go from an English village to here, then maybe I can be a ballerina.'

'I'm sure you can. If you want it enough.' Leo found her hand reaching out to take Alice's. It was an impulse, a simple gesture of compassion, and it made her throat tighten to be talking to Alice of such things, to be holding her hand.

'I do. I really do. Saying it aloud like this makes me even more sure. The fight with my mother to go to Balanchine's

school was so difficult that it's just been easier to go along
with what she wants since then. But maybe not any more.' Alice
gestured to the photographs on the wall. 'May I?'

'Yes. Take a closer look.'

Leo caught her breath as she watched Alice jump up. She
was so young. So innocent, so untouched by the world. If only
she could stop time so that Alice would never know heartbreak
and loss and everything else that time promised.

'I want to do the advertisements,' Alice said determinedly.
'I'll convince my father, then he can help me convince my mother.'

Leo sipped her champagne. 'You're close to your father?'

'Yes. He's the best. My hero, I suppose. You probably think
that's silly.'

'I can think of no better hero for you to have.' Leo willed
her voice to remain steady.

'Do you know him?'

'Richier Cosmetics are sold in Forsyths stores,' Leo said,
which was not really an answer.

Alice finished her champagne. 'When would you take the
photographs?'

'Whenever you have time.'

'We're rehearsing for the gala right now and I need to
rehearse a lot. There's another dancer, you see – Irina – and
she's very good.'

'Better than you?'

'I don't know. Maybe not if I practise enough.'

Leo moved to stand beside Alice. 'We can do it after the
gala. I don't want to get in the way of you going after your
dream.'

'No. I don't want to put it off. I don't want to lose the
courage. I'm going to talk to my parents right now.' Alice picked

up her purse. But she didn't cross to the door. 'A new male dancer started today,' she said in a rush of words. 'He's our new principal. I'd . . . I'd like to dance with him, I think.'

'Is he handsome, this new dancer?' Leo said lightly, noting Alice's blush.

Alice blushed even more furiously. 'Very.'

'More handsome than Robbie?'

Alice laughed. 'I can't believe you asked me that! But yes, he is. Much more handsome. Dark hair, dark eyes. I think he's Italian.'

Leo looked at Alice's strawberry-blonde hair, her blue-green eyes. 'You'd look quite glorious dancing with him. Perhaps we can do a *pas de deux* shot for the advertisements?'

'I could never ask him to do that.'

'You wouldn't have to. I will. Then we can find out if he really is as charming as he looks.'

'Really?'

'Really.'

Alice's face looked as if it couldn't quite hold all of the happiness she felt. 'So that I don't squeal like a little girl in front of you, I'd better go.' Alice leaned over to kiss Leo's cheek. 'I'll let you know what my parents say.'

'Good luck!' Leo called as Alice left the salon and walked jauntily down the street. Then Leo leaned her head against the glass door and whispered, 'What the hell am I doing?'

Alice opened the door of her house, Leo's letter in hand, and knew immediately that her father wasn't home but her mother was. It was something to do with the vibrations in the air; each left behind an echo of themselves, her father a valiant symphony, her mother a set of cymbals waiting to strike.

'You're home.' Mattie Forsyth wiggled down the stairs in that way she had of being too much, her curves on opulent display in a figure-hugging suit of black and leopard skin.

Alice tried to shove Leo's letter into her pocket.

'What do you have there?' Mattie asked in the honeyed tones that covered a sting worse than any bee's. 'Something you don't want me to see?' She held out her hand, smiling all the while.

Alice reluctantly gave the letter to Mattie.

Mattie's eyes lit up as she read and, for a moment, Alice thought that perhaps she'd misjudged her mother. That maybe being the star of an advertising campaign would give Mattie something to brag about to the ladies she lunched with. A smile sparked on Alice's face but Mattie's words lashed it away.

'The only place this letter belongs is in the trash, like its author,' Mattie said.

Ordinarily Alice would have slunk off. But she'd told Leo she wanted to be more courageous. 'Please,' she said, hating the neediness in her voice.

The front door opened behind Alice and she whirled around, seizing her father's arm. 'Please, Daddy, can you read the letter?'

'What's going on?' Everett Forsyth touched his daughter's cheek and looked from her to Mattie.

'Yes, you should read the letter,' Mattie said, smiling as if this was the most fun she'd had in a long time.

Alice watched as her father read, her hands clasped tightly together, willing him to placate her mother, to take Alice's side, as he always did.

But he sighed and folded the letter into ever smaller pieces. 'Your mother's right,' he said, eyes fixed on Mattie rather than Alice. 'You can't do this.'

'Why not?' Alice exploded as Mattie sauntered off.

'Why not?' Alice whispered again, eyes full of tears, staring at her father in disbelief.

Everett pressed a finger to his lips. 'Shhh,' he said. 'Let me go and talk to Leo ... Mrs Richier. I'll find out some more about it. Then we can decide.'

'Thank you,' Alice said. 'I know if you talk to Leo, she'll persuade you.'

But a grim, 'We'll see,' is all her father had to say before he left the house.

⌒

'What the hell are you doing?'

Three hours after her conversation with Alice, Leo started and almost tripped on her way up the steps to her house. Everett was waiting for her at the front door.

'You told me to leave you alone,' he said. 'And I did. But now you've sent a letter to my daughter.'

She'd never seen him look so angry. And she was so stunned to find him there, to be talking to him for the first time in fifteen years, that she couldn't speak.

'Why did you contact Alice?' Everett's voice was steely.

God, he hated her. At least that was how it sounded. 'I ...' she started.

'What?'

How could she say it? How could she say any of it to him when he was so irate, when it was clear he had no feelings left for her at all? But the words left her mouth before she could stop them. 'I have something I need to tell you.'

He waited for more, eyes blazing at her, but she couldn't do it now. She needed to be composed when she told him, not so completely unready that she felt she would mess it up, that he would stalk off down the street, away from her, and never once look back. And she would be left feeling utterly eviscerated.

Leo spoke quickly. 'There's a Horn and Hardart automat at Union Square. Let's meet there at six tomorrow morning when we're both a lot calmer.'

Everett turned and walked down the steps. He had reached the sidewalk before she called out, 'Will you come?'

'I don't know,' he said, then he disappeared.

Chapter Twenty-three

After she went inside, Leo pulled herself together slowly, as if she had to stitch her limbs back into place, button skin over bone. She found a note from Joan to let her know that she'd stayed until Faye fell asleep. Leo couldn't stop the sigh of relief; if Faye was asleep, she wouldn't have to check on her. But the letter also said that Joan had coaxed Faye out of her room, that, in fact, someone had telephoned for Faye. Leo stared at the note in astonishment. Faye no longer spoke — well, not to Leo, anyway. She was always in a drunken stupor by the time Leo arrived home and Leo assumed this was how she spent her days.

She was about to turn out the lights and go to bed when the telephone rang. She could tell by the way Burton, her lawyer, said, 'Some news has reached me,' that whatever he had to say wouldn't be good.

'What is it?' she asked.

'It's the factories.'

'An accident?'

'When you hear this, you'll wish it *was* an accident.'

'Tell me.' Even though she wanted to say, *I can't deal with this right now*, she didn't. She kept her voice level, betraying nothing, with the poise she'd perfected over the last fifteen years: Leo Richier, the cool-as-a-cucumber executive who never let her emotions get the better of her.

'Your factories are coming under scrutiny. Someone could make a lot of money out of them over the next few years. If there's another war.' He spoke as if he was easing her in like a new pair of shoes, trying to soften the inevitable blistering that was coming.

'I've said I'm prepared to allocate two factories to any war efforts, if required,' Leo said. 'Only one would then be producing cosmetics.'

'But you still own the factories. Therefore, you'd take the profit.'

'Which I've said I'd donate back to the war effort. I don't want munitions money.'

'Somebody would like that profit for themselves.' Burton cleared his throat. 'You must remember that the ownership arrangements for the business were never made clear in the will. That all I have is the agreement drawn up giving both you and Faye each a thirty percent share of Richier Cosmetics, with Benjamin keeping the remaining forty percent.'

'But what does any of that matter?' Leo asked. 'If I own seventy percent of the company, then how can anyone take it over?'

There was a long pause. 'Do you own seventy percent of the company? Of Richier Industries? Do you have that anywhere in writing?'

'I don't need to. I've been running the company for the last seventeen years.'

'Because nobody cared. Until now.'

Leo pressed her hand against her forehead, trying to remember the details of what had happened back when Benjamin had lingered on and then disappeared from her life forever.

'I own the house. You told me the inheritance law made certain of that. And I have my shares in Richier Cosmetics, and Faye's by proxy because she isn't capable of making any decisions. And Benjamin's too, surely? So I practically own the entire company.'

'You don't necessarily own all of Benjamin's shares.' Burton spoke kindly, patiently, but the words were still a blow. 'Not in Richier Industries, and quite possibly not in Richier Cosmetics either. It's never been contested. Nor do you have a signed document giving you Faye's proxy. And now that people want factories, they're digging into the ownership arrangements.'

'If I don't own all of Benjamin's shares, then who does?'

'If ownership of the business were to be contested, it's likely you'd be entitled to half of Benjamin's share and Faye would be entitled to the other half.'

'Giving us each an equal fifty percent share of the business,' Leo said slowly.

'Yes.'

Leo's stomach turned and fear came swooping in like an eagle, claws outstretched. She leaned back against the bedhead, thinking through everything Burton had said. She remembered he'd raised questions about the ownership of Richier Industries, including the cosmetics business, when Benjamin was still unconscious in hospital, barely alive. He'd told her that because she and Benjamin had never had children, Leo and Faye were the only ones entitled to a share of Benjamin's estate. But Faye was incapable of getting out of bed, let alone running a business. His advice to Leo was to do what she could to woo the key managers in the business, to promise them vice-presidential positions in the different divisions if they allowed her to keep running the cosmetics side of the business. She'd told them she had Faye's proxy and nobody had questioned this because nobody could speak to Faye. And nobody could speak to Benjamin either.

So Leo had found herself responsible for Richier Industries, but with the help of excellent staff who'd been trained impeccably by Benjamin, and she was able to spend most of her time in the cosmetics division. She had twice-weekly meetings with the heads of the other divisions, but they were capable businessmen so she let them work autonomously and everyone was happy – until now. Leo's thoughts circled around and came back to one person.

'Only Faye could take this to court though,' she said.

'Technically, yes. Or someone working on her behalf.'

Leo swore, more vehemently than she'd ever sworn in her life, but only in her head; she needed Burton on her side. 'Who?'

'The rumour is that it's one of the big steel companies. Austin Ironworks.'

'Austin's,' Leo repeated. She'd been talking about Austin Ironworks with someone only recently. And then, as if the bed beneath her had given way and she'd dropped to the floor, the wind knocked out of her, she knew. Robbie Austin was Alice Forsyth's intended. Intended for her by Mattie. How oddly coincidental that as soon as Leo had made contact with Alice, this takeover attempt would arise. Leo swallowed. 'I'll deal with it.'

'I'd advise you not to delay,' said Burton in his typically understated manner, which Leo ordinarily valued.

As she hung up the telephone, she made herself stand. It wouldn't do her any good to fall to pieces now. In the morning, she'd find something fabulous to wear, apply a perfect face of make-up and go to her meeting with Everett, then she'd talk to Faye about the shares in the afternoon and nobody would know she was more terrified than she'd ever been. Terrified of losing not just her company, but any respect Everett had left for her once she told him about their baby.

'Did you speak to her? What did she say?' Alice pounced on her father the minute he walked in the door, but her joy evaporated when she saw the grim expression on his face and smelled the whiskey on his breath. Whatever had happened in his meeting with Leo, it didn't look good. But how could that be? How could the glamorous and stylish Leo fail to convince anyone of anything?

'Your mother will hear us if we talk out here,' he said brusquely, and he led Alice into his study, where the first thing he did was pour himself a whiskey. Alice frowned. He didn't look like he needed another — and why on earth should the idea of a few photographs upset him so much?

'What is it?' she asked, hearing loud and clear the anxiety in her voice.

Her father smiled at her but the warmth didn't reach his eyes and she could tell it was only to cover up what he was really thinking. 'I love you, Alice,' he said.

'That means you're going to say no.'

'It was hard enough convincing your mother to let you go to ballet school. I don't know if even I'm wily enough to convince her about this,' he joked, but he turned away and she could have sworn his eyes were glittering with tears.

'But if you let me do it, she won't stop me. So it's really up to you.' She knew she was asking him to take her side over her mother's. But she was aware her parents didn't love one another. And she didn't expect them to. Most people her parents' age were married to someone they barely saw or spoke to, someone with whom they shared a name but little else. It was what her mother wanted for her with Robbie. And she didn't think it would cost her father that much to back Alice instead of his wife.

Her father put his hands on the windowsill and looked out at the splendour of Central Park, darkened now by nightfall, small orbs of lamplight scattered like pearls across the park. He shook his head. 'I don't think so. Not this time.'

'Why not? It's all very decent. Man Ray is taking the photographs. And it's Richier Cosmetics. Everybody uses them. You sell them in your stores. It will be good for me as a dancer too. I'll be noticed if I do this.' Alice approached her father and willed him to look at her. But he kept his gaze fixed on the view out the window and she could tell that whatever he was seeing was something private and he didn't intend to tell her anything about it.

'Your mother and Leo knew each other a long time ago. But they don't . . . they don't get along. There is absolutely no way your mother will let you do anything that involves Leo Richier.' He pushed himself away from the window. 'I need another drink.'

'I don't think you do,' she said pointedly.

He looked at her serious face and gave her a half-smile. 'Coffee?'

She nodded and called the maid. Then she sat down in a chair and waited for her father to say something more. The five-minute wait for coffee went on forever, her mind spinning through what she'd do if he said no. Would she defy him? She'd never thought there'd be anything she wanted that her father disapproved of.

Finally the coffee arrived. Her father didn't speak until the maid left the room, then he came to sit in the chair beside her. 'I do love you, Alice,' he said.

Inexplicably, Alice felt her own eyes fill with tears. She could see that she'd hurt him, hurt her father, her champion, her steadfast supporter in all things, and she didn't know how she'd done it. 'I'm sorry,' she whispered.

'There's nothing for you to be sorry for,' her father said, and he smiled at her in that way he had, tender and almost maternal, as if she was the most wonderful thing in the world. And even though she was too old to do so, she sat in his lap and he held her tight while she cried for something she didn't even understand, head tucked against his chest.

He kissed the top of her head. 'I'm seeing Mrs Richier again soon,' he said. 'About . . . business. I'll discuss it with her some more.'

'Thank you!' Alice kissed her father's cheek. Then she said, 'I want a different life to Mother's. She won't understand that, but I hope you can. And I want to do the advertisements.'

'I know you do.'

'And you know I love you too.'

'Thank God,' her father said, and the catch in his voice almost broke Alice's heart.

The next morning, Leo woke up at four o'clock. Two hours to go until her meeting with Everett. Two hours until she had to tell him she'd had his baby nineteen years ago. Two hours until she told him what Joan had said. Two hours until she would find out if he thought the hope she was holding on to was a real one, and whether it mattered at all to him the way it did to Leo.

Even though it was far too early, she got out of bed and began to get ready, because dressing gave her something to concentrate on besides what he might say when he found out. She chose a Lucien Lelong gown in black-and-white silk crepe with a bold chevron print. It had a high neckline, covering her collarbones and the base of her neck, and the skirt was a marvel;

the top of it draped to a point just below her waist, then the fabric fell in a cascade of folds almost to her feet. Red lipstick, of course, to contrast with such a strong print.

She looked in the mirror when she'd finished and took a step back. She looked so completely different from the Leo East who'd first met Everett Forsyth, from the girl with the tangled hair wearing a dress of sturdy navy wool, and her childish combinations beneath. She'd had red lips then, too, but that was the only similarity between Leo East and Leo Richier. She shivered. Did she look so unlike the woman he'd fallen in love with that Everett would think her a stranger now? And what did it matter? There was no prospect of them ever being together. Except . . . Leo shut her eyes. Except if Alice wasn't Faye's daughter or Mattie's. Except if Alice was Leo and Everett's child.

Leo drove to the corner of Broadway and Fourteenth and entered the Horn and Hardart automat, where she approached the cashier to change her dollar bills for nickels. In front of her in the queue was Everett Forsyth, changing his money as if he'd been dining in automats all his life.

'Eat here regularly, do you?' she couldn't help teasing as she came up behind him, anxious not to repeat the anger and hurt of last night's meeting.

He caught the mischief in her eye and he actually smiled. The relief that flowed through Leo was a tangible thing; her breath slowed, her hand loosened its grip on her purse, the tension in her neck released just a bit.

'This is my first, and maybe last, automat dining experience,' he said wryly.

He waited for her to collect her coins and as they walked over to the glass windows protecting the plates of food, he said,

'So, out of the macaroni and cheese, the baked beans and the creamed spinach, which do you recommend?'

'It's all terrible,' Leo said. 'I ate enough of the stuff back when I first came to New York, so I should know. Which is also how I know we won't run into any acquaintances here.'

'Well, is the coffee any good?'

'Awful too. But I'm having one anyway.' Leo slipped her nickel into the slot, turned the handle, lifted up the glass case and removed her coffee. Everett did the same. They found a table beside the rows of indigestible food and sat down.

Leo was surprised at how easily they'd slipped back into conversation. There'd been no awkwardness. Not like the night before. Thank God. If she could just keep the conversation going like this, then perhaps he might forgive her, might also yearn for Alice to somehow be their child.

'How's business?' Everett asked. 'I saw your speech at the Yale Club was a success.'

'You mean the one where I exhorted all the men in the room to let their wives keep spending as much money as they wanted to on lipstick?'

Everett laughed. 'Yes, that's the one. I always knew the woman I met in an inn in the rain would become something spectacular.'

Had he really said that? She looked across at him and felt the desire tear through her and she wished she could lean across and loosen his tie, undo the top button of his shirt, see the intake of his breath and know that he still wanted her as much as she wanted him. But she couldn't.

'I'm sorry.' Leo picked up her purse. 'I shouldn't be here. I'm destroying whatever peace we've been able to find.'

'I haven't found any peace,' Everett said, watching her. 'Have you?'

'You have with your daughter.'

Everett nodded. 'I have. And we're here to talk about my daughter.'

'I might get more coffee.'

'Leo,' Everett said, and the voice he used was the one she missed — not the harsh tone of the night before, but the one that felt like a gentle hand running along her naked spine. 'You haven't drunk that one yet.'

Leo's eyes roamed the automat, taking in the sleepy faces of those who were up early and couldn't afford breakfast anywhere else, the congealed plates of ready-made food, and she knew she couldn't say what she had to say to him here. 'Come with me.'

Everett followed her out the door and they walked block after block along Broadway without speaking until they reached Chinatown. Leo turned on to Canal Street, which hit her in the face with the intermingling smells of the fish shops, the produce stalls and the ever-present incense. Everyone was awake, even though it was early. Accompanying the shouting of the stallholders was the voice of Judy Garland singing 'Somewhere Over the Rainbow', drifting like a promise through the open door of one of the buildings.

'What are we doing?' Everett asked at last.

'It's up here,' Leo said in reply.

She led him down a laneway that threaded between the tenement and Greek revival facades, which were crossed with the black tracks of fire escapes, like broken train lines on a road to nowhere. They reached a set of stairs and Leo started down them. 'It's a bar I used to drink at,' she said by way of explanation.

Everett stopped on the bottom step, taking in the magnificent room, which had silk-covered walls, patterned with gold thread. Paper lanterns hung from the ceiling, wafting gently in the breeze which had followed them in through the door.

The tables and chairs were black lacquer, Oriental porcelain vases sat in clusters along the bar filled with bell-skirted peony blossoms. A few people were still gathered at tables, evidently not yet ready to believe it was morning and time to go home. Leo sat down at a table.

The waiter came over to serve them as if it was perfectly reasonable to appear at a bar at half past six in the morning, which was exactly why Leo had come. She knew from experience that the warmed rice wine was strong enough to singe one's eyebrows, so she watched as Everett picked up his glass and swallowed the drink, wincing as the fire hit him in the back of the throat. She laughed.

'I should have warned you,' she said, tossing hers back and grimacing as she felt the liquor scour her mouth. 'Goddamn, the first glass is always more than one can bear.'

Everett laughed too and reached up to loosen his tie and undo his top button. He ran a hand through his hair so that it fell across his brow and Leo knew she'd done the right thing, that she could say what she had to say in a place like this, when Everett looked like her Everett, not like the man from Forsyths who was married to Mattie.

'Another?' she said. 'It gets easier, I promise.'

'In that case, why not?'

The waiter poured another shot. This time, they clinked glasses and Everett said, 'One, two, three,' and they swallowed the wine at the same time.

'That's better,' said Leo. 'Now I feel like I can tell you.'

'Whatever it is, it can't be good if we need wine that strong to prepare us.'

Leo fidgeted with her glass as she spoke. 'Remember when you told me that Alice wasn't yours? That Mattie had fallen pregnant to somebody else?'

Everett nodded slowly. 'Of all the things I'd thought you'd say, I wasn't expecting that. But yes, I remember.'

'On my wedding day, Faye shared a different version of those events.'

Everett summoned the waiter. 'If whatever you're going to say involves Faye, then I need another.'

'Good idea,' said Leo, knowing she was going to be extremely drunk in about twenty minutes, but that it was probably the best way to be. She finished her third wine quickly. 'Faye told me that Mattie was never pregnant. That she had made the whole thing up to force your hand, that she used pillows and props so you wouldn't know. But *Faye* was pregnant. She gave her baby to Mattie. Faye said Alice is really her child.'

Everett didn't say a word. He was throttling his glass with his fist and Leo could tell he was furious, but she wasn't sure if he was furious at Mattie and Faye, or furious at Leo for not telling him sooner. She ploughed on. 'Did Mattie have Alice in a hospital? Were you there?'

'No,' he said shortly. 'She gave birth to Alice at home. I was at work and apparently it was complicated. She had a midwife to help her, or so I was told.' Every word of Everett's was tipped with steel, a little dart of pure anger.

Leo fumbled over her next words. 'I didn't tell you back then because you loved Alice and it wouldn't do anybody any good to know this. You'd only hate Mattie, but you had to live with her for Alice's sake.'

'Then why are you telling me now?'

How to say what she had to say when he was sitting across the table glaring, most likely because he wanted to strangle her? And if he wanted to strangle her now, then he'd tear her to pieces once she told him the rest of the story. She blinked hard. 'I had a baby at the same time as Faye,' she whispered.

'What?' His eyes were shining with tears and he looked as though someone – Leo – had just ripped out his heart.

'I fell pregnant after we were together. I gave the baby up for adoption.'

His silence was worse than the bitterest accusation.

She tried to explain through a throat tight with tears. 'You were married and I was pregnant with an illegitimate child. If I'd had the baby, I'd have been destitute. I'd be living in a tenement with a dozen other people because nobody would give me a job or rent me a decent room. I'd be taking in laundry which wouldn't earn me enough to feed a child, and it would have been dead within a year. You know that's what would have happened. And you know what Mattie would have done if she discovered you'd had a child with me.'

Finally he spoke. His voice was so low she could barely hear it and she wished the tears in his eyes would fall because then she could wipe them away, could do something to take away the terrible pain she'd caused him. 'Where is the baby now?'

Leo slid across to the chair beside Everett. 'I never knew Alice's birthday was February fourteen,' she said haltingly. 'You see, last week I saw my friend Joan for the first time in nearly twenty years. She delivered my baby. And Faye's. She told me . . .' Leo stopped and drew in a long breath, terrified of saying it aloud because it was both too preposterous and too wonderful to even consider.

'Told you what?'

And Leo repeated Joan's tale. That Faye's and Leo's babies were both born on Valentine's Day 1920 and were adopted out from the same home. That Joan thought Faye's baby was too ill to be adopted out immediately, possibly too ill even to have survived for long. But Mattie had still taken home a baby that very day. 'So I wondered,' Leo finished, 'I wondered if . . . if Faye was wrong. Perhaps Mattie doesn't have Faye's child. Perhaps our child is . . .'

'Alice?'

As soon as Everett said it aloud, Leo realised how ridiculous it sounded. Was it really likely that Everett could have been raising their child for nineteen years?

Everett stood up. 'I have to go.' He strode towards the door.

Leo felt ill. Too much liquor and too little food. Too many lies and too little truth. How despicable he must think her for never telling him he had a child. But she'd hoped that he'd see through the utter illogic of it all and tell her that yes, Alice must be theirs. That he'd divorce Mattie. That the three of them, Alice, Leo and Everett, would live together as a family. What a stupid goddamn joke it all was. Why the hell was she scratching at the scars of the last twenty years until the wounds opened up again?

'Dance with me.'

Leo looked up through her tears and saw Everett's hand outstretched to take hers. He led her over to the dance floor, while the waiters continued polishing the glasses impassively as if they were used to crazy people dancing together at seven in the morning.

Everett drew her into his arms as Glenn Miller's 'Moonlight Serenade' wound around them. She stretched her hand up to the back of his neck and rested the top of her head against his cheek. Neither spoke. They just danced, circling the floor, the length of their bodies touching, her chest pressed to his, his breath sighing past her ear. He shifted a little so her body tucked in even closer and it was the most glorious torment to dance with him like this, to feel that the hunger was in him too.

'Everett,' she whispered, drawing her head back a little so she could see his eyes shining with two emotions: desire and determination.

'I had to do that,' he whispered back. 'I had to feel you again because it's been so long and I had to know that you felt the same . . .' He stopped and stroked her hair. 'In twenty years I've never touched you like this because I'm married. But Mattie's told so many lies that I don't care about doing the right thing any more. We have to find out. Because what if it's true?'

'Then it would be the most marvellous thing in the world.'

'And then there'd be no reason why . . .'

Why we can't be together. Leo touched a finger to his lips. 'Don't say it aloud. Not yet. I don't think I can bear to hear it and then not have it happen.' She moved her finger, tracing his lower lip, and saw his mouth open a little, felt his fist clench at her back. 'You can't kiss me,' she said. 'I don't have the willpower to resist and we need our wits about us.'

Everett closed his eyes. 'You're right,' he said. 'I'm going to find a bucket of cold water to throw over myself.'

'Or perhaps we should talk about Mattie and what she knows. That's sure to douse even the strongest fire.'

Everett winced. He turned and rested his forearms on the bar. 'Every day I wake up wanting to divorce Mattie. But I've known that, if I so much as threatened it, the first thing she'd do is tell Alice that I'm not her father. And even though it doesn't make sense, I've never wanted her to know that. Because what if she decided to find out who her father really was? What if she decided she wanted nothing more to do with a man who wasn't related to her at all? And after losing you, I couldn't bear the thought of losing Alice too. So to find out that she might really be mine . . .'

He blinked once, twice, and could no longer speak.

'Everett,' she said, desperately wanting to hold him again, to soothe away all the myriad torments the years had inflicted upon him, upon them.

He straightened, and when he spoke again, his voice was steadier. 'We need to find this Mrs Parker from the home, or the nurse who looked after Faye's baby. And our baby.'

'I'll talk to Joan.'

'And I'll see if I can find any papers at home about Alice.'

He turned to leave, clearly as eager as she to start the search, to find something that would tell them incontrovertibly that Alice was Leo and Everett's child, but then he stopped. 'I love you,' he whispered, a gentle smile on his lips, and the tiniest spark of a flame in his eyes.

Leo's breath caught. 'I love you too,' she said, and she knew it was the truest sentence she'd ever spoken, that she'd do whatever she had to do to be with him this time.

Chapter Twenty-four

'Alice?'

A voice roused Alice from reliving the previous evening's conversation with her father. She was blocking the entrance to the studio and Jesse was standing behind her. He smiled at her and she couldn't help smiling back.

'Are you all right?' Jesse asked.

Her habit of speaking before thinking got the better of her and she replied, 'I had a disagreement with my father last night and . . .' She stopped. Jesse wouldn't be interested in that.

'What about?' he asked, surprising her. He followed her into the studio.

Alice sat down and put on her shoes for the warm-up. Jesse waited expectantly, as if he really *did* want to know. 'Richier Cosmetics wants to photograph me for some advertisements,' she confessed. 'My mother thinks it's totally unsuitable.'

'What do you think?' he asked as he placed his foot on the barre and stretched his hamstrings.

'I want to do it. Wouldn't you?'

'Yes, but nobody would ask me. I don't know the right people.'

Alice looked up at him. 'I don't know anybody at Richier Cosmetics either,' she snapped. 'Leo Richier has seen me dance and that's why she wants me. I'm going to warm up over there.' Alice pointed to a space far away from Jesse.

Jesse put out a hand to stop her. 'Sorry. I didn't mean it like that.'

'How did you mean it?'

Jesse had the grace to colour slightly. 'You're a lot fiercer than you look.'

'And how exactly do I look?' she retorted.

'Right now, even more beautiful than Alicia Markova.'

Alice blushed right down to her toenails. Thankfully the piano began to play and everyone had to take their positions at the barre. She was stuck with Jesse behind her and she tried to do each exercise perfectly, so he'd see she'd been chosen by Richier Cosmetics, and by Balanchine, for her grace and flexibility, not for any other reason. Her turnout was the thing she had to work on the most and she always liked to give her hips an extra warm-up before class began, but she hadn't had time this morning. And, for some reason, it mattered more than usual that her turnout should be the best in the class. She pushed herself and soon found her hips relaxing and her feet achieving the position she wanted them to.

'For me, it's my shoulders that I have to work on the most,' she heard Jesse say.

'You must need a lighter ballerina for a *pas de deux*,' she said, keeping her eyes to the front of the room.

'I do.'

Irina was light. But so was Alice. Though Irina was shorter by a few inches, which could easily tip the balance in her favour.

The class was told to practise their promenades and Alice found herself paired with Jesse. She moved *en pointe* and his hands fitted into the curve of her waist. She tilted into an arabesque and then dropped, *en penché*, all the way to the floor with one arm; one leg lifted straight up into the air, forming an exact vertical line with the other leg from the ground to the sky. Jesse walked, turning her in a circle, and she felt the thrill of knowing that their technique together was flawless. They were pulling against each other just the right amount so that neither her leg nor her body dropped, so that the line of her leg and arm remained impeccably straight. He had somehow found her centre without even having to shift his hands or his weight, and she could sense the strength of his back holding him upright as she twirled.

'Mademoiselle Forsyth!'

Alice's head shot up and her leg dropped to the floor.

'This is how it should be done,' the ballet master said.

For a moment Alice thought she was being corrected, but then she realised he was holding her up as an example to the rest of the class.

'Again!' The ballet master clapped his hands and the music started and everyone stopped their own promenades to watch Alice and Jesse.

Once again Alice stepped *en pointe* and felt Jesse's hands touch her waist. She smiled at him and he smiled too, as if he was feeling her exhilaration at being chosen. She lifted into an arabesque then dipped her hand to the floor and raised her leg to the sky. Again she felt Jesse judge her centre perfectly, so that she was in alignment and she was able to hold that alignment without the slightest curve or wobble as he promenaded.

The ballet master pointed out the line of her leg, her position in relation to Jesse, the placement of Jesse's hands, the way he stood straight and didn't lean towards her, but she hardly listened, so enchanted was she with the way her body moved beside Jesse's. If this was what it was like to practise one exercise together, she could only imagine what it would be like to dance an entire ballet with him. Or what it would be like to have his arms wrapped around her in the seductive glory of something like the Black Swan *pas de deux*.

Alice felt flushed all over and she knew it wasn't just from the exercise. She lifted her body upright and lowered her leg. In the split second that it took for Alice to place both feet on the ground and stand straight she saw Jesse's face; he looked more flushed than he ought to be too.

But the day went from sublime to terrible very quickly. Balanchine came in for the gala rehearsals and had Irina and Jesse dance together – Irina's reward for being the one to hold up her leg for the longest time the day before, he said. They danced so well together that Alice was sure she hadn't a chance. But it was Jesse making Irina dance so beautifully; Irina didn't have the same line in the promenade as Alice had had, but Jesse adjusted his body to accommodate her and correct her alignment. Irina's leap was too long into the supported *grand jeté* so Jesse had to work harder to control the jump than he should have.

He was a generous dancer, Alice realised, not like some of the other male dancers who would complain and point out their partner's mistake so the blame wouldn't fall on them. But for Jesse, she could tell, the important thing was the dance.

At the end of rehearsal, Irina walked out to the change rooms with Jesse. Alice sat on the floor and waited until she was sure most of the company had gone home. Then she began to dance, to practise all the steps Irina had danced with Jesse, pretending she had a partner there beside her, a ghost man, darker than Robbie and vastly more alive, unafraid to touch her, wanting to be right there with her in the dance. If any step was even slightly less than it should be, she repeated it ten more times, twenty even, until it was faultless. Until she didn't have to think ahead and remember the next step, until her muscle memory took over.

She pirouetted, ready to move across to her ghost partner, to pretend to be raised high in a one-handed presage lift, something Irina hadn't been able to pull off, unable to hold her legs straight in the split. As Alice moved, she realised her ghost partner had become real, that Jesse was standing in the centre of the studio, ready to catch her, ready to lift her into the air. Alice had no idea if she could actually do a split in second while balancing in a one-handed presage lift but she didn't stop to worry about it. She spun towards him and felt his hands shift to take her and then she was flying and, rather than practising the lift first with two hands as he should, Jesse moved one hand away as Alice swung her legs into the splits and hovered like a cloud in a brilliant summer sky. It was magnificent; *they* were magnificent. She smiled at the wonder of it all and so did Jesse.

Alice always felt the story of the ballet when she danced, but this was different. She was no longer Alice. She was fearless; Jesse too. When she pulled away from him to leap a series of *grand jetés* across the floor, he was right there to draw her back beside him; where Alice could see that Irina had made her face look as if she was feeling passion, Alice had no need to falsely arrange her features.

The final position was a boat lift, which they executed superbly, and then she was supposed to glide down Jesse's body so they would end clasped together. Irina had fumbled a little, not quite caught up enough in the dance to relax, given the degree of bodily contact required, but Alice knew there was no other way to end that wouldn't seem like a disappointment. Jesse began to lower her to the ground and he pulled his arms in so that she wouldn't land traditionally, a foot away from him. As her body slid down his, instead of turning away and ending the dance with his arm clasped around her waist, they both moved their heads towards one another. And they kissed the same way they had danced: without inhibition.

Alice opened her mouth instantly to Jesse's. She felt his tongue flick against hers and she moved nearer to him, unable to stop from gasping when she felt the full force of his hard dancer's body melded to hers. Jesse wasn't wearing a shirt – he'd pulled it off after a few minutes of dancing – and she ran her hands down his back, feeling the ridge of each glorious muscle, fingers revelling in the sensation of his skin beneath her hands, his mouth pressed fiercely against hers.

Fortunately, the wooden floors of the School of American Ballet building always sounded the arrival of anyone not wearing ballet shoes. As the approach of footsteps became apparent, they jumped apart. Alice bent down and pretended to tie her shoe ribbons. Jesse turned away and began to towel the sweat off his body so that when Natalia poked her head through the doors, there was nothing to betray what they'd been doing besides their flushed skin and panting breath, which could just as easily be a result of dancing.

'I thought everyone had gone,' Natalia said cheerily.

'Just getting in some extra rehearsal time,' Alice said lightly, as if she hadn't been about to remove her clothes, and Jesse's too. Her cheeks burned. What had come over her? She'd never done anything like that before. Jesse probably thought she was easy; she'd known him for two days and there she was, letting him touch her and kiss her in a way no man ever had.

'I'm going to lock up upstairs. Then I'll lock up here if you're finished.'

'Yes, we're finished,' Alice replied.

'Goodnight,' Natalia called as she walked away.

'How did you know I was still here?' Alice asked Jesse, daring to glance up at him.

He smiled at her and she could tell that he didn't think she was easy; like her, he'd wanted to know what it would be like to do more than promenade together: to dance a *pas de deux*. And now they both knew. Explosive.

'I was waiting for you outside but you didn't come out. I checked the change rooms and no one was there so I figured you'd be in here,' he said.

'Why were you waiting for me?'

'Let's get changed. Then I'll show you.'

Alice's stomach leaped as if he'd lifted her up to the sky.

⁓

Alice showered quickly and changed, grateful that she'd worn her favourite dress that morning. It was a deep shade of wine-red, with a nipped-in waist and flared skirt that fell to her knees, a swirly, fun yet graceful dress that emphasised her narrow waist and the curve of her breasts. She slipped on her white gloves and her hat, marvelling that only moments before it had been acceptable for her to be wearing just a leotard and now she had to cover her hands and her head just to go about in the world.

She stepped outside onto Madison Avenue.

'Cookie! You've been a hard woman to catch.'

The man waiting for her on the steps was not Jesse Valero but Robbie Austin, an awkward dancer whose chief loves were golf, and shooting ducks, deer and anything else ornamental and helpless.

Alice's smile vanished. 'What are you doing here?'

'I haven't seen you for a week, Cookie. Your mother said the best place to find you was here.' Robbie lunged forward to kiss her.

Alice searched the street frantically for Jesse, while trying not to look as if she was searching for anything. 'I've been busy,' she said. 'We're rehearsing for the gala, remember?'

Robbie shook his head uncomprehendingly and Alice knew that he either hadn't heard her mention it to him before or he'd forgotten all about it. 'In fact, I'm late for . . . a thing,' she said. 'Rehearsals ran over time.'

And then she saw Jesse, waiting down the footpath and laughing at what he'd overheard, knowing the real reason why rehearsals had run late.

'I don't think we should date any more.' The words rushed out and even though she wanted them said, she knew she hadn't chosen the time and place at all well. 'I'm sorry,' she said, putting her hand gently on Robbie's arm.

But Robbie just grinned. 'This your way of making me propose? Message received, loud and clear. I thought I might have a few more months of bachelorhood left to enjoy. But it looks like I'd better head to the nearest jeweller.'

'That's not it at all,' Alice said. 'I don't want a ring. How can you even want to marry me when you don't know the first thing about me?'

'My family's known your family for years. How can you say I don't know anything about you? You're upset with me. I should have proposed earlier. You're right. I'm contrite. See?' And he arranged his face to look like a naughty child pleading with its mother for clemency. For all Alice knew, it probably worked with his mother. But it only made her shudder.

'When's my birthday?' she asked. 'What's my favourite ballet? My favourite piece of music? Your birthday is November twenty-two, you don't have a favourite ballet because you've never been to one and your favourite piece of music is Joan Blondell singing "The Girl With the Ironing Board" in *Dames*.'

'Look at you – you know everything there is to know about me!' Robbie cried, shaking his head in admiration. 'This is why we have to get married. You're the best, Cookie.' He moved in to kiss her again but this time Alice was ready.

'I have to go,' she said firmly. She'd been clear. If he chose to wilfully misunderstand her, that was his problem.

'I'll call you,' he shouted after her. 'I'll take you someplace nice for dinner and give you that ring.'

Alice strode down the street, hands shaking with fury at his refusal to listen to her. All her anticipation of what the afternoon with Jesse might hold had gone. She wasn't even going the right way, was just marching away from Robbie.

After a minute, she felt someone come up behind her and take her hand. 'He's gone,' Jesse whispered. 'Friend of yours?'

'Oh God. To think you had to see that.'

'Did you mean it?' Jesse asked. 'What you said to him?'

'Of course I did!' Alice said. 'I've never been in love with Robbie Austin, which I know isn't an impediment to marriage among the set my mother moves in, but it's not what I want.'

'So what do you want?'

'I want to find out where we're going,' she said.

'We'd better hurry then.' Jesse began to run and she ran too, holding his hand and also her hat, and she noticed people looking at them and smiling at the way they were laughing and hurrying hand in hand down the street as if they were lovers. He stopped at the Fourth Avenue subway station at Fifty-Ninth and bought two tickets, and as soon as Alice realised they were taking the Sea Beach Line, she knew where they were going.

'We're going to Coney Island?'

Jesse smiled. 'We are.'

'I've never been,' Alice admitted sheepishly.

'I thought as much.'

'Why Coney Island?'

'Because it's a place where anything can happen.'

Alice and Jesse took their seats on the train. He held her hand, running his thumb along her palm to rest at her wrist. Even that small movement made her stomach clench. She didn't want to move her eyes away from his face but she thought that if she looked at him any longer, she'd be unable to resist moving closer and kissing him in a way that she shouldn't when aboard a very public train.

'I need to stare out the window for a while,' he said. 'You're too beautiful to look at for very long.'

Alice found it hard to believe that a dreamboat like Jesse Valero thought *she* was beautiful. 'Let's talk instead,' she said. 'I know nothing about you other than that you're the best dancer I've ever seen.'

'What do you want to know?' he asked.

'To start with, maybe . . . where do you live?'

'To start with?' Jesse grimaced. 'This'll be a long interrogation, won't it?'

Alice laughed. 'I'm not interrogating you. I just want to know who you are.'

'And knowing where I live will tell you who I am?' Jesse was staring at his hands now and Alice wondered how she'd made him so uncomfortable.

'Of course not.' She was expressing herself badly and she sounded like her mother, who *did* think that where a person lived told you everything you needed to know about them. 'You don't have to tell me where you live if you don't want to.'

'Sorry,' he said. 'I'm being a jerk. But this is the part where you find out I'm nothing like you and you decide you want to take the next train back to the city. I live in Queens.'

Alice could have thrown herself from the train when she heard herself say, 'Well that's not so bad.' She clapped her hand over her mouth. 'I didn't mean that. I just meant I don't know why you'd think that was something you couldn't tell me.'

'Irina told me about you.' He was watching the streets of Brooklyn swing past, rather than Alice.

She sighed. 'She may not necessarily want to present me in the best light.'

'Well, the light was pretty fine. A wealthy heiress. You live in a mansion on the Upper East Side. Your father owns Forsyths.'

'Like you said, where I live and what my father does isn't who I am.' She leaned across, trying to catch his eyes, and when she did, she saw something like fear in them. And she understood that he was trying to protect himself in case all she wanted was to amuse herself for a day with a guy from the wrong side of town.

She tried to be as honest as she could. 'It wouldn't matter to me if you lived in Spanish Harlem. I've never kissed anyone the way I kissed you.'

Jesse lifted her chin gently and she saw that the fear had gone from his eyes. 'I've never felt that way when I've kissed anyone before either.'

Alice smiled wryly. 'That wasn't quite what I said. I said I *hadn't* kissed anyone like that before. But you obviously have.'

Jesse grinned. 'Robbie has a lot to learn. I'm glad you won't be the one teaching him.'

'Me too,' she said as the train stopped at Coney Island. 'Where do we start?'

'The fat lady?'

Alice laughed. 'There isn't really a fat lady!'

'Of course there is. It's Coney Island. Come on.'

Jesse led her through the crowds and stopped in front of a booth advertising grotesque splendours.

A man with a megaphone shouted, 'Hurry, hurry, hurry. We've got the show if you've got the dime. The strangest sights on the island, picked from the four corners of the world. What about the lady without a head? There are thin ones, there are fat ones . . .'

'We have to go and see the headless woman,' Alice said, grinning at Jesse.

She was about to step up to the ticket counter when Jesse caught her arm. 'Your eyes are so green when you smile. They're like . . . they're like the pictures you see in books of tropical seas. They're alive.' He leaned in close to her.

'If you kiss me now, we'll hold up the queue, because I don't think I'll be very good at making it quick,' she whispered.

He brushed back a strand of her hair. 'Okay, no kissing.' Then he added, 'For now,' which only made her imagine the moment when they'd be free to kiss again.

They wandered through the Hall of the Strange and Wondrous, then Jesse raced her in the bumper cars and she lost miserably, having rarely had the chance to drive anywhere.

'But you don't have a car, surely?' she protested as he helped her climb out. 'Ballet dancers can't afford cars.'

'No, but I used to live across from a garage and Vic, who ran the place, let me and the rest of the neighbourhood kids climb in and out of the cars and even drive them around the lot when the owners' backs were turned.'

'Did you ever crash into anything?' Alice asked.

Jesse pretended to be hurt. 'Didn't you see how well I handled that car?'

'I saw you crash into the back of my car more than once!'

'I just wanted to make sure you knew you were alive.'

'Oh, I certainly know that,' Alice said softly.

Jesse's hand reached out to draw her closer but then he caught himself. 'No kissing. That's the rule. How about the worst Italian spaghetti you've ever tasted?' He held open the door of the Italian Kitchen, which was advertising spaghetti for twenty cents a plate.

'How could I say no to that?'

They sat down at a greasy table and Jesse ordered red wine and spaghetti, which came served in a mountain so high she could barely see over the top of it.

'You won't be offended if I don't eat it all?' she asked.

'If you ate it all, you'd be the Fat Lady of Coney Island,' he said with a grin. 'Just don't think this is proper Italian spaghetti.'

'What should proper Italian spaghetti be like?'

'You'd have more garlic. Fresh herbs. Just a swirl of sauce through the pasta.'

Alice sipped her wine. 'You sound like a man who's eaten a lot of spaghetti.'

'With a name like Valero, how could I be anything other than Italian?'

'When did your parents immigrate here?'

'In 1919. Just after the war.' He expertly twisted his spaghetti onto his fork.

'Do you live with them?' Alice asked at the same time as Jesse said, 'I'll cook you spaghetti the way it's meant to be cooked one night.'

Alice forgot her question in her astonishment. 'You cook?'

'You can't?'

Alice's face flushed and she stared at her plate. 'I've never tried.'

'Hey.' Jesse leaned across the table. 'I was teasing.'

'I know. It's just that today I've realised how incompetent I am at living. I can't drive. I can't cook. I've never been to Coney Island. Perhaps I should be the one apologising for growing up a spoilt child on the Upper East Side.'

'You're not spoilt. You only have to do one performance at the Palais Garnier and have the rich Parisian girls come see you after the show to know what spoilt is.'

'I don't know which part of that sentence to pick apart first,' Alice said incredulously. 'You've danced at the Palais Garnier? I'll ask you about those Parisian girls too, but the dancer in me is more interested in everything else.'

Jesse blushed. 'I've danced at the Palais Garnier.'

'You're very good.'

'I know,' he said, and she knew he wasn't boasting. He was simply stating a fact. He was a magnificent dancer. And he deserved to be proud of that.

Alice pushed her plate away. 'I can't eat another thing.'

'You did well for a tiny ballerina.'

'I'm hardly tiny. I'm taller than most women.'

'I've felt your body. You might be tall, but you're tiny.'

Alice raised her eyebrows. 'We need to find something to do to stop you from flirting. Let's try the Big Wheel.'

But when they arrived at the Big Wheel, Alice discovered the ground they were on was even more dangerous than that at the Italian Kitchen. They were locked in a carriage together, heading for the sky. At first Jesse sat well away from her and she looked at him quizzically.

'You'll see,' was all he said.

And she did, soon enough. The carriages began to move up, but also across, swinging crazily from side to side, so that Jesse slid down the seat and almost landed in her lap.

'You knew that would happen!' she said laughing.

He smiled. 'I couldn't let a chance like this pass me by.'

Day vanished into night while they rode the Big Wheel and the coloured lights of the amusement park patterned the sky with thousands of miniature rainbows.

'My parents are dead,' he said, looking out over the sea and into the darkness beyond, and she knew he was continuing their conversation from earlier, that he *had* heard her ask about his parents but he hadn't been ready to answer, not then.

'I don't want to say I'm sorry. That sounds trite. What happened?'

'They had typhoid. So did I. And my brother. I'm the only one who survived.'

Alice's breath rushed out of her. She couldn't imagine what it would be like to have no family. To not have her father especially. 'How old were you?'

'Five.'

'Five,' Alice repeated. She wrapped her arms around Jesse. 'Who did you live with afterwards? And how did you become a dancer with nobody to help you?'

Jesse shrugged. 'It was an Italian neighbourhood. People looked out for one another. I stayed with a family across the hall for a while. Then I went to see Vic at the garage one day and I forgot to go back. He let me stay. He was old, around fifty or so back then, and his wife had been a ballerina. She'd died of typhoid too, at the same time as my folks.'

Jesse paused for a moment, as if the words had become too difficult to say. Then he continued. 'Vic used to take me to the ballet because he'd always gone with his wife and I think it was his way of not just remembering her, but of being with her. He played music from all the great ballets on the gramophone and I used to try to dance to it. He told me I was a natural and sent me to one of his wife's friends for classes. It was either that or fix cars, and I knew once I'd heard the music from *Don Quixote*, I couldn't give that up to work on motor engines.'

Alice wiped her eyes and sniffed.

'Hey, don't cry for me,' Jesse said.

'I think you're the most admirable man I've ever met.'

'I'm just a dancer from Queens who'll leave no great mark on the world.'

'You've left an immeasurable mark on me,' she whispered, and that did it.

His thigh was pressed against hers. All she could see were his dark, dark eyes, and the pulse in his throat beating fast. Alice reached out a finger to touch it. She heard the sharp intake of his breath and he began to kiss her again and this time it was all the more electrifying because she knew how good it would feel. He kept his hands courteously fixed at one point on her back until she reached around and brought one hand to her lips. She kissed the tips of his fingers and then his hand moved down to stroke her breast and her nipple hardened against his touch. She worked her hand under his shirt and touched the muscles of his back.

Jesse's hands dropped to his side. 'Alice,' he said, his forehead touching hers. 'I'm this far from taking off your dress and making love to you here on the Big Wheel, but given that would land me in jail quicker than the ninety-foot drop on the coaster we have to stop.'

His words made the heat in her body burn harder, stronger. But she knew he was right so she reluctantly moved away. And just in time. Their carriage had reached the ground.

'Tell me about Robbie – that should do the trick,' Jesse said with a wry grin as he took her hand and they began to walk back towards the station.

Alice groaned. 'Do I have to?' Then she sighed. 'You're right. The least I can do is be honest. My mother wants us to marry. But I'm not going to. I promise.'

'Don't change too many things in your life because of me. I'm not the kind of man your parents would want for you. I work at the garage with Vic most evenings and on weekends to pay my way. You're the only person I know who owns anything that could be called a company.'

'I had a huge quarrel with my mother two years ago when I told her I wanted to dance with Balanchine. She didn't even know who he was. Nor did she care.' Alice shrugged as if it didn't matter but Jesse squeezed her hand and she knew he understood how she'd felt. 'Anyway, what I'm trying to say is that I don't think my mother is a good judge of what's best for me.'

They boarded the train and, once they'd found a seat, she went on. 'My mother had let me take ballet lessons up until then because she thought it was good for my deportment and that, being tall, I needed to know how to move with grace rather than clumsiness – of course that's all a lady needs in order to marry a wealthy man. She didn't know I was any good at ballet.' Alice rested her head on Jesse's shoulder. 'My father knew; he used to come to all of my performances and he said I could join the company but that I should keep dating Robbie for a bit, to let Mother think she'd won something. So I did, because it didn't seem like such a bad thing. But now I can see that I've rarely fought for anything because I've always known my father would do it for me. Which really does make me a spoilt brat. But not any more.'

'What if your mother says she doesn't want you to see me?' Jesse asked.

Alice slipped her arm through his. 'Then I'll find someplace else to live.'

'I'll ride back with you,' he said as the train neared Manhattan. 'And walk you to your door.'

'It's out of your way.'

'I want to.'

And Alice knew it was those things that made him a gentleman, not where he worked or lived. It gave her the courage to ask something she'd been wanting to ask all day. 'Who do you think Balanchine will choose?'

'Out of you and Irina?'

Alice nodded.

Jesse sighed. 'Don't take this the wrong way, but I don't know who he'll choose. I dance better with you than with Irina, but that might not matter. Balanchine likes to put his dancers in roles that challenge them. I know you want me to say it'll be you, and I hope it will be, but . . .' He shrugged.

One look at his face told her he was just being honest with her, in a way few people ever were. She had to take it on the chin. 'Thank you for a wonderful day,' she said, smiling, as the train pulled into the station.

They reached her street too quickly. Alice knew she couldn't let him go without sharing one more kiss. But she also knew that she couldn't kiss Jesse on the front steps of her home.

'Come here,' she whispered, pulling him into a laneway that was so shadowed by night she could see nothing except his eyes, glittering like tiny stars. She drew him closer to her, her back pressed against the wall of a building, and slipped her arms around him. His lips met hers, mouth opening eagerly.

His fingers drifted down her cheek to the base of her throat, sending a glissade of heat through her body, making her shift her leg so that his groin pressed right against her.

Then his hand moved away from her neck and before she could miss his touch, he found the hem of her skirt and stroked his way up her thigh, finally cupping her buttock in his hand, and she couldn't help but move her leg up and around him. He stroked the skin of her hip ever so lightly, his eyes open and hers too, and Alice could see the yearning on his face, a yearning which matched her own. They both became still; it took all of the strength she had, and perhaps he felt the same, to look into the eyes of the man she'd fallen in love with that very day.

'Not like this,' he whispered and withdrew his hand. 'Not in a laneway at night as if it was something to hide. When I make love to you, I want it to be in a bedroom with the lamps lit so I can see all of you and feel all of you and make sure it's what you want too.'

And she had to kiss him again for saying that — that and the words: *When I make love to you.*

Not if. When.

⌒

'Where were you?' Her mother's eyes were like two spotlights stripping Alice's face to nakedness the moment she stepped through the door. Alice's hand moved to her chin, which felt grazed from Jesse's stubble.

Mattie took hold of Alice's chin and turned it both ways before saying, in a voice that would make an iceberg shiver, 'Who have you been out with?'

Alice blushed from her collarbones to her hairline. But here was her chance to say everything she'd told Jesse she would. Time for her to unsheathe an *épée* and fight her own battle. She swallowed. 'I went to Coney Island with Jesse Valero.'

'Did you?' said Mattie, eyes widening, lips twisting upwards into a smile. 'Let's move into the drawing room. We can discuss it over a drink.'

The drawing room, a room Alice thought of as uniquely Mattie's, a room she and her father avoided as much as possible. To walk directly through it was impossible; one had to weave through antique chairs and spindly tables holding vases of flowers that always seemed to dive onto the floor whenever Alice passed by. The walls were papered in yellow and gold and there were so many lamps that it felt brighter than a stage lit up for a grand finale. Alice knew that if she went in there with her mother, she would lose. Mattie would sit in a chair and smoke a cigarette and let Alice stand awkwardly, terrified of knocking over some ridiculous ornament, and her mother would have all of the power and Alice would have all of the fear.

She put out a hand to stop her mother and let courage fill her the way music did when she danced. 'Let's get it over with here and now. Jesse Valero is a dancer.'

'You look as if you've been doing more than dancing with him.'

Her mother's smug voice did fill Alice with something, but it was anger, not courage — anger of the kind that forced the truth finally from her mouth. For the last nineteen years she'd put up with her mother's stinging waspishness, the bile directed at her father, and she'd had enough. 'I kissed him,' she snapped. 'In fact I did more than kiss him. Would you like to know what I did with him? Things you probably couldn't imagine doing because when was the last time anyone kissed you?'

Alice shut her mouth; there was so much more she could say, but then she would be mean, just like her mother, a person she never wanted to be. But Mattie's expression didn't change from contemptuous amusement; she gave no indication that

Alice's words might have hurt her. Her suit must be made from rhinoceros hide, Alice thought. 'I'm not going to marry Robbie,' Alice said.

'Then I'm afraid I won't be able to provide you with a roof over your head,' Mattie purred sweetly, but Alice knew her mother was more alley cat than leonine queen. She could wait for her father to come home and he would manage Mattie for her, force her to sheathe her claws. But she couldn't expect to, on the one hand, be the woman who might make love to Jesse Valero, and on the other hand, be a child who needed her father to put things right.

'I've spent two years cultivating the Austins for you,' Mattie continued, 'and I won't have you embarrass me with a refusal now.'

'I'm going to pack a bag,' Alice said, expecting her mother would probably laugh at her.

But she didn't. Instead she said, 'You have no idea what it's like to have no money, Alice. To have nothing. To have to do whatever you can to make sure you marry a man with so much money that it will never run out. Robbie Austin is that man. Jesse Valero certainly isn't.'

'I don't care.'

'Because you've always had everything you've ever wanted.'

'So have you,' Alice bit back.

This time Mattie did laugh, a malevolent sound that Alice would rather not have heard, that she didn't understand. 'You won't survive on your own. I'll give you three days to discover that you need money to live somewhere other than this house. So I'll see you on Sunday.'

Alice didn't bother to reply. Instead she went to her room and packed some dancing clothes and a couple of dresses into a bag, along with her toiletries and the few scraps of dignity that her mother hadn't yet taken from her. She knew her mother was watching her as she walked back down the long flight of stairs. But Alice kept her head high and her back straight, using every bit of the poise she'd acquired as a dancer to hide the fact that she wanted to weep, wanted her mother to put out a hand to stop her and say, 'I'm sorry.'

It didn't happen. Mattie's eyes tracked Alice's every step towards the front door. No words passed between them; no words were needed. If Alice had spent all her life wondering whether her mother felt any affection for her, she didn't wonder any more.

As soon as the door closed behind her, Alice knew where she'd go. It was probably ridiculous, but she felt sure she'd be welcomed, at least for a night. And it wasn't far. Just a few blocks downtown. She arrived fifteen minutes later, was admitted by a butler, and heard the lovely, musical voice that perfectly suited its owner say, 'I wasn't expecting anyone.' And as Leo caught sight of Alice, the voice changed in timbre to the tenderness Alice had hoped for from her mother.

'What happened?' Leo said.

At those words, Alice's self-possession fluttered away. She ran straight into Leo's open arms, unable to stop the tears from falling, feeling at last defended, like a single musical note that had finally found the symphony to which it belonged.

Chapter Twenty-five

$\mathcal{F}$inding Alice Forsyth on her doorstep was the last thing Leo had expected the previous night, but when she peeped into Alice's room the next morning, she thought it was by far the nicest way to begin a day: seeing the tranquillity on Alice's face, as perfect as the flat surface of a lake in the moment before the wind blew.

Leo leaned her head against the doorframe, suddenly overcome by a feeling so intense she wasn't even sure how to describe it. Love? No, it wasn't quite love. It was devotion. She would do anything for this child and she didn't even know if Alice was hers. It was almost too wonderful and also too opportune, not least for the fact that it lessened somewhat the wretchedness of giving up her baby to see that she'd become such a beautiful creature.

Leo felt a crack in her chest and she wondered how many more blows a heart could suffer before it gave up. She almost didn't want to look for evidence because, right now, she could just believe, whereas if the evidence proved that Alice was Faye's child, then Leo would lose something irreplaceable.

She closed the door quietly and went downstairs, where Joan's voice sounded from the drawing room. She checked her watch and realised she was much later than usual, having stayed upstairs in case Alice awoke and wanted to talk.

Leo went to say hello but stopped dead when she found Joan and another person playing cards. A person whose hair was done and whose face was made up. A person wearing a stylish black suit.

'Faye?' Leo gasped.

Faye smiled at Leo.

'You're out of bed,' said Leo, stating the obvious, but she was so shocked at the sight of Faye sitting up as if the last seventeen years of silence hadn't happened that she could do nothing else.

'I had a visitor,' Faye said, indicating Joan.

Leo sank into the nearest chair. 'You're feeling better then,' she managed to say, which was the most ridiculous understatement ever uttered.

'I didn't have a reason to get up before,' Faye said.

'But now you do?'

'Yes.'

'What is it?' Leo felt dread reach out and place its hands around her neck as she remembered her conversation with Burton.

Faye didn't answer. She stood and turned her back to Leo. Leo looked across at Joan, who shrugged. 'She was dressed like this when I arrived,' Joan whispered.

'I might go out,' Faye announced.

'Go out?' Leo repeated. 'But you can't. Last time you went out . . .' Leo's voice trailed off and she tried to push away the memory of how Faye had looked when Leo had found her after the only other time she'd gone out, years earlier.

Leo shook her head. 'Who is Alice Forsyth?' She cringed as she said the words. She hadn't meant for them to come out that way, raw and unadorned, her need for an answer so painfully clear.

'I told you who Alice was.' Faye's voice was mocking, just as it had always been.

'She couldn't have been your daughter. Your daughter . . .' *Was too ill to be adopted out. Might even have died.* To say either of those things out loud was cruel beyond measure. 'It doesn't matter,' Leo said.

'If you'd cared about Benj as much as you care about the Forsyths, he'd still be here,' Faye lashed out. Then her voice sweetened, though her words didn't. 'You should be careful, Leo. There are some people who don't like you very much.'

'You and Mattie?' Leo said, trying to suggest that the petty jealousies of Faye and Mattie were but a minor irritation.

'That's all it takes.' Then Faye stalked from the room and out the front door, calling for the car, just as if she hadn't kept herself confined to one room for so long.

'Is she all right?' Leo asked Joan.

'I think so. She was talking about old times. As if we were friends. She didn't even have a drink.'

'That *is* remarkable,' Leo said drily.

'Perhaps seeing me jolted her out of the state she'd got herself into. She certainly doesn't strike me as mad. Just overcome by shame. Or sadness.'

'Or both. But not any more.' Leo stood up. 'I should go after her.'

Joan shook her head. 'She's a grown woman, Leo. Leave her. Enough of the guilt.'

Leo closed her eyes, shutting out the vision of Faye dressed to kill and on the loose. 'I need to speak to Mrs Parker.'

'She'll have shot through. You don't run a place like that for more than a few years before the police come after you. I mean, it's not legal, what she did. Making money like that. It's a shame, because her home was one of the cleanest and best run around. And I doubt that Mrs Parker was even her real name.'

Leo opened her eyes. 'Well, what about the nurse who was working in the nursery that day? The one who looked after Faye's baby?'

Joan thought. 'Sarah Mackay. She was new, I remember. I gave her your baby when I arrived at work, as well as a long list of instructions because I wanted to make sure the baby was looked after. She's also the one who was in the nursery with Faye's baby.'

'Do you know how to get in touch with her?'

'If she's still nursing in Manhattan, then I should be able to find someone who knows her. Can I use your telephone?'

'Of course.'

'I can't promise anything.'

'I know. But thank you. I might leave you to it. If I stay here, I'm bound to pace and smoke and annoy the hell out of you.'

'The minute I find something, I'll let you know.'

❧

Leo went to work in an effort to distract herself. She frittered away the morning moving piles of paper around her desk until she received a call from Joan mid-afternoon. 'You have a meeting with Sarah Mackay tomorrow night.'

'Tomorrow? Really?' Leo jumped up from her chair as she spoke. 'I can't thank you enough times.'

'I don't know how much she'll be able to tell you, so don't thank me yet. Oh, and Faye hasn't returned.'

Leo tapped her fingers on the desk. 'If I don't hear anything from her by tomorrow, I'll call the police.'

'Or you could just let her go.'

'I can't have her die as well.' Leo's throat tightened inexplicably. She hung up the phone, collected her purse, gloves and hat, and left the office, needing to walk, glad of the roaring noise of the city's cars and people and commerce filling her head with sound so she was incapable of thought.

When she pushed open the door of the Richier mansion, she found herself stopping dead in the drawing room for the second time that day. Alice was in there, talking to her father.

'Leo,' he said politely, shaking her hand as if they were mere business acquaintances.

'Everett,' she said, just as formally. 'Lovely to see you again. I'll leave you two to talk.'

'Please stay,' said Alice.

Leo hesitated. 'How are you feeling today?' She couldn't help but look, really look, at Alice now. Couldn't help but devour her, examine every contour of her face for something that reminded her of Everett. Or of herself. Of course, now that she wanted to find it, she could see similarities everywhere. Alice had Everett's smile. Leo's build. Everett's charm. Leo's hair. But Faye had flame-coloured hair too.

'Still furious with Mother,' Alice admitted.

'I wish you'd come home,' Everett said. 'Who cares what Mattie said? We've always found our way around her.'

'I don't want to always be apologising and tiptoeing past her. I want to do the things that make me happy,' Alice said.

'You're welcome to stay here as long as you need,' Leo said to Alice. 'I have plenty of room and I enjoy the company.

Besides, the photo shoot is next week so you might as well be here for that.'

'What will you say to Mother?' Alice asked her father.

'That you're staying with friends and will contact her when you're ready.' Everett kissed his daughter on the forehead and said goodbye.

'I'll walk you out,' Leo said. Once they were out of the drawing room, she said quietly, 'I have a meeting tomorrow with one of the nurses.'

'I'm coming with you.'

'You don't have to.'

'I want to.' Everett leaned back against the doorframe and she smiled at him.

'Thank you,' she said.

'I wouldn't miss it.'

Leo could feel the billowing of her heart against her chest, so full of love and of hope that there might be a better future waiting for both of them, and for Alice, that it almost hurt. Her eyes revelled in the sight of him, back resting against the wood, the top button of his shirt undone, shirtsleeves rolled up, tie loosened, just like when she'd first met him – although his hair was cut a little shorter now. His blue eyes were alight with hunger and an expression as close to joy as she'd seen in them since the one night they'd spent together.

'I should go,' he whispered.

'You should.' She smiled.

He straightened up. 'When Mattie was out to lunch today I looked through her room but there were no papers to do with Alice.'

'Maybe Faye has some record of the birth?' Leo said. 'I put everything of hers in the attic.'

'I'll help you look.'

Leo grinned. 'As much as the thought of being alone in the attic with you is very appealing, it's probably not a good idea.'

Everett laughed. 'You're right.' He leaned forward and kissed her cheek. It was a chaste and decorous kiss but she felt her eyes close, savouring the gentle rub of his stubble against her skin, breathing in the scent of him.

'Alice thinks she's in love with someone,' Everett said, lingering on the doorstep, speaking to Leo like a father might speak to the mother of their child. 'I've never even heard of Jesse. They've known each other for five minutes. She's nineteen. How can she possibly know anything about love?'

'Alice is the same age as I was when I first met you. And I think I'd known you for maybe six minutes before I knew that I loved you.'

Everett smiled. 'It only took me one minute to fall in love with you.'

Leo's throat tightened. 'I have to close this door.'

'I know. Goodbye, Leo.'

She shut the door, turned and gasped. 'Alice!'

Alice was walking out of the drawing room and into the foyer. Even though Leo knew that nothing unseemly had happened between her and Everett, the intimacy of their tones, their expressions, would have given them away to anyone.

Alice looked at Leo, puzzled. 'Were you talking to my father that whole time? I'm sorry – you were probably begging him to take me home.'

'Not at all,' Leo said. 'Did you see Jesse today?'

The change of subject worked. Alice's face lit up. 'I did,' she said. 'And we danced together and we were perfect. Even Balanchine said so. Irina missed the lift. I didn't. The casting for the gala is announced in two days.' Alice bit her lip. 'What will I do if I'm not the lead?'

Leo smiled wistfully. To be young and to want a thing so much was something she remembered all too well. 'Come here,' she said and opened her arms.

Alice walked into the embrace and rested her head on Leo's shoulder. 'No matter what happens, you'll be fine,' Leo said. 'You might be sad, but use that sadness to make your dream bigger, to make you try for more.'

'I will.' Alice kissed Leo's cheek. 'That's good advice.'

Then Alice went up to her room and Leo to the attic, a room she'd hardly been in since Ben died. She had no idea what was up there – artefacts of Richiers past, she assumed. The boxes with Faye's personal effects, which the staff at the Plaza had packed up for Leo when it became clear Faye wouldn't be returning there, were nearest the door, in front of the boxes of Ben's things, which she hadn't been able to throw away. She supposed Faye would want all her things unpacked now, if and when she returned.

Leo sat down on the floor, opened the first dust-covered box, and peered inside. It was like finding her way into a tunnel that moved between now and then. There was the phosphorescent dress Faye had been wearing when they'd first met on the ship and there was the blue dress Faye had lent Leo for the impromptu party, a dress that had only reminded her of the colour of Everett's eyes. Leo pushed the box away. She'd choose another, one that she knew less about and felt less for, and she'd come back to this box of times long dead later.

The rest of the boxes revealed nothing. More dresses than Leo could have imagined. Cosmetics – it was like a museum of Richier Cosmetics' early inventions. Very little that was personal. No letters, keepsakes, mementoes; just shoes and clothes and, at the bottom, a jewellery box stuffed with diamonds and a pair of silver cufflinks engraved with the initials *EF*. A memory beckoned and she followed it back to a conversation she'd had with Everett at the 300 Club, when he'd told her about Faye stealing a pair of his cufflinks. Why had Faye kept them? But, then, why did Faye do anything? Her motivations were always opaque.

Leo sighed and stood up. Her mission had been fruitless. Whether Faye or Leo was Alice's mother, the evidence was not in these boxes. She went down to her room and was about to get changed when there was a knock at her door.

'These came earlier, Ma'am,' the housekeeper said.

'Thank you,' said Leo, holding out her hand for the letters.

The first was a note from Faye to the housekeeper, asking her to transfer all of Faye's things to the Carlyle, where Faye would be staying from now on. Leo felt an awful relief at the thought that Faye and Alice wouldn't meet under this roof, that she wouldn't have to deal with the fallout of that preposterous meeting. She opened the second letter then let it drop to the floor. It was a summons. She was to appear in court; Austin Ironworks was contesting her ownership of all the Richier businesses.

Leo spent the next day locked in a meeting with her lawyer.

'We have to get ready for court,' Burton said.

Leo almost couldn't speak. Fury clogged her throat, and instead of replying, she cast her eyes around her office, over the images on the walls of the famously beautiful Richier Cosmetics advertising campaigns, over the display case that housed every single Richier product sold. Through the closed door of her office, she could hear the bustle as people designed packaging, sent out bills, made sure products got onto trucks and trains and ships. Everything in her office and outside her office, everything that happened in this building, in the salon, in the

Richier Cosmetics sections of department stores, was the hard and joyous work of twenty years. 'I'll be damned if Mr Robert Austin Senior is going to have any of this,' she said.

Burton managed a rare smile. 'Then let's see what we can do to stop him. It won't be easy.'

'I wasn't expecting anything less,' Leo said darkly as she sat down beside him to go through all of Benjamin's documents and the law, ready to find an ambiguity that would mean she didn't have to give away her life. All the while she tried not to think about the meeting she was to have with a nurse that evening who might be able to tell her something about Alice.

Later, she drove to Forsyths department store and waited outside for Everett, wondering how it was that just last night she'd felt so hopeful. Burton hadn't found an ambiguity, or a loophole, or any black-and-white evidence that Leo owned the entire company. And Faye still wasn't showing either her face or her hand to Leo.

Then Everett slid into the car with a smile and Leo drove them to the same automat they'd met at two days earlier, fingers tapping the steering wheel.

'I was served a writ yesterday,' she said abruptly.

'What for?' he asked.

'Austin Ironworks want my factories. They're disputing my ownership.'

'Austin Ironworks is Robbie's father's company.'

'I know. I didn't say anything about it before because Burton said it was just a rumour. But now it's real.'

Leo wondered if he'd come to the same awful conclusion as she had the night she'd spoken to Burton: that Mattie was using Faye, and Robbie's company, to send a clear message to Leo: *Leave my daughter and my husband alone.* She could imagine Mattie cosying up to Robbie or his father at a dinner party, mentioning that things at Richier Industries might not be quite what they seemed with regards to ownership, casually hinting that she and Faye were such close pals, that Faye owed her a favour and might help to deliver them a serve of Richier's on a bloodstained platter. And of course Faye would relish the chance to wrest the company from Leo.

'It seems very close to home,' Everett said slowly. 'But how?'

'Faye's out of bed now. She's been gone since yesterday.'

'They could only have got to Faye through Mattie. Goddamnit,' Everett swore.

'Do you think it's just an empty threat? That if I back away from Alice and the photo shoot, she'll stop?'

'I don't know.'

'And is it just about the photos? Or does she suspect . . .' *That we're trying to prove Alice is ours.* She felt suddenly ill at the thought of what Mattie might do, given her long history of lies, deceit and vindictive acts, if she discovered what Leo and Everett were up to.

'I hope not.' Everett's voice was grim.

'Was it really so bad, what I did to her without knowing?' Leo whispered. 'Making you fall in love with me.'

'Leo.'

She made the mistake of looking at him, of seeing on his face the agony of twenty years of love, concealed but not forgotten.

She drew the car to an abrupt halt at the kerb. 'We're here,' she said, forcing her eyes away from his.

Inside the automat, she could see a woman in a nurse's uniform drinking a milkshake.

'I'll get coffee,' Everett said.

'Thanks.'

Leo sat down opposite the woman. 'Are you Sarah?'

'That's me,' the woman said.

Everett returned with the coffees and Leo plunged in.

'Did Joan tell you we're interested in a baby she brought in to Mrs Parker's home back in February 1920?' she asked.

'She did,' Sarah said. 'It was awful.'

'Why?' Everett asked, and Leo could hear the alarm in his voice.

'It was my first day on the job you see, and Joan arrived, ordered me to look after a baby she'd turned up with, then disappeared to help someone in labour. Soon after, I was handed another baby and everyone was yelling at me: Joan was yelling about all the blood and Mrs P was screaming about needing me to sort out the baby because it was worth a lot of money, and in the end I just started crying. I was only nineteen.' Sarah sighed. 'I'd never done anything more than bandage a few cuts and I took the job because I have five sisters and we needed the money, but it was more than I'd bargained for.'

Everett took out his cigarette case, handed it to Leo and then to Sarah, who put one in her mouth and one behind her ear. Everett lit their cigarettes and said, 'Do you know what happened to the babies?'

Sarah shrugged. 'Mrs P shooed me out of the nursery in the end. Told me I was more trouble than I was worth. I went and had a cup of tea in the kitchen.'

Was that it? Leo stared mutely at Sarah. Everett didn't speak either.

'What about when you finished your tea?' Leo asked at last.

'I didn't go back to the nursery. I was too shaky. Eventually Mrs P came in and told me to take the rest of the day off. She said the babies had gone and luckily she'd got her money for one of them or else she mightn't be so kind. That next time she'd send me off to the Foundling with the baby she couldn't give away.'

'The Foundling?' Leo said, horrified that a baby who might be hers would be taken to an orphanage.

'That's where they sent the ones they couldn't adopt. One of the babies was sent there that day.'

Leo gazed at her, aghast.

'Thank you,' Everett said to Sarah. 'Here's some money for your drink. And your taxi fare.' He handed over a fifty-dollar note and Sarah's eyes lit up.

'If you want to ask me any more questions,' she said, 'I'd be more than happy to answer them.' She finished her milkshake and made for the door, clutching the money.

Leo let out a long, slow breath.

'So one baby was adopted,' Everett said. 'Most likely by Mattie, if this Mrs P was so pleased with the money. After all, Mattie would have paid an awful lot to make sure she had a baby, given that she'd told everybody she was pregnant.'

'And one baby was taken to the Foundling,' Leo finished. 'You don't think . . .' She swallowed. 'You don't think Mattie somehow found out one of the babies was ours and she had it taken to the Foundling out of spite?'

Everett didn't answer straight away. 'Or perhaps Faye's baby was so unwell it could only be taken to the Foundling. Both are possibilities.' He rubbed his face with his hand. 'And you look like you need something stronger than what they serve at an automat.' He took a flask from his pocket and poured a generous slug of whiskey into Leo's coffee.

'Maybe another cigarette too.'

She had to move closer to him so he could light it and his eyes flared a sultry blue in the flame.

Then, because they'd survived for so long on stolen moments, because they didn't need splendid romantic backdrops to buttress their love, in that instant of sitting in the oily stink of the automat, drinking coffee so strong it felt like swallowing the worst of Chinatown's hooch, Everett reached out and took her hand. 'I still can't believe that nothing, *nothing* has changed,' he said, his voice low, husky, private. 'That I feel even more for you now than I ever have. How is it possible that it hasn't just faded away with the years?'

'I don't know,' Leo said, holding tightly to his hand.

'Every day, after Benjamin died, I'd look out for an engagement announcement in the newspaper, thinking you'd surely find somebody else. That any man alive would want you. Or believing that even if you hadn't married, there was no way you'd still be thinking of me.'

'I've never wanted anyone except you.' Leo slipped her hand out of his; she could feel his pulse beating against her skin, right at the very edge of self-control. 'Which is why I can't hold your hand.'

He drew hard on his cigarette, then blew smoke out into the already hazy air of the automat. 'So what do we do now?'

'Besides hope that the baby taken to the Foundling was Faye's and not ours?' Leo said. 'But that's such an awful thing to wish upon Faye. I almost don't want to know that for sure either.'

'We can go to the Foundling. See if anyone there remembers anything.'

'I need to talk to Faye first. It's the right thing to do. And she might know more about it than she's ever let on.' She couldn't help the sudden shudder at the thought of having such a conversation with Faye.

'We can stop now if you want to. Whatever we find out is going to hurt someone, and you've been hurt so much over the years that maybe it's best to . . .' Everett's voice cracked a little on his last words. 'Leave it.'

'Do you really believe that?' Leo asked softly.

He shook his head. 'But I'll do whatever you want.'

'I want to find out. We have to.'

Chapter Twenty-six

*A*lice hurried off to the School of American Ballet filled with optimism. Today was the day! She and Jesse would be chosen as the principals for the gala.

There was a huddle of dancers in the hall, staring at the noticeboard. The casting was up. Alice shouldered her way through and realised that everyone had stopped their excited chatter and was looking at her. She must have done it. She flicked her eyes over the typed page and saw Jesse's name at the top. Her smile was huge. Then her heart stopped. There, under Jesse's name, was Irina's. Not Alice's. Her name appeared further down, as a soloist. She turned away from the board. Jesse was standing a short distance away, watching her.

'Alice,' he said.

She shook her head and marched back down the hall, out the doors and onto the street with Jesse following her. What was she thinking? That she could really be a ballerina? That she could stand on her own two feet? So few were chosen and she hadn't been.

'Alice,' Jesse said again. 'It doesn't mean anything.'

'It's easy for you to say that,' Alice retorted. 'Your place in the gala was always assured. You're there to make Balanchine shine and to get yourself a place in an American ballet company until it's safe to go back to Europe. I don't have that luxury. I needed to be the *première danseuse*.'

'I know you did,' he said gently.

Alice knew she was angry at the wrong person, but she couldn't help it. 'I have to stay away from you. You take up too much room in my head. I danced with you yesterday at rehearsals as if I already had the part. I didn't try as hard as I should have.'

'You always try harder than you need to. It felt easy at rehearsals because we're so good together. But that didn't mean it *was* easy. And you know he doesn't decide who gets to be principal based on one day's dancing.'

'Oh, so you're saying I've been consistently terrible? That yesterday was just one in a long line of below-par performances?' All Alice could think of was her mother, of Mattie's serpentine smile when she found out that Alice had failed, of how Mattie would humiliate her if she had to move home because she couldn't afford to live anywhere else.

'Of course not!'

'I have to work on my dancing more than ever now,' Alice said. 'I need a job. I have nowhere to live and no money to live on. I have to put all my energy into rehearsing. I can't see you again outside of this building.'

She strode back inside. How stupid she'd been. She'd spent all day yesterday thinking about Jesse when she should have been fixing her turnout. Being stuck on Jesse Valero had just cost her dearly.

In the change rooms, everyone fell quiet when they saw her. Irina looked as happy as Alice would have done if only Balanchine had chosen her.

'Congratulations, Irina,' Alice said, forcing out the words as she bent down to remove her shoes.

'Thanks.' Irina grinned.

Rehearsals began soon after and Alice moved through her part, messing up the double *fouetté*, her timing all wrong. Irina, on seeing Alice's fumbled attempts, moved into the centre of the room and executed the turns perfectly. Four times. The other dancers clapped.

'Damn,' Alice muttered, vigorously rubbing sweat from her neck with her towel until her skin was almost raw, making sure she didn't look at Jesse, or anyone else, so they wouldn't see her mortification.

When it came time for Irina and Jesse's solo, she sat on the floor with the rest of the dancers and watched. Irina was good, there was no doubting it; Alice could see it clearly, despite her anger. She had that way of seeming to be as light as a dust mote; she truly did appear to be dancing on eggs, as Balanchine was always exhorting them to. But with some dancers, even at their level, it was still possible to see that they were thinking about what they were doing, that they weren't yet able to surrender to the music, to let it lead them.

'Expression comes from the steps you are dancing; there is no need to emote; the emotion is already there in the dance,' Balanchine said to Irina, who nodded.

But Alice could see the separation; Irina's body wasn't yet a shadow of each note. All her attention was given to technique – technique that was, Alice conceded grudgingly, far better than that of anyone else in the room. And there were still two weeks to go until the performance. Irina would soon have the steps mastered and the emotion would come, no doubt.

As soon as rehearsals were over, Alice fled to the change rooms and threw on her clothes without even bothering to towel down. She passed the rehearsal room on her way out and could hear voices inside. Jesse and Irina, getting in extra rehearsal time. Then there were no voices. The door was open just a crack and she could see, as she rushed past, that the reason the voices had stopped was because Irina and Jesse were kissing.

Alice pressed her hand over her mouth to stop herself gasping aloud. How was it possible that Jesse had gone from that shared moment of understanding at Coney Island to kissing Irina just days later? A sharp sound from the rehearsal room made her start; it was Jesse's voice. Her head was in too much of a whirl to make out what he was saying but she had to get away before he saw her. It was bad enough that he was kissing Irina; to have him know Alice had witnessed the kiss was a humiliation she couldn't bear.

She made her legs move towards the door. Made herself walk out onto the street, the hot August afternoon making it seem as if the redness of her face, the dampness on her cheeks, was an effect of the heat, not of hurt. If she could just get home to Leo's house, then she could forget what she'd seen.

Anger dried her tears. She knew there were many male dancers who had passionate affairs with their leading ladies, affairs which ended when the performance was over. It was said that one could weave more emotion into the dance if there was emotion between the dancers. Jesse had been more than happy to kiss her when it looked as if she might be the *première danseuse*. But he'd been quick to transfer his interest to Irina when he knew she had the part. What a bastard. It was not a word Alice had ever used before, but right now she wanted to shout it out into the street so everyone would know.

She put her hand on the door at Leo's house. She'd call Robbie and apologise. She'd meet him later, share a drink. And a kiss. She wouldn't think any more about dancing. She'd live the easy life, the one that she could slip into like an old silk dress and feel nothing for whatsoever.

~

An hour later, Alice came downstairs and said to Leo, 'I'm going out with Robbie.'

'Is it a good idea to look so beautiful when you're telling Robbie you don't want to see him any more?' Leo asked, referring to Alice's dress, which was sapphire blue and sensational. It had a low neckline that plunged to Alice's sternum, a nipped-in waist and a thin column of a skirt.

'I made a mistake. I'm going to keep dating Robbie,' Alice replied.

'Oh, Alice.' Leo could tell there was deep hurt hiding beneath the bravado. 'How did things go today?'

'Irina is the principal ballerina. She'll be dancing with Jesse.'

'But it's not Jesse's fault,' Leo said gently.

Alice bit her lip. 'It's like I'm going mad,' she burst out. 'It's torture. To be unable to focus on anything else for more than a few minutes. To have every thought lead back to him. To want him so much that I'm prepared to do anything, things that I never thought I'd do.' She sat down. 'I'm sorry. You must think me shocking.'

Leo sat down beside Alice. 'Once upon a time, when I was the same age as you, I met a man and I fell so hard and so deeply in love that I've never been able to see the world the same way again. It was 1919. The war was over, just. I was supposed to be mourning, not being brought suddenly to life. So yes, I know what it is to feel as if you're going mad. It's love — love of the rarest and most unfathomable kind.'

The doorbell rang. Leo kissed Alice's cheek. 'Remember

that you have only one life and it will seem very long if you live it with someone you don't really love.'

'What happened to the man?' Alice asked.

'Our timing was off. He was engaged to somebody else. Now,' Leo said, 'you'd better answer the door. Unless you want me to tell him you've changed your mind?'

Alice shook her head.

But Leo could almost sense Alice's recoil as Robbie whistled and said, 'Hubba-bubba. Look at you, Cookie.'

Still, the door closed and Alice left with Robbie.

~

The next day was the photo shoot and Leo had no time to talk to Faye about Alice or to do anything about the writ. She moved forward as if her life was split into two halves: one in which she ran Richier Cosmetics and everything was fine, and one in which all of the seams had come apart and if even one more thread was pulled, she'd be left as raw and exposed as the water-worn rocks at the edges of the river that ran beneath her feet.

She was standing on the Brooklyn Bridge; she'd wanted the romance of the Gothic arches, the colossal Manhattan Tower and the spiderweb of steel suspension cables as a backdrop. They'd been given permission by the city to set up on the bridge and they were starting early, at six in the morning, when the light was rose-coloured.

Leo waited with Alice while her make-up was done and her hair brushed into a length of fiery silk. She helped Alice slip on the black tutu which, against her blazing hair and creamy skin, made her look as if she was truly the queen of those rare and beautiful birds, the black swans.

'I need to tell you something,' Leo said as Alice tied up her ballet slippers. 'Jesse is coming to the shoot. I'd asked him to come before I knew about the gala casting and I didn't think I could retract the invitation. I'm sorry.' It wasn't entirely true. Of course she could have told Jesse he was no longer required. But then Alice might let go of the one thing that mattered.

Alice didn't reply straight away. Then she sat up, tall and unbending, and Leo could tell that beneath Alice's beautiful exterior was a steel as strong as that of the bridge on which they stood, even if Alice didn't know it yet. 'One of the first things you learn as a ballerina is how to dance with anyone, no matter if you dislike them,' Alice said. 'I'm a professional. I'll do it.'

'Thank you,' Leo said, her attention caught by the man standing beside Man Ray. He was tall, with tanned skin and hair as dark as Alice's tutu, and when he turned around, Leo could see why Alice felt so strongly about him. Jesse Valero was unquestionably, unequivocally handsome.

⁓

'You can do this,' Alice repeated to herself when she saw Jesse. But God she wanted to reach out to him, to take his hand and dance along the bridge with him into one of the towers, where they'd be alone and she could see what might happen if she wrapped her arms around him and kissed him.

Instead she remembered what he'd been doing when she'd last seen him, lips locked with Irina's, and she nodded at him as if they were barely acquainted. He nodded back and she saw his jaw tighten.

The shoot that followed was the most exquisite torture. Torture because it meant holding a position for longer than one would when dancing on the stage, so Jesse's hands were on her body for the entire day. Exquisite because the sky was cobalt, a brilliant and inscrutable shade of blue accented here and there by purple clouds. It was as if a storm was threatening just off stage but, for now, they were able to revel in the drama of the moment before the rain swept in.

Man Ray asked them to dance in front of the Gothic towers of the bridge, which were brooding and spectacular. Alice found herself flying up into the theatrical sky, suspended against the archways that soared more than a hundred feet upwards like the magnificent granite windows of a cathedral. Her body did the impossible that day, as did Jesse's; she used all of her strength to stay aloft for as long as she had to, Jesse's body poised strong and powerful beneath.

Then Man Ray asked her to slide down Jesse's body, holding her palm to Jesse's face, and she felt every slow inch of movement as her legs and then her hipbones and then her stomach slipped over his chest. That one shot seemed to take hours, the two of them standing there, her hand touching his cheek, his eyes fixed on hers, thigh locked against thigh. She could feel her heart racing and could feel his too, could sense his breath high and fast like hers. She didn't know how much longer she could remain chastely there, pretending to feel nothing. Jesse's eyes flickered as if he'd caught her thought and she blushed, feeling his grip tighten.

'Let's have a break,' Leo called, and Jesse strode off to the refreshments tent without even a backwards glance.

'Are you all right?' Leo asked, and Alice nodded, watching Jesse but recalling her date with Robbie: how he'd arranged to meet some friends at the 21 Club and how he'd sat drinking whiskey and talking war with his pals while she'd been stuck at the end of the table with a group of women who didn't work, who spent their days shopping, and whom she didn't really like.

Robbie felt no need to stay beside her, nothing happened when they held hands, there was no urgent desire to be together.

When he'd walked her back to Leo's, he'd kissed her and grabbed her breast, squeezing hard. Rather than her nipple leaping at his touch, like it had with Jesse, she felt her body turn away from his hands, and she'd laughed and pushed him back as if she was too demure to be touched like that when she knew she was not.

'If it's too hard to dance with Jesse . . .' Leo's voice trailed away.

'It's fine.' Alice shook her head. 'I might just get some water.'

After the break, they danced a *pas de deux* against a blackening sky as the storm moved ever closer to the city. The silence of the dance was unbearable for Alice and she found the words had left her mouth before she could stop them.

'I saw you kissing Irina,' she murmured into his ear.

'Irina kissed me,' he replied. 'If you'd waited around, you would have heard me ask her to stop, heard me tell her I wasn't interested.'

'Really?' she asked.

'Really,' he said.

'Oh.'

Then the rain came without warning, a sudden drenching downpour, and Man Ray wanted to shoot on, through the rain, and somehow the rain washed away the driving tension of the day so that they danced as they had in the rehearsal room, unrestrained and boldly, as if they had nothing to lose. In the end they were both laughing, soaked through, her hair wrapped wet around her shoulders, his hair falling into his eyes, hands slippery but never letting go, never letting her fall. At last the dance was finished but they couldn't stop laughing, and after they had bowed and curtsied to one another out of habit, Alice moved to embrace him.

But he stepped away, his laughter stopped abruptly and something more like anger crossed his face. 'You can't keep changing your mind, Alice,' he said, and he stalked off, leaving her standing in the rain, bedraggled, open-mouthed, full of unsatisfied desire, hurting just as much as she'd hurt him.

Chapter Twenty-seven

A very wet and soggy Alice sat on the sofa in Leo's drawing room, crying. 'How is it possible to feel so much for one person?' Alice asked through her sobs.

'I don't know,' Leo said. 'I suppose you could resign yourself to marrying and then sleeping with a man you don't love, like Robbie, and always wishing it was Jesse's arms around you. But that doesn't sound like a life you'd want to live.'

'That's not what my mother would say to me,' Alice said soberly. 'In fact, I would never have this conversation with my mother.'

Leo had to turn away. *That's not what my mother would say to me.* She couldn't sit by and watch this girl who could be her daughter repeat her own and Everett's mistakes and waste the love she might have.

The doorbell rang. The butler entered with a man whose appearance made Leo smile. Jesse.

'I have to go out,' Leo said. 'Make yourself at home, Jesse.'

'You're staying here?' Jesse's voice expressed his disbelief as he tipped his head back to look up at the ceiling.

'Just for a while,' Alice said, smiling, trying to make him see that while it was a grand home, she was still Alice within it. 'Why did you leave so quickly today?' she asked.

Jesse turned his face away from her. 'I had to leave before I did something I shouldn't. I can't be the man you toy with when you're bored with all this.' He waved his hand at the room, at the chandelier, the furnishings, the photographs. 'You want to concentrate on dancing, fine. But don't keep changing your mind.'

'I'm not toying with you. I . . . I learned something today. That I'm not used to following my heart or good at being disappointed. I need to get better at both things.'

'I should go home.'

Alice took a step forward. 'Please don't go.' Then she kissed him, and his mouth opened straight away, his tongue seeking hers, his hands moving up her back to pull her close against him. Oh God, how could anyone stop themselves after a kiss like that? Alice knew she couldn't, knew she didn't want to. 'Come upstairs with me,' she said.

'Do you really want me to?'

She nodded and took his hand, leading him towards the stairs, but she couldn't walk more than two steps without turning back to kiss him again, to undo the buttons on his shirt. He slipped the collar of her dress down over one shoulder, leaving the skin exposed, and moved his mouth down her neck. Her head tipped back against the wall and she cried aloud.

Then she dragged him all the way to her room, where she pushed the door shut. 'Now we can do whatever we want.'

'Jesus, Alice, if you keep saying things like that I might not even make it to the bed.'

His hands touched her thighs, pulling her dress up and over her head so that all she was wearing were her brassiere and knickers, and she tugged at his shirt until it too came off. She reached around and unhooked her bra, letting it fall to the ground so that her breasts lay bare before him.

'I know I keep saying this, but you are so beautiful,' he said, running his hands down her neck, across her shoulders and back along her collarbones to meet in the middle of her chest, where one hand moved down to cup her breast, to stroke her nipple, and the other hand reached up to her neck so he could kiss her.

'Come over here,' he said, leading her towards the bed. 'I want to lie down beside you, not make love to you standing against a wall.'

His hand went to her knickers with a question in his eyes and she nodded. He slipped them off and she lay down on the bed, Jesse lying beside her, propped up on one elbow, not kissing her, not touching her, just taking in her legs, her belly, her breasts.

'What are you doing?' she asked.

'Admiring you,' he said. 'Worshipping you, adoring you. I can't take my eyes off you.'

'Oh, but you can,' she protested, wanting his hands and mouth on her again.

He stroked her cheek. 'Is this your first time?' he asked softly and she nodded, so glad he was the kind of man who would ask, who would care. 'I'll try to make it as enjoyable as I can.'

'I don't think you need to worry about that,' she said.

Then she undid his trousers, undressed him, seeing the parts of his body that had been hidden from her. 'My God,' she said quietly.

'We can stop if you want to,' he said, voice strained.

She hastened to explain. 'I didn't say that because I was frightened but because ... my God,' she said again. 'You're divine.'

'So are you,' he said, and he drew her back to him, turned her onto her back and began to make his way slowly and delightfully down her body, stopping to kiss every inch of skin, fingers trailing back over the places where his mouth had been. By the time he reached her belly, she found herself arching towards him, every part of her aflame, unable to be silent, hands clutching the sheets.

He opened her legs, watching her eyes all the time, and while she wasn't exactly sure what he meant, she nodded because she trusted him. His fingers moved first, stroking lightly, eyes on her to make sure she wanted it too, but the sensation was so strong that she found her eyes closing, her head tipping back. Just when she thought she could bear it no longer, she realised he'd moved his mouth to the place where his fingers had been. And she couldn't hold it in any more. 'Jesse!' she cried out as everything around her dissolved.

She opened her eyes to find him watching her, a grin playing on his lips. 'Did you like that?' he asked, and she laughed.

'You know I did,' she said. 'But come to me now. I want you to feel the same.'

'Alice,' he whispered against her ear, and he moved inside her. She felt only a momentary sting, which vanished in the pleasure of him rocking against her, his clever fingers straying back between her legs again, so that as his body shifted back and forth against hers, she felt the rapture build up once more, felt her legs wrap around him, heard him cry out, just as she had.

Neither spoke for several minutes. Then, with a reluctant sigh, Jesse moved off her and lay on his back. 'Are you all right?' he asked.

She laughed. 'All right is a very poor way to describe how I'm feeling.' She rolled onto her side. 'Is it always like that? I had no idea. My mother's friends whisper about sex as if it's like going to confession, a duty that requires great mental fortitude. I mean, you're obviously . . . experienced. So you would know.'

Jesse had the grace to blush. 'I'm not really that experienced. But no, it's not always like that. In fact, it's never been like that.'

'Really?' Alice said doubtfully.

Jesse put his arms around her. 'Really. I've never felt like that before. It's not even been five minutes and I want you all over again.'

She smiled at him, then frowned. 'I'm sorry about what I said. About it being your fault I didn't get the part.'

'It's okay. You were upset. And maybe . . .' He stopped.

'What?'

'Maybe Balanchine's testing you. To see how you deal with failure. Everyone has a moment when they either give up or get better. Maybe this is yours.'

Alice considered this. 'What was your moment?'

'It was in France last year. I hurt my back. I wasn't being careful, I was trying too hard to be the best and I couldn't dance for a month. I lost so much tone and strength that I thought I'd never get it all back. Then I realised I'd been lucky, that everything had come easily to me and that if I stopped at the first injury I'd be shipped back to New York and stuck working in Vic's garage for the rest of my life. So I spoke to other dancers. Found out what they'd done to come back from injury. And I worked slowly and carefully to get better and I taught myself to be patient. My first time back on stage, Balanchine saw me, and offered me the role in the gala back here.'

'So it was all worth it.'

'Yes.'

Alice traced her fingers across Jesse's chest, marvelling that she could do that, that she could take her hand and place it anywhere on his body and that he would let her — would want it, in fact — that his body was as much hers as it was his. 'I should do the best job I can with the part he's given me.'

'Maybe.'

Alice smiled. 'You're very wise and probably right. Balanchine's always been concerned about my background, that I'm biding my time until I get married. Maybe he *is* testing me. Do I quit because I didn't get what I want and marry Robbie? Or do I accept his decision and help make the gala spectacular in the role he wants me to dance?'

'Given that I'm lying naked on a bed next to you, I'm hoping you're not really considering the first of those two questions.'

'There's no man on earth I want to be with except you.'

'God, Alice.' Jesse brought her head down to his and kissed her, a long and hungry kiss that could lead to only one place.

'Is it really possible to do this so many times in one night?' Alice whispered.

Jesse grinned. 'We can always stop if it's too much.'

'Don't even think about stopping!'

Later, when they were lying exhausted, bodies still entwined, he said to her, 'You were right about Leo. No one could be as beautiful as you, but she reminds me of you. How do you know her?'

'In some ways I don't really know her at all, but in other ways I feel like I know her better than my own mother. She's an old friend of my father's. I hadn't realised what good friends they were until I heard them talking the other night. I didn't hear what they said, just the sound of their voices. They were speaking like lovers.'

She had said the words thoughtlessly, but once they were spoken she remembered Leo talking about a man she'd once fallen deeply in love with, a man engaged to be married. She remembered the melancholy, the look on her father's face that night in his study when they'd talked about Leo Richier and he'd said that she and Mattie didn't get along. Realisation washed over her. 'Oh,' she said. 'Leo and my father . . .'

'Leo and your father what?' Jesse asked.

'I think they were lovers once. I think she loves him, the way I love . . .' Alice stopped and blushed. Could she really say that aloud?

'The way I love you?' Jesse finished the sentence for her, eyes searching hers, wanting to know if he'd gone too far, but she nodded.

'Yes.'

They slept after that, which was another kind of bliss. To feel his arms around her, to know that he was there beside her, made her sleep soundly, erotically dreaming of him.

A knock at the door finally woke her and she sat up with a start, realising by the light outside that it was well and truly morning, time to get up and go to rehearsals. Jesse stirred beside her. 'I'll just open the door a little,' she said. 'It's probably the housekeeper.'

'What will Leo say if she finds out?' Jesse asked, and Alice shook her head because she didn't know.

She slipped on her robe and padded over to the door, opening it a crack. The housekeeper handed her a breakfast tray, which Alice took from her, laughing. For on the tray, obviously prepared under Leo's instructions, were two glasses of juice, two bowls of oatmeal scattered with raspberries, and two cups of coffee.

'I don't think Leo minds,' Alice said.

Jesse smiled. 'That's good. I wasn't looking forward to being thrown out onto the street, clothes in hand.'

They sat in bed and ate breakfast together, talking about Jesse's time in France, about how Alice became a ballerina, but they both knew they had to be quick because they were due at rehearsals in half an hour. When they'd finished eating, Alice reluctantly prepared to take a shower, but Jesse suggested he join her, which she thought was a wonderful idea, especially when the shower ended the way everything did when they were together.

They dressed quickly after that and hurried downstairs, not wanting to be late and face Balanchine's wrath. They met Leo at the foot of the stairs.

'Good morning,' she said, as if she was quite accustomed to her young, unmarried house guest coming downstairs with a man in the morning.

Alice blushed to the roots of her hair but Jesse smiled and shook Leo's hand. 'Thanks for breakfast,' he said, and Alice blushed all the more when Leo said, eyes twinkling as if she knew exactly how they'd spent their night, 'I thought you'd need the sustenance.'

Jesse laughed and so did Leo and even Alice allowed herself a small smile.

'I'll drive you,' Leo said to them. 'Otherwise you'll be late.'

Once they were in the car, Leo began to talk about the previous day's photo shoot, but after just a few minutes Alice couldn't help asking, 'Is it my father?'

Leo paused, her eyes fixed on the road, but Alice knew she understood the question. Finally she nodded. 'It is. I'm sorry.'

Alice shook her head. 'Don't be. I wish things had been different.' And she felt her eyes fill when she saw two tears drop from the corners of Leo's eyes, leaving a mark on her dress that coloured the silk dark purple like a bruise.

Chapter Twenty-eight

*L*eo decided to talk to Faye that very day, but she arrived at work to find Burton's serious face awaiting her. 'We're in court tomorrow,' he said without preamble, setting his briefcase on one chair and sitting down in another.

Leo dropped her purse onto her desk. 'Tomorrow? I thought we had another week?'

'It's been moved up. Mr Austin must have the judge in his pocket.'

'Well that's reassuring,' Leo said sarcastically. 'So what's our strategy?'

'We don't have one,' Burton said, unease cut deeply into every line of his face.

'You haven't found a loophole.'

'If the outcome one desires is that Faye takes on half of the company, then the paperwork is all in order. There is no paperwork to support your claim to own more than half.'

She pointed to the headline of the newspaper on her desk. BRITAIN AND FRANCE STAND BY POLES: RUSH PREPARES FOR WAR. 'There really is going to be a war, isn't there? That's why they've had the case moved up. They want capacity for munitions contracts.'

'I think so. But we'll still fight this, Leo. If there's one thing I know for sure, it's that you deserve to run this business.'

In all her years of dealing with Burton, she'd never heard him say anything so warm. Their meetings never veered towards the personal; they always stuck to business, which made Burton a clear-headed and valuable ally. 'Thank you,' she said.

Burton stood up. 'I'll see you in court at midday tomorrow.' The door closed behind him.

There are some people who don't like you very much. So this was what Faye had meant. That Leo would have to sit in a courtroom and watch while a lawyer working for Austin Ironworks, at the prompting of Mattie and with the assistance of Faye, proved that she didn't own her business. By the end of tomorrow, the office she sat in, the products she loved, products that adorned the faces of more women in America than any other cosmetic brand, might be run by a steel company, by men who hadn't a clue what a woman wanted, by men who desired factories, nothing more.

Leo picked up a piece of paper and a pen. Perhaps if she wrote to Mattie, told her she wouldn't use the photographs of Alice, that she'd back away again, give in, then Mattie would let it go. Perhaps if she let Faye come back to the business in a capacity where she felt important but couldn't destroy too much, then Faye would relent. Perhaps if Leo fought less and acquiesced more, then everything would work out.

Dear Mattie, she wrote. But how would she explain her decision to Alice? How could she tell Alice that, in order to save herself, she was going to sacrifice Alice's advertising campaign?

The door to her office opened and Lottie burst in, carrying a large envelope. 'I was too excited to knock,' Lottie said.

'I don't know how he did it. But here are the contact sheets from the shoot.'

'Already?' Leo asked.

Lottie passed the envelope to Leo.

Leo carried it over to the lightbox in her office, opened the envelope, placed the first contact sheet down and examined the print with a loupe. It was a picture of Alice, soaring, atop the Brooklyn Bridge in the arms of her lover.

Leo stepped back. 'Take a look.'

Lottie peered into the magnifying glass and drew in her breath. 'It's magnificent.'

'It is.'

Leo switched places with Lottie, moving the loupe across the sheet, studying each image. And she knew, without question, that Alice deserved to see herself as she really was. Beautiful. And that Mattie needed to know what her daughter had become. Astonishing.

Leo straightened. 'We're going to use them everywhere,' she said. 'Send the contact sheets to JWT and tell them this is their priority. I want a billboard in Times Square in a week, and advertisements in all the magazines by the end of the month.'

Ten minutes later, at her request, Leo's office was filled with staff.

'You might have heard rumours that someone is trying to take over the business,' she said. She could see that most of the staff, even Lottie and Jia, wore worried expressions. 'Twenty-one years ago, I stood in the back room of a chemist in a small English village making mascara from soap flakes and lampblack. I dreamed of having a shop one day, just something small, but more than that I dreamed of a time when nobody would call a woman immoral for wearing lipstick, when nobody would fire a woman from her job for wearing rouge, when mascara wouldn't be sold only in secret and by mail order. I dreamed of a time when women would be free to wear cosmetics if they wanted to and wouldn't be labelled fast or loose or wanton. With the help of my two friends –' she smiled at Lottie and Jia '– and the Richiers, and all of you –' she spread her arms to take in the crowd of people gathered before her '– that dream has come true. I don't intend to let anyone steal it away.'

The staff cheered and clapped, their faces relaxing into smiles. Leo was glad. It was just one punch in a much larger fight, but it was a start.

Alice dressed in her rehearsal clothes, determined to be more than the spoilt girl who quit when she didn't get what she wanted.

The corps de ballet took their positions and she allowed herself to exchange one small, private smile with Jesse before he took his place next to Irina. Alice took her place with the other two soloists. She extended her hand to the music and let it lead her, made herself forget, as Balanchine was always saying they ought — *allow the music to move your body and the technique will follow,* he said — and that's what she did. She almost closed her eyes, so caught up was she in the dance. Then the music came to an end and it was time for Jesse and Irina to take the floor. Before they did, Balanchine clapped his hands. 'That is how it should be done,' he said to Alice.

Alice didn't blush from the compliment as she might once have done. She accepted it gratefully and graciously and was so glad that Jesse was wiser than she, that she'd let go of ego, accepted failure, and used it to make herself better. She glanced over at Jesse and he caught her eye, nodded, and Alice knew she could do it. She could watch Jesse and Irina dance and she could applaud them. She could be happy with the part she had because she'd done it well and her time would come.

Jesse and Irina moved into the centre of the rehearsal room and began to dance. Balanchine stopped them a few times to correct a slight flaw in technique, but mostly he let them dance, interjecting every now and again to say, 'Reach for gold,' to Irina when her leg began to shake in the *arabesque penché*, so that she had something to think of other than her aching leg, or, 'Scoop the water,' to Jesse when his hand wasn't as fluid as it should be.

As Alice watched, she thought she understood why Balanchine had done what he had. The part he'd given Alice to dance was sculptural and precise; it needed perfect technique, which Alice compensated for with passion and emotion so that the audience could always feel the story of the ballet when she danced. Irina was the opposite; her movements were finely honed and exact – she could leap higher than Alice, she could turn faster because her feet and her arms were always in exactly the right place, but she lacked expression. Irina found it hard to dance the music. Balanchine had given them the roles they needed to become better dancers.

At the end, Alice walked over to Irina. 'Can we practise together this afternoon? I need help with my double *fouetté* and you really are the best at those.'

Irina studied Alice for a moment and then smiled. 'Of course. Perhaps you can help me with the expression.'

'That'd be great,' Alice said, marvelling at how much easier it was to be friendly than jealous.

The dancers began to leave but Balanchine summoned Jesse and Alice over to him. Alice shifted her feet nervously while she waited for him to finish dispensing advice to one of the other dancers. Did he know about her and Jesse? Was he going to ask them not to become involved with one another because he didn't want to have to deal with tension in the company if things went wrong? And would Alice be able to acquiesce, to give up Jesse right when they'd just begun? She didn't dare look at Jesse in case she gave anything away.

Finally Balanchine was ready for them.

'I have extended the gala program,' he said. 'There will be one final dance, just a short piece, only five minutes, at the end of the program.'

Alice glanced at Jesse to see if he understood what Balanchine meant but he seemed as puzzled as she.

'It is a *pas de deux*,' Balanchine continued. 'I have written it for the two of you. You will close the show.'

Balanchine's words washed over Alice like the glorious unshackling rain that had poured down upon them at the photo shoot the day before. She and Jesse would have their own dance. They would be the finale.

She turned to Jesse at the same moment that he turned to her and she didn't care what Balanchine thought; she let Jesse pick her up and spin her around and then, finally, kiss her in front of everyone. Then she stepped forward and kissed Balanchine's cheeks. 'Thank you,' she said, still holding Jesse's hand.

'Dance as well as you love and you will be spectacular,' he said.

Alice laughed. 'I think we can manage that.'

After her speech to the staff, Leo drove straight to the Carlyle. She asked at the front desk for Faye's room number and the manager called up to Faye to see if it was all right. Fortunately, Faye agreed.

When Leo arrived at Faye's room the gramophone was playing – in some kind of strange irony – Louis Armstrong's

'When the Saints Go Marching In' and Faye held two gins, one of which she handed to Leo. 'Cheers,' she said.

Leo sipped. 'Do you really want Richier Industries?'

Faye smiled. 'I told Mattie you'd figure it out. Not that it matters.'

'Why are you helping her this time?'

'You killed my brother.'

There it was. The accusation Leo had charged herself with years before, but which hurt all the more when it was said aloud by someone else. The gin burned the back of her throat and she swallowed hard. 'I'll buy your shares,' she said, 'for more than the market price. It's a good deal. You should take it. You'll need money now that you're up and about.'

'Eager to be rid of all the Richiers in your life, aren't you?'

'Only because I think we are, neither of us, any good for one another. You'll be a wealthy woman. You can do whatever you like. But let Ben rest in peace without us fighting over him for the rest of our lives. Don't destroy his company just because you hate me.'

'Don't pretend you cared about Benj. You married him to get your hands on his company and then you all but ignored him.' Faye's voice was easy, relaxed.

Leo wanted to slap her, to shout: *But you were the one who grabbed the steering wheel!* Instead she let fly. 'So all it takes is one visit from Mattie, one call for help in her constant battle to trounce me and the nervous breakdown that rendered you speechless is gone?'

'I wasn't pretending,' Faye said.

'Yet you've recovered so quickly.'

'We were talking about Benj. About the fact that, if you'd actually loved him, maybe he'd have been happy to go home with you that night.' Faye kept her smile pasted on, but Leo could hear the sound of heartbreak every time she said her brother's name.

'You miss him,' Leo said. 'And I'm sorry for that.'

Faye's intake of breath was sharp and loud.

'How do you know that Alice is really your daughter?' Leo asked, turning the conversation to the place she needed it to go.

Faye knocked back the contents of her glass. 'Like I said to you years ago, Mattie and I had an agreement from the time I knew I was pregnant.'

'But do you know for sure that she took your baby home?'

'Don't scrabble in the dirt, Leo. It doesn't suit you.'

Still uncertain if Faye was dissembling, Leo said, 'Our babies were born on the same day. Joan took mine to the same home where yours was born. She said yours took some time to breathe after it was born, that it mightn't have been well enough to be adopted. That Mattie might have had to take home a different baby.'

Faye's face was a map of shock, her mouth a circle of stupefaction. Was it possible that she didn't know? And that she might care?

'You think Alice is yours?' Faye's voice shook and Leo's throat tightened as she remembered the vital Faye who'd stood on a ship and called Leo's lipstick the berries, radiating health, beauty and fortune. Faye reached for irony but she wouldn't let Leo see what was hidden in her eyes as she spoke. 'Wouldn't that be . . . convenient.'

'Do you remember anything from that day? Anything at all? Please,' Leo said. 'Apparently only one of the babies was adopted. The other was taken to the Foundling.'

There was a pause.

'It was a long time ago, Leo.'

And Leo knew she couldn't keep pushing this woman who suddenly seemed as frail as the child might have been, as if Faye's insides, the deepest and most hidden part of her suddenly lay atop her skin, flayed by Leo's lack of mercy. If Faye had known her child's hold on life was precarious, then perhaps it hurt too much to remember.

Leo reached out and took Faye's hand, held it gently, like a mother might hold a child's, or a sister might hold her sibling's. In that moment she almost wanted Joan's story to be proved false, anything other than see Faye like this, raw, excoriated. 'It's all been such a mess,' she said. 'You won't believe me, but Ben told me he didn't want me to love him; that he didn't want to love me. That love carried with it the potential for heartache and he didn't want to feel that ever again.'

Faye stared at Leo's hand. She wriggled her fingers a little, as if reacquainting herself with the sensation of being held with compassion rather than need or lust or greed. 'He said that?'

'He did.'

There was a long pause. Faye looked as if she'd been smashed to pieces and recomposed from eggshells, a porcelain beauty past her time, frangible. Powder had collected in the crevices on her face, crevices left behind by the years and the drugs, crevices that betrayed the fact that Faye might be in one piece but the glue wouldn't hold for long. When she finally spoke, her voice was bloodless. 'Let's go,' she said.

'Where?' Leo asked, bewildered.

Faye didn't reply. So Leo followed her into the elevator and then into a car. It was only when she heard the address Faye gave to the driver that she baulked. 'I'm not going to Mattie's house.'

'Yes, you are,' Faye said firmly.

She's finally lost her mind, Leo thought. *But why now?* And she knew she couldn't let Faye go in to see Mattie alone, not in this state. So she took Faye's arm and climbed the steps with her, waited while they were announced and then led by the butler to an overfull drawing room where Mattie was waiting.

'So,' Mattie said, 'looks like you two have finally worked out that you both had babies on the same day. I couldn't believe it when the woman at the home told me the name of the mother of the other baby she had there. She was very careful to make sure I took home *the right one*.'

Mattie's last three words were slaps that made both Faye and Leo stiffen.

'Faye gave you her baby,' Leo gasped. 'That's the most loyal thing anyone could do. How can you speak to her like that?'

'Did she give me her baby?' Mattie grinned. 'Or did you give me yours? Isn't that what you're here to find out? Besides, Faye's persistent flirting with my husband doesn't really make her the world's most loyal friend.'

'You wanted this,' Faye said to Mattie, and Leo ached at the vulnerability in her voice. 'You knew I liked believing I had a daughter like Alice. Not one like me. You wanted me to come and ask you because that would make you the one with all the power.'

'For the first time in my life,' Mattie said bitterly.

Leo wanted to cover her ears. As if it wasn't enough to see Faye exposed, now Mattie was too. The woman who'd tricked a man into marrying her and, in so doing, had ensured that he would never love her, that she would live a life without affection for the sake of money and security.

'Let's go,' Leo said to Faye, stepping away.

But Mattie's voice stopped her. 'I have a safety deposit box. In there is everything you need.' She threw them a key, which Leo caught. Then she walked out of the room.

Leo stared at the key. It was inscribed with the words: *Chase Manhattan Bank.* Was it possible that Mattie had relented? In playing out her game, Mattie had only hurt herself. Did that mean she was going to let them find out who Alice's mother was?

Leo picked up the nearest telephone, dialled Everett's number and told him she was on her way. Faye followed her outside without speaking.

When they pulled up outside Everett's offices, Leo could see him pacing on the sidewalk. He did a double-take when he saw that Faye was in the car too.

Leo climbed out and told Everett everything that had happened. That Faye had been hurt. That his wife had known about Leo's child all along. That they still didn't have an answer – but that they might soon. She showed him the key.

'What do you want to do?' he asked, studying her face, which she knew must show every wretched emotion of the morning.

'Will you just kiss me?' she said.

'Leo.' He reached for her then and her lips met his with something that wasn't passion; it was beyond passion, beyond intimacy, because intimacy implied they were two separate people coming together whereas Leo knew that she and Everett were one and the same. Tears flooded her cheeks. When she reached up to place her palm on his cheek, she felt dampness there too.

She leaned her forehead against his, her breath high and fast, her hand still touching his face, his hand still woven into her hair. A long moment passed before either had recovered sufficiently to pull away, to open the car door and step inside, to take their seats beside Faye.

Minutes later they were standing inside the bank. Everett summoned the security guard. After a few grim words, they were led to the safety deposit box whose number matched that on the key.

The key was inserted and the box opened.

There was nothing inside.

Leo heard Everett breathe out, winded. Faye made a choking noise.

Leo sank to the floor. 'What does it mean?' she whispered.

'That Mattie's still playing a game,' Everett said, sliding down to the floor beside her. 'She doesn't want to give any of us the satisfaction of knowing.' He put both his arms around Leo, drawing her head into his chest as if he was sheltering her from the coming storm, a storm she thought she'd weathered, only to find it had blown up again, worse than ever.

Faye turned away. 'You can have my shares,' she said. 'I don't want Mattie to have them now.'

Leo struggled for a moment to work out what Faye meant. The writ. Of course. 'You should keep them,' she said dully. 'You don't need to give them to me.'

'What would I do with them? Something else for me to ruin.'

'Faye,' Leo said, tears in her eyes, reaching out a hand to her.

'I don't hate you,' Faye said, ignoring Leo's hand. 'I envy you, in fact.'

'I have nothing worth envying,' Leo said.

'You've had love,' Faye said. 'It doesn't matter what Benj said — when you were in a room, you were all he could see.' She looked at Leo and her eyes held tears, the heartsore tears of a woman who'd idolised her brother, a brother who'd also been like a father to her. 'And you have Everett. Two men I would have done anything for.'

Leo's intake of breath was like Faye's had been earlier: sharp and loud and sorrowful. She felt Everett freeze beside her. Had Faye's flirting with Everett really hidden a much deeper affection? Why else would anyone keep a pair of cufflinks for twenty years unless they meant something?

'I'm sorry,' Leo whispered. 'I didn't know.'

Faye shrugged. 'Doesn't matter any more.'

And with that, Faye walked away, on the surface still seeming the same as she'd always been, bold and brash, but the puzzle of the woman beneath was at last a little clearer to Leo, and she wished for the thousandth time that things had somehow been different. She and Everett might have only shared one night twenty years ago, when everything changed, when two bodies met and two hearts married, but the repercussions continued to flow, on and on and on.

'We can still try the Foundling,' Everett said in such a low voice Leo could hardly hear him.

She shook her head. No. It was all her fault. She was the one who'd given Everett hope, the one who'd snatched away the hope Faye had held on to for so long. Leo had delivered to all of them only questions and uncertainty. 'No,' she said, voice husky with tears. 'I don't think I can bear to hand you any more disappointments.'

Chapter Twenty-nine

Alice threw herself on Leo when she arrived home, eager to share her news about the gala. Leo forced a smile onto her face and tried hard to be thrilled for her, to share her joy. She managed to open a bottle of champagne, to drink a glass, and not let on that she'd just suffered the cruellest disappointment of her life: that while she might desperately want Alice to be hers, it seemed she would never know for sure. Mattie had covered her tracks too well.

Watching Alice now, talking and laughing and bubbling over with pleasure, quickly became too painful to bear. 'You need to tell your parents,' she said, putting down her glass. 'They should know about this.' Because Leo still didn't have the right. And Mattie did.

Alice sighed. 'I suppose you're right. Gosh, it's hard being grown-up and doing all the things you'd rather not. But if tackling my mother head on works out as well as it did with the gala, then I suppose there's no time like the present. I'll go and talk to them now.'

'I'll organise the car for you.'

'No, I'll walk. If I plan to move out on my own, then I need to get used to walking. Best I start now.'

'Good luck, Alice,' Leo said softly, aware of how final it sounded, how much like the farewell it might have to be.

Alice hugged Leo and kissed her cheek. 'You'll come to the gala, won't you?'

'I wouldn't miss it,' Leo managed to say.

Once Alice had left, Leo tried not to think about what it would be like to receive that kind of daughterly embrace every day of her life. She felt the tears start and she vowed to herself that it would be the last time.

When morning came, she would concentrate on her work, the work that had always saved her before. She reached for the whiskey decanter. And she would drink, quite a lot.

~

Alice let herself into the house, the home of her childhood. She crept into her father's study, where the lights were all on.

She was about to open her mouth, to surprise her father with the wonderful news of her *pas de deux*, to take his hands and pull him up from his chair and make him waltz with her around the room. But she stopped short at the sight of him. His face was broken. *He* was broken. Cracked, torn asunder. By what?

She ran to his side. 'What is it?' she cried. She couldn't imagine her father, her champion, this lion of a man, brought to such grief.

He blinked and smiled and shook his head. 'It's nothing, darling.'

'Are you thinking about Leo?'

'Yes.'

Such a simple word, but it meant so much. It meant that for all of Alice's life, her father had truly been her hero, staying with a wife he didn't love, sacrificing the woman he adored, so that he could be with Alice and not leave her to Mattie. It was all for her.

Alice hugged her father. There were no words. Because she knew she'd look exactly the same if she ever lost Jesse.

~

The rest of the week was a carnival ride that spun Alice's entire world around. The Richier Cosmetics billboard went up on the day of the gala and Jesse and Alice skipped out of rehearsals for half an hour so they could see one of them. They caught the subway to Times Square and when they emerged onto the pavement, they stood completely still.

There they both were, up high, strung across buildings, dancing so close to the edge of desire that it seemed as if Jesse had lifted Alice above his head for one thing only: to throw them both over that edge and into one another.

Alice grabbed Jesse's hand. 'It's us,' she said, awestruck.

'Get a load of that,' was all Jesse could manage.

They watched other people walking past, arrested too when they caught sight of the billboard, unable to continue on past such an illustration of love and longing without having to catch their breath, to wonder if anyone had ever looked at them the way Jesse was looking at Alice, dwelling for a moment in the fantasy of flying against a New York sky and landing in the arms of a man who wanted you more than anything.

Alice turned to Jesse and kissed his cheek, smiling when he moved his head to catch her mouth. When they broke apart, she looked across at the billboard and then back at Jesse, the memory of her father's face still fixed in her mind. 'Let's get married,' she said.

Jesse laughed and kissed her again. 'Are you serious?'

Alice nodded, eyes sparkling.

'Then let's get married,' he said.

~

Leo went to the gala because Alice had been insistent and because she did want to see Alice and Jesse dance together. She'd managed to avoid Everett's telephone calls, but she couldn't avoid her own crippling feelings of guilt for dragging him into what had turned out to be the worst kind of emotional quicksand.

Luckily the show was spectacular and it made her forget, for a short time, everything that had happened. Jesse made Irina look like the star she might become with just another year or two behind her. But of course the thing everyone wanted to see was the grand *pas de deux*, especially now that the billboards had gone up and Alice and Jesse were the couple everyone wanted to be.

It was exquisite, almost unbearably so. In fact, Leo had to close her eyes midway through because it was more than she could stand to see the kind of love she knew existed played out right there on the stage before her and to know that she might never be able to live it as Alice and Jesse could.

She slipped out while the crowd was applauding, the standing ovation drumming on and on. She hurried through the foyer and had made it all the way to the doors before she felt a hand on her arm.

Of all the things she'd thought might happen that night, Everett bending his head towards her and kissing her with more passion than she'd ever felt in him was so difficult to comprehend that for a long, long moment she lost herself in the kiss, let her mouth open hungrily to his, let his arms draw her to him.

Then her senses took hold and she jumped back. 'What are you doing?' she hissed, thankful that the doors of the theatre had only just opened and that the people coming out would see them talking, rather than kissing.

'What are *we* doing?' he said. 'Watching Alice tonight I realised that she doesn't need me any more. She has ballet and Jesse, she's looking for an apartment. She's out of Mattie's reach; I don't need to protect her any more. So it doesn't matter if I divorce Mattie. It doesn't even matter if Mattie carries out her threat and tells Alice I might not be her father. Alice will survive. But I won't survive being without you for the rest of my life.'

Everett's words whirled around in Leo's head as the theatre crowds hurried past, talking gaily about Jesse and Alice and the entire gala performance. Was it really possible, this thing that until five minutes before had seemed so desperately out of reach? Of course it wasn't.

'But we still don't know if Alice is ours. We might never know,' Leo said slowly. 'You wouldn't want me unless . . .'

'Are you crazy?' Everett cupped her face with his hands. 'My love for you has never been dependent on having a child. I want you. I love you. The rest was only ever going to be a lovely and unlooked-for blessing.'

'You're certain?' she asked, because it seemed too easy now, when all of their life it had been so hard.

'I'm certain.'

Two words, without embellishment. Because they needed none.

And then suddenly she smiled and Everett laughed and that was all it took. 'My God,' she said as the realisation of what was to come finally hit her. That she could wake up in the morning beside Everett. That she could come home to him at night, sit beside him, head tucked into his shoulder, his hand weaving into her hair as they talked. That she could touch his body wherever and whenever she wanted. That he would be hers, truly.

Leo slipped her hand into his. 'Is this really happening?'

'I think it is.'

Leo bit her lip and saw Everett's eyes trace her mouth hungrily, wanting what they hadn't had for so long.

She squeezed his hand. 'Not tonight. Tonight is Alice's night. You should go to her, be proud of your daughter. Celebrate with her. And tomorrow, you'll tell Mattie. Then you'll come to my house and take me to bed.'

Chapter Thirty

The doorbell rang at six o'clock the next evening and Leo rushed to answer it herself, having sent the staff away on a week's holiday. She didn't want anyone else in the house, just her and Everett, alone together for an entire week. The things they would do! But the smile died on her face when she saw that it wasn't just Everett on the doorstep; Faye was there too.

'Faye?' Leo said warily. 'Why are you here?'

'Let me in and I'll tell you,' Faye said, in the swashbuckling voice of her youth, a voice that had always got her what she wanted. Faye pushed past Leo, who was unable to move, suddenly certain that, whatever hopes she and Everett had held for that night, Faye was about to disrupt them entirely.

Everett looked as perplexed as Leo felt. 'Her car pulled up at the same time as mine,' he said. 'I thought you must have invited her.'

'Why would I do that?' Leo said. 'I don't want anybody here except you.'

'Let's go see what she wants,' he said grimly, slipping his hand into hers.

Of course Faye had helped herself to a gin in the drawing room by the time they reached it, and had also poured one for Leo and Everett.

'Will I need this?' Leo asked.

Faye shrugged, downed her drink in one swallow and turned her back on Leo and Everett. 'I thought you might like to know how I spent my day,' she said conversationally, but Leo could hear the same brittle tone that had pervaded her last encounter with Faye, and she was once again filled with the sensation that the woman in front of her was almost at breaking point.

'Your day?' Leo repeated, glancing at Everett, who shrugged and squeezed her hand.

'I went to the Foundling.'

'Why?' This time, Everett spoke.

'It turns out that one of the sisters who's there now was also there in February 1920,' Faye said. 'They don't stray far, those sisters; there's nowhere else to go. Anyway, she's old and sick now, too ill to speak. When I saw her lying in her bed in her nightgown, I thought I'd wasted my time. Because if she couldn't speak, how could she tell me anything?'

Leo needed more than Everett's hand. She slipped her arm around his waist and he did the same.

'But the sister was wearing a necklace made from baroque pearls. I noticed it, because how often do nuns wear pearl necklaces?' Faye gave a small laugh. 'The nun in charge said she had no idea where she'd got it from, that she must have been wearing it under her habit for years, unbeknownst to all. That they'd only seen it when she fell ill and they didn't have the heart to take it from her. Most people want their pearls round, not imperfect. But I always liked a bit of irregularity.'

A memory flickered. Faye on the deck of the ship wearing a strand of pearls. Faye moving her hand to her throat at the meeting when Leo first went to Ben with her business proposal, the pearls no longer there.

'You see,' Faye said, voice falsely bright, 'I gave Mrs Parker the pearls. I wanted them to go with my baby, so it had a keepsake. I thought that was what Mattie had put in the safety deposit box.'

'But if the nun was wearing them . . .' Everett began.

'Then the baby that went to the Foundling was mine. And Joan was right; it was too sick . . .' It was Faye's turn to stop mid-sentence. Because if Faye's baby had been too unwell to adopt out, so sick that the only place it could go to was the Foundling, then it had most likely died a long time ago. And the baby Mattie had taken home – Alice – was Leo and Everett's child.

Nobody spoke. Then Leo saw Faye's shoulders twitch, a movement she knew came from smothering a sob.

'Faye.' She hurried over to her sister-in-law with her arms outstretched, wanting to gather her in, to hold her.

But Faye held out a hand to ward her off, and Leo saw that Faye couldn't tolerate an act of tenderness; it would utterly undo her.

'Don't pity me,' Faye said. They were the exact words that Benjamin had used the night he revealed himself to Leo.

'I don't pity you,' Leo said. 'I love you, and that's a different thing altogether.'

They regarded one another for a moment, Faye with tears on her cheeks – it was the first time Leo had ever seen her cry. They could perhaps never start over and be the friends they might have been, but Leo now thought that maybe Faye regretted the lost opportunity as much as she did.

'Thank you for coming to tell us,' Leo said.

The tiniest smile broke over Faye's lips and Leo was certain she'd never see her again. This moment of painful camaraderie would prove too much, and Faye would, like Benjamin, run from the possibility of loving because hand in hand with that went the possibility of hurting.

As if to prove her right, Faye swept past Leo and Everett and disappeared.

Leo dropped onto the sofa, a trembling beginning in her hands that spread through her whole body.

'God,' Everett said, sinking down beside her, arms wrapping around her.

Speech was impossible for a long time, but finally Leo felt her body stop shaking and relax into Everett's. She felt him pull back a little and run his thumbs over her cheeks.

'I can't believe it,' he said.

'Nor can I.'

'Alice is ours.'

'I know.'

Said aloud like that, the magnitude of their blessings once again left them silent. They were together in a room in each other's arms and they had a daughter.

'Should you go after Faye?' Everett said, at the same time as Leo said, 'Should we tell Alice now?'

They laughed and the weight of tension from the last half-hour lifted a little. Leo shook her head. 'I don't think Faye wants me to go after her.'

'I think you're probably right.'

'What about Alice?'

Everett kissed her suddenly, softly at first, and then harder, hungrily, mouth pressing against hers. 'We can tell

Alice tomorrow,' he murmured. 'She hasn't known the truth for nineteen years. One more day isn't going to make any difference.'

Leo smiled. 'Do you remember what I asked you to do tonight?'

Everett smiled too. 'I'm afraid I have to break my promise,' he said. 'Because it would be impossible for me to wait right now until we found a bed.'

'Then please, go right ahead and break that promise.'

Finally he drew her in as close as he could, lowering her back onto the sofa, his body on top of hers. There was that kiss again, that starving kiss, the one she'd been wanting for half her life. There was her dress, on the floor, and his clothes too. And there was his body, his strong and beautiful body. And here was the man with whom she was, at last, going to spend the rest of her very long and happy life.

Author's Note

*M*any years ago, I worked at the Australian head office of L'Oréal Paris in Melbourne. I was the marketing manager for the Maybelline brand and one of the first stories I ever heard about the history of the brand was that of young Mabel, who was in love with a man who only had eyes for someone else. Mabel's brother Tom helped her to mix coal dust with Vaseline to put on her lashes in an attempt to turn this man's head. Whether or not it worked is the subject of much debate, but this was the first mascara to be widely retailed to consumers. That story has stayed with me for fifteen years and was the spark that lit the idea for this book: to write about the time when cosmetics moved from illicit to everyday.

Her Mother's Secret is a work of fiction, but many sources provided useful information to help me reconstruct the era and way of life depicted in the book.

For information about the history, use and manufacture of cosmetics I referred to: *Cosmetics Science and Technology Volume I*, edited by Marvin S. Balsam and Edward Sagarin; *A History* of *Cosmetics in America* by Gilbert Vail and S.L. Mayham; *War Paint: Madame Helena Rubinstein and Miss Elizabeth Arden, Their Lives, Their Times, Their Rivalry* by Lindy Woodhead; *Inventing Beauty* by Teresa Riordan; *Classic Beauty: The History of Makeup* by Gabriela Hernandez; *Beauty Imagined: A History of the Global Beauty Industry* by Geoffrey Jones; *Hope in a Jar: The Making of America's Beauty Culture* by Kathy Peiss; and *Compacts and Cosmetics: Beauty from Victorian Times to the Present Day* by Madeleine Marsh.

References that informed the sections of the book dealing with department stores and their display windows included: *The Grand Emporiums* by Robert Hendrickson; *Service and Style: How the American Department Store Fashioned the Middle Class* by Jan Whitaker; *Holidays on Display* by William L. Bird; and *The World of Department Stores* by Jan Whitaker.

For information about New York City during the time the book is set, I used many sources, including: *New York in Seven Days* by Helena Smith Dayton and Louise Bascom Barratt; *Only Yesterday* by Frederick Lewis Allen; the *Ask Mr Foster* map of New York City 1922; *New York Nights* by Kurt Wiese; and *Guide to New York*, published in 1926 by the New York Credit Men's Association.

Balanchine's School of American Ballet has been documented on the George Balanchine Foundation's website, and in the books *George Balanchine* by Robert Gottlieb and *In Balanchine's Company* by Barbara Fisher.

Mr Grundy's words on pages 206 and 207 were first published in May 1920 in an *Atlantic Monthly* article called 'Polite Society'. The quote on page 157 comes from F. Scott Fitzgerald's *This Side of Paradise*. On page 175, Leo and Lottie discuss two advertisements from the time, one of which they quote; this quote is taken from an advertisement for Boncilla Beautifying Preparations.

Acknowledgements

First and foremost, I have to thank Rebecca Saunders, fiction publisher at Hachette, who helped me transform this book from a muddle and into the novel you're now reading. I don't think I'll ever stop saying this, but Rebecca really is the best publisher any author could ever wish for and I'm enormously lucky and grateful to work with her.

There are many other people at Hachette who have been very supportive of me and my books and I'd like to thank all of them. I still can't quite believe that I have the huge good fortune to work with such an incredible publishing house.

To Jacinta di Mase, my amazing agent, who is always the calm, reassuring voice of reason and who provides an incredible amount of support, thank you.

My family are my rocks and they put up with my glazed expression and my lack of attention and they understand that I'm apt to disappear at any moment into an imaginary world inside my head. I thank them for giving me the time and space to write my books, and for always being interested in what I'm doing, and for doing whatever they can to help.

To booksellers and readers, I wouldn't be writing this book if it wasn't for you. Thank you for always doing your utmost to support writers and for enabling me to do the thing I love most in the world.

Read on for an extract of Natasha Lester's
deliciously evocative love story of a small-town girl
with big ambitions in 1920s New York

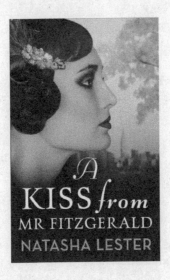

It's the Roaring Twenties in the Manhattan of gin, jazz and prosperity.

Women wear make-up and hitched hemlines and enjoy a new
freedom to vote and work. Not so for Evelyn Lockhart, who is
forbidden from pursuing her passion to become one of the first
female doctors. Chasing her dream will mean turning her back on
her family: her competitive sister, Viola; her conservative parents;
and the childhood best friend she is expected to marry, Charlie.

In a desperate attempt to support herself through Columbia
University's medical school, Evie auditions for the infamous late-
night Ziegfeld Follies on Broadway. But if she gets the part, what
will it mean for her fledgling relationship with Upper East Side
banker Thomas Whitman – a man Evie thinks she could fall in
love with, if only she lived a life less scandalous . . .

$\mathcal{P}$rologue

NEW YORK, 1925

ow did I get here? How did I get here? The words reverberated between each click of Evie's heels as she stepped off the moon and executed a perfect Ziegfeld strut. Her arms were extended as if to lift the skirt of a dress she wasn't wearing, and her head was pulled back by the halo of a hundred silver-dipped stars. She smiled at the audience, who thought that what she did was, at the least, entertaining and, at the most, foreplay. Her neck ached but she concentrated on the sound of the dollar bills that Ziegfeld would flick into her hand at the end of the night, like a baccarat dealer at a high-stakes table.

The music changed to the big, belting fanfare of the finale and Evie curtseyed, then took her place near the centre of the line of showgirls. She knew what she had to do: join arms, scissor-kick the legs, emphasise the breasts, and damn well make herself look so delicious that no one in the crowd remembered the New York that existed beyond the doors of the theatre. That was a place of discreet money and manners and hidden mistresses, where a woman called Evie Lockhart fought a battalion of men every day for permission to become a doctor. Inside the theatre, the men had no manners, the mistresses were out on show, the money was splashed around like whiskey, and Evie Lockhart was once again fighting, this time to remember that an exchange of dignity for college fees would be worth it.

Where did it all go? Evie thought as she spun around. All my joy, all my wonder. New York used to knock the breath right out of her. Now it was a daily struggle just to get enough air. But she slapped her smile back on, because Florenz Ziegfeld was glaring at her, and Evie needed to be a Ziegfeld Girl more than Ziegfeld needed her. She'd better give someone in the audience a sultry wink to show she was still playing the game. As she looked for a man to dazzle, she got a feeling like an itch at the corner of her eye; she blinked once, twice, but the irritation was still there, narrowing her focus to the man in the fourth row from the front – centre seat so he must be important.

When she saw who he was she got what she wanted – the breath knocked right out of her.

It was Thomas Whitman. Tommy. Back from London.

Would he recognise the girl from Concord, Massachusetts, who used to live next door – oh, such a long time ago? He'd never expect to see Evelyn Lockhart dancing a cancan with a line of beautiful girls whose long legs shimmered from toe to thigh in a way you'd never see in a drawing room on the Upper East Side.

Evie knew she should look away. But two and a half years in London had transformed Thomas into the cat's whiskers. He'd been handsome before, but now he was heart-stopping, and he looked all the better for not slicking back his hair like the rest of the Valentino imitators in the crowd. His eyes were like black marble, and unlike those of most of the men around him, they were studying her face, not roaming her body.

Then he stood up and began to step past the people seated beside him. He strode towards the exit, even though the show wasn't over. It could only mean that beneath the thick kohl lining Evie's eyes, the red lips, the leotard and the stars, Thomas had seen someone he used to know.

Luckily it was the last number of the night. The curtain was about to come down and Ziegfeld's Girls would be officially off duty, unless they wanted to don a sheer, lacy robe and go up to the bar and pout because the cigarette dangling so elegantly from their quellazaire was unlit. Evie never joined them and she certainly wouldn't tonight. Instead she'd lie awake, remembering how often she'd dreamed of kissing Thomas Whitman. And she'd try not to think about the fact that now he knew she worked for Ziegfeld, he'd never want to see her again.